M.K. HUME

THE WOLF OF MIDNIGHT

TINTAGEL BOOK III

REVIEW

First published in 2018 by
HEADLINE REVIEW
An imprint of HEADLINE PUBLISHING GROUP

2

Cataloguing in Publication Data is available from the British Library

ISBN 978 1 4722 1586 4

Typeset in Golden Cockerel by Avon DataSet Ltd,
Bidford-on-Avon, Warwickshire

Printed and bound in Great Britain by CPI Group (UK) Ltd,
Croydon, CR0 4YY

HEADLINE PUBLISHING GROUP
An Hachette UK Company
Carmelite House
50 Victoria Embankment
London EC4Y 0DZ

www.headline.co.uk
www.hachette.co.uk

M. K. Hume is a retired academic, who is married with two grown-up sons and lives in Queensland, Australia. M. K. Hume completed an MA and PhD in Arthurian Literature many years ago and has now written a magnificent series of novels about the legend of King Arthur. For more information visit: www.mkhume.com.

Praise for M. K. Hume:

'Hume deftly navigates the Arthurian legends, populating them with likeable and despicable characters, and casting them in a fully realised historical setting' *Publishers Weekly*

'Hume brings the bloody, violent, conniving world vividly to life ... will appeal to those who thrill to *Game of Thrones* and other tales of intersecting, ever-warring, noble lineages' *Kirkus Reviews*

'An altogether totally original version of the Arthur legend, owing more to Cornwell and Iggulden than to Malory, with a sense of reality pervading it that keeps you interested. It's a slice of history that's totally, utterly believable. Magnificent' www.booksmonthly.co.uk

'It's always good to come across another great historical series and this new trilogy from M. K. Hume looks set to be one. Exciting, violent and bloody and full of historical facts to keep you gripped throughout. Up there with Conn Iggulden and Bernard Cornwell' www.lovereading.co.uk

By M. K. Hume and available from Headline Review

King Arthur Trilogy
Dragon's Child
Warrior of the West
The Bloody Cup

Prophecy Trilogy
Clash of Kings
Death of an Empire
Web of Deceit

Twilight of the Celts Trilogy
The Last Dragon
The Storm Lord
The Ice King

Stormbringer's Voyage (e-novella)
The Last Dragon's Voyage (e-short story)
The Emperor's Blood (e-novella)
The Warrior's Blood (e-short story)

Tintagel Trilogy
The Blood of Kings
The Poisoned Throne
The Wolf of Midnight

This book is dedicated to those warriors, male and female, who struggle to fight for the values that enable the human condition in a violent and sectarian world.

To those zealots whose madness and religious fervour leave death and chaos in their wake, may you discover the futility of mindless violence and learn that Lady Fortuna will repay your cruelty with cruelty twice over, bigotry with all the torture you enact in its vile name and religious intolerance with the ultimate failure of false religions.

Order is the governing factor in the great dance of the universe, just as God, by whatever name that He/She is called, will repay the perpetrators with *exactitude* for those sins that evil people commit in His/Her name.

The mills of the gods grind slowly, but they grind exceedingly small.

M. K. Hume
June 2018

ACKNOWLEDGEMENTS

This book would never have been completed if it weren't for the efforts of a number of people.

In May 2016, I suffered an allergic reaction which resulted in oxygen deprivation. It played *merry hell* with my hand–eye coordination. I was seriously ill and, to all intents and purposes, my prospects of continuing as an author were severely limited.

My thanks go to my son, Brendan, and my friends, Roger and Penny, who dragged me back from the brink.

So many people were responsible for my recovery that it would be impossible to mention them all. Suffice it to say that I am very grateful for the assistance and support I was given, especially by the doctors at Royal Brisbane Hospital, the therapists at Brighton Rehabilitation Centre and, most of all, the wonderful nurses who assisted me as I grappled to re-learn all that I had known and accepted as my right.

This book only exists because my husband, editor and indefatigable bully, Michael, spent every day with me. He wrote the text in long hand while I dictated it to him.

My family and friends have been towers of strength during my illness and this book exists because of their support and expertise.

M. K. Hume

DRAMATIS PERSONAE

Aeron ap Iorweth	King of the Dobunni tribe. Aeron is the son-in-law of King Caradoc, the deceased king of the Dumnonii tribe. Married to Queen Endellion, he is the father of Prince Pridenow and foster-father of Queen Severa. This branch of the royal family resides in Corinium.
Ambrosius	Ambrosius is the son of Constantine and Severa and is the elder brother of Uther (Pendragon). The brothers are exiled to Hispania after Vortigern, king of the Demetae tribe, usurps the British throne and marries Severa, their birth mother. He intends to kill the children.
Brisen	Severa's personal maid in the palace at Venta Belgarum.
Cadoc	The infant (first-born) son of Pridenow and Creidne.
Calindre	A special knife used by Severa for her personal protection.
Constans (Prince)	Constans is the son of Constantine III (Constantinus). The youth travels from Venta Belgarum to join Constantine in Gallia where his father is trying to usurp

the throne of Honorius, the emperor of the Western Roman Empire.

Vortigern (pretender to Constantine's throne of High King in Britannia), assassinates the youth during a battle with a Roman force near Vienna.

Constantine I
The long-dead emperor of the Roman Empire (both Eastern and Western branches) in the early fourth century.

Constantine II
The emperor of the Western Roman Empire from AD 337 to AD 340.

Constantine III
The emperor of Rome (co-emperor with Emperor Honorius) between AD 407 and AD 411.

As Constantinus, a centurion, the young Roman officer marries Princess Severa (the daughter of Flavius Magnus Maximus, the deceased High King of Britannia and, later, co-emperor of the Western Roman Empire). Constantinus seizes the title of High King of the Britons in his own right before taking a combined British–Roman army to Gallia and Hispania in an attempt to usurp the Roman forces of Emperor Honorius.

He is successful initially, but suffers a major defeat at the last hurdle and is assassinated by Rome's stranglers.

Constantinus
Flavius Claudius Constantine. Constantinus assumes the nomen of Constantine during an attempt to usurp the throne of Honorius,

	Emperor of the Western Empire.
Creidne	The daughter of Cael ap Cynog, a trader whose caravan is ambushed by Saxon raiders on a road outside of Venta Belgarum. She is rescued by Pridenow and they fall in love. They marry and she has a girl-child, Ygerne, who will become the birth mother of King Arthur after a rape at the hands of Uther Pendragon.
Daire	A sea captain whose ship is based at Burdigala in Gallia. He ferries Paulus's party from Burdigala in Gallia to the relative safety of Donostia in Hispania.
Dara	One of three serving-maids who care for Ambrosius and Uther during the children's escape into exile.
Dilic	One of three serving-maids who care for Ambrosius and Uther during the children's escape into exile. Dilic is their nurse.
Elen (Queen)	The deceased wife of Magnus Maximus. She is the mother of Severa.
Endellion (Queen)	The wife of King Aeron of the Dobunni tribe. She was the illegitimate daughter of King Caradoc and Saraid, the Wise Woman of the Red Wells. She is the foster-sister and lifelong friend of Severa, Queen of the Britons.
Etain	One of three serving-maids who care for Ambrosius and Uther during the children's escape into exile.

Fortuna (Lady)	The Roman goddess of fortune.
Gorlois (King)	A young warrior from the west (the Boar of Cornwall), who becomes King of Cornwall in later life.
	He is destined to marry the beautiful Ygerne, who becomes the birth mother of King Arthur after a brutal rape in Tintagel Fortress at the hands of Uther Pendragon.
Gratian (Emperor)	The co-emperor of the Western Roman Empire who is defeated in battle by Flavius Magnus Maximus.
Helguerra	Aeron's wealthy associate in Hispania who provides a safe haven for Ambrosius and Uther during the children's exile. He resides in Donostia in Hispania and owns a large estate in nearby Apollodorus.
Hibernians	The native tribesmen of modern-day Ireland.
Honorius (Emperor)	The ruler of the Western Roman Empire from AD 393 to AD 423.
Jael and Sisera	Jael and Sisera were biblical characters. Jael killed Sisera to save the Israelites in ancient times.
Joseph the Trader	Also known as Joseph of Arimathea. Joseph was a Jew who was known to have travelled throughout Britannia and he is reputed to have visited Glastonbury. His wooden staff is believed to have been the source of the famed thorn trees of Glastonbury.
Katigern	The second son of King Vortigern. He is

sired on Caitlin, a British servant.

Macsen Wledig	The Celtic nomen of Flavius Magnus Maximus, a co-emperor of Rome.
Marcus Britannicus	An early suitor of Princess Severa. Known as *Shithead* to the troops in his command, Marcus is assassinated while attending a brothel in Corinium.
Mavourna	The amorous spouse of Daire, a ship's captain who resides in Burdigala.
Maximo (Tribune)	The commander of Roman forces in Britannia.
Maximus (Magnus)	Flavius Magnus Maximus was a Roman tribune who served under the Roman governor of Britain.
	Ambitious, he became the emperor of the Western Empire in Rome and came into conflict with Theodosius, the Emperor of the Eastern Empire in Constantinople.
	Maximus is eventually defeated and assassinated by forces loyal to Theodosius.
Otto	The headman of a fishing village at the mouth of the Loire River in Gallia.
Paulus	Constantine's Roman decurion. Paulus takes Prince Ambrosius and Prince Uther from Venta Belgarum to Hispania where they will go into exile. He will care for them for the remainder of his life.
Picts	The native tribesmen of modern-day Scotland.
Pridenow (Prince)	The son of King Aeron and Queen

Endellion of the Dobunni tribe.
While still a child, he learns that he will become an important personage in some future events regarding the future of Britannia.

Pridenow's family line will lead directly to the birth of King Arthur, the future High King of the Britons.

The Red Dragon	King Arthur, who will become the High King of the Britons.
Saraid	The Wise Woman of the Red Wells. She is the birth mother of Queen Endellion, but abandons the child as an infant. A white witch, she is a notable healer.
Scythians	An ancient European tribe. Their warriors were famous for their ability to ride their steeds while firing their bows with deadly accuracy.
Severa	The daughter of Flavius Magnus Maximus and Queen Elen, she is raised in the household of King Caradoc of the Dumnonii tribe. She marries Constantinus and bears two children, Ambrosius and Uther Pendragon, who will later become High Kings of Britannia in their own right.
	She is also the stepmother of Constans, the son of Constantinus by a previous marriage. Later still, as Constantine's widow, she will marry Vortigern, who also aspires to Britannia's throne.

She bears Vortigern one son, Vortimer.

She is important to the Arthurian legends in that she gives validity to a number of claimants who strive to achieve various thrones in Britannia.

Tello (Fulvius)	The captain of *Sea Queen*, a ship that ferries Severa's young sons from Cornwall to Gallia at the beginning of their exile.
Uther	The younger brother of Ambrosius, Uther is the second son of Severa and Constantinus, the High King of Britannia. The two brothers are exiled to Hispania after Vortigern, king of the Demetae tribe, usurps the British throne and marries Severa, the children's birth mother.

In later life, Uther will follow Ambrosius on to the throne and both will (in turn) become High Kings of the Britons. He will adopt the name of Uther Pendragon.

He will carry out a vicious rape of Queen Ygerne in Cornwall, which results in her impregnation.

This union results in the birth of Arthur, High King of the Britons.

Vortigern (King)	In early life, Vortigern is the ruler of the Demetae tribe of Britannia and, as a young soldier, he serves in Constantine's armies.

Later, as a senior officer with Constantine in Gallia, his ambition impels him to assassinate his commander's son, Constans.

Returning to Britannia, he weds Queen Severa and becomes the High King of the Britons in his own right.

He fathers a son, Vortimer, on Severa.

Later still, he will father further children on one of his Saxon servants.

Vortimer   The legitimate son of King Vortigern and Queen Severa.

MAJOR ROMAN SETTLEMENTS
IN BRITAIN (c. 360AD)

■ Roman Fortress and Legion
◉ Roman Settlement

Bremenium

Vallum
Hadriani
Onnum

Magnis

Vinovia

Bravoniacum ●   *Lavatrae* ◉

Verterae ◉

Caractonium ◉

Eburacum
VI VICTRIX ■

Bremetennacum ●

OCEANUS HIBERNICUS

Melandra ◉

Mamucium ◉

OCEANUS
GERMANICUS

Mona ◉   *Canovium* ◉   *Deva*   *Lindum* ◉
◉ *Segontium*   **XX**   *Aquae* ◉
   VICTRIX ■

Venta Icenorum
(Cerdicsand)
◉

Margidunum ◉

Letocetum ◉   *Ratae* ◉   ◉ *Causennae*

Viroconium ◉ **FOREST**   ◉ *Durobrivae*
   OF
   ARDEN ◉ *Venonae*

Salinae ◉   *Camulodunum* ◉

Moridunum   *Venta Silurum*   ● *Bannaventa*
◉   **II AUGUSTA**
Isca ■ ◉ *Glevum*

SABRINA AEST   *Abone* ◉ *Corinium*
◉ *Londinium*
Aquae Sulis ◉   *Calleva*
   Atrebatum

Lindinis ◉   ◉ *Venta Belgarum*
● *Glastonbury* ◉ *Sorviodunum*
● *Cadbury*   *Durnovaria* ◉   *Noviomagus* ◉   *Anderida*
● *Tintagel* ◉
Isca Dumnoniorum ◉   *Vectis*

BARBARIAN ATTACKS ON
ROMAN BRITAIN (c. 380AD)

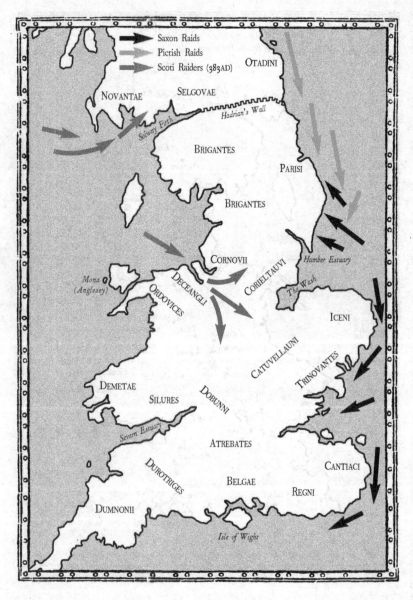

Saxon Raids
Pictish Raids
Scoti Raiders (383AD)

OTADINI

NOVANTAE   SELGOVAE

Hadrian's Wall

Solway Firth

BRIGANTES

PARISI

BRIGANTES

CORNOVII   CORIELTAUVI   *Humber Estuary*

Mona
(*Anglesey*)   DECEANGLI

ORDOVICES   *The Wash*

ICENI

CATUVELLAUNI   TRINOVANTES

DEMETAE

SILURES   DOBUNNI

Severn Estuary

ATREBATES

CANTIACI

DUROTRIGES   BELGAE
REGNI

DUMNONII

Isle of Wight

THE TWIN ROUTES FROM ARELATE
TO VENTA BELGARUM

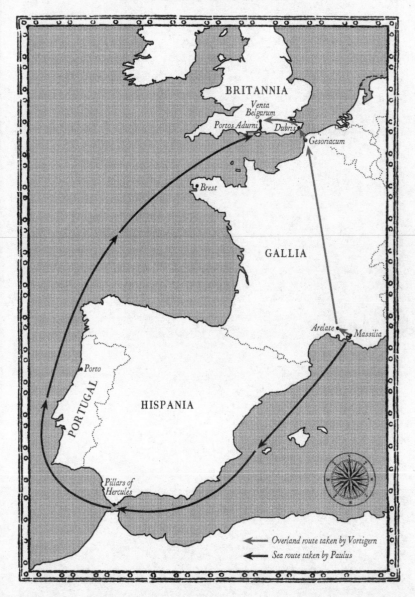

Overland route taken by Vortigern

Sea route taken by Paulus

PROLOGUE

Do not try to find out, for we are forbidden to reveal those things that the gods might bestow on you.

Horace, *Odes*, Book 1:11

Vortigern used every curse-word he knew, but the weather was unfavourable and the Briton was forced to bide his time in his dirty room in the Gallic port of Gesoriacum. Outside, the autumn skies were grimy with grey cloud, but the long-anticipated rains and onshore winds that could take ships across the Litus Saxonicum had not yet arrived. As soon as he had eaten what passed for a stew in this filthy hovel, he would return to the wharves. There, he would seek out a trading vessel's captain who might be enticed into taking him across the forty miles of open water that would give him a landfall at one of the ports on the eastern coast of Britannia. He didn't care which one; his luck had held throughout his flight across Gallia, so he was confident that he'd eventually find a ship that was prepared to risk the voyage.

Damn the weather! Damn Gesoriacum! And damn that fool, Constantinus.

After years of bowing and scraping, and deferring to that ambitious Roman and his delusions of glory, Vortigern was no longer prepared to recognise the emperor's newly acquired nomen of Flavius Claudius Constantine. The Demetae's respect for his erstwhile master had dissipated and his lupine grin would have curdled milk as he wondered if the usurper had finally been captured and strangled by his Roman enemies.

Vortigern took a sombre pleasure in thinking of the failed emperor as Constantinus, the name the would-be emperor had used when he was still a humble centurion in Rome's legions. The usurper was probably dead by now, so Vortigern was anxious to forget the many occasions when he had been forced to pay homage to a man whose ambition exceeded his ability.

The British kinglet again grinned like the wolf harboured within his rapacious heart.

'Your son is dead, Constantinus, and I hope you choke on your impotence,' Vortigern spat into the stiff breeze. 'I sent the boy into the shades, you Roman sod, so he's worm-food by now. I wish I'd told you in person that your precious boy will never sit on Maximus's throne at Venta Belgarum. But you can be assured that I'll keep the throne warm for him.'

Even this expression of hatred couldn't relieve Vortigern from the hot bile that sat in his windpipe and burned its way into his stomach. The boy, Constans, had worshipped his British mentor, so the Demetae king should have felt some vague feelings of regret when he drove his spear into the lad's back in the thick of the battle for Vienna. But he had felt no sense of shame. Constans hadn't expected treachery from his mentor and, even as he lay dying, he had begged his murderer to protect and care for his pregnant wife and unborn child. Vortigern had no intention of carrying out the boy's wishes, but he was happy to make a vow to the dying boy that would ease his pathway to the shades.

The memory made Vortigern erupt with mirth, for he'd certainly taken care of them.

As his merriment began to fade away, a small rain shower struck the windowsill and the Demetae king was forced to struggle with the swollen shutters before he eventually forced them to close. In doing so his sleeves were soaked and he cursed in frustration. Constans might be dead and Constantinus was under sentence of death, but Vortigern was still many leagues from his destination in Britannia. The last thing that he wanted was for news of the High King's death to reach Severa *before* he arrived in Venta Belgarum to resume his stewardship of the British throne.

Awake or sleeping, Queen Severa had become the focus of Vortigern's cunning mind. Something about her extreme calm had drawn him to her from the very beginning; her composure and self-confidence challenged his ability to dominate her and break her unnatural self-control. She had sat on her gilded throne like an effigy of a Roman empress and he was obsessed with the cold restraint she displayed whenever he was in her presence. If she gazed in his direction, the faintest trace of fear in her pale eyes would drive him to distraction. Her very appearance excited him, but he had always been capable of schooling his face to mask his true feelings. In his earlier sojourn in Venta Belgarum as Constantinus's regent, Vortigern had forced himself to play with her infant brats while praying to Lady Fortuna that her absent husband might yet be killed in far-off Gallia. Prince Constans had become aware of the Demetae's passion for his stepmother, but the lad accepted that this ardour was a part of Vortigern's loyalty to the joint Romano–British cause.

But Vortigern had been instructed to join his master in Gallia, while Constans was left in the care of Queen Severa. She would be given the task of preparing the youth to step into his father's boots.

A year later, Constantine had called for his son to join him in Gallia, so the Demetae had been certain that his own time was coming. The Demetae kingdom was small and its fields bore more seaweed, flint and slate than crops that could be sold for profit.

While still in his teens, Vortigern had been sent to the Romans at Isca to receive an education in the ways of the outside world. This declaration of loyalty to the Roman cause was intended to gain Vortigern some preferment and influence, attributes that might eventually enrich his impoverished kingdom.

In Tribune Maximo's headquarters, Vortigern had made the acquaintance of Constantinus, a centurion who would become High King of the Britons and, later, co-emperor of the Western Roman Empire with Honorius. Impressed with Vortigern's competence, Constantinus had invited the warrior to ride to Corinium with the troop that escorted Marcus Britannicus, the Shithead of renown, to meet his betrothed.

Here, the ill-fated betrothal between Marcus and Princess Severa had taken place with due pomp and ceremony but, with the assassination of Marcus in a filthy brothel, the fulcrum of Vortigern's life had begun to shift.

Now, as Vortigern strode through the light, drizzling rain to reach Gesoriacum's harbour, he remembered the day that Constans died. Both men had been a part of Constantine's force aligned against the defences of Vienna, a fortified town that had stubbornly persisted with its loyalty to Emperor Honorius.

Earlier, Constans had begun to distrust Vortigern's motives and aspirations during the long journey from Arelate to Vienna. After a few minor disagreements between the two men, Vortigern realised that Constans would never accept the role of a puppet ruler. As such, he was of no further use to Vortigern.

During the Battle of Vienna, Constans had been in the forefront of the initial cavalry charge but, afterwards, he had positioned himself among the foot soldiers so he could watch and absorb the ever-changing patterns of the conflict taking place around him. In accordance with his father's teachings in those early days when the lad first showed promise of becoming a capable field commander, Constans was using this experience to understand essential battle strategies and tactics.

In truth, the young man was an excellent strategist and his father followed the boy's studies with interest. He also realised that Constans was fiercely proud of his Roman ancestry, despite his quiet and reasonable demeanour. The prince hadn't shied away from revealing a growing scorn for the native tribesmen, including Vortigern's British warriors.

Constans had relinquished his horse as soon as the final charge was ordered, so he joined the infantry as they made a direct charge at the enemy's defences. Hungry for glory, Constans was eager to earn a reputation for heroism, and therefore Vortigern had no doubt that the lad would put himself in harm's way.

The Briton was given a perfect opportunity to cut the lad down while the attacking force was embroiled in the chaos of the final melee. Vortigern waited for his chance and then seized it. In such a press of men and wildly swinging blades, his treacherous blow with the spear was one of many that went unnoticed by the warriors around him.

With one well-aimed stroke, Constantinus's hopes and dreams had withered on the vine.

Abandoning his post and pausing only to steal Constans's war chest, Vortigern had returned to Arelate to ensure that Constantine was made aware of his son's heroic actions during the attack on Vienna and the sad loss of a young man who was a good friend and companion.

Later, when Fortuna changed her fickle mind and Constantine's enemies trapped the usurper inside the walls of Arelate, Vortigern knew that the time was ripe to turn his ambitions into reality. He must return to Venta Belgarum at full speed and seize the British throne from the wreckage of the emperor's dreams.

Committed to this treachery, Vortigern made his escape from Arelate by crawling through its stinking sewers. He struggled under the weight of Constans's strongbox, but he knew this treasure would be needed as a buffer against future financial disasters.

As the Briton was making his way through the mud and the slime, Constantine's defence of Arelate was turning into an unmitigated disaster. The newly integrated legions in Honorius's army had arrived on Constantine's doorstep from out of nowhere, so the newly acknowledged co-emperor had found himself surrounded by a superior force from which there was little hope of escape. If Vortigern wished to live and prosper, he must take to his heels and run for his life.

His scouts had already informed him that the town's sewers came out of the earth in the middle of the swamplands where the Rhodanus River wound its way towards the Middle Sea.

Here, quicksand and clouds of stinging insects made passage difficult, meaning this isolated spot would be perfect for his needs. But Vortigern knew that the Romans would soon become aware of this escape route and they would send scouts to secure the tunnels that lay below the city.

One way or another, Vortigern was determined to profit from the deaths of Constantine and Constans. The war chest entrusted to the boy would go a long way towards funding mercenaries and arms for his future enrichment. The gold might weigh heavily on his shoulders as he slogged his way through the vile sludge of the sewers, but residual feelings of discomfort or humiliation that remained would soon be washed away.

But he must decamp immediately if he was to escape with his life.

It took four hours to find his way through the sewers, a time that seemed like a year as he followed the slow flow of water that would eventually bleed into the swamps.

Then, once the Briton reached the swamps, he had found a suitable spot to hide the chest while he searched for horses to carry him to safety. Once again, Lady Fortuna was smiling down on him. He had discovered a careless scout who was relieving himself near a thicket outside the margins of the swamp. After making short work of the incapacitated cavalryman, Vortigern gratefully accepted the man's uniform and all three of his horses. Then, with a sigh of relief, he retrieved the treasure chest and began to make his way upriver by following the wide, heavily frequented Roman road.

Safe within his disguise and mounted on good horseflesh, Vortigern travelled north. While this road was an open thoroughfare with a great deal of traffic, anything was better than crawling through the slime of the swamps and trusting to his luck in the south.

Vortigern wasn't stopped, or asked to account for himself, during the entire journey.

He found that Gallia was in ruins, for every kinglet had been forced to shore up his own walls rather than pay attention to nondescript scouts in the service of Honorius. He made his way through Gallia like a mud-stained ghost.

Once he reached Gesoriacum on the northern coast, Vortigern was close to success and safety. He could almost smell the green fields of Britannia that lay across the waters of the Litus Saxonicum, but the prevailing winds remained fixed and they would give no assistance to those ships that sought to travel into the west. He knew that Severa would be waiting nervously for word of her husband, so he was forced to gnaw at his bottom lip in frustration. If the queen received word of Constantine's death prematurely, she would realise that human raptors were about to swarm over the gates of Venta Belgarum to take her by force and lay claim to her husband's kingdom. He must reach the city before another opportunist did so.

Vortigern's plans depended on Severa being caught by surprise in Venta Belgarum, a place where she was separated from her powerful kin. As a bonus, her infant sons would lie in the palms of his hands and she would know she was a defenceless pawn in his game.

A brief gust of rain hit him with force but, on this occasion, the sudden torrential downpour struck him from behind. Hell, the wind was beginning to change! What were rain and discomfort, though, if a kingdom was waiting for him in Venta Belgarum? Smiling, Vortigern turned swiftly towards the wharf.

Eventually, one of the port's unemployed ship's captains was cajoled into trusting his luck on the narrow stretch of water between Gesoriacum and Dubris. With his horses securely tethered on the deck and his strongbox under his lean flanks, Vortigern sat at the prow of the wallowing vessel and willed the breeze to fill the patched sail and drive the old vessel towards the shores of Britannia. When the white-chalk cliffs near Dubris eventually came into view, he spat into the surging waters and luxuriated in a feeling of nostalgia when he saw the British sentinel fires rising sullenly through intermittent sheets of rain.

He was coming home.

'Those other fools can hunger for glory in Gallia and Italia. Those old lands aren't for me and I'll take my chances on a smaller prize. Severa and Britannia are enough for any man.'

Vortigern laughed when he saw that the ship's captain was staring at him with an odd expression on his face; he realised he must have spoken aloud.

'I suggest that you should remember my name, Captain. I, Vortigern, will rule these isles before the year is out.'

The captain dropped his eyes to hide his embarrassment and superstition, causing Vortigern to laugh with a rasping irony that made the hairs rise on the back of the hapless sailor's neck. A lifetime of experience told him that passengers such as this man should be given a wide berth, for they are unpredictable and violent, and almost inhuman in their capacity for cruelty.

'Take care that I've no reason to remember you, Captain,' Vortigern added, and winked with pleasure as a rainbow caught the dim afternoon light and lit the way towards a small harbour still wreathed in mist. Finally, after the best part of a decade away from his lands, Vortigern had returned to claim his birthright.

CHAPTER I

BANISHMENT

Maybe one day it will be cheering to remember these
things.

Virgil, *Aeneid*, Book 1

Paulus stared out into the black water that encircled the ancient
fishing boat. Impatience creased his face into deep, lugubrious
wrinkles while his old skin, like a too-large tunic, fell in folds
towards his softening gut. Deep in contemplation, the old
decurion ran his hands over the white whiskers that stippled his
cheeks and jowls, and the touch made him feel unkempt and
filthy.

I hate being furred like a barbarian, he thought glumly as he
felt the week-long growth of facial hair. I should have died with
my master!

His mind returned to those terrible days when Britannia's
army was besieged within the enclosing walls of Arelate. Caught
like a rat in a trap, Constantine had to choose between facing

Honorius's forces and making a fighting retreat through a morass of swamps and quicksands, or surrendering the remnants of his army to an implacable enemy.

Constantine had begged Paulus to escape the siege of Arelate by making his way through the sewers and taking his chances outside the walls. After all, Vortigern had taken the same route some hours earlier when he had opted to desert his post. Paulus had blanched at Constantine's unintended insult and refused the order out of hand, for no legionnaire with hard-earned rank would consider abandoning his fellows in the face of an impending defeat.

'I'll be a soldier till my dying day, master, and I refuse to run away like a mongrel dog. I won't desert my men, not even for you!'

Constantine had looked at him as if he was searching for a telling argument that would convince the decurion to take to the sewers and make good his escape. As always, those black eyes seemed flat, but Paulus had known his commander for many years and their friendship stretched back to a time when they had first served with Rome's armies in Britannia. The decurion was familiar with that studied analysis and personal manipulation that Constantine exercised whenever he wanted to achieve his own ends, even when he was trying to coerce a reluctant friend. The commander's hawkish nose, handsome cheekbones and black eyes were much as they had always been, similar to the centurion of old, a man whom Paulus had loved with all his being.

'Constans is dead, Paulus,' Constantine said. 'My son has gone to the shades and I have been the architect of his death,' he added starkly. 'I'm aware of the mistakes I've made and I must bear the guilt for my failures, but I won't allow my other sons to have their throats cut by assassins if I can save them from an undeserved fate. You're my only hope, Paulus, so I intend to place their lives into your hands. Who else can I trust?'

'But Queen Severa will do everything in her power to save your sons and she has the ways and means to protect them. She also has kin who will stand between the boys and any enemies who would inflict harm on them. I'm just an old man, sire, one who has no place in a world that has moved beyond his understanding. Who would listen to an old man who has lived beyond his allotted span on God's earth?'

Constantine turned his back on Paulus and stared out from the unshuttered window that gave him a clear view of the empty streets of Arelate and the walls that lay beyond them. He could see the huge, black shadows that were slowly approaching the town walls; enormous, box-like constructions that groaned as their wheels bit into the loose earth. He could hear the sharp protest of heavy, creaking timbers as the multi-storeyed siege machines were pushed and dragged towards Arelate's defences. Constantine felt a renewed sense of urgency when he saw his troops scatter to the new defensive positions that would confront these fearsome threats. Honorius's general had been provided with the means to rain death on his legionnaires and the ultimate fate of his army would then be sealed.

'Are you able to lift your sword, Paulus? Can you kill your enemies as you would have done in the days of your youth? Of course you can! Roman soldiers are required to face every kind of death that might consign them to the shades, but there's no doubt that we all have fears for our own mortality. You've lived a long and fruitful life and you've learned how Fortuna can desert us in the twinkling of an eye. Who else should I send to save my babes? Who else could I trust to carry out this last duty to a friend of long standing?' Constantine's voice revealed nothing of the fears that were jerking at his nerve endings.

Ever the realist, Paulus could only shrug and accept his master's orders. Constantine was caught in an iron trap and he would have to gnaw off his own foot if he was to extricate himself from Arelate. Even if the emperor escaped, the carnage and bloodshed inflicted on the citizens of the city would be terrible and the common people would pay a price for their loyalty to Constantine. The decurion understood the strategic position and he knew in his heart that the arrival of these siege machines would bring an end to Constantine's defence of Arelate.

'I intend to relinquish the title of Augustus and I will beg the bishop to ordain me as a priest in the Church of Rome. Once I've made my peace with God, I will bargain with Honorius's general for the lives of my men. Have pity on me, my friend, for the last thing I want is to trample my honour into the mud of Arelate. I hope to gain some redemption for my hubris by saving as many of my legionnaires as possible, even though this will come at a cost to my pride and dignity.'

He grinned ruefully and turned to face his decurion.

'You can understand my predicament, my old friend and sword-companion. At the end of the day, I will always be a centurion and I'll never desert my men.'

Paulus was appalled. He tried to devise a better option than making a cowardly retreat into the doubtful sanctuary offered by the Roman Church. He racked his brain to devise an alternative strategy that Constantine could use to escape with his life, but every method of escape led to closed doors. Was there any hope for his master?

'Vortigern has already deserted his post and slipped out of Arelate,' Constantine continued. 'He escaped in the last hour or two and I've no doubt that he'll ride like the wind to the nearest port. He intends to find a boat there that will take him to Britannia and, once safely ashore, he'll make his way to Venta Belgarum. When he arrives in my city, he'll force Severa into marriage at the earliest opportunity, whether she is willing or not. Ambrosius and Uther will have no chance of survival if Vortigern can assume the role of regent.'

Paulus tried to protest, but his logical mind told him that Severa's boys were in mortal danger. Eventually, the decurion accepted the inevitable and agreed to abide by his master's wishes. 'I'll do whatever I can to protect your boys, but Queen Severa will also be in great danger without a capable man to protect her.'

'I have no fears for Severa's personal safety,' Constantine said. 'She is a resourceful woman and she'll find some way to bend Vortigern to her will. I could almost feel sorry for the bastard!' His voice had a bitter ring and his face had twisted from an emotion that was akin to hatred.

'But your lady has always been loyal to you, sire. From what I've seen, she has supported you in every way and I've seen nothing in her nature that would warrant criticism from any man.' Paulus's rebuke caused Constantine to shift his weight from one foot to the other in shame, but the bitterness he felt towards Severa remained obvious to the decurion.

Now, on the high seas, Paulus's ship was heading towards an unknown landfall on the southern coast of Britannia. As he stood in the prow of the vessel and tried to cope with the waves of seasickness that threatened to overwhelm his stomach, he refused to dwell further on his own departure from Arelate.

While the decurion was staggering through the slime and muck that fouled the walls and floors of the old sewers, the disgusting stench had threatened to overcome him. But the sights and smells of the sewers were as nothing when compared to the thoughts that flooded his imagination when he recalled the shame of Constantine's retreat and his subsequent surrender to their enemies.

When he finally climbed out of the sewer and lowered himself into the swampwaters with the shambling gait of an old man, he had cursed the ties that bound him to his master and the habits of disciplined obedience that would force him to feel shame for the remainder of his life. As it happened, Paulus's aged and careworn appearance proved to be an excellent disguise, for he experienced little difficulty in passing through the bands of legionnaires who patrolled the lanes and byways between Arelate and Massilia.

In the port city, he used some of Constantine's store of gold coins to purchase a berth on a decrepit trading vessel that would take him to the Pillars of Hercules, Western Hispania and onwards to Portus Adurni on the southern coast of Britannia. Seasickness had racked his exhausted frame, but a small core of obstinacy began to quicken Paulus's spirits. With luck, he could reach Venta Belgarum before Vortigern if the Briton had actually travelled by the overland route to Gesoriacum.

Discreet questions asked of the denizens of Massilia's lowlife hadn't revealed any information about a Briton seeking to take ship for Britannia, so Paulus decided that Vortigern must have taken the road leading to Gesoriacum and was by now a long way into Gallia's north.

* * *

When Paulus had finally arrived at his destination, he realised that the citizens of Venta Belgarum must have been surviving on a knife edge of fear for many months. Clad in filthy civilian clothing and astride a nondescript old horse, the decurion had taken pains to ensure that he wouldn't be recognisable as Constantine's erstwhile Roman servant who was newly returned from the Gallic wars. He'd even taken the precaution of hiding his gladius in the pack on his spare horse, a luxury he'd been reluctant to purchase, despite knowing that an extra mount would be essential if he was forced to run from Venta Belgarum with two young children in tow. For his personal protection, he had thrust an evil-looking stabbing knife through his old legionnaire's belt. He was trying hard to look harmless and senile.

With an old man's openness, Paulus smiled amiably at the gatekeeper who halted him at the walls of the town.

'Where do you think you're going with that nasty weapon in your belt, Grandfather?'

The gatekeeper must have been a bully boy in his younger days, but his body had run to fat from advancing age, laziness and gluttony. Still, he managed to display an aggressive manner that was better suited to a younger and more dangerous man.

'Look at me, young sir!' Paulus forced his mouth to smile affably. 'Would you begrudge an old man the protection of a weapon? My daughter's a maid up at the big house.'

The gatekeeper spat on to the cobbles with the bravado of a man who won't be taken to account. 'So she's one of them that live on the hill, is she? It's a sad day when British lands are ruled by a bitch while her man is away in the wars. We'd like her better if we knew what she's doing to keep innocent citizens safe from them Saxon bastards that beset us.'

Paulus's palms itched to strike out at this florid servant whose bearded chin and bulbous nose were thrust out in his direction. Instead, the decurion bit down on his anger and stayed for a brief gossip. The exchange was profitable, for he realised that no word had reached the town of the disasters in Gallia.

And nothing had been heard of Vortigern.

Paulus grimaced. He was fated to be the storm crow that must tell the citizens of Britannia that many of their young warriors had died on the fields of Gallia. Inevitably, the women of the town would rend their tunics and curse him with their eyes when the terrible losses became common knowledge.

'It's time I was on my way, my friend,' he announced before kicking his horse in the ribs and riding off into the heart of Venta Belgarum. Surprised at the sudden dismissal, the gatekeeper watched him pass through the gates to enter the town.

Paulus had fond memories of Venta Belgarum from previous visits to the city. The flavours of Rome had been successfully blended into the British tribal culture, so the best attributes of both races had coalesced into the sense of purpose, wealth and security that lived within the hearts of those citizens who resided within the city's walls. Tired after his time in the saddle, the decurion still noted that a flock of fat gulls had taken up residence in many of the open areas and the aggressive birdlife was demanding food from passing citizens or snatching at morsels of garbage. The birds' search for treasure was accompanied by raucous screams of self-satisfaction and scorn.

But where were the ordinary citizens of the city?

Once he was close to the King's Hall, Paulus found an inn that offered stables for his horses. Then, after paying a few coppers to the hostelry, he left his possessions in the landlord's care with a warning to ensure their safety. Having made these preparations, he found a water trough where he could cleanse his face, hands and feet of the grime he had collected during the overland journey from Portus Adurni.

Squelching in his wet half-boots, Paulus made his way toward the paved forecourt and the King's Hall that opened directly on to it. By this time, noon had passed and the afternoon was well advanced. His stomach grumbled hungrily.

As Paulus approached the large, dragon-decorated doors that led into the King's Hall, he was stopped abruptly by two tall warriors. With no respect for Paulus's age, one of them placed a muscular hand on the decurion's chest to bring him to a halt.

'Don't you recognise me, lad? I'm Paulus, decurion to Constantine Augustus. I come with a message for Queen Severa from her husband.'

'I've never seen you before, old man, so you could be anybody,' the grey-eyed warrior answered evenly. Paulus was close enough now to see the face below the shadow of the guard's helmet and he decided that this lad was no older than sixteen years and could, perhaps, have been even younger. 'I'll inform the steward of your arrival. If you are who you claim to be, he'll remember you. If he acknowledges you, I'll accompany you to my sister. Wait here!'

Sister? Severa was an only child, Paulus had thought; he was nonplussed at this new development. Still, the Britons had a habit of extending their families through fostering, so it was difficult to unravel the snarled threads of tribal relationships.

Paulus shrugged in acceptance of the situation as the guard hurried away. While he waited, he remembered his sketchy history of Roman military commanders. The very first emperor of Rome, Augustus, had used his relationship with his foster-father, Julius Caesar, to validate his claim to the throne of Rome, so how should Paulus be permitted to criticise the machinations that occurred among the families of the British rulers?

The guard returned and asked the decurion to follow him to the queen's private courtyard. Although the young man's manner was courteous, this breach of normal protocol and etiquette caused Paulus to raise one eyebrow in surprise. Still, he let his guide lead him through the great hall and into the maze of corridors and renovated apartments that had turned a modest villa into a confusing, two-storey hybrid of a royal palace. Paulus was convinced that he would never be able to retrace his steps unassisted.

The two men made their way along a dark corridor and through a heavy door, emerging into the suddenly blinding light of an early autumn afternoon. Even the slight chill was unable to dim the golden dazzle of the warm sun.

The queen's walled courtyard was bathed in bright sunshine and this hideaway served as a warm refuge from the cares and darkness of the Hall of Justice and the weight of Severa's royal duties. An oasis of calm in the dark complexities of her palace, the queen's courtyard was open to the weather except for a number of vines entwined through the bare rafters so they could drop their late blossoms on to the cobbled courtyard below. As well, pots of fragrant late-blooming roses stood among the vines, so the perfumed air and clear skies washed over Paulus with an illusion of freedom and gracious civilisation.

The queen was sitting among her women like a widow in a crowd of bridal guests. To Paulus, she seemed dowdy in an all-encompassing robe while her ladies were wearing every pastel shade that fashion could create. Their laughter as they busied themselves with embroidery or mending contrasted with the queen's utter stillness as she waited for Paulus to join her in the courtyard.

As if the gift of clairvoyance had made her aware of the news that was about to arrive with a hapless courier, she was clad in deepest black.

Paulus scanned the faces of the ladies' maids and other aristocratic attendants, but he failed to find a single familiar face. Nor were her children present. Paulus wondered if some other disaster had befallen this sad woman while he'd been travelling in foreign lands. There was no possible way that news of Constantine's fate could have reached her before his arrival.

As Paulus entered the courtyard with her foster-brother, the queen turned towards them, her face pallid and expressionless.

'What has happened, Paulus? Tell me your news this very moment, for my guesses have turned into nightmarish imaginings. Does my husband still live? What of Constans? Has he truly perished?' Her words were almost desperate, yet her features remained as stiff as a mask.

'Constantine was still alive when I left Arelate, Highness. However, we had suffered a series of reverses and he was forced to surrender himself into the hands of Emperor Honorius. By now, he will have relinquished the purple and accepted the robes and tonsure of the Church of Rome. Your husband hopes to save the lives of the men who followed him into battle seeking the blessing of the good fathers. Whether Honorius honours these requests is debatable, but I doubt that he will show mercy to my master. You must prepare yourself for bad news.'

'Thank you for speaking so truthfully, Paulus. I'm surrounded by kindly folk who try to keep my spirits high with promises that Constantine will survive. He won't return, will he?'

'Not in this life, Highness. Perhaps we shall be reunited in the next world, if the words of Jesus are true . . . but Venta Belgarum will never again welcome its lord and master.'

He paused delicately.

'With regards to Constans, I must confirm that you were advised correctly. Constans was killed in the battle for Vienna, Highness. Unfortunately, your husband blamed himself for this particular tragedy.'

Paulus kept his eyes fixed on the queen's strong-boned face while he searched for any signs of the flawed character that had angered his master and caused him to abandon his wife during the latter years of his life. All that Paulus could see was a woman who was bowed down by troubles, even as she struggled to find the strength to meet her responsibilities. The effort to remain untroubled and serene for the sake of her people was crushing her spirit.

The queen turned to face the young bodyguard. 'Sit with me and hold my hand, Pridenow, for I can tell that Paulus bears more bad news that must be shared with us.'

As an afterthought, she introduced the young man as her foster-mother's second son.

'I can confirm that Constans met his death during the battle for Vienna,' Paulus repeated. 'There was some talk that he was struck down from behind.'

'I am already in receipt of that news, but I had hoped that word of his death might have been sent to me in error. What else, Paulus? What of Vortigern? Did the Demetae king survive the battle?'

Severa's eyes had hardened as she asked these last questions, so Paulus deduced that the queen was aware of her vulnerable position and Vortigern's duplicity. She was trying to put a brave face on a dangerous situation, for everyone who knew the Demetae kinglet had learned to distrust him.

'Yes, Highness, he survived. Vortigern was seen after the battle for Vienna was over, but he deserted his men and rode back to Arelate with the news of Constans's death. I'd been made aware that the boy, Constans, had taken his fatal wound from *behind*, and this information added itself to rumours among the legion-naires that Vortigern's hands were stained with Constans's blood. I was told that there had been harsh words between the two men on the road from Arelate to Vienna, but no warrior in their century had the balls to accuse Vortigern of murder. In the days that followed, Vortigern must have felt that Constantine would take him to account for the assassination of Constans, so the Demetae decamped from his post after the Roman legions mounted their siege on Arelate. He did so on the same day that I made my own escape. To the best of my knowledge, he plans to travel via Gallia to Dubris and thence to Venta Belgarum. I've managed to outpace him, but his arrival must be imminent. Before I left Arelate, Constantine extracted a vow from me that I would travel to Venta Belgarum, find your sons and protect them with my life. Are the children still in the palace?'

'No, Paulus! I've taken the precaution of sending the boys to King Aeron in Corinium in anticipation of a disaster occurring in Gallia. Aeron has arranged for the boys to be spirited away to a place of safety if they should be threatened. Are they in immediate danger?'

Paulus could only nod, as the prospect of another long ride to the Dobunni town of Corinium loomed before him. Fortunately, the road between Venta Belgarum and Corinium was well maintained.

'Fetch some writing materials for me, Pridenow,' Severa ordered, before turning back to continue her conversation with Paulus.

'I'll give you a missive for my foster-parents that will explain your arrival in Corinium and ensure that you're taken into their confidence. I'll leave it to them to explain the arrangements that have been made for the safety of my sons. I admit that your arrival has eased my fears, Paulus, for you have always been well loved in my household. My husband often described you as the rock on which he could always rely. Like Constantine, I am forced to ask one last service from you in memory of the man you have served for most of your adult life. Please, Paulus, accompany my sons to that place of sanctuary that Father Aeron has selected for them and, once there, cherish them and see to their future. They must not be permitted to forget their birthright.'

Paulus lowered his head in case she should see the moisture in his eyes.

During the days of the Republic, Roman women were expected to be stoic and courageous, just like this woman. As a small boy, Paulus had heard tales of the courage and exemplary character that Julius Caesar's wife had displayed, as this queen now did.

The decurion considered the crosses that she was forced to bear. Her children, little more than infants and wholly dependent on strangers to provide for their welfare, had been torn from her breast. To add to her woes, Severa had loved her stepson, Constans, and had laboured hard to teach him the rudiments of rule. But the lad had gone into the darkness now and he would never return. Her husband, absent and estranged from her in recent years, had also been swept away by fate in recent times. Now she would be forced to hold a fractured throne together with no expectation of praise. Paulus recalled the gatekeeper's scornful description of the queen as a bitch and felt a frisson of shame for the man's lack of respect.

'You must flee, Lady Severa. At the very least, you must make some provision for your continued safety. Vortigern will arrive sooner, rather than later, and any fool can tell you that he'll use your political standing to his own advantage.'

His protests fell on deaf ears. She had made up her mind and the decision was irrevocable.

'I'd be breaking my trust with the citizens of Britannia if I deserted the King's Hall and left the people of Venta Belgarum to their own devices. I intend to reason with Vortigern if such a course of action is possible. He does have affection for me, so I may be able to temper some of his cruelty. It's my duty, Paulus. You, more than most others, are able to understand that.'

'Vortigern has no softness or generosity in him, my lady. You'll be throwing your life away for little reward. You'll be raped and turned into a puppet ruler who will be forced to preside helplessly over the destruction of all you know and love in Britannia.'

Severa smiled, and Paulus drew in his breath as he saw her hidden loveliness suddenly exposed.

'I've already decided that I shall keep Vortigern fully occupied in Britannia. The Saxons come every summer and they swarm in the east like gnats that are sucking at our blood. We already have vicious killers battering at our doors, so I'll send my rapacious wolf of a husband to beat them at their own game. With any luck at all, I'll rarely see him. I'll survive, Paulus, as long as Vortigern can be kept occupied with hordes of enemies on the point of his sword.'

Paulus was unable to stifle a sudden chuckle. Severa had read Vortigern's character exactly. This queen was clever as well as courageous, and he was left to wonder why Constantine had rejected her.

'But Vortigern mightn't need you once he becomes High King, my lady. He'll kill you if your beauty fades, or if he should tire of you.'

'As God wills!' Severa answered resolutely. 'It will be interesting to see if Vortigern offers me protestations of love and concessions to gallantry if he attempts to win my favour. I understand my worth to him, both now and in the future, so any betrothal between us must have mutual value if it is to be acceptable to both parties. Vortigern isn't stupid! He wants the crown and, should he take it by force, his relationship with the British kings will lead to civil war if his newly wed queen is seen to be other than compliant.'

Severa giggled and the sound reminded Paulus of a child playing at games.

'If he gives me the chance, I'll act as Jael did when she saved the Israelites in biblical times. I'd happily dispatch Vortigern into the shades to save my Britons, just as Jael saved the Israelites by slaying Sisera with a nail driven into his forehead. My greatest fear would be the chance that Vortigern might sire a child on me. My hands would be tied then.'

'Any pregnancy would be awkward, Highness,' Paulus answered levelly before changing the subject. 'I must set off for

Corinium as soon as I can, but I must rest for a few hours while this old body of mine recuperates a little. My horses were exhausted by the time I reached Venta Belgarum so they too will need some time to recover their strength.'

The queen gasped. 'I'm sorry, Paulus. I've been dwelling on my own problems and I've failed to consider your plight. You're exhausted and you must be ravenous with hunger.'

As she spoke, Pridenow returned to the room with a writing box in one hand, so the queen turned to one of her handmaidens. 'Lydia, ask Jerome to see to food and accommodation for our decurion.' Severa paused and considered her next instructions carefully before continuing. 'Jerome can arrange a warm bed, some new clothes and a change of horses for our Roman friend. He can also arrange more weaponry for him.'

She turned back to Pridenow to issue further instructions. 'You, Pridenow, will organise a small troop of ten cavalrymen under Paulus's command to accompany you on your travels throughout the isles with Paulus and the boys. You must understand, Pridenow, that you are under the direct command of Paulus and you'll carry out the decurion's instructions as if I was personally issuing his orders. Paulus will also be given sufficient coin, in both gold and silver, to ensure his survival, and that of my boys, for the foreseeable future. Further funds will be made available as they are required.'

Severa turned back to Paulus as her ladies scattered to carry out her instructions.

'I may not be able to achieve much, but at least I have the power to make decisions that will ease your journey and ensure your safety. One matter that must be stressed, Paulus, is that Pridenow is not permitted to leave the shores of Britannia under any circumstances. Should you accept him as the commander of your bodyguard, this requirement is sacrosanct and will not be disobeyed – regardless of the situation.'

Pridenow scowled briefly at the last instruction.

'I'll protect the decurion with my life, sister,' he swore. 'But it seems I'll be forced to abide by this vow in Britannia – because you won't allow me to leave your clutches.'

Pridenow gave a wry grin; he and his foster-sister were sharing long-standing banter. Despite a slight tremor of fear that betrayed her hidden terrors, Severa responded to his teasing with a reluctant smile.

'You're a scamp, Pridenow, and your attempts to escape your destiny can sometimes be foolish and very trying. Off you go now, because you have much to do before you leave in the morning. Complete your preparations and planning tonight, because Paulus will need to make his departure at first light.'

She glanced towards the door, as if she half-expected Vortigern to stride into the room at any moment.

'Don't worry, sister, I'll deploy some of our scouts to alert us if your Demetae suitor is making an approach to the city. If that happens, I'll ensure that Paulus is spirited away before Vortigern arrives. Now, good sir, where might I find your horses and your packs?'

With a pleasurable sigh, Paulus sank into a pallet made from soft linens and pillows stuffed with goose-down. The luxury of a hot bath and a face that had been scraped clean by a servant filled him with a sense of well-being. He'd gorged himself on fresh food after weeks of hard-tack rations, and his whole body relaxed with a rare contentment.

'Good ale, a full belly and a clean bed are all that a soldier really needs from life,' Paulus said to himself as he thanked the servant who escorted him to his quarters. 'My task begins tomorrow but, for tonight, I'm a free man,' he added to the servant, who was surprised at the candour of this grandfather who was obviously a valued guest.

Paulus was enjoying the sheer pleasure of using his voice in the company of others. He had been alone for a long time until this afternoon, so he had gabbled on for far longer than was his habit. When Severa had asked about his history with Constantine, in his loneliness he had told her everything that he could remember, including his childhood in the north of Italia where he had been the second son of a blacksmith. He could still remember the heat of the forge and the magic of bending hot iron to his will, but he had always been determined to join the legions. Eventually, he had left the river valleys and the fields of grain that moved like green water in the scything winds.

In all the years that had passed, he had never returned to that long-lost home.

Perhaps Paulus was talking too much, but much of his garrulousness was the prerogative of advancing age.

While Paulus was catching up on his much-needed sleep, Pridenow selected a small troop of warriors who would accompany the Roman on his travels. After briefing them on their duties, he began to prepare his personal equipment and the full set of kit that would be placed at the decurion's disposal. This last task was particularly pleasing for the impressionable young warrior when he learned that Paulus was one of those rarities, a free-born legionnaire who had served with Rome's legions for all of his adult life. In thirty years, he had never again set foot on the soil of Italia.

When he finally looked into the old man's room at midnight, Pridenow noticed that Paulus was sleeping lightly, even in such a safe place. He had barely taken two steps into the room when Paulus catapulted himself to his feet in the crouch of a knife-fighter, with his weapon upright and ready to draw blood.

'I don't think I'll ever try this again, will I?' Pridenow responded with a wink. 'I've brought your gladius and your saddlebags to your quarters. I understand how much it pains a military man to be separated from his weapons, so I've taken the liberty of preparing a full set of kit; you can make a selection of what you're likely to need. I've also brought a small whetstone with me for you to sharpen your blades with before we set off on the morrow.'

Carefully, and with his eyes never leaving the old man's face, Pridenow placed the sword and scabbard at the end of the pallet, then added a sharpening kit that was identical to the one normally used by legionnaires of all ranks.

Paulus lowered his knife with a wry smile and gave the lad a brief nod of thanks.

'Sorry about my response, lad! I'm afraid that I've retained some old habits. But I thank you for the consideration you've shown me,' he added to qualify his reaction to the sudden awakening. He smiled again as he realised that the prince no longer considered himself a boy. 'There's no need to colour up at being called a lad, Pridenow, for every warrior seems young to an old bastard like me. You're a sharp young man with a very pleasant manner about you, and I believe that you'll go far in this world. We shall mix well together, you and I.'

'I won't travel at all if my family has any say in the matter,'

Pridenow retorted and, when the old soldier looked inquiring, the youth laughed ruefully. 'I'll tell you the whole superstition when we're on the road to Corinium. For the moment, sir, you must go back to sleep. It's still hours before I can go to bed and I'd like to continue with my preparations.'

When he eventually made his way to his spartan soldier's pallet, Pridenow realised he was relishing the prospect of travelling with this Roman legionnaire. Imagine the marvels that can be learned from such a warrior, Pridenow thought. His heels clicked on the wooden floors with renewed vigour at the prospect of his wonderful luck.

Paulus slept the sleep of the truly innocent for the remainder of the night.

In the morning, he woke to one of those perfect days that occasionally dusted Venta Belgarum with a golden haze and he was overjoyed when he clambered to his feet without the usual joint pains and regrets for lost youth that had beset him in recent months. Distinct rays of light entered his room from the small windows and caressed his highly polished gladius and the precious metal inlaid into his scabbard. Paulus dressed quickly in the soft clothes of a prosperous townsman. The fabric allowed his chain-mail vest to fit comfortably over his tunic without any chance of bare skin chafing against metal. After lacing up a set of the leather half-trews used for riding, he donned a full red cloak that had once belonged to his master and had been found by the queen in her clothes chest. The decurion was grateful to Severa for providing him with this symbol of Rome's military heritage. After a lifetime as a legionnaire, he would have felt naked without a cloak, and his own one had been left behind in Arelate.

One of Severa's servants entered Paulus's room with a tray on which porridge, honey and a bowl of nuts awaited his pleasure. With a sigh of contentment, Paulus broke his fast with a will as he sampled the excellent ale that came in a horn mug. He spooned the porridge into his mouth with the single-minded concentration of a soldier who understands the need to ensure his body is well fuelled. Afterwards, the servant returned with a bowl of warmed water so he could cleanse his face and hands in preparation for a long day in the saddle.

Paulus sallied forth into the morning sunshine to find that the forecourt of the King's Hall was a hive of movement and disciplined bustle. As he checked the harness of the team of horses that would haul a clumsy, two-wheeled wagon, Pridenow raised one hand in greeting. Ten British warriors were waiting with their horses on the cobbles. All young men and all seconded from Severa's personal guard, they had prepared their kit and were ready to undertake an exciting adventure for which they had received only the vaguest of briefings. They watched intently as the queen's servants loaded baskets of supplies into the tray of the wagon.

'Are you well rested, Paulus?'

Severa stood behind him, her funereal skirts drawn up to avoid the mud and dung that had been churned up by the horses in the forecourt.

They spoke briefly of nothing in particular as Paulus's new horses were led up to him for his approval. He smiled delightedly to discover that the mounts were young, frisky and well muscled. As he inspected them, he noted that each animal's long-lashed eyes were alive with spirit.

Grateful, he thanked the queen for her generosity. 'I'd be

failing my master if I didn't make one last appeal to you, Highness. You're far too important to the citizens of this kingdom to throw your life away needlessly. Please make provisions for your safety.'

'I matter very little, Paulus. It's a fact that I'm now of less importance than you, for you have the task of saving my boys from those who would harm them. My path was set before I was born. Indeed, I am more of a Briton today than a Roman. I've chosen my road and it lies with Britannia.'

Paulus longed to present her with a gift of some worth that would show the esteem in which he held her. But he possessed no coin of his own to purchase the smallest of trinkets. Instead, he bowed low and knelt on one knee in the mud, careless of fouling his clean clothing.

Severa made a small cry of protest, but Paulus took her hands in his own and felt their strength under the sheath of soft skin.

'I've seen Roman women aplenty in a long life, my lady, and some of these have been high-born while others have come from the peasantry. Yet I can swear to you, my lady, that no Roman matron has matched your honour and your gravitas. I believe the wife of Julius Caesar would have been a woman such as yourself as well as his famed mother, who was also noted for her piety. I pray that those men who stand against you will come within reach of my sword.'

Severa blushed hotly, giving her the animation of a young girl. 'You do me too much honour, Paulus. Please rise, for I'm only a woman who tries to do the best she can.'

'Good for you, Decurion,' a male voice interrupted them. 'I often tell my sister that she is too good for this world, but she won't believe me.' Pridenow strode through the press of men to assist the old soldier to his feet.

Severa drew a fat purse from the folds of her robe and pressed it into Paulus's hands. He tried to refuse the offering, for he could tell by its weight that many gold coins were straining the heavy leather.

'Your husband has already given me funds aplenty and those coins are more than ample for my needs, Queen Severa. You may need his gold to fulfil your own needs, if I've correctly judged the grasping nature of Vortigern.'

Her eyes were steady and unafraid as she gazed up at him.

'All being well, you will have the responsibility of training, educating and caring for my boys. You will need to hire tutors, protect them from harm and love them. To provide the basic necessities, you will have to hire women who can help you with their persons, as well as bodyguards who can ensure their safety. Your expenses will be heavy, especially when the boys are approaching manhood. When this gold is gone, you must send word to Pridenow and I will contrive to send more coin to you. I want Ambrosius and Uther to be raised like princes rather than as peasants.

'Please make sure that I remain in their memories, Paulus, for I'm fearful that I'll never see them again in this life. I beg you to remind them daily how much I have loved them during their short lives.' She took a deep, shuddering breath. 'One other matter is troubling me. I ask that you take special care of Uther. The boy is noisy and hot-tempered, and he is less stable than his older brother. He must be schooled to become a gentler person.'

'I'll try to do everything as you would, my lady,' Paulus promised. He felt his eyes prickle and cursed the streak of sentiment in his nature that had grown with advancing age.

I'm about to become a grandfather, an old man who sits beside the fire and weeps into his ale for long-dead friends, he thought in wonder when he realised his life was about to change.

'Come, Paulus! It's my limited experience that extended farewells are painful for everyone concerned.' Pridenow guided Paulus towards his new horse. Taking the old man's left boot into his linked hands, he boosted him into the saddle. This action was conducted so naturally that Paulus was not in the least offended by the assistance.

'Farewell, Lady Severa. We who are soon to die . . .'

Paulus allowed his words to peter out. After all, little else remained to be said.

On this bright morning, the small column moved along the quiet streets of Venta Belgarum, through the city gates and out into the countryside. Although he longed to turn his head, the decurion kept his face turned towards the north and the heavy weight of duty that lay before him.

CHAPTER II

A WOLF IN SHEEP'S CLOTHING

I see the better things, and approve: I follow the worse.

Ovid, *Metamorphosis*, Book 7:20

Pridenow was happy. The journey to Corinium would be of sufficient duration that he'd have Paulus to himself for a few days while this well-kept, safe and uneventful road stretched out before them. He felt the assigned task of guarding this Roman decurion was child's play, so he looked forward to the prospect of extracting a number of stories from Paulus's memory.

'Your weather shows no mercy to an old man's bones, lad,' Paulus muttered as he stretched his aching legs to regain some feeling in his feet. Long hours in the saddle were no longer as easy or as pleasant as they had been in his younger days and Paulus was grateful when Pridenow had finally brought the column to a halt.

The small contingent of riders made camp before the end of the first day's travel and Pridenow ordered the young warriors to prepare a defensive perimeter in case they were attacked during the hours of darkness. Paulus approved the plan, for no road or province should ever be considered entirely safe in these days of barbarian invasions. Such measures did no harm and served the purpose of keeping his warriors on their guard. Paulus had favoured the young Briton with his praise by explaining that security must always come before comfort whenever Roman soldiers were on the march.

'Aye! I've been fortunate in that my father gave me many lessons in Roman tactics and strategy during my learning years, but I know that I still have much to learn now that I've been given this first command. I've also been able to obtain some advantages of birth from my grandfather, King Caradoc, of whom you may have heard stories. He was Maximus's dearest friend in Britannia.'

Impressed by these revelations, Paulus asked the young commander to consider the need for scouts to the north and the south of their bivouac, riders who could alert their small force if strangers approached their camp during the night.

Pridenow agreed, although he doubted if there was any real need for such precautions. He detailed four of his warriors to find observation points a mile or so from the camp in both directions, taking turns to snooze during the coming night.

Then, satisfied that every security consideration had been considered, Paulus stretched again and repeated his complaint about the weather.

'Pardon, Lord Paulus? I don't understand!'

'Let's have no more of this *lord* nonsense, Pridenow! I'm Paulus, plain and simple! Do you hear me? Good! When I spoke of the weather before, I was referring to the unpredictable nature of the rain that is ever-present in these misbegotten islands. I've served in many places where there's torrential rain, but I've never experienced a landscape where the rain is always with us. And it's not just the rain, mind! The skies piddle, mizzle, drizzle and then they drip, drip, drip. Rarely do the heavens open up with a good, cleansing downpour. Instead, we fighting men must spend all our time being damp and miserable. I can swear that there have been times when I could hear rust growing on my armour.'

Pridenow had no measuring stick to judge British weather, because he'd never been permitted to leave the shores of Britannia.

Dismayed, he felt mildly insulted at Paulus's comparisons.

'The sun's shining now, Paulus, so why are you complaining? My father has always warned me against constant whining about things over which we have no control, for he believes that the listener will eventually cease to hear the complainant, or the nature of his complaints. *Don't tempt the gods*, he always said, although he claimed to be a good Christian. I think my father saw too much violence at the Battle of the Save and the campaign in Italia. I don't think he'll ever trust in a kindly god again.'

Paulus had turned away, arranging his sleeping pallet, but his attention was caught by the lad's mention of a kinsman who had been a friend of Magnus Maximus.

'So the Dobunni king followed Maximus into the east?' Paulus said. Like all legionnaires, he was fascinated by tales of the great Maximus and how the usurper had come to grief. 'Did your father actually know him well?'

'He did, but I must explain that my father's service was given with some reluctance. He was betrothed to my mother at the time, but Maximus required a scribe and historian who could provide him with an accurate record of his campaigns. My father served Maximus with absolute loyalty for some years. Fortunately, Maximus was grateful for this service and arranged for my father to be spirited away to a place of safety towards the end of the campaign. The man who escorted him to safety was the famed Andragathius, the warrior who assassinated the Roman emperor, Gratian, inside his own encampment.'

'I've been told that Maximus mounted a particularly noble campaign,' Paulus stated, his eyes aglow with fervour. He could recall that Maximus's legionnaires had laughed long and loud over the ruse that had resulted in the death of the emperor, Gratian, a lascivious fool who had been more concerned with his women and gold than securing his personal safety.

'Aye, I learned this while sitting on my father's knee. Father believed it was only the Scythians and their devilish horsemanship that brought Maximus to grief. He convinced me that Maximus was a man of contradictions but, for all that, he was brave and honourable.'

Paulus's eyes grew misty for a moment.

'Your father was fortunate to take part in such an important campaign with such an honourable general. Maximus was an aristocrat in his own right, but he received the accolades of his peers when they awarded him the Grass Crown. That is the highest honour that any legionnaire can receive on the field of battle. Nor did he display any foolishness when he ruled over Gallia and Hispania. I've seen many coins with his face stamped upon them. Maximus the Great! I was stationed on the Germanic border at the time and my commanders kept themselves remote from the dispute over the throne. But we know from rumours how highly Maximus was worshipped by the rank-and-file legionnaires. As it turned out, it was only the politics of Constantinople that brought about his undoing. I would have wished that Constantine's drive for glory was based on such a legitimate foundation.'

Pridenow's eyebrows rose at this extraordinary statement. Despite his personal thoughts on Constantine's ambitions, Pridenow had heard few complaints about Constantine or his motivation when he stripped Britannia of her men and arms in a fruitless quest for the throne.

'I don't understand, sir. I was led to believe that you were Constantine's loyal servant.'

'Aye! But loyalty to a friend and a commander doesn't make me a fool, lad. Constantine reached far too high and we all paid a huge price of his hubris.'

Paulus wandered off to the cooking fires where a warrior was throwing chopped root vegetables from their stores into a bubbling pot. He could smell the familiar aroma of salted meat, the dried staple of soldiers.

If Paulus wanted to avoid the topic of Constantine, he had underestimated Pridenow's interest in the subject.

Pridenow was busy for the next half-hour as he carried out the many duties required of a commander, so Paulus was left staring into the cooking fire and feeling useless. By the time Pridenow returned, crisply efficient and confident despite his tender years, the warrior tasked with preparing the stew at the cooking fire decided the meal was edible and went off to eat with his friends. Faced with a fresh meal, Paulus felt his mood begin to improve.

'You seem glum, Decurion. Is the cook's stew not to your liking?' Pridenow asked as he used a piece of stick to stir the thickening mess. 'As it happens, I have something here that will improve the taste of even the crudest soldier's fare.'

The young prince retrieved a small leather box from his kit. From it he took a few pinches of a crude, crystalline powder which he then dropped into the stew, stirring vigorously as he did so.

'You've brought salt with you!' Paulus exclaimed in an amazed tone of voice. 'How did you find such a blessing?'

'My sister had the sense to anticipate that our food would be tasteless when we were on the march, so she gave me some of her precious rock salt. It's rarely found in these isles, my friend, so even the smallest pinch must be savoured.'

All soldiers, regardless of race or rank, dream over food and the next meal that will come their way. Hard-tack rations, plain beer and meat caught on the road tended to consume their thoughts, but a princely feast such as this, with fresh vegetables and salt, was a luxury to be savoured, even if the meat was already salted. Like ravenous animals, the men fell on the cooking pot and spooned goodly dollops into their tin bowls before devouring every morsel with gusto. Once they had filled their bellies, they belched contentedly and leaned back against their saddles.

'Good food and good company! Who could ask for more! I've slaked my thirst and hunger, and I couldn't eat another thing,' Paulus murmured and sighed with satisfaction.

Without answering, Pridenow gathered up the utensils and carried them off to a streamlet in the woods for cleaning, although Paulus insisted he could wash his own. 'I'm not totally decrepit, young man,' he complained.

'Remain seated, old man! It's my intention that you will recompense me for these chores by recounting your adventures with Maximus, Andragathius and Constantine. I intend to learn of these legends by hearing the tales from the horse's mouth, so to speak.'

Pridenow matched his demands with an impish grin, so Paulus relaxed. 'You're a horse's arse, young man! Fact is, there are some things I want to learn about you. I'd especially like to know why your sister won't allow you to cross the waters and leave the British lands.'

'*Quid pro quo*, sir! *Quid pro quo!*' Pridenow retorted and disappeared into the tree line with a jaunty stride.

When Pridenow returned with the tin plates that he'd scoured clean with river sand, Paulus was completely relaxed and replete. He had decided that Pridenow's request was a small repayment for the young man's cheerful efficiency and the respect he had shown to an old warrior. Paulus spent the next few hours recounting everything he knew of Maximus's campaigns in Gallia and Italia, while Pridenow sat and listened with rapt wonder. Every so often, Pridenow asked sharp, intelligent questions as he sought to understand how such an able and experienced general as Maximus could suffer such a humiliating defeat by the forces of Rome. Paulus answered the young man's questions as best he could.

'I wasn't there when many of these things happened, boy, so I can only tell you what I later heard from others who were present at the time. Fact is, your own father knew a damned sight more than I did, because he was always with his master whenever strategy was planned.'

'I don't know why, but Father refused to speak of those days, except for the few times when I made sure he had too much to drink and I caught him when he was off his guard.'

Paulus nodded. 'Such is often the way with those men who see terrible things. They hide such sights into deep pockets that lie around their hearts and then try to forget what they've seen. It doesn't work, of course.'

'I might have been able to understand my father a little better if I'd been acquainted with what happened during those historic years.' Pridenow's mobile face was momentarily troubled, but the sad expression quickly evaporated.

'I'm fairly certain I know why Maximus failed, although my reasoning mightn't be to everyone's satisfaction. Don't say I didn't warn you!'

Pridenow shook his head impatiently.

'Two critical factors defeated Maximus, and these were in evidence long before he left Gallia to begin his campaign in Italia. We spoke earlier of the sin of hubris, a flaw which can drag a man down to ruin quicker than any other fault. Lady Fortuna becomes angry if we take her for granted. Maximus had already won those honours that he craved. He was already the co-emperor of the Western Empire, but his hubris impelled him to attack Italia in a bid to rule Rome alone. Foolishness! Sheer foolishness!'

'Why? Father told me that I must interpret the causes of this tragedy for myself.'

'Two powerful men had divided the Roman Empire between them,' Paulus went on. 'In the east, Theodosius was the ruler of the Eastern Empire in Constantinople, while the weaker man, Gratian, was accepted as the ruler of the Western Kingdom. Then Maximus came along. He was a Roman, but he was born in

Hispania. And the unthinkable happened! Maximus defeated Gratian's forces and killed him, so Theodosius brokered a new treaty that anointed the young heir, Valentinian, as the new co-emperor with Maximus. The Eastern Emperor was committed to this means of propping up a weak emperor as a buffer between his own kingdom and the tribes who were competing to gain influence in the west. Maximus was a handy tool.'

'I can understand Theodosius's motivation.' Pridenow felt a little insulted at the simplicity of Paulus's explanation.

'Well, when Maximus rejected Theodosius's solution and advanced into Italia, he sent Valentinian scurrying for his life. How would you expect Theodosius to respond?'

'I can see that Maximus was in error if he expected the Eastern Emperor to stay out of the conflict.' Pridenow's forehead furrowed and he toyed with his knife and whetstone while he listened to the decurion's explanation.

'Which leads me to the second error that sealed Maximus's fate. He couldn't imagine how any force could defeat his beloved cataphractii. Heavy cavalry is a deadly weapon that can bludgeon one's enemies into oblivion, but Maximus should have sent scouts to learn the composition of Theodosius's army. Your father would have mentioned the Scythians, but you would need to see those devils in action before you could appreciate how dangerous they were. Maximus was so overconfident that he broke the most essential rule of strategy. You must know your enemy! Instead, he hastened to meet the forces of the east at the earliest opportunity. He would come to pay in blood for this error.'

Pridenow held his breath, unwilling to speak a word that might distract the old man from his reflections on those long-lost and sorely missed legions.

'I've seen the Scythians at their murderous work and I'm certain that few bodies of troops could stand against their special skills and fighting spirit. But, despite my admiration for them, I'm still convinced that Maximus could have devised a plan to counter them, if he had known that Theodosius had ordered his Scythians into battle. Instead, Maximus struck out blindly at his enemies and the heavy cavalry was drawn into a deadly trap. I've no doubt that you're aware of the final result of the confrontation between the two forces.'

'I've heard tales that Scythian warriors can control their horses with their heels while using their arms and hands to fire their small bows. I've never seen such wonders, so I find it hard to imagine that men from such backward lands could develop such skills.'

Paulus tapped Pridenow's forearm and felt the iron in the boy's long muscles. He sensed that this young Briton was showing more physical aptitude and military nous than the young Constans, a stripling who had been trained to fight with the legions for all his life.

'I pray that you never have to face the Scythians, young man. They can fire arrows so quickly that the eye can barely follow their flight. And they rarely miss their targets. No! Maximus's two errors were fatal. You're the coming man, Pridenow, so I suggest you learn from the mistakes of the great ones and consider the men who fight for you as something other than wooden counters in a board game. You must learn to be a leader of men and use your strengths to maximise the efforts of your forces.'

The sound of the crackling fire was the only sound that intruded over the sudden silence that followed. Beyond their own fireplace, other warriors were damping down their fires and curling up in their bed rolls within any nests of leaves that they could find. To Paulus's mind, the forest seemed to be full of eyes that followed him and pleaded with him to save them.

'With your leave, boy, I think I'll place these old bones of mine into my bed roll. I'll wait till tomorrow night to hear your story, when my wits are sharper.'

If Pridenow was disappointed, his amiable expression gave no evidence of it. Paulus rolled himself into his blanket and closed his rheumy eyes.

The hours were far advanced when Paulus was suddenly dragged out from a deep sleep, roused by a sound that his befuddled state failed to recognise. At first he thought the sharp scream was the sound of a wild animal, but silence had fallen over the encampment once again. He heard several warriors stirring nervously but, otherwise, the encampment was as quiet as death.

Yet Paulus's senses were quivering. It was almost as if he was carrying sensitive antennae that warned him of movements in the air or vibrations in the earth around him. His muscles tingled, although he tried to relax and avoid panic by using all the old soldier's tricks he had learned during his long military service.

'Aghhhhh!'

The cry came again, but this time it sounded so close, so sudden and so agonised that Paulus almost jumped as for a brief moment his heart stuttered in his chest. With all the agility of constant practice, he rose to his feet with his gladius drawn. Around him, the other warriors got up while hissing to each other in their tribal tongue.

'Aghhhhh!'

This time, Paulus was able to pinpoint the source of the

half-roar and half-scream that seemed to be in their midst. Alarmed, he crossed the few body lengths to stand over the prone form of Pridenow who was curled up into a tight, foetal ball within his tangled blankets.

'Pridenow! Pridenow! What ails you?' Paulus asked as he extended his arm to shake the huddled form.

Another arm snaked out from the darkness as one of the prince's warriors arrived to brush Paulus's hand away from the unconscious Briton, who was lying in a trance at the decurion's feet. The cavalryman quickly placed his own body between the decurion and Pridenow.

'Please, sir, you mustn't startle him into wakefulness. His father swears that such a shock might send his wits wandering on the wind while they're out of his body and we'll be left with an empty shell. We've seen these fits before, my lord, so please don't touch him ... please!'

'What are you talking about, young man? Does Pridenow suffer from night terrors? If he does, it's no shame. Speak up, man!'

The cavalryman shook his head. 'No, sir, he doesn't exactly have night terrors. He has some other affliction, but I'd prefer to wait and allow Lord Pridenow to explain his infirmity to you in person.'

An infirmity? The boy seems to be as healthy as a carthorse ... and twice as strong, Paulus thought, but he stepped back, sheathed his gladius and sat on his makeshift bed. The other warriors gradually drifted back to their own pallets without any particular surprise, their actions telling Paulus that they had seen one of these fits on previous occasions.

Just when Paulus was considering returning to sleep himself,

Pridenow sat bolt upright and turned to face the decurion as if he could see him. With a thrill of superstitious alarm, Paulus realised that those wide grey eyes saw nothing but the images that scrolled within Pridenow's own skull.

'Why must it be so, Caradoc? You can't love any of us if you doom us to slavery.'

Pridenow's voice was clear and expressionless, regardless of the passionate nature of the words he had uttered. In fact, the lack of emotion in Pridenow's voice and flat facial expression caused the hair to rise on Paulus's arms.

'I tell you, Caradoc, she's far too beautiful to be anyone's pawn and, as my daughter, I won't permit her to be married as a child,' Pridenow continued. 'I don't care if she is meant to be the mother of a hundred heroes or all the Dragons of Satan. I'll not permit her to be destroyed by you – or by anyone!'

'Never fear, lad, for you'll be well,' Paulus interrupted as comfortingly as he could. Somehow, he felt impelled to say something – anything – that would soften the edges of some unknown or even unknowable threat to the younger man.

The lad's eyes sharpened like gimlets and fixed themselves on Paulus's worn face.

'Your duties will often be long and thankless, but you will fulfil your master's orders to the best of your ability. But you must be warned, Paulus! The golden dragon is fair of face and mind, but he will always be blind to the evil that lies under his nose. His destiny demands that he should learn to be strong – always – and not just with those who lie within the scope of his power. He will always be balancing out the good and the wickedness, as he tries to find the middle ground. But there is none for him!'

Paulus drew in a ragged breath. A golden dragon? What nonsense was pouring from the mouth of this boy?

'But the brother – red in claw, hand and heart – is the beast that you must tame. Spare him the lash occasionally and avoid crushing his spirit, for much will depend on this man's courage. But be warned, man of the legions, that you must never turn your back on this boy. This dragon will kill you, even if he loves you.'

Paulus uttered an exclamation of disgust so pointed that the boy's ice-hard grey eyes flickered momentarily.

'Even in your place of safety, the Wolf of Midnight will kill you all, unless you free the Man of Glass from his bonds. Do not forget! There is no place of safety for you if you're unable to free the Man of Glass.'

'What did you mean, Pridenow? Stop talking in riddles and answer my questions,' Paulus demanded as he rose to his feet and strode towards the rigid figure. Even as his hand reached out to grip the younger man's shoulder, Pridenow's eyes softened, blurred and then rolled back into his skull. He was comatose.

As if he had been felled by a blow, the Briton fell back on to his bed of leaves. He might easily have been dead.

Into this horrified silence, a fox screamed in the woods as it made its kill.

CHAPTER III

A LITTLE WISDOM

The glory of God is man fully alive.

St Irenaeus

Pridenow returned to full alertness in an instant, as had been his habit over many years as a legionnaire in so many dangerous troublespots in the Roman world. This acquired skill had saved his life on any number of occasions when a lesser warrior would have died in the gurgle of his own blood during surprise attacks in the darkness of the night. For now, it was only a remnant of a former life, but a reminder of his competence as a legionnaire.

As he climbed to his feet, Paulus stared across the dead fire pit to an empty scattering of leaves where Pridenow had spent the night. A rolled blanket and folded field pack beside the remains of the fire were the only indications that the Briton had slept there at all. Several of the other warriors approached the campsite, carrying leather buckets of water, while two other men setting fires looked up at him with friendly smiles.

'Good morning to you,' Paulus said amiably to no one in particular as he ambled into the nearest thicket and its privacy to relieve his strained bladder. Satisfied, the decurion used his ears to locate the sound of the nearest flowing water, a shallow spring that burbled cheerfully over pebbles in the cool shadows of the trees.

As he approached the water, Paulus plucked a suitable twig, stripped off the bark and began to clean his teeth by chewing on the fibrous wood. He spat reflectively before entering the shallow stream, while examining the water for clarity. Satisfied, he scooped up a mouthful to rinse away the furry taste of sleep.

Discarding the twig, Paulus reached down to the streamlet's bottom and gripped a handful of grit and sand to scour his hands and bare feet. He was at peace with his world as he scrubbed away at the hard skin on his soles and heels. His calloused hands, tempered by a lifetime of swordplay, ran another handful of sand over his naked legs and then, using his soaking-wet neck scarf, he washed his face and chest thoroughly, careless of the water that soaked into his tunic. Always thorough with his ablutions, Paulus used his cupped hands to soak his recently trimmed hair. Then, having wrung out the scarf, he retied it around his neck and waded back to the weed-slick bank.

Back in the camp, Paulus donned his mail and armour. He had only just finished lacing his sandals when Pridenow strode purposefully into the clearing clutching a basket of apples. With a deft swing of the arm, he threw a large piece of fruit underarm towards Paulus's chest. The decurion caught the treat with equal deftness.

'Freshly picked from the tree,' Pridenow explained with a smile. 'There's a ruined croft across the steam. It's just another casualty of the many drafts of young men who were dragged away by Maximus and Constantine. The parents die off and there are no sons to work the farm, so a lifetime of effort dies with them. I've found some late peaches, scores of apples and wild onions, so tonight's evening meal will have some taste to it. Oh – and cast your eyes over these wonders!'

Pridenow fumbled inside the folds of his cloak and pulled out a cloth-bound package containing some twenty speckled brown eggs that he'd collected near the abandoned farmhouse.

'We'll share these beauties this evening, shall we? It's a shame, Paulus, because the land attached to this croft still bears as richly as ever. But there are no hands left to break the soil in late winter or to collect the bounty that the trees give us. Everything is wasted!'

Paulus was puzzled by the young man's nonchalance.

Nowhere on the lad's open face was there any sign of the convulsions and fits that he had suffered during the earlier hours of darkness. Paulus wondered if Pridenow could even remember what had occurred. Unwilling to broach the topic, Paulus engaged in meaningless and pleasant conversation, while one of the young warriors tried to coax the fire into sluggish life and heat a tin of water. Once the pot had been placed over the fire, Pridenow threw in some aromatic herbs and lemon pulp, so that the soft morning air was soon filled with the smell of peppermint, rosehips and lime.

'I have an unreasoning liking for hot water laced with herbs, especially early in the morning. My mother used to give me this hot lemon drink when I was a mere lad. She swore it brought calm to the spirit and a better digestion to the body.'

Paulus raised one eyebrow. His inquiring mind attempted

to devise a sensitive way to raise the embarrassing topic of Pridenow's infirmity.

'Were you sickly as a child, Pridenow?' Paulus asked. 'I've heard that many herbal remedies and infusions can be used to assist infants and children who experience poor health.'

'No, not really! I was a normal scapegrace of a boy, so I was always in and out of trouble.' The young Briton's eyes sharpened. 'Why do you ask?'

Paulus was weary of dancing around the problem of Pridenow's strange fits. 'You went into a trance last night in the death hours of early morning. You screamed and yelled while you were convulsing and the disturbance woke the entire camp. I wanted to wake you and return you to your senses, but your men warned me not to interfere. You were speaking in riddles during your rambles, especially when you were addressing me directly. You warned me of *wolves at midnight, men of glass* and *coloured dragons*. I couldn't fathom your warnings.'

'Oh! Is that what you've been worrying about?' Pridenow's face showed understanding, but no concern whatsoever. 'Yes, I've had night terrors since I was very small – and not always when I am asleep.' He laughed as if he was free of care.

Surprised, Paulus stared blankly at him. In the normal course of affairs, any Roman with such an infirmity would be barred from the military and only the most aristocratic of sufferers would be permitted to take part in public life. Such an illness would blight a young man's hopes for the future, yet Pridenow was mildly amused at Paulus's shocked expression.

'Drink some of my lemon and herb water to cleanse your blood, Paulus. Mind you, it's hot to the taste! Then, once we've resumed our journey, I'll explain the whole tale to you. You'll see that my fits might be inconvenient, but they aren't a threat to me or to any other person in my care.' Pridenow smiled engagingly as he filled Paulus's mug with his medicinal concoction. 'You'll discover that today's Pridenow is still the same as yesterday's person.'

'True! But...' Paulus stuttered to a halt as he took the tin mug. Without thinking, he raised it to his lips and sipped at the infusion, before recoiling with a curse when it burned his tongue.

'Ow!' he exclaimed. 'Fuck it, Pridenow, that brew was damned hot! You scared me shiteless last night when you were screaming and now you're doing your best to scald my gullet! I thought you were some kind of demon who'd been sent by Satan to drag my mortal soul from my body. My imaginings might seem foolish in the light of day, but—'

'But you can't be sure,' Pridenow finished for him. 'If you wait for a while, I'll convince you that I'm just a young man who's trying to make his way in the world. Drink up, Paulus, and we'll be on our way.'

'Even at the best speed of our wagon, we'll still be in Calleva Atrebatum long before darkness arrives. It's a perfect opportunity for you to have a comfortable night in one of the town's inns.'

Pridenow was grinning with theatrical exaggeration, so Paulus's memory of the previous night's incident seemed trivial in the face of the young man's obvious good health. The column had been on the road for several hours since the dawn cup of hot lemon juice and herbs, but Paulus's tongue was still tender from the scalding liquid. The promise of a soft bed, even after two days on the road, was a very attractive proposition.

'Calleva Atrebatum! I've heard of that town. Many of the

supplies for the legions were prepared there and sent off to the Roman fortresses across the island, or what remained of them.'

Paulus stared along the rod-straight road which was still relatively flat, although hills could be seen on their left in long, rolling ranks. The weather remained pleasant, even though it was still a little too hot and sticky. Paulus was glad that he'd washed his scarf because it already felt damp and grimy from sweat. The pale-blue sky revealed a line of large billowing clouds that marched towards them from the south, but the grey and green in the lower cloud banks promised heavy rain in the afternoon, especially if the heat persisted.

'How many Roman soldiers remain in these isles?' Pridenow asked abruptly and Paulus was surprised at his deadly serious expression. 'Can we expect any assistance from Rome in our struggles against the northern savages?'

'I couldn't even guess, lad, but I'll wager my balls that Britannia's current Roman governor has little more than his personal guard to give him any feelings of consequence. The bean counters and public servants have deserted Verulamium, the administrative centre, so that's a sure sign we've reached the beginning of the end. In fact, many Romans have made a good life here in Britannia. Many of our soldiers have married British women and set down roots, so they intend to live or die with the Britons. But the legions themselves will have disappeared into the past.'

'Will they ever return?' Pridenow asked. His eyes were chill and hard, but they reminded Paulus that Pridenow was only sixteen, a man in body, yet still ignorant of the realities of politics and good governance. He was searching for confirmation of his unspoken fears.

'I'm not privy to the thoughts of Honorius, but I'd be surprised if he allowed any of Constantine's legions to return to Britannia. Even the Roman governor of this province would know where these lands fit into the long-term strategies of the emperor, for it's a fact that the men who went to Gallia with Constantine will have perished with him. There is no hope that a reprieve will be granted to those legionnaires or tribal warriors who raised their swords against the might of Rome, even if she is a pox-riddled old whore who can hardly protect herself or her dependants. Honorius has delusions of grandeur, but he couldn't give a fuck about Gallia or Britannia. You must kill off any hope that the emperor will send an army to save you from the Saxons, because this is a crazed dream. Your sister understands. She knows in her heart that your only salvation is to fight the barbarians off, again and again, until one side or the other ceases to exist. For these very reasons, Vortigern might well become a possible, if unpredictable, saviour for your people.'

Pridenow bit on his thumb and this small, familiar action reminded Paulus of Queen Endellion in Corinium, although his last sighting of her had taken place many years earlier, when he had accompanied Constantine and Shithead, the loathsome Roman patrician who had been betrothed to Severa. Paulus realised that Endellion was Pridenow's mother and they could share any number of physical mannerisms.

'So, what we have now is the most favourable political and military situation that we'll ever have, unless Lady Fortuna intervenes. The Saxons will hardly be so obliging as to give us the time to reinforce our towns or give us an opportunity to grow a new generation of young warriors.' Pridenow sighed deeply. 'A whole race of people is at risk of foundering because of the hubris of two men who sought to achieve their own selfish senses of destiny.'

'Aye, lad! Unjust as it is, harsh reality is the future that awaits the British people.'

'But that fate isn't for you, Paulus. You'll have disappeared with Constantine's young princes to a safe place far removed from the shores of Britannia.'

Paulus could hear a sense of yearning in the youth's fair young voice and he understood the powerful surge of desire that Pridenow was feeling. The boy hungered for skies and hills that were remote from these islands, places where the air smelled of danger and excitement, and a warrior's future was unpredictable.

'I've reached an age where I look forward to enjoying an extended period of peace and I relish the freedom and luxury to grow old,' Paulus said. He could hear the desire in his own voice and he suddenly felt ashamed. 'But we aren't given the chance to choose our own selfish fates and I have a number of duties that must be fulfilled before I can finally take my rest. Still, I'd happily trade places with you, Pridenow, because there are many forms of imprisonment. Be assured that my words are spoken in truth.'

Both men rode on in a silence that was no longer easy and companionable. Neither man was happy with his lot, because both men longed for futures that were moving further out of their reach even as they tried to capture them.

The first peals of thunder began to roll in from behind the small column, while the air smelled of ozone and the fresh scent of crushed leaves and grass. The Roman road leading into Calleva Atrebatum began to fill with farm carts and hand-wheeled barrows, mostly empty, as farmers hurried to reach their homes before the first raindrops started to fall and catch them on the open road. Market day in Calleva Atrebatum had obviously drawn the farmers into the town, so the rural folk had taken their fill of the town's hospitality while selling off their produce.

With a pang of guilt, Paulus noticed that the men and women who hastened past the column with nervous, averted eyes were mostly of middle or advanced years. The absence of young men among the throng sent feelings of pointless shame skittering along Paulus's nerves, although he had no idea why he should have been overconcerned about the crofters' vulnerability.

Then, as the first of the town's potteries and workshops came into view, the heavens opened and a deluge fell from the blackened clouds to drench the warriors in moments.

'Is this enough mizzle, piddle, drizzle or drip for you, Decurion?' Pridenow joked as the column's mounts meandered their slow way towards the promise of stables and sweet hay.

Embraced by the warmth of a large room above the horse stables, the ten guards settled down to enjoy their evening in the fresh, clean hay and reasonably pleasant surroundings of their billet. Nowadays Paulus never overlooked the opportunity to sleep in comfort, so he had purchased a bed in one of the local inns. As expected, Pridenow opted to spend the night with his men, but he was willing to share a meal with Paulus in the alehouse and enjoy the hearty fare provided by the innkeeper. Their bowls filled with a tasty chicken stew, the two men ate with all the shared gusto of soldiers, men who always appreciated every good meal that came their way.

'I'll say one thing about this town – the food is substantial and the wine is surprisingly good,' Paulus remarked, as he finished his second bowl. 'But the bread's rather gritty. You'd almost think the baker had mixed some sand into the flour.'

Pridenow shrugged. Merchants weren't averse to adding any number of substances to food and drink that would maximise their profits. Like all good traders, they were prepared to engage in judicious cheating.

'At least the bread is edible,' Paulus added, ripping the flat loaf into two halves, while ignoring the texture of the grain. 'At least it sops up gravy, which is all that I care about. However, I'll be really annoyed if our host adds water to the beer.'

Both men knew that no sensible landlord would have the courage to serve adulterated beer to trained warriors, so they had little to fear in this regard. The ale had a rich golden colour, without the usual cloudy, almost milky appearance that promised an oversweet brew. They drank from their earthenware beakers with pleasure.

'Now, my young friend, tell me about your fits,' Paulus began bluntly. In a long life, he had learned that tact rarely served a useful purpose, except to waste time.

'My grandmother was Saraid, the White Witch of the Red Wells, a pagan seer who protected a series of wells whose waters were blood-red when seen in the sunlight. Despite this oddity, the waters were found to be clean and unadulterated when the liquid was poured into a mug for drinking. My mother, Endellion, was the offspring of a casual coupling between Saraid and Caradoc, who was the king of the Dumnonii at that time. When Endellion was still a babe in arms, Saraid gave the child to Caradoc and he raised the girl as a legitimate member of the royal family. The White Witch relinquished her responsibilities as a mother because she feared for the child's safety. Saraid lost all memory of events whenever the fits of prophecy came over her, even the existence of her own daughter.'

Pridenow described all this in a bland voice, but Paulus could easily imagine the witch, her wells and the prophetic episodes that were sometimes suffered by soothsayers when they plied their trade. 'I always thought such trances were a result of good acting, rather than a physical affliction,' he commented, without considering how insulting this response must have sounded to Pridenow.

'Saraid wasn't a charlatan! In fact, one of her prophecies so frightened Caradoc that he decreed that this prediction must be repeated to every member of the Dumnonii royal family and their heirs to this very day, although the great man has been dead for many years. Every family member had been warned by Saraid that no grey-eyed boy-child should ever be permitted to leave the shores of Britannia for fear that some cataclysmic disaster would befall the family and the British people. Being a grey-eyed descendant of Caradoc, I am forbidden to travel to the continent. I'm doomed to remain in Britannia forever because of the credence given to Saraid's prophecy.'

Pridenow paused to allow Paulus to absorb the import of his revelations.

'Caradoc told my mother that he never intended to seduce Saraid. She insisted on the coupling and convinced the king that the gods demanded payment for the care and treatment she had provided for one of Caradoc's servants who'd been mortally wounded. The king heard her prophecy when she fell into a trance at the Red Wells and, ever after, he continued to believe her warnings and feared the power she had at her command. My mother swore that Caradoc wasn't gulled by Saraid and, to the end of his life, cherished her memory with a strange kind of love. Still, Saraid's other gift is a complicated inheritance for me to carry, so my plight is difficult to explain to normal men who don't have experience of the Sight.'

'I can understand your reluctance to speak of your gift,' Paulus said. He felt the hairs on the nape of his neck stirring now as if they had a life of their own. An odd sense of familiarity reminded Paulus of another wise woman in Dacia, decades earlier, who had promised Paulus a long and productive life. Something in the clear hazel of that woman's eyes reminded him of Pridenow, but he dared not think too deeply about matters that involved the designs of the gods. Good Christian that he was, he was sensitive enough to pay lip service to the religion of the Old Ones, just in case.

'Saraid would speak with opened eyes, although her senses had fled from her flesh. Years later, Caradoc repeated the witch-woman's warnings to Endellion, after she had grown into womanhood and was able to understand the burden that she would be forced to carry.'

Paulus stirred nervously and rotated his beaker in small, wet circles on the table top, afraid to break the train of the younger man's recollections. After all, Paulus had asked for the truth, so he could hardly complain that he was becoming alarmed at Pridenow's words.

'Saraid warned Caradoc not to leave Britannia with Magnus Maximus, the first High King, who would eventually join Gratian as a co-emperor of the Western Roman Empire. Meanwhile, Caradoc remained at Tintagel as Maximus's regent and Saraid's prophecy ensured that the king, and the Dumnonii tribe, would remain safe within his ancestral lands. But her prophecies concerning myself were far more detailed. They were exacting and frightening!'

The young warrior paused and collected his thoughts.

Pridenow was unmoved by the family curse, for the lad rejected any possibility that he was less of a man because of the bloodline he inherited from Saraid. Paulus was certain that, if asked, the young prince would express pride in sharing such a distinguished legacy. But the enforced imprisonment that kept him in Britannia was causing him more pain than the other prophecies that affected his future.

Perhaps he's never considered the fear that his inheritance can engender in others, Paulus thought, while waiting for Pridenow to consider his next revelation.

'When I was still a child of some ten years, Mother Endellion insisted that I should learn the words that Saraid passed on to Caradoc. She wanted reassurance that I would never forget the importance of Saraid's threats.'

Paulus said nothing, fearing that any sound could break the flow of words that seemed so strange, yet so right. Had the God of Jesus, or Mithras, or any of the strange British pantheon sent him to meet this grey-eyed man-boy? Was Pridenow's future set in stone? Had Constantine sent Paulus a message from the shades with a prediction that used Pridenow as a conduit? How could any man of flesh and blood hope to know?

'"Another man with grey eyes will come to you. You must protect him because he will be of great importance to your house and your people. He will only be a boy when you first meet him, whereas you will be very old."'

'Did you ever discuss these matters with Caradoc, Pridenow?' Paulus felt a need to interrupt the flow of the young Briton's words to satisfy his own curiosity. For some inexplicable reason, he wanted an answer to this particular question.

The decurion was afraid that *he* might have been chosen by the fates to be interchangeable with Caradoc during the convulsions. Although the idea seemed crazed, Paulus had felt as if Pridenow was speaking to *him* when he was in his trance, and the illusion persisted, although common sense indicated otherwise.

'No! Grandfather survived his friend, Maximus, by some years, but he had the good fortune to breathe his last in the comfort of his own bed. He was quite old and infirm by the time my parents were betrothed. I never met the great man.'

'Hmmm! No matter! Was there more to the prophecy that Endellion passed on to you?'

Pridenow looked up from the beaker he was clutching so tightly in his hand that Paulus was surprised the sturdy vessel remained unbroken.

'Caradoc was promised that his tribe would survive through many generations of upheaval and foreign invasion,' Pridenow said softly and sighed.

'"Remember the red dragon, Caradoc, for he shall come out of Tintagel and all the tribes of Britannia will tremble at his birth."'

The young man sighed again. 'For such a promise, I must stay pinned within these shores.'

'I acquit you of lying, Pridenow, or of trying to impress me,' Paulus said eventually. But he was unable to meet the lad's troubled eyes. 'I can see traces of your description of your grandmother's condition in your own trance. The gift of prophecy is a heavy burden to carry, my boy, if you can refer to it as a gift.'

'My mother bears this same gift and has done so since she

reached womanhood. She often sees shadows of what will come on the roads, in the towns and in her own house, but she has been unable to understand the meaning of her visions. Imagine, Paulus, she sees the roadways populated with shadows yet to be born and she traces the actions of men and women who will love and live when her bones enrich the soil. When the gift inside her is strong, she barely knows what is real and what is not. I am the luckier one, for my visions slip away from me like bad dreams. I live my life as I choose and I pay them no mind.'

Wrapped in his red cloak, Paulus sat at the fireside for some time without speaking. Two farmers arguing over the value of a ram could be heard through an open doorway, while the crackling of logs, spitting and burning away to ash in the grate, seemed inordinately loud.

'You've spoken to me of red and gold dragons, but I can't believe that my red dragon is the same as the beast described by Caradoc. The old king's dragon is destined to be born in Tintagel, whereas my dragons sound young – and they are already in existence. I've been warned that I must take care in raising the two children, who I assume are Severa's sons. She said as much when she warned me that her younger son would need an ocean of love if he is to fight the violence that lives within his blood.'

'Severa's youngest child wasn't born in Tintagel!' Pridenow stated with certainty. 'Her sons were born in Venta Belgarum in the south,' he added. 'This implies that Saraid's red dragon is destined to be born at some time in the future. It's entirely possible that the red dragon ascribed to you could be Uther, and this child is destined to become the forerunner of a hero who is yet to enter our world. But I'm only guessing! When I am experiencing my trances, the truth can sometimes run through my fingers like water. The goddess's warnings are always ambiguous, because I don't understand what I'm saying.'

Paulus scratched warily at his chin.

Pridenow had been more than honest and he had given the decurion more information than he required. Paulus supposed that such disclosure was rare for this young warrior, and that speaking of his trances helped him to bear the strictures of his life, especially if he shared those loads with others who cared for him. At any rate, no threat could strike at Paulus, or the princes, from this quarter, so Pridenow was in no danger.

Paulus said as much to the Briton, who seemed surprised that Paulus should be disturbed by some aspects of their discussion.

'Few men are totally honest in the world in which we live, Pridenow. Most of them can stare you in the eyes and twist the truth into falsehoods that will catch you out and bind you to a false premise. You're an honest young man and few warriors would willingly admit to the burdens you carry, so I know I can place my trust in you. May you always be a fine young man!'

Before Paulus sank into blessed sleep, despite a suspicion that lice were sharing his pallet with him, he decided that the prophecy related during the previous evening was aimed at him. If prophecies were easily understood, then no man would ever fear the darkness of unpredictability. Seers often spoke in riddles, as if the powers that were placed in them during trances wanted to shroud the precise nature of the future from normal human beings.

'I always hated riddles, so it's strange to find that I'm a part of one,' Paulus observed to the wall on the opposite side of his itchy pallet. Scratching his armpits reflectively, he began to consider the individual elements of the prophecy related to him by Pridenow.

Doomed to slavery? The Dumnonii tribe and the heirs of Caradoc had been promised survival but, with a little reflection, Paulus realised that freedom and survival weren't necessarily the same things.

Paulus decided that Pridenow could easily father a daughter who would grow into womanhood and fulfil his role in the prophecy. This child could marry young and bear the predicted boy-child who could become the future hero. Pridenow might rail against his fate and he might argue with the dead Caradoc and his heirs as he liked, but Paulus was convinced that he had interpreted the prophecy correctly.

But the decurion was still puzzled by the oblique references to gold and red dragons. Were they Severa's sons, as seemed obvious?

Regardless of this riddle, Paulus accepted that the reference to the red dragon was of little import to himself. Still, his mind refused to allow him the luxury of sleep. He could see Pridenow's stark, grey eyes whenever he began to drift off, the young man's message continuing to run in a loop within his brain.

The golden dragon is said to be even-tempered and will be blind to the realities of evil, Paulus thought as he lay in his pallet. Ambrosius, perhaps! I can't believe that such a mild flaw could be dangerous, even if I am correct about the identity of the child. But I'm certain that the red dragon is Uther, despite his tender years. The suggestion in the prophecy that I should never turn my back on the red dragon is disconcerting, even alarming.

Paulus's thoughts ran crazily as he waded through the essentials of Pridenow's prophecies, but he gained some comfort from the young man's assurance that Paulus would eventually fulfil the wishes of Constantine, his erstwhile master.

'But who is the Wolf of Midnight? And who is this Man of Glass? I'm supposed to free this man, but I have no idea who he is. If I don't free him, the Wolf of Midnight will kill the princes – and me! Oh, by the gods, I hate riddles!'

Paulus continued to tear at his bites with his nails, convinced that he was sharing the pallet with several fully armed legions of bedbugs.

'Fuck it all! I could tease my brain throughout the night and still be none the wiser. I'll still be lice-ridden in the morning. No, Fortuna! I thank you, but I'll take my chances without trying to learn more answers. I do best when I muddle through by myself.'

And then, like a blessing, sleep fell over him as a heavy burst of rain began to fall in long, drenching gouts on the reed roof. The gods were kind and the leaks missed his old body as he dreamed all night of a beautiful woman astride red and golden dragons that flew into the sun with a great bolt of fire.

CHAPTER IV

TWO DRAGONLETS
IN THE NEST

Count it the greatest sin to prefer mere existence to
honour, and for the sake of life to lose the reasons for
living.

Juvenal, *Satires*, Number 8

Corinium had scarcely changed during the decade that had
passed since Paulus had last seen it. In those distant days,
Constantine had still been Constantinus, a humble centurion
who was investigating the murder of Flavius Marcus Britannicus.
The Roman aristocrat had been betrothed to Severa, the daughter
of Magnus Maximus, but his lust and stupidity had led to his
untimely death at the hands of a group of British assassins. Paulus
shivered, because the walls of this town still held memories of
torture and violence that he would rather forget.

'Are you unwell, Paulus?' Pridenow asked as his sharp eyes

caught the decurion's apprehensive expression. Few things seemed to escape from this lad's gimlet observation.

'I still have unpleasant memories of my last visit to Corinium. I haven't come back to the city since Marcus Britannicus met his end here. Some ten years have passed now and the events of those terrible days have left a bad taste in my mouth. I imagine you're familiar with the tale of Shithead and his assassination in one of Corinium's brothels.'

'My kinfolk have familiarised me with the details of the crime and its aftermath. Your Constantinus extracted information about a treasonous plot that had been devised by a group of disaffected Britons to usurp the British throne. One of Corinium's brothel-keepers and her girls were numbered among the conspirators. My parents told me that your master carried out their torture as neatly and as easily as if he was skewering a winkle in its shell.'

Paulus's expression darkened and he spat on to the roadway. 'My master never got his hands dirty during the entire investigation. I was his decurion, so I was the one who had to extract the information that Constantine needed. I can tell you, boy, that torture is an all-round dirty business.'

Pridenow's brow furrowed as he considered the cost the torture had exacted on the man who had been ordered to carry out the task. Because of his youth, Pridenow had never been forced to consider the particular conflict that could exist between duty and cruelty.

'I wouldn't really describe torture as a task that can be neatly done,' Paulus added reflectively. 'Yes! We extracted the information we needed from those avaricious folk and my master made sure that their suffering and terror unlocked their memories, but

I was left to live with the guilt over what we had done to stupid peasants who had no idea what they were doing when they took a bag of gold from a ruthless traitor. The consciences of some of the participants had been placated by the results of our investigation, but neither Constantine nor I could claim credit for our actions during those ugly days. Have you ever burned and beaten a woman until she was near to death? Have you ever been forced to remove the eyes of a prisoner with a white-hot metal spoon? I have! And I've always regretted acting like a barbarian.'

Pridenow could sense the deep resentment that lay behind Paulus's words. During this painful episode, Pridenow's parents had managed to keep their own hands clean at the decurion's expense, but Paulus was too tactful to point an accusatory finger at those who ruled in Corinium.

Pridenow's parents had profited from the soiled hands of their servants and allies but, for their part, the king and queen understood the debt they owed to Constantinus and Paulus who had ensured that they were spared from Roman revenge over the attack on a senior Roman officer. Pridenow, a warrior in his own right now, could imagine a similar situation where he might be required to use torture. He would hate to obey such orders but, if he was required to comply with them, he wouldn't hesitate to do his duty.

'The tower room and the cellars that we used for our interrogations were situated in the guards' quarters at the northern gate. We could tell by the bars and the chains attached to the brick and stone walls that the local rulers had used this building as a prison in the past, so the prisoners from the brothel weren't the first unfortunates to be tortured there. I hope I don't set eyes on the place while we are in Corinium.'

'I mean no disrespect, Paulus, but I wouldn't have judged you to be a squeamish man.' As the decurion turned in the saddle to face him, Pridenow hastened to add, 'However, I can appreciate how difficult it must have been to inflict torture on other men.'

Pridenow grinned ruefully; his inadequate experience and inarticulate comments were only making the situation worse.

'Especially when women were involved!' Paulus said emphatically.

An imaginative young man, Pridenow paled a little as he thought of these events.

'I'd rather we spoke no more of torture or the murder of Shithead Britannicus,' Paulus declared firmly. 'We've more pressing problems to worry us, lad, dangers that occupy the minds of better heads than ours. Shithead's remains are mouldering in his urn, so he's best forgotten. He was never very important anyway and, ultimately, he became a foolish pawn who was used by wealthy and powerful men.'

Wisely, Pridenow kept his mouth shut and said nothing further.

As they rode through the city, Paulus saw that Corinium had become a bustling metropolis under Aeron's benevolent rule. He was immediately impressed by the newly erected shop fronts and displays that had been set up around the hub of the road network that radiated outwards from the commercial centre. Roman roads from Corinium led to Glevum, Aquae Sulis, Ratae, Venta Belgarum and Londinium, so vigorous trading took place in the marketplace for goods that would eventually reach all parts of Britannia. In contrast to the untrusting features of the citizens of Venta Belgarum, the townsfolk of Corinium seemed to be well fed, satisfied and free from fear, and work for the peasantry appeared to be plentiful; Paulus decided that the city's prosperity was due to stable and sensible rulers who dispensed justice with fairness and common sense.

He said as much to Pridenow in an effort to smooth over their earlier contentious conversation.

'Aye! My parents believe that their rule should benefit all Dobunni citizens, so they take pains to govern with light hands,' the lad said as he flushed with pleasure at the indirect compliment. 'Mother guides a group of women healers and aristocratic wives who treat the sick and indigent in the city, while Father takes his responsibilities with tribal judgements very seriously. He insists that justice must be seen to be even-handed.'

Paulus nodded his approval. This well-tended town reflected the loving hands of a ruling class who did far more than divest the city's merchants of their coin through taxation.

The column made its slow way to Aeron's Great Hall where the king and queen dispensed justice to the citizens. Their official home was an ancient British and Roman structure with a haphazard layout that resulted from its hybrid history. The palace, for want of a better description, was dry and well maintained, even though the roof was made from interconnected bundles of bound reeds. The original circular components of one building, known as the Round House, had probably served the kings of the Dobunni tribe in the long-gone days before the first Roman legionnaires set foot on the shingle beaches of the south coast. Such buildings were now an uncomfortable reminder of an archaic past.

Aeron and Endellion strode out on to the forecourt from the Great Hall before the column had time to dismount. The rulers were soon surrounded by other members of the court, as well as ogling servants who were determined to see one of the few Romans remaining in Britannia. With a pang, Paulus was struck by how much Endellion had aged in a single decade, as if she had moved directly from youth to old age. The queen seemed to have missed the middle years endured by most women, although she was no older than forty.

Her hair was starkly white at the forehead, but its bulk was swept back into its usual rich black at the rear of her head and her pretty face and kindly eyes mitigated the harshness of her piebald hair colouring Her husband's body was bent, considering his age, but he was still hale and young in spirit. The king blamed the aches in his swollen joints on the campaigns with Maximus's legions and the scores of uncomfortable nights when he'd slept on cold and damp earth. Even so, his handsome visage and guileless eyes spoke eloquently of his generosity and fairness. Despite their age, the king and queen made a handsome couple who were still loved by their subjects. Paulus bowed low after dismounting from his horse.

Embraced enthusiastically, and with every courtesy showered on him, Paulus insisted that he would forget how to live the rough life of a soldier if the queen continued to spoil him so thoroughly. The king and queen laughed gently at his diplomacy, but Endellion's eyes were serious.

'There'll be scores of stony pallets and privations aplenty that'll test you in the days and weeks ahead, my dear Paulus, so you should enjoy this brief period of comfort while you can. Unfortunately, we've received word that Vortigern has landed at Dubris and will soon be riding to Venta Belgarum at speed. When he arrives on Severa's doorstep and learns that the children have been spirited away, he'll pursue you in a trice. For safety's sake, it's essential that you leave with the boys on the morrow.'

This information caused Paulus to reconsider the safety of his charges. If a courier had reached Corinium with this bad news, then Vortigern could be in Venta Belgarum already. After all, Corinium was a long way from Venta Belgarum and even further from Dubris.

Endellion pressed his hand urgently after exchanging a telling glance with her son. 'No, Paulus, you've mistaken my meaning. Vortigern has only just left Dubris with a small column of mercenaries at his back, men that he has recruited to escort him to Venta Belgarum. I have my own spies and couriers, so you can trust me when I say that the information I'm passing on to you is accurate. Vortigern has decided to spend three days in Dubris to hire a group of ruffians to protect him during the overland journey to Venta Belgarum. He also needed to purchase a team of horses to provide suitable mounts that can speed him to his destination.'

This statement successfully cut the discussion short, although the hair rose on the decurion's neck at the implications of her statement.

The queen gave Paulus a charming and dismissive smile. 'Do you wish to meet your charges? They've been told who you are and have been made aware of the journey they must endure. They are eager to speak with the man who will become their guardian.' Paulus had no choice but to follow her lead.

He swallowed a sudden lump that appeared in his throat. As far as he was aware, he'd never fathered a child nor felt the slightest urge to become a parent. In the next few minutes, he was about to be judged by two children who were still in the care of wet-nurses.

Constantine had, in effect, made him a surrogate father at a time of life when he was old, grey and very set in his ways.

'Come forward, boys! I'd like you to meet Decurion Paulus,' Endellion called, beckoning to a young boy of some five years who appeared in the open doorway that led into the hall. This child stood squarely with slightly parted feet, while he examined Paulus carefully with wide, hazel-green eyes. Behind him, an adult woman, somewhere in her thirties, held the hand of a younger boy with red-gold curls that tumbled over his shoulders. The younger child was notable because his expression was so thunderous. The air seemed to crackle and seethe around him, a remarkable feat for a child so young. Inwardly, with a silent groan of worry, Paulus marvelled at the strength of character that totally eclipsed that of the older brother.

'The elder lad is Ambrosius, Decurion. He has been eager to meet the great man who will become his foster-father,' Endellion said as she led the older boy forward.

'I am very pleased to meet you, young man,' Paulus said solemnly in his clipped soldier's voice. He offered his right arm in a soldier's clasp as a manly greeting between equals. After a brief moment of consideration, Ambrosius stepped forward and also extended his arm. He gripped Paulus's thick wrist in a surprisingly strong grasp, even though his fingers were unable to encircle Paulus's wrist guards.

'I am pleased to make your acquaintance, sir. I hope we shall be friends.'

Paulus examined the open face below him and saw no guile in Ambrosius's clear eyes. In fact, the boy seemed far older than his five or six years. His hair was dark blond in colour, shading to white-gold at the tips, his skin hues golden. Although he was a handsome boy, Ambrosius's face had none of the harsh angles of his younger brother's features. Paulus decided that this lad would always think carefully before he committed himself to any plan of action, a quality that would be both a blessing and a curse for any aspiring leader of men. He felt a growing respect and liking for this boy who looked directly into his eyes. This prince, Paulus decided, must be the golden dragonlet.

'I don't want us to outdo each other in the nonsensical extremes of courtesy, lad, so you shall address me as Paulus or Decurion. For my part, I will call you Ambrosius. This befits my position as your personal protector and guardian.'

'I believe you were a friend of my father, Paulus?'

Paulus was careful to reply with complete honesty. He intended to abide by his promise to Constantine and Severa that these children would never forget the legacy of their parents. Paulus would never lie to the boys, but nor would he tell them the unvarnished truth until they had grown to manhood. If his younger brother was inclined to be difficult, Ambrosius would make a good ally in the days that lay ahead of them.

'Yes, Ambrosius, your father and I were friends and comrades for near to fifteen years. We served together in the legions until he bade me to leave him at Arelate before that besieged city fell to his enemies. Constantine ordered me to remain alive and to ensure that no harm came to his sons. I have sworn to obey him and I will protect you for as long as I can lift my gladius.'

Man and boy examined the truth in each other's eyes and Paulus was pleased by what he saw in the lad's expression. If Ambrosius was too fair and apt to believe in the goodness of others, these flaws could be fine characteristics in a man, although they might well be dangerous in someone fated to become a future king of the Britons. Paulus decided that he would do his very best to prepare the boy-child for the role he must play.

As Ambrosius stepped back into the shelter of Endellion's skirts, she called the children's nurse and instructed the second boy to step forward.

'This maidservant is Dara, Paulus. She is the boys' nurse. They will tell you that they are too old for such a servant, but she has agreed to travel with you and care for the boys for as long as you need her services. Her name means *oak tree* in the ancient language of the Britons. Dara bears a venerable name because the oak was sacred to our ancestors before the Romans brought Christianity to our shores. Like her namesake, Dara is strong and will faithfully serve you and the boys until death comes to her.'

Both Dara and Paulus nodded politely to each other, although Dara bowed her head far lower in deference to the superior rank of the Roman officer. Younger than Paulus by twenty years, she was long past the foolish romantic dreams that immature girls cherish. Her husband had gone to war with Constantine and Dara knew all too clearly that he'd never return from Gallia.

'And this young man is Uther, our scapegrace,' Endellion added cheerfully, although her expression was unusually nervous. Paulus realised immediately that Uther may have been last of the siblings, but he would never be the least.

'Greetings, Uther,' the decurion responded and extended his hand. Uther ignored the gesture completely and impaled Paulus with his leonine amber eyes. Paulus had once seen a small pride of those huge cats in a circus in Cyrene when he was a newly trained boy-soldier. The three lions, a male and two females, had been loosed against a pair of gladiators to amuse a provincial crowd in a stinking-hot, crowded township on the edge of the

African desert. Paulus had been bored at first, but the drama in the arena soon captured his attention.

A female with dark-tipped markings on her ears and feet taunted one of the gladiators, keeping just out of reach of his trident and net. Her eyes had spoken of fierce, inhuman intelligence as she lured the overconfident warrior to move away from his friend, until Paulus realised that the other lioness and the huge, black-maned male were edging towards the exposed flanks of that second warrior who was armed with a sword and shield. The crowd screamed warnings and encouragement at the men until the gladiator with the net and trident caught the audacious female a glancing blow across her shoulders.

The crowd howled at this first sign of a blood flow on the animal's pelt.

The female continued to prowl her way across the arena, pausing to crouch and watch her prey for a few seconds, before surging forward to a spot that was just beyond the reach of that wicked trident and the entangling net. Her tail twitched angrily. When she began to limp and blood stained the sand of the arena, Paulus almost crowed with amusement. Surely this gladiator would be too experienced to believe she was weakening.

But, with all the arrogance of young men who have under-estimated their enemy, first the gladiator with the trident and then his companion with the sword began to advance on her, forcing the lioness to move slowly backwards. Meanwhile, both men appeared to forget that, by their own forward momentum, they were allowing both the male and the second female to outflank them. Nor did they realise the error of their ways until the lioness behind them ripped her claws through the net-man's tendons at the back of his knees and spilled him into the dust.

Meanwhile, the male lion rose like a wave over the swordsman and brought the gladiator down on to his stomach, as all four feet and their curved claws raked at the hapless man's torso and sides. As the huge male finished off his victim with brutal skill, the two lionesses played with the other gladiator like domestic cats tormenting a mouse. Unable to run on legs that no longer obeyed him, the poor man screamed and lashed out with his trident and net in a vain attempt to stave off the inevitable.

Finally, the lioness with the dark points ripped her claws through his throat and stalked away to lick her wound in peace. To Paulus's immature eyes, the lioness had seemed like an all-powerful queen disciplining a fractious slave with indifferent cruelty.

As Uther gazed into Paulus's features, the child's eyes were as cold and pitiless as those of any lioness. 'We don't need you, Roman! I have my knife, so I'll protect Ambrosius.'

Endellion looked skyward for a moment and then grinned apologetically at Paulus in an effort to enlist his understanding of this precocious child.

'The plans we've discussed were made by your parents, Uther. Do you intend to disobey your mother?'

Uther pushed out his bottom lip pugnaciously, but he frowned in sudden anger when Ambrosius added his own criticisms.

'Your knife is very small, Uther, and all you've done with it is to wound our grandmother's cat. You made Grandmama cry, Uther, so beg for Paulus's pardon!'

'I won't!' Uther hissed at his brother in fury. 'I won't!'

Paulus chose to intervene and establish his authority from the outset. It was important that he started with the same control that he intended to maintain during their entire association. For now, Uther was small and powerless; but one day he would be a man – and he would be powerful.

'You'll be quiet, Uther, or I'll gag you. You will not throw tantrums in the presence of your grandmother or the king in childish displays that will cause them shame. You will soon learn that you would be unwise to throw those same tantrums in my presence, or in the presence of acquaintances who might be embarrassed by such foolishness. For shame, Uther! You are the son of a Roman emperor who was also the High King of the British lands, so it is your duty to ensure that your lands are stripped bare of those enemies who would take its bounty from your subjects. To do your duty, you must become strong, clever and talented. Your father gave me strict instructions that I was to beat you without mercy if I need to instil good manners in you.'

'You wouldn't dare!' Uther screamed as his face and body tensed like a metal spring.

With far greater speed than the boy expected, Paulus stepped forward, grasped Uther by the front of his short tunic and lifted him bodily into the air while Endellion and Dara gasped with surprise. By contrast, both Aeron and Pridenow looked pleased, as if they had longed to box Uther's ears for some time. Only Ambrosius seemed upset on Uther's behalf and the lad moment-arily raised one hand to stop his guardian before he thought better of it.

Uther's eyes flared with surprise and apprehension, but the decurion could see the effort with which the child was trying to control his panic and stare back at Paulus in defiance. Paulus shook Uther until the boy's teeth began to chatter before setting him down on his backside without ceremony.

'I'll put you over my knee, bare your arse and beat your

backside with the flat of my sword on every occasion that you speak out of turn. Regardless! Do you understand?'

Uther nodded, but Paulus knew in his heart that this particular battle had resulted in a stalemate. Realising that his language had been inappropriate in the presence of the queen, he apologised immediately.

'You'll also apologise to the queen, Uther. I understand temper and how it goads us to say things we don't really mean, but such bad behaviour in front of your grandmama is unacceptable from any young prince. You've shamed your parents and all of your kin by such lack of control.'

This stern speech actually broke through Uther's steely resolve and penetrated his immature armour. His eyes fell and he shuffled his feet like the child he was.

'I'm sorry, Grandmama! I'm sorry, Grandpapa! I'll try not to embarrass you again.'

Endellion lifted the squirming, embarrassed child and kissed him on both cheeks, which made Uther wriggle in her arms even more.

'You've begged our pardon, sweetheart, so I forgive you for your words. You'll make me very happy if you learn to obey Paulus like the young warrior that we want you to become under his tuition. That's all that can be asked of you. It's for your benefit that Paulus is a Roman legionnaire, because they're the best warriors in the world. You have a chance to become a fine young leader under his tutelage, so I hope you won't be fighting with him along the way.'

'I'll try,' Uther began, even as his doubtful eyes suggested that he expected to fail. 'But I don't want to leave here, Grandmama. Why can't we stay in Corinium?'

'We've already decided on the options that are available to us,' Aeron said. 'There are bad men coming who intend to hurt you because they hated your father. Whether you agree or not, it's their intention to assassinate you if you remain in Britannia. It's imperative that you and Ambrosius are taken to a place where you can learn the art of kingship in safety. If you should survive, you'll both have an opportunity to seize the throne when you grow to adulthood. Regardless of your own wishes, you will abide by your father's instructions – no matter how unhappy it makes you feel. I, too, had to suffer and give up things I wanted to do, so that I earned the right to rule over my subjects. You, Ambrosius, as the heir to the throne, and you, Uther, as Ambrosius's heir, have special obligations to the citizens of Britannia. You must do everything in your power to make them safe and strong.'

'King Aeron offers wise counsel,' Paulus added. 'You must spend the coming years learning your craft and working on the skills you'll need if the Britons are prepared to place their trust in you. Your mother is sacrificing herself to keep you safe, so you must act as men, even at your tender ages. For my part, I'll be forced to hide from your mother's enemies until such time as you're old enough and strong enough to wrest power from them.'

The decurion spoke with such gravitas that both boys watched him with fixed stares, for his words came hard on the heels of King Aeron's description of the responsibilities of high birth. Paulus's challenge laid out their futures and his words explained why they should obey the one man who was able to help them and protect them.

Into this short and poignant silence, the sound of a woman clearing her throat suddenly intruded into the discussion. As if responding to a threat, Paulus turned his eyes away from his two charges to a striking woman who was standing in the doorway.

'I'm sorry, Dilic, for I've failed to present you,' Endellion said in a flat voice. 'This lady, Decurion, is Mistress Dilic. She's the personal maid and friend of my foster-daughter, Severa. Dilic has been asked to accompany the boys into their exile.'

Endellion glanced enigmatically towards Paulus as the woman bowed low, although her bold eyes showed no trace of respect.

This wench must be a servant or the widow of a tribal lord. What now? The bitch seems far too bold for my liking and she isn't a woman who'll take orders willingly. Paulus's thoughts were visible in his furrowed brows and thinned lips. She moved forward sinuously with a derisive smile.

The woman was handsome by any yardstick. Her coal-black ringlets fell to her thighs, except where her mane was constrained by bronze combs. Her green eyes watched the decurion with a determined gaze. She was letting him know from the very start that she wasn't fooled by his apparent lack of interest in her presence or her appearance.

I know you, she seemed to be saying. *After all, you're only another man.*

Paulus felt his temper begin to rise at her arrogance.

'Can I assume that Mistress Dilic will be assisting Dara with the boys' personal welfare?' Paulus asked the queen.

Before Endellion could answer, Dilic interrupted her mistress with a bright smile. Endellion bridled visibly, but forced down her glance of displeasure.

'Queen Severa has made me duty-bound to ensure that the boys receive their personal tuition from her family friend. I was at my mistress's bedside when the boys were born and I have cared for them throughout their short lives. They are used to my presence and they are beholden to me when I order them to obey me. My mistress is determined that they will not be permitted to forget her and their birthright, Master Paulus, so I have been given the task of teaching them the manners and history of her family and her household. She means no disrespect towards you by allotting this task to me. My mistress has given me my instructions in great detail, and I intend to obey her commands out of my love for her.'

'Hmmmf!' Paulus grunted his annoyance, but he knew that he had been presented with a fait accompli and had been saddled with the wench. In truth, she might be useful in adding a veneer of polish to Ambrosius and Uther, a skill that was beyond Paulus and Dara.

'Very well then!' the decurion said at last. 'I'll expect you to be ready to travel at dawn.'

Once again, Endellion and Paulus exchanged glances and the swift, silent communication between them spoke volumes of her exasperation with Dilic and the difficulties the maidservant had caused since her arrival from Venta Belgarum. With a brief smile of triumph, Dilic bowed low to the royal family and Paulus before backing away into the gloom of the Great Hall.

As soon as she had vanished, Endellion sighed with ill-humour.

'Drat the girl! She arrived on my doorstep with the boys and Dara, and I must admit that she is very fond of them. Of more importance, she is correct when she says that the boys mind her instructions and obey her every command. She irritates me intensely, but I am loath to have her removed because Severa is beholden to her. Nor is any man with a hint of red blood in his veins safe when he is in her presence. I'm afraid that the bitch has the morals of an alley cat and she'll be a source of constant trouble when you're travelling to your destination in Gallia.'

'She also has claws!' Aeron added with a snide laugh. 'The steward's son decided to touch a certain part of her anatomy without her express invitation and he now has a scar across his nose as a memory of the incident.'

'Aeron! The boys are in your hearing!' Endellion protested, at which the subject of Dilic was temporarily forgotten.

Uther's eyes had opened wide at the exchange that had taken place between Dilic and Paulus, though Ambrosius merely looked puzzled.

Paulus wasn't fooled. Uther might be the red dragon, but he was only a small boy. He would prove to be a handful as he grew older, the decurion thought; perhaps Dilic could actually be of some use to him if the younger son was prepared to obey her commands.

He grinned wickedly at the prospect.

Soft-footed and welcoming, other servants led the decurion to a warm room that was more sumptuously appointed than the simplicity of its construction suggested. Had he been asked the route that they'd taken to reach it, Paulus could never have answered because the circuitous corridors, rooms within rooms and circular spaces that seemed to have no purpose completely defeated his sense of direction.

With a sigh of gratitude, he sank back on to the pallet as soon as he'd removed his armour and half-boots. He'd finally been given an opportunity to think.

Paulus was slow to sleep, so his mind retraced the written directions he had received from King Aeron. The Dumnonii king had used every blood debt owed to him (and Constantine) over a long and fruitful life. He had planned their journey meticulously, although Paulus was certain that a disaster could confound Aeron's carefully wrought instructions.

The decurion carefully unrolled Aeron's scroll and perused it again in an attempt to memorise the detail. He knew that this whole enterprise depended on his understanding the detail of Aeron's plans, and he would soon be obliged to destroy this precious piece of vellum and ensure that its information could not be delivered to the ears of Vortigern.

Decurion Paulus,

You are about to embark on what could be a tedious and dangerous journey, one which will take many months. I pray that God will protect you during these travels.

I have a special friend in Hispania who owes me a blood debt that goes back to our youth. He is a stern Visigoth warrior and a fine man, one who is more than capable of protecting my grandsons from an animal such as Vortigern.

My friend's name is Helguerra and he is the chieftain of a tribe whose citizens live in the small villages and ports scattered along the Vasconian coast in the north-east of Hispania. He has become a wealthy man through trade and has adopted the Roman culture, so you will not feel completely displaced in his company. He has a large estate near the small town of Apollodorus, which is inland from the port of Donostia. This estate is your ultimate destination.

Your first task is to find a trading vessel which will carry you to a port called Portus Namnetum, which is on the coast of Armorica in Gallia. I suggest you travel to the western or southern coast of Britannia to some suitable place where you can find a vessel that will take your party to Gallia.

From Namnetum, you will need to follow the Roman roads to the port of Burdigala in the south-west of Aquitania. I will leave the exact route in your capable hands, but I fear the distances you will be forced to travel will be long and arduous. But so it must be if we are to protect the children.

Once you have reached Burdigala, you must seek out a sea captain by the name of Daire. This man is indebted to Constantine's family and he can be trusted not to betray you. He will gladly do his duty and will take you all on board his vessel, Neptune's Kiss, for the next stage of the route which will take you to Donostia in northern Hispania.

The journey from Burdigala to Donostia would best be undertaken by sea, to ensure that no prying eyes become aware of your precious cargo or your destination.

Donostia lies on the Vasconian coast where southern Gallia meets northern Hispania. You will find a guide here to take you to Helguerra. Show him Severa's missive and explain my wishes. I'm certain that he'll adopt our cause with enthusiasm.

There is one further matter that I have failed to discuss with you. I don't know what Severa has asked of you, but I can guess. May I add my voice to hers and beg that you stay with the children during their formative years and, if possible, guide them during their journeys into manhood. I would ask that they be trained as warriors and as leaders. I can think of no better mentor for them than a Roman decurion.

These boys are princes of Britannia, so the day will come when our people will have need of them. Use your wisdom, my friend, and teach them to become the rulers of tomorrow.

More than this I cannot ask.

Aeron, King of the Dumnonii tribe of Britannia

* * *

Vortigern pulled his horse to a ragged halt on a low hill overlooking the walled town of Venta Belgarum. Behind him, a troop of twenty multiracial mercenaries, light cavalrymen who had been hired in Dubris with coin stolen from Constans's war chest, pulled their horses to an undisciplined halt as they awaited the pleasure of their new master.

The face of the Demetae ruler revealed nothing of his thoughts as he stared across the roofs of the town and the hall that lay at its centre. The next stop in his journey to achieve his heart's desire was spread out before him like a naked woman. The bitch who ruled Venta Belgarum would agree to any demands that would save her sons, but the brats had no place in his plans. So, once they were safely in his clutches and under his total control, they would perish in a tragic accident. Vortigern would weep bitterly and console Severa in her time of tragedy, while reminding the bereaved mother of the care and concern he had displayed while acting as Constantine's regent. His mouth curved in its perpetual smile, although he took no pleasure from the murder of small children. A pragmatist to his core, Vortigern understood that the victors always destroyed the families of the vanquished and obliterated their seed, if only so they could sit safely on their newly won thrones without fear of retribution. Vortigern would do whatever was needed to achieve his aspirations and ambitions, without any qualms.

He remembered something of the boys he had played with and amused in those days when he sought to pacify their mother's suspicions. Ambrosius was much the same as any child from a royal family, although he was a little taller and fairer than most. But Uther was a different matter entirely. Vortigern knew that

Uther would grow into a man who would never rest until he had taken back all that he considered to be his own, even if he had to kill the whole world to attain his desires.

After taking a deep breath, he squared his shoulders and kicked his horse's ribs. The big bay gelding responded with a surge of speed while the mercenaries straggled along behind him. He winced at their slovenly discipline and their shoddy dress.

'You get what you pay for,' he hissed to himself and swore inwardly that the attitude of these ragtag dogs would improve before the month was out. Still, their presence spoke more loudly than words and Severa would understand the significance of their arrival at Vortigern's back. The Demetae king had returned to Britannia to claim a kingdom. He would not be denied.

Inevitably, Vortigern's column was halted at the city gates by a self-important, overweight fellow who sauntered up to Vortigern in a manner guaranteed to offend the returning warrior. But Vortigern was no Paulus, nor was he a low-ranking officer who was prepared to overlook the arrogance of a mere servant.

'You lot can't come into Venta Belgarum. The queen has issued an edict that forbids any group of warriors larger than six from passing through the gates and entering her city.'

This news was delivered with a sneer that grated on Vortigern's nerve endings.

'Is that so? Perhaps you should send word to the queen that a courier has come with news of her husband.' The door-keeper hawked and spat out a globule of phlegm that narrowly missed the Demetae's booted foot. A red haze appeared behind Vortigern's eyes, but the gatekeeper totally missed this warning sign.

'It doesn't matter! I've been told that no groups of armed men larger than six can enter the city. I'll send a message to the queen that you're here, but she won't change her mind.'

'You'd do well to learn some manners before I see you again,' Vortigern began amiably as, suddenly, his left hand was holding a long, curved knife. 'Trouble is that I can't see you ever controlling your stupid tongue, if I don't leave you with a gentle reminder of who I am.'

Vortigern's right hand gripped the gatekeeper by the straining woollen tunic that barely covered his hard belly. Then, in a display of raw strength, he raised the man on to the tips of his toes so that his contorted face was dangerously close to the blade. The gatekeeper struggled like a gaffed fish, while the bunched tunic began to choke off his breath. The mercenaries exploded with mirth in a surge of admiration for Vortigern's show of brute strength.

Vortigern shook the frightened man several times to show his displeasure, while the gatekeeper begged and pleaded to be released. But the Demetae's eyes were ruthlessly cold.

'I didn't . . . mean . . . nothing disrespectful . . . like . . .'

Vortigern's knife sliced through the mottled red face from forehead to chin with a single flick of its blade. As blood streamed from the man's face, the Demetae fastidiously dropped him with an exclamation of disgust and began to wipe his bloody fingers on his kerchief.

'We'll have no difficulty in recognising each other's faces when next we meet and you'll take care to show me the proper respect,' Vortigern hissed. His face showed a slight grimace of distaste, as if he could smell something that was rotten. 'Now open the gates to my fucking city . . . and let me in.'

Ignoring the blood that was running down from the deep gash in his face, the gatekeeper scrambled to his feet and began to drag open the heavy gates. Before he had finished grappling with the huge timbers, Vortigern and his mercenaries galloped through and entered the town. In front of the riders, citizens ran for their homes and, with a sense of satisfaction, Vortigern heard the sounds of locks and bars falling into place behind the doors, even as the hoofs of his horses sent stones flying through the air.

'We're home again,' Vortigern said with a lopsided grin, as he thundered towards the Great Hall at full gallop. His destiny was waiting.

THE JOURNEY INTO EXILE FOR AMBROSIUS AND UTHER

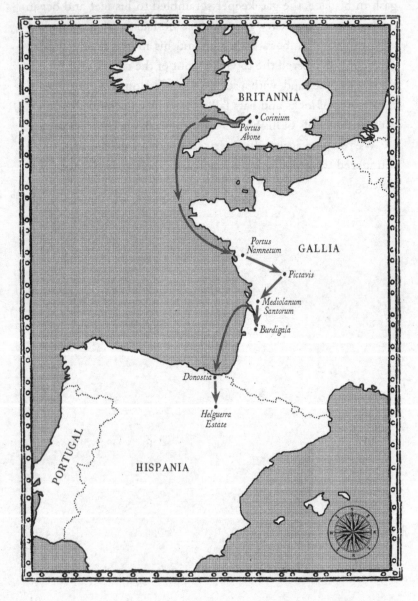

CHAPTER V

INTO EXILE

Everything flows and nothing stays.

Heraclitus

By any definition, the small fishing village outside of Portus Abonae could only be described as a ramshackle and grubby settlement that was just one step better than a rubbish midden. The drying racks for fish, the smokehouses that preserved the catch and the village's small boats were all decrepit, dirty and in desperate need of repair. Those same boats had been drawn up on the shingle above the high-tide mark with its garlands of seaweed and driftwood, all of which added to a miasma of decay in the village. Small groups of fishermen idled along the sloping sand dunes as they waited for the next break in the weather that would allow them to make their way into open waters. With weather-beaten faces and gnarled hands twisted and scarred from years of dragging on heavy lines, these fisher-folk seemed like bleached scarecrows as they bragged about the huge catches they had achieved in bygone days.

This village was a sad memory of a disappearing past where dwellings had been built from raw stone, thatch and mud. Narrow, overgrown lanes linked circular and oval houses that were filled with smoke and the smell of fish oil. Stunted children ran on bared feet between the huts and screeched like young animals when they made violent attacks on the strangers with handfuls of mud, dung or clumps of weed.

Paulus ducked as one missile whistled by his ear. He glared at the culprit, an urchin who scuttled away with an awkward squawk.

'What a useless blot on the face of the earth,' Paulus said aloud in a voice that expressed his disgust at everyone who inhabited the hovels. Both Pridenow and the wearisome woman, Dilic, turned in their saddles as one.

'It has no name that I've ever heard,' Pridenow responded drily. 'The local peasants refer to it as either the Home of Fishermen or, more often, as Home.'

'All the necessary information was included in my mistress's instructions,' Dilic added pugnaciously. 'Can't you read?'

Paulus had come to expect such crude responses from Dilic during the slow journey that had brought them from Corinium to Aquae Sulis, before continuing to this tiny speck of human habitation that lay on the very edge of vast waterways.

The first major disagreement between Paulus and Dilic had occurred when Corinium was barely out of sight. Dilic provoked a fist fight between two young warriors who were determined to woo her, albeit at the cost of their previous friendship. The conflict had been short, but bloody, for Pridenow and Paulus had waded through the other troopers who were enjoying the fun and had separated the warriors by force. In the process, a swinging fist had hit Paulus on the bridge of his nose, drawing tears and blood aplenty, and souring his mood.

Paulus hadn't hesitated to dress her down in front of the men, for he was careless of her protests or humiliation. He warned her to refrain from placing temptation in the path of his troops. She had sulked ever since.

The decurion stared at the village, if such a grand term could describe this collection of hovels, and he began to wonder why Aeron and Endellion had saddled him with this she-devil and instructed him to make his departure from Britannia from such a remote and backward place. Dilic might have been an attractive woman and she was truly beloved by the two boys who had been placed in his charge, but she was all vanity and immorality when it came to young men, especially handsome warriors.

Paulus was disposed to dislike all ports at the moment, but the Home of Fishermen failed to reach the basic requirements of a trading port. At the extreme end of a low headland, he could make out the outline of what seemed to be a rickety wharf made from tree trunks. This primitive construction had been built by driving long tree trunks into the mud and then securing them with a framework of roughly cut and split logs. Smaller timbers had then been attached to the structure to provide a deck that could be used to load or unload cargo. The poor state of the pier showed that the structure had been buffeted by strong winds, rough seas and vicious tides for many years. It was fortunate for the local fishermen that the waters in Sabrina Aest were better protected than those in the wild ocean that lay to the south-west.

He grumbled deep in his chest like an irritable old bear. There would be no inn here and no comfort. Without windows, and with only low doorways and ragged holes in the thatch to disperse the smoke from the fire pits, these tiny basic dwellings were small, foetid and would smell of the livestock which shared the limited space with their owners during the long winters. Suddenly, a blanket on the cold ground seemed far more luxurious than these lice-ridden nests of purgatory on earth.

The decurion swore as a sympathetic itch began in his right armpit. He scratched at the nonexistent bite with growing bile.

'I'm familiar with Queen Severa's instructions, Mistress Dilic, but I'm at a loss to know why the children weren't sent to Portus Adurni to catch ship and sail away from the British lands. We'd be long gone from Britannia if we'd followed that course of action.'

'The port would be the first place that Vortigern would have looked for you. Even a Roman should know that.'

Pridenow coughed and shot a sharp glance in the maidservant's direction. His intervention should have warned her that insulting Paulus was an unwise thing to do.

'I'm ever so sorry!' she continued in the same sarcastic tone. 'I suppose you wouldn't have survived to become such an old man if you'd been a complete dolt.' Of a sudden, Paulus began to realise where Uther had learned some of his worst mannerisms.

Pridenow watched in amazement while Paulus considered the response that the maidservant's insults warranted. The young warrior could see that Paulus's mailed left fist had been cocked and he realised that Paulus was close to making a violent response to her ridiculous taunts. Then Pridenow heaved a sigh of relief. He knew from his observations of the Roman that Paulus always kept his anger under control, for he believed that violence against women was unmanly. Dilic was probably safe from the decurion's fists. With some reluctance, Paulus embarked on an almost reasonable venting of his spleen.

'You seem unable to act with even a pretence of manners in my presence, woman, so you'd best get back to the wagon where you belong. There'll be no more riding for you. Your sullen face and obstructive attitude are telling me that you've outlived your usefulness on this journey. If it continues, I'll send you back to your mistress.'

Pridenow was aware that King Aeron had ordered this difficult woman to obey Paulus in all matters. It was important to ensure that good order and discipline prevailed during this period of exile, which meant that Dilic mustn't be permitted to erode the decurion's authority. Why she had declared war on Paulus was a mystery to the young man, but Paulus must solve the problems brought on by this fractious woman – and he must do it soon.

Belatedly, Dilic realised that her conversation and manners had been over-combative when she noticed that Pridenow was mouthing warnings in her direction. Aware now that she might have been a little foolish in making a direct attack on the man who was responsible for the protection of her charges, she opted to retreat and obey the decurion's orders for now.

For his part, the decurion was unimpressed by this stupid maidservant who'd been foisted upon him at the last moment, along with the hastily scrawled missive that Pridenow had scribed for Severa in a heartfelt appeal to Paulus's better nature.

To Decurion Paulus.

Hail, friend. I trust that the roads have been kind to you and this message is in your hands before you make your departure from Corinium with my boys.

My maid, Dilic, who has cared for the boys since their birthing, carries a small cloth packet which contains all the information I can give you, as well as my parting gift to you, an exquisite gold jewel in the shape of the Christian fish symbol. I would be pleased if you were to wear this gift in memory of Severa, Queen of the Britons.

Dilic is in possession of a small ivory chest in which I have placed all the extra coin I could amass at short notice. This sum should be used for the boys' education if their exile should be of long duration. Take the coins and use them well to ensure that my sons become true Roman citizens in the image of their father and grandfather.

It's likely that I'll never see my boys again in this life, so it is my dearest wish that Dilic will address this lack. She will tell them my story and relay to them my great love.

I know that she can be a very trying girl and she has no taste for authority, but I trust her with my life and the lives of my sons. I ask that you overlook her many faults, Paulus, for her heart is good.

We shall not meet again, my friend, but this is a fate I can bear if I am certain that my boys will grow to manhood in the care of such a worthy patron.

I thank you for your service, Paulus, which exceeds everything that has been asked of you. I will speak to the Lords of the Underworld and the Christ when we eventually enter the shades and tell them of your honesty and steadfast service.

I pray that you will stay safe and well.

Queen Severa

Written at Venta Belgarum.

For one brief moment, Paulus was very angry. The queen and her problems had intruded into what should have been a quiet and peaceful retirement.

Paulus glanced downwards to his scarred soldier's hands.

Severa's request amounted to a huge responsibility, for so much would hinge on his cool head and his ability to protect the children.

King Aeron's written instructions had also been stored in Paulus's pouch, but the decurion had a rational mind and his soldierly acumen held no truck with a journey that might be fraught with danger. Too many things could go wrong. The instructions from the Dumnonii king nestled beside Severa's missive and, with every word from the old king, Paulus's hopes of a quiet retirement had faded from view.

Paulus sighed deeply as he reread Severa's message. As his eyes moved down the precious vellum, he could just decipher Pridenow's spidery hand. Time stood still.

On this delicate page, his life hung in the balance. Dim with presentiment and concern, Paulus saw his duty stretch out before him.

He looked at the vellum again.

It seemed so fragile, for something that would change his life in the name of duty. But there it lay and nothing would ever be the same again.

Severa's short message, in conjunction with the packet of instructions and the golden fish-shaped Christian amulet, had softened Paulus's heart to the extent that he was able to withstand an impulse to punish the girl. However, her persistent insubordination would cause problems if he couldn't eliminate the chasms that lay between them. He would have to confront her as soon as they were away from Britannia. She would be far more amenable to discipline when the society that she knew was behind her.

In the meantime, Paulus must find a vessel that was large enough to sail to Burdigala, the port and fishing village that lay on the coast of Aquitania in Gallia. Many problems lay ahead of him before they set foot on the continent, for the likelihood of finding a vessel larger than a coracle or a wooden rowing boat was negligible in this tiny village.

The decurion swore with colour and imagination, simple vulgarity that forced a discreet smile from Pridenow as he stared morosely at the battered wharf on the headland. 'I'll try to find out if any vessels are likely to pause here when they are sailing into the south,' Pridenow volunteered politely. He could see that Paulus's facial expression was thunderous.

'While you're talking to the local fishermen, the rest of us will be making camp at the top of the hillock where we can keep a lookout,' Paulus ordered curtly, while pointing towards a low rise in the ground that overlooked the village. 'At least we can enjoy the view from there and we'll have the advantages of clean air and fresh grass for the horses.'

Pridenow nodded, dismounted and ambled off to speak to the fishermen who were mending their nets on the mound overlooking the foreshore. His iron-studded boot soles crunched on the shell- and kelp-strewn pebbles, while the small group of men eyed him nervously.

'Are the fish running for you, good folk?' Pridenow asked, out of a desire to put the men at their ease.

'No more than usual, sir,' one grandfather answered, while shading his eyes to lessen the glare of the afternoon sun.

'But we'll catch a goodly share if the weather stays fair.'

'Good! Good! Then there should be lots of ships plying the sea to the north and the south, if the winds and the seas continue to be fair, although I imagine that their captains would only rarely stop into a small settlement such as yours.' Pridenow's words were accompanied by a cheerful grin, his boyish freckles and wide, guileless eyes easing any nervousness that the fishermen might have otherwise felt at his questioning.

'Some of the trading ships put into the wharf whenever they have a need for fresh water,' one young lad offered, although an older man, probably his father, nudged him with his bare foot as a warning to keep his silence.

'Oh! That might be of some help to my charges. I've been given the task of escorting some noble children who have been staying with the Dobunni king in Corinium. We've received word that their kinfolk in Gallia have been taken down with a deathly illness and there's a need for the children to return to the care of their maternal grandmother. I decided to find a vessel that might be able to transport them back to the continent. Their need is great, as you might imagine, so we would be happy to reward your people for any arrangement that can be made.'

The eldest of the fishermen nodded agreeably, although none of them cared whether the boys returned to their homes or not. The arrival of these grand folk was merely a new topic of conversation, a juicy titbit that could be masticated and enjoyed for many days to come.

'Aye!' the original greybeard answered. 'That's bad luck for them young 'uns of yours.'

The other fishermen agreed with him. Pridenow noticed that the fisherfolk possessed scarcely a mouthful of teeth between their total number, except for the young lad who used his incisors to snip away at the twine that he was using to mend his section of the net. This boy's sharp, white teeth clicked together audibly as the strands of twine parted with every bite.

It's no wonder their teeth have broken or fallen out! Pridenow thought as the young fisherman grinned at him. Life must be hard along this coast, God knows, for they live in much the same ways as their ancestors survived in long-gone centuries.

But Pridenow was too sensible and far too tactful to allow his thoughts to reach his eyes. His smile never wavered as he lowered himself on to his hams to spare the older man's eyes from the harsh afternoon sun.

'Are any vessels due to stop off at the village for water or supplies? I'm certain that you'd know what traders pull into the wharf while on their way back to Gallia or Hispania.'

'Mayhap! They come and they go from year to year without any word of their intentions. You mustn't take too much notice of what we say about these things,' the older man added, as the others nodded in agreement.

'Surely they do some trading with your villagers,' Pridenow prodded, for he guessed that these villagers maintained the wharf, such as it was, to facilitate the trade that arose from its occasional use.

The old grandfather began to chortle through his two remaining incisors.

'They traded two piglets of mine the last time they came here, but I held them to a good trade. The buggers wriggled a bit, but the captain told me that they'd been away from home for six months and his crew were famished for some sweet, soft piglet. I got a bronze pot and a bolt of good cloth for those little beasties.'

The other fishermen thought the deal was a good joke, presumably because piglets were born every spring in large litters and a provident housewife could do well out of a fertile sow. In an impoverished village such as this, trade goods could mean the difference between subsistence living and a fruitful life.

Pridenow laughed as if he had heard a very good joke. 'Do you know of any vessels that are likely to arrive in the immediate future, Grandfather? As I said before, our need is great and we would be willing to pay you well for any assistance you can give us.'

The face of greed was immediately apparent in four pairs of eyes.

'The harvest has come and gone,' the youth muttered to his father.

'Aye! The winds will freshen soon, so the traders will want to return to their homes in Gallia and Hispania,' the older man replied while biting on his thumbnail in concentration.

'Has *Sea Queen* passed yet?' another elder asked, while the grandfather twisted his lips and narrowed his eyes in painful thought.

'The *Sea Queen* be a trading vessel that comes in every year on her return from Hibernia. That black-hearted captain always stops here and tries to rob us blind, while they collect enough fresh water to complete their voyage. They must be due soon, so I'd say that *Sea Queen* is your best chance for a passage to Gallia. But the captain is a rogue. He'll steal yer women and yer gold as soon as look at yer.'

Pridenow wasn't put off by the prospect. 'Good enough! We'll wait for *Sea Queen* to arrive.'

To show his appreciation, Pridenow searched in his pouch for a handful of base coins which he distributed to the four fishermen, who bit them and looked satisfied. The coins vanished, like the objects of a conjuring trick, into their ragged clothing.

Bidding the fishermen a good day, Pridenow made his way back to his horse, climbed into the saddle and followed the churned earth to where the column had sent up camp on the small hill that overlooked the sea.

Once Pridenow informed Paulus of the intelligence he had gained from the fishermen, the decurion sent a brace of scouts to search out the well and make a signal fire near the ramshackle wharf on the headland. One warrior would be rostered to stand by the signal fire for as long as they were required to wait on this inhospitable coast.

During the lazy afternoon, the boys had finally been given a release from their prison in the travelling wagon and had been allowed to play like puppies in the long grass beside a copse of trees. Dilic was with the boys, filling her arms with the last wildflowers that bloomed in the long grasses in white and yellow drifts. Paulus watched this bucolic scene with unreadable eyes.

'With any luck at all, the trader will appear within the week,' the decurion remarked to Pridenow. 'While I'm not likely to enjoy the voyage on board a ship, I'd rather be moving than sitting on my arse and waiting for Vortigern to pick up our trail and make an attack on us. I've known that young fellow for some years and I know how his evil mind works.'

Paulus's voice dripped with sarcasm and something that sounded almost like hatred. The emotion was so strong that Pridenow felt curious to know more.

'Oh, yes, our Vortigern is a fine fellow. He's a truly talented fighter, boy! In fact, you'll rarely see a more competent warrior. But he has no honour – none at all – because it's foreign to his nature. He'll pretend well enough, but loyalty means nothing to him. He'll always go his own road and will act in any manner that's right for him, regardless of any oaths of fealty that he might have sworn in the past.'

'You know him well then,' Pridenow answered slowly. 'I was sent to train under his tutelage in Venta Belgarum and I'd have to agree he's a superb tactician and warrior. He was called to Gallia with Constans before I could gauge the kind of man he was. Besides, I was barely more than a boy at the time he was called away by Constantine.'

Paulus spat towards the newly lit camp fire, while the remaining eight warriors hurried to make an encampment for their noble charges. In the distance, Uther was screaming war cries in a high-pitched, excited treble. Ambrosius was shouting orders in boyish excitement, as the children fought their battles against imaginary enemies.

'Vortigern betrayed Constantine, who was his king and my master. He proffered his love and loyalty towards my master, while treating Prince Constans as if the boy was his own son. Yet, after all that, he murdered Constans from behind and deserted Constantine when he was at the mercy of his enemies. The bastard will do anything to have his own way, anything at all, so I pity Queen Severa, who will be unable to escape from his clutches.'

Pridenow furrowed his brow and worry dragged his mouth down into an unpleasant scowl. Although he had known that his foster-sister was in some danger, he had failed to consider just how brutal and villainous Vortigern had been in the recent past.

'I'll return to Venta Belgarum as soon as we have you and the boys safely aboard your vessel. I'll do my best to protect her, so Vortigern would do well not to make an enemy of me.' Pridenow's bravado wavered a little, for the lad knew that Vortigern outclassed him.

The threats elicited a snort of scorn from the decurion, an insult that caused the younger man to scowl even more thunderously.

'You probably think of me as a young man who cannot carry out any threats I should make. I might be young in years, but I'm capable of controlling my mind and emotions. I'm not a fool, Paulus, and I know how to wait for a fortuitous time. Sooner or later, Vortigern will make a mistake and I'll be waiting in the wings to do him harm. My heart would be fixed on Vortigern's death if he harmed my sister.'

Paulus nodded, but he was unconvinced. He had been dreaming of wolves and men who were made of glass for night after night, so he was weary of his responsibilities.

'Vortigern must be the Wolf of Midnight who appeared to you in your fits, although I'll never know what that description means. Beware, my young friend, for superb warriors and wise men have been taken in by Vortigern.'

Pridenow nodded and the conversation passed on to more pleasant matters.

'Mistress!' a female voice screamed from the corridor that led to the rose arbour. 'Mistress! Armed men are riding towards the Great Hall.'

Severa stood so abruptly that she almost fell from dizziness and was forced to steady herself with one hand. 'So it has begun,' she whispered to herself and walked through the doorway, past the terrified maidservant and onward to the King's Hall. Her skirts rustled gently as she moved, seemingly without haste.

Pale faces appeared before her as servants hurried to be elsewhere, bobbing their heads in respect to the queen as they hurried past her. Servants are always wise to impending changes in the structures of power, she thought sadly.

'The situation must be grave,' she murmured to the empty air.

Regretting the absence of Pridenow, yet grateful that he and Paulus must now be with her sons, Severa called for her personal guard to attend her. Only two young warriors responded to the summons, young men of fifteen and sixteen years of age respectively. Swathed in shining armour that was just a little too large for their growing frames, the lads came running. They would have drawn their swords to protect her, but Severa insisted that no bloodshed should begin on her account. She ordered them to keep their weapons sheathed. Then, as she walked towards the internal doorway that led into the King's Hall, she felt her knees stiffen with resolution as her two guards swung in behind her as an escort.

'Follow my instructions, lads, and don't allow yourselves to be provoked. Depending on who is disturbing my peace, we shall walk on eggshells. Obey me, and we may be safe.'

Severa paused at the small door that was normally used by those servants to run errands for the king and the queen, when the Hall of Justice was in session. Severa drew in a deep breath, straightened her skirts and composed her face.

Then, before her courage could fail her, she opened the door and entered the King's Hall, a place where every shadow held a memory of long-dead kings. She could almost see them. Caradoc was there, along with her father who was a huge and heavily armed figure without a face. Constans was there also, smiling wistfully from the gloom after dispensing justice for the first time. Another woman with golden hair and pale eyes was gliding from shadow to shadow as she smiled across at Flavius Magnus Maximus. And there, too, was Constantinus before he set his eyes on Rome.

She shook her head with despair, until her plaits trembled and all her ghosts had gone.

She had barely made her way to the throne and seated herself in the gloom before the outer door was opened to give entry to a rush of weapons, huge men and direct sunlight. Severa shaded her eyes, momentarily blinded by the brilliant light.

Strange, roughly uniformed men were standing in the doorway of the King's Hall, their numbers obscured by the glare and the relatively narrow space. There were too many of them for resistance, now that Pridenow was absent with Paulus on their mission into the south with the boys. Her shoulders slumped for a second or two, and then squared again as her confidence returned. She was a Roman – and she was British. Let these dogs see how true noblewomen died. She sat on her throne and refused to blink or flinch at the sound of iron-nailed boots thudding over her floors, or the male voices that were raised in raucous amusement to disturb the peace of her hall. Eventually, these dark shapes would join those ghosts who already lingered there . . . as would she.

'I hadn't thought I'd find you were waiting for me, my lady. I'm touched!'

That voice, of all others, she had dreaded to hear. Vortigern had come!

The Demetae's dark shape loomed out of the press of men and he reached the dais in a few quick strides, as if this place had always been his goal. Every nerve and sinew of his powerful body had tensed because he was anxious to claim the prize that was finally within reach. He mounted the three steps and then, as Severa's senses accepted the shock and disruption of his arrival, he seated himself beside her on the High King's throne.

Behind her, Severa heard a collective, indrawn breath as her attendants acknowledged the interloper's challenge. She turned her head slowly to face the wretch who had her at his mercy. As always, he was smiling.

'Your presence in my husband's chair informs me that Constantine, your emperor, is dead,' Severa said with utter finality in her voice. She was determined not to allow a trace of grief to be seen that would give any pleasure to this man who had once been a trusted friend.

'Of course, Highness! You must be eager to know the fate of Constantine, who died so far away and so alone. I confess that I wasn't with him when he died, but I heard of his end from a Frank courier who swore he was present when Constantine was sent so propitiously into the shades. We met in Gesoriacum, at a time when the cowardly dog was trying to escape into the north and avoid Rome's retribution for desertion.'

Vortigern's face showed a fleeting trace of wonder, as if the treasons committed by the barbarian courier were far worse than his own crimes. No sins or evils that were extant in this world had the power to touch the Demetae, but the Frank's treason, for little reward other than personal safety, had caused him some consternation.

'The Frank believed that the murder of an unarmed priest

would bring the wrath of God down on all things Roman, so he was determined to make his way to Frisia, or some backward pigpen where he would be safe from heavenly retribution, or that of his Roman masters. Still, the man did have his uses!'

Vortigern fears what he can't easily understand, Severa thought, as she stored this fragment of information away in a special vault inside her mind.

'Your husband was beheaded on the roadway just outside of Ravenna. He was executed on the direct orders of the emperor. When he died, he was dressed in a priest's cassock and my courier friend told me that Constantine begged for his life like a coward.'

For a brief moment, Severa was forced to close her eyes against the pain and humiliation that Constantine must have suffered when faced with his dishonourable fate. I wish you had died more fittingly, my love, she thought with as much regret as was left to her. Then she pushed all thoughts of Constantine out of her mind. Her husband was dead and she would mourn his passing at a time when she had the leisure to do so.

'Where are your boys, Lady Severa? I've been looking forward to gazing on their faces again so I can resume their training and education. That task gave me great pleasure when I was their regent, so I intend to become their tutor again now that their father is no longer with us. I recall that the boys spent much of their time following that attractive nurse of theirs, the one with the overbold eyes. Dilic? Was that her name?'

Severa permitted her face to fall into an expression of innocent regret.

'I'm sorry, Vortigern, but I decided that the boys should be taken to a place of safety in the north where there is a strong Roman influence. The southern parts of Britannia have been under threat from the Saxons and the Jutes, and their incursions into our lands have increased during the last couple of seasons. My husband has friends in the north who are prepared to protect them and educate them in the Roman way. Constantine initiated these arrangements some time ago in anticipation that some unforeseen disasters might befall either of us.'

Choke on that, you turd! she thought in a most unladylike fashion.

Neither of the combatants' faces gave an inch or showed a flicker of emotion, other than to reduce the amiability of what might have been a pleasant conversation.

Vortigern raised his hand then, and beckoned to one of his officers. This fur-clad barbarian stepped forward, eager to obey his commander and have done with this useless talk.

'Make a thorough search of the palace and bring any children to me,' Vortigern instructed the thug, before turning back to face the queen. 'Not that you'd lie to me, Severa, but I've never trusted the veracity of women's utterances. Some people can't be trusted.'

The mercenary acknowledged his orders with a grin that was twisted by an old sword cut. The man was tall, red-headed and obviously descended from Britannia's mortal enemies.

'Afterwards, you will question the steward and the household servants. I want to know if the children have been sent away – and where they've been taken.'

The mercenary disappeared into the back of the King's Hall with three of his fellows loping in his wake.

Vortigern's attention returned to Severa. 'A wise man always checks the veracity of information that is passed to him. It contributes to his self-confidence.'

Severa brushed the insult away with a gesture of her hand. So far, Vortigern was acting in the exact manner that she expected of him. She would be forever grateful to her God that she'd trusted no one with the boys' itinerary, other than Dilic and her parents. Even Endellion hadn't been given the full contents of Aeron's packet of instructions, for she chose to be kept ignorant of them, knowing she could never betray secrets, deliberately or otherwise, if she wasn't familiar with the details of the plot to deceive Vortigern.

'Do you plan to stay here for some time, Vortigern? I admit that I didn't expect so many armed visitors to appear on my doorstep without an invitation. I hope my steward can arrange suitable accommodation for your men during this visit.'

'They'll manage! I'll be staying in the palace for an indefinite period of time, Lady Severa. As you have just said, the Saxons and their allies are becoming bolder by the day, so it is beholden on me to protect your sons' inheritance. Such an arrangement would be temporary, of course, until such time as I can devise a permanent arrangement that is satisfactory.'

Satisfactory to you, Severa thought waspishly.

'Of course,' she responded in the same smooth tones as the interloper, but her mind screamed in shame at the impotent position where she'd been placed by Vortigern's caprices.

'Am I not welcome, Lady Severa? I can put my hand on my heart without hesitation and swear that I am the answer to the prayers of your long-suffering subjects. I expected a little more enthusiasm and gratitude from you.'

'My pardon, Vortigern, but the tidings of my husband's death have wiped away all pretence of good manners from my feelings. I will try to do my duty in future.'

This small, subtle insult was acknowledged when Vortigern raised his finger to his forehead in a comic gesture, checked it for blood and then grinned amiably.

'The next few months will be most interesting, Lady Severa, for I will be learning the disposition of our defences. I'll make our people ready for the Saxon attacks that will come when the spring winds bring their ceols to our shores. If they don't meet my expectations, they will die under my lash, rather than the heels of the northern barbarians.'

'Yes, Vortigern, I agree with you that we must make ourselves ready. But, for now, you must forgive my rudeness because I must go to my room and mourn my husband in private. I scorn to display my tears before the servants and your men. Everything you need from Venta Belgarum will be placed at your disposal by my steward, Jerome.'

Vortigern stood and bowed with a sincerity that Severa automatically distrusted. As she also rose, she tripped on her own skirts and Vortigern's arm reached out to steady her. She noticed that his forearms were brown, hairless and very strong. His flesh was quite warm under her fleeting touch, as if a furnace was raging beneath the confines of his skin.

The queen walked at her usual unhurried pace as she moved from the King's Hall to the solace of her own apartments, but her mind was awash with questions and unstated fears.

She had expected Vortigern to make an aggressive and crude invasion of her body. She had assumed that the Demetae would rape her and force her to capitulate to him in an attempt to validate his assault on her throne, but no overt approaches had taken place. She had imagined dozens of large and minor indignities that would be designed to break her spirit and push away any thoughts of rebellion, but Vortigern had preserved a veneer of respect for her. They both knew he was trifling with her, but he seemed to enjoy this subtle game that he was playing. Rape would have been easier to understand and, while her dignity would have been shattered, her flesh would have healed.

But this tortuous game had stretched her nerves until she longed to scream. His dark eyes had been lambent in the half-darkness and his curls had seemed like the shaggy winter coat of a large and primeval beast.

He's toying with me as if I'm a mouse and he's a large and playful cat, she decided.

No! He isn't a cat. Severa amended her image of him. He's more like a large wolf who is prepared to tear away at my flesh without any thought of delicacy once he's found himself aroused. For the moment, however, he's happy just to stare me down. The images raced through her brain in the darkness.

So much was resting on her shoulders. She must continue to resist this treasonous and murderous warrior, because that was the role that fate had allotted to her. Every polite riposte gave Vortigern pleasure, even if she defied him, because the game for dominance was so compelling to him. He would have slain a male opponent without compunction, but the inclusion of Severa in his plans was more of a challenge than instigating a simple murder.

Severa wanted to scream. Under her pillow, Calindre offered the cold comfort of a slit wrist and the peace of an easy death. She could imagine Vortigern's rage if she could elude him through suicide.

The blade burned her palm with an icy fire. But the Roman solution was barred to her, for there would be no one to care for her people if she perished. All hope of seeing her sons again would also vanish in the tide of her blood.

To her cost, Severa had misjudged Vortigern, the man. Now, she must play his games and try to win, even if she knew that resistance was hopeless.

Vortigern was far more dangerous than she had ever imagined. She had known he was using her as a plaything, but she had misjudged his ability to play the role of saviour. Within his silken gloves, his claws would tear her defences apart, but her people would only see an affable face with an ever-present smile.

Yes, he would become the saviour of the British people, no matter what he did. With luck, he would spend little time in Venta Belgarum and life would return to normality under her quiet reign.

Severa had barely prostrated herself in her bed before her body began to shake and she shivered like a woman who was suffering from ague. Confused and afraid, her women covered her with warm blankets and heated bricks to take the chill from her bed, but nothing could stop her involuntary tremors.

Severa was suffering for all her subjects, yet her eyes remained stubbornly dry. She was truly a Roman queen and tears were for those fortunate citizens who had no responsibilities.

CHAPTER VI

THE WILDERNESS

He was covetous of other men's property, and prodigal of
his own.

Gaius Sallustius Crispus, *Cataline*, Chapter 5

The seas pitched and reared like a maddened horse as the trading
ship slid down the waves with a crazy swoop that left Paulus's
stomach in his mouth. Then the long-suffering vessel slammed
upwards into a wall of water with enough force to drive the
decurion's spine into his brain. He retched from side to side,
although he little cared if his vomit blew back into his face.

'Help us, you bastards!' he yelled at the gods, real or imagined.
'We're on God's mission here and we're carrying out your work.
We deserve better than drowning in your ocean!'

Unfortunately, the gods must have been unable to hear his
call over the howl of the wind or, alternatively, they were
deliberately ignoring him. A scrawny ship's boy, one of the three-
man crew who toiled on *Sea Queen*, was trying to secure a barrel

116

that had come adrift in the wild seas. From the smell, the salted fish in the barrel were threatening to escape from their wooden coffin and swim to belated safety in the scuppers.

With some reluctance, Paulus helped the young crewman to secure the loose items of cargo on to the deck where they could be kept from harm's way. Then, while holding his heaving stomach and abused ribs, he staggered his way midships, where an unused sheet of old sailcloth had been lashed to the tray of the wagon to provide shelter for the two women and the young boys on the main deck. The wagon itself was secured to the mast and the captain's small deck cabin by stout ropes that allowed no movement from the old farm cart. Four woebegone faces looked up at him as he dived under the sailcloth, while four pairs of eyes seemed to accuse him of complicity with the fates that were responsible for this foul weather.

'Are we going to S – I – N – K, Paulus?' Dilic spelled out that frightening word in an attempt to deceive the terrified boys. If that result had been her true intention, she failed, for it soon became obvious that Ambrosius was familiar with his letters. Paulus watched in amazement as the boy put the word together in his mind.

'S . . . S . . . Sink?' the boy stuttered.

As he stroked Ambrosius's trembling shoulders, Paulus stared at Dilic. The decurion had been surprised to discover that the maidservant possessed the rudiments of learning, and even more taken aback to find that Ambrosius had mastered the first steps of an education.

The child's eyes had flared in a nameless fear that Paulus was unable to drive away. Huge seas towered over the creaking and groaning vessel, while every blow from the gigantic waves deposited more and more salt water on to the deck and into the scuppers. Ambrosius and his brother were saturated from the freezing water with their teeth chattering from the cold. Their lips were turning blue and their bodies had begun to tremble uncontrollably.

'Hold your head up, Ambrosius,' Paulus ordered the young boy, who stiffened automatically. 'So far, this old bucket has been floating like a cork but, like that cork, it manages to bob and bounce around without any control from the captain. I can promise you that I'd rather be anywhere else than here, for I've been woefully seasick. The only thing I do know is that old tubs like this boat rarely seem to sink. I think we'll survive.'

Paulus managed a sickly smile and Ambrosius's lips twitched for a brief moment in a reluctant response. If the decurion could pretend to be terrified of the ocean's power and then share this confidence with the boy, Ambrosius might feel better about the dangers they were facing. Paulus was content to exploit his own fears for a good cause.

'I can swim a little, but I'm not very good and I never feel comfortable at sea. Still, we men must pretend, for the sake of the ladies, who'll be terrified if they see that their menfolk are afraid.' Paulus winked at the boy as if they were conspirators. 'So we have to be brave, Ambrosius. Can you do this for me?'

Ambrosius nodded. Leaving his nest in Dilic's lap, Uther crawled across to huddle behind his brother.

'I can be brave too,' Uther said manfully, although his eyes rolled with fright when he saw the size of the waves that were attacking *Sea Queen*.

'I'm sure you can, Uther. Dilic will need your strength to help her get through these trials we are facing. Real men are always frightened when threatened with danger, but the best warriors fight on, regardless of how difficult the struggle becomes.'

Uther squared his small shoulders and looked up at the decurion with a steadfast, determined expression. Paulus recognised the powerful man who was already developing within the childish body and realised why Severa held such concern for this son, who could be so upright and yet so vicious. Paulus clasped the boy's shoulders as if he was already a grown man.

'I'll become a real man, Paulus,' Uther stated, while setting his jaw as firmly as any young warrior. Paulus smiled at the little boy, who responded with a shy, unfamiliar grin of his own making.

Paulus hunkered down into the narrow slit of the sailcloth, careless of the water that continued to lash at his back. He addressed himself to Dilic and Dara. 'The storm is beginning to abate. I know it doesn't seem to have lessened, but I've just seen some light in the west when the clouds parted. The worst of the storm has passed over us. I know you're wet, cold and uncomfortable, but we'll be dry soon and the seas will begin to become calmer.'

Dilic looked up at him and, for once, her eyes seemed less aggressive than he'd come to expect from this argumentative woman. He even imagined that there were signs of a grudging respect in their depths, but his past experiences with her reminded him that any improvement in her attitude towards him was probably of short duration.

'Does the captain know where we are? He doesn't seem all that clever to me.'

'Let's hope so. He's an experienced seaman, so he must have passed through scores of storms during his life on the oceans. I'll speak to him later,' Paulus replied drily.

The captain was a greasy, overweight parody of a seaman, a drifter by choice, whose person had run to seed in too many foetid bars and dirty inns on the waterfronts that criss-crossed the Roman world. His age and his race were indeterminate, because of the layers of body hair, grime and grease that obscured his features and darkened his hair. A layer of overstuffed belly protruded over a straining belt and more folds of fat, deeply creased and black with grime, obscured his jawline. Paulus knew that this man could never be trusted.

After paying far more coin for their passage than the uncomfortable journey was worth, Paulus soon realised that this unpleasant creature was reluctant to provide the party with the least pretence of comfort. He was forced to accept that the passengers and their wagon would be offloaded at a point along the coast of Gallia that would be convenient to the captain, rather than their preferred destination of Burdigala. Nor would the captain take action to avoid the storm front. His belated departure from the waters of Hibernia and Britannia and the success of his earlier trade negotiations had already placed his vessel at risk, so he was desperate to make a safe landfall at a place where the vessel could be safely berthed during the coming winter.

Paulus's small party had already been forced to endure several pauses in the voyage while *Sea Queen* had been crammed with trade goods, including pigs of lead from the Dumnonii villages where lead had been extracted from the earth since time beyond counting. Uther had laughed with boyish enjoyment when he realised that the lead ingots were described as pigs.

Slowly and ponderously, *Sea Queen* had wallowed her ungainly way around the south of Britannia until the storm had overtaken them on their course towards the lands of Gallia.

After easing the residual panic that remained in the minds of the two ladies and their charges, Paulus returned to the deck and the gelid waters that continued to spray over him from the sea and the icy rain that buffeted the vessel from above.

Grumbling and brushing raindrops from his reddened nose, he made his way along the deck to speak with the captain in his ramshackle cabin amidships where he spent most of his time. Paulus struggled to dodge the worst of the water as he swayed against the pitch and roll of the vessel, his temper beginning to fray.

'The light's beginning to overtake us to the west,' he shouted, pointing towards the sky in that direction to ensure that the captain could understand the words that the wind was endeavouring to blow away. 'Where are we going once the winds abate?'

'It depends on where we are,' the captain shouted over the wind. As he had failed to supply Paulus with his name, the Roman had been forced to sound discourteous whenever they spoke. Not that Paulus was overconcerned with the captain's feelings.

'So! Where are we then?' Paulus asked as he stepped into the shelter of the small cabin which was open towards the stern of the vessel.

'How can I know? Look up at the skies, Roman. Are any stars visible? Look towards the land. Can you see anything that tells you where we are? Well, neither can I! We'll have to wait until nightfall when the stars become visible.'

The fat, self-satisfied face of the captain made no attempt to disguise the sneer that relegated this no-account legionnaire to irrelevancy. On the high seas, the captain was king, so Paulus could ask all the questions he wanted but would learn little for his efforts. The Roman officer could turn blue for all that the ship's captain cared.

Paulus resisted an impulse to sink his fist into the man's bloated stomach.

'My women and the two children are cold and hungry and their safety is of great concern to me. It's important that I know when we can expect to make our landfall in Gallia, so can you give me some sort of guess?'

'There'll be no guesses from me, Roman. I'm busy now and you're dripping water on my charts.' The captain had been playing at dice with his subordinate while the ship's boy was bailing water from the vessel in the wind and the rain, so the likelihood of any meaningful work being undertaken on this poorly managed boat sent a tremor of amazement through Paulus's stretched nerves. Perhaps the steady decline in the level of wine in the captain's jug might be considered hard work by a disinterested observer.

Paulus noticed that a meal of bread, cold meat and cheese was spread over a greasy table that was fixed on to the deck. He realised that the children were in need of food.

'You're the master of your vessel while we are at sea, Captain, but once we reach port, you should take care that I don't use my own powers to have your cargoes checked for contraband. I have a certain amount of influence in the Roman establishment and I don't hesitate to use my powers, especially when your guests are in need of sustenance,' Paulus responded with a casual smile. He threw the man a lopsided grin, but his fists were clenching behind his back.

The captain controlled his fury and gave the decurion a plate laden with old bread, some hacked-off portions of meat and a piece of cheese to feed the women and children. With a sour laugh, Paulus accepted the plate filled with the almost inedible food.

'I'll remember your generosity,' he muttered, for the situation was more one of farce than force.

Then, after retreating to the covered section of deck used by the passengers, he divided the rations between the two boys, who began to suck on the food with their sharp milk teeth.

Well satisfied with his efforts, Paulus watched the sky lighten as he waited for the cessation of the storm's fury.

Several days after Paulus's party had departed for Gallia on *Sea Queen*, a horseman rode into Corinium bearing a message for King Aeron. Fortunately for his mother's peace of mind, Pridenow had returned to the palace without difficulty and, even as the stranger demanded entry, the young man was practising his archery in the apple orchard. He was under strict instructions from Endellion to refrain from frightening the gardeners.

The courier was a tall, fair-haired man with bright blue eyes. Aeron looked at him and his heart fell. This man was more Saxon than Briton, his appearance a subtle, wordless and menacing message from Vortigern.

'My master has instructed me to demand the return of the High King's sons so they can be protected with his strong right arm.'

This request, which was no real request at all, was spoken in such an arrogant tone that King Aeron immediately bridled with insult.

'My grandchildren aren't here. Even if they were, I'd never release them to your master without a very good reason. These children are my only grandsons. Nor are they blood kin to your master, so he has no right to detain them. I suggest you relay that message to him with as much courtesy as you can muster.'

The courier made the barest nod of his shaggy head and held out a scroll that was wrapped in a hide cover.

'From my master!' he explained economically and, as Aeron accepted the scroll, the messenger took three steps backwards to await a reply.

Aeron unwrapped the scroll, untied the thong that held it in a tight roll and began to read the light, flourishing calligraphy presented in the document.

Aeron, King of the Dobunni tribe,
> *Greetings.*

Queen Severa suffers because of the absence of her children and, belatedly, fears for their safety while they are far from the protection of Venta Belgarum's walls and my strong right arm.

Therefore, as Regent for the sons of Flavius Constantine, the erstwhile Emperor of the West, I must respectfully demand the return of Ambrosius and Uther to the arms of their mother. As a loyal subject, I expect you to pass on any information that will assist Severa to retrieve her boys and hold them to her bosom, safe and well, if they have been removed from your care.

As the foster-grandparents of these children, it is your duty and your filial responsibility to be frank with my appointed courier. Any prevarication or reluctance on your part could be construed as treason by any strict upholder of the High King's justice.

The Dobunni people have always been strong allies of the High Kings of Britannia and, as you have raised the queen when her noble father was executed, I would regret any cessation of the amity that has existed between us.

Please consider the nature of the treaties that have long existed between the Kings of the West and inform my trusted courier what you know of the whereabouts of the royal children.

I await your information and aver that no bad blood should be allowed to exist between us.

Vortigern. King of the Demetae Tribe,

Regent of the sons of Constantine III,

By the hand of Drusus Rusticus, Scribe of the Royal House of Venta Belgarum.

Aeron longed to spit out his righteous anger at the unwarranted demands and barely concealed threats contained in Vortigern's peremptory message. The Demetae king, who had deserted his liege lord in order to save his own skin, was now threatening Aeron with accusations of treason if he refused to turn his grandsons over to this northern scoundrel.

A crooked grin suddenly spread over Aeron's face, while the courier responded with an expression of brutish surprise at the king's sudden amusement.

'Your master has made his position on this matter perfectly clear in his use of this scroll, so I must reply in kind. Do you know your letters?'

The courier shook his head in a scornful rejection of a need for personal literacy.

'Then I will reply to your master explaining my position, but I expect you to carry my message to Vortigern accurately in a manner that is faithful to my intentions. I assume that you were chosen for your task because you have a good memory?'

The courier nodded brusquely. He could see no need to waste words on a lowly king of a minor tribe. His scorn was palpable.

'You can tell your master, Vortigern, that the boys are no longer here. It is my intention to ensure that you and your guards will carry out a search of Corinium that extends from the cellars in the buildings to the turrets on the walls. You'll find no trace of them! They were sent away into the land of the Picts and will remain in exile beyond the Vellum Antonini to ensure their safety. Their mother insisted on this transfer, so I entrusted their journey to a steadfast friend of the family and two nurses who have vowed to raise the boys. The children's ultimate sanctuary in the north is known only to their protector.'

'Do you wish me to impart this nonsense to Lord Vortigern?' the courier asked with such an obvious lack of respect that Aeron clambered to his feet from his throne. Obviously offended, Aeron's reaction to the courier's arrogance would remain unknown, for Pridenow swept aside the curtains that hid the internal door leading into the hall and strode, fully armed, to stand beside his father. The courier's right hand sought out the empty scabbard on his belt as soon as his eyes met the glacial stare of the British prince. The Saxon courier, Hoffa, had sold his battle skills across the northern world and he could recognise a fellow killer when he saw one.

'This fool seems to doubt the word or the honour of a British king, Father, so I'd take great pleasure in dealing with his demands.'

Aeron nodded and sank back on to his throne with some relief. Personal honour demanded that Aeron should respond to the insults that came from this lout, but the British king was a practical man. Neither his ageing body nor his doubtful skill with the sword would save him from harm if he became involved in any physical confrontation with the courier. In any event, a lowly courier's status precluded Aeron from entering a dispute with him.

Pridenow walked down the two steps that raised the dais above the eyes of petitioners and citizens alike to face Hoffa, and the Saxon responded by drawing himself up to his full height.

'I heard the statement and the challenge that you issued to my father. It should be perfectly obvious to any competent warrior that King Aeron is well past his middle years and he obviously suffers from the disease of the joints that restricts his use of weapons. Provocation of an incapacitated opponent is, without doubt, a cowardly action on your part. On the other hand, I suffer from no physical impediments and I am quite prepared to discuss this matter further, either in private or in public. For the moment, I would advise you to keep your insults behind your teeth and refrain from careless opinions that offend my sensibilities. Do I make myself clear?'

In truth, the Saxon only understood half the words thrown out so casually by Pridenow in his complaint. Still, the young man's tone was sufficient to convey the gist of his threats. The courier clenched his fists in frustration and gritted his teeth. He had been forced to surrender his weapons to King Aeron's guard before he was allowed to enter the hall. Unable to respond to Pridenow's courage, this pup with the eyes of a wolf was making him feel like the landless and penniless mercenary he had been before Lord Vortigern had offered him a future.

'I stand by my words, Briton. Lord Vortigern will not tolerate harm done to an envoy who is acting on the High King's behalf. I came to you in good faith and I placed my trust in your father's honour.'

'Honour? I doubt that you understand what that word means. But never mind! Let us stick to the bare essentials. I was the captain who led the guard that accompanied the boys and their guardian to Abonae and the fishing village that lay beyond it, there to meet with an itinerant ship that would take them away from Britannia. If you have any doubts of the truth of my statements, then you should voice your questions and insults to me. I will be happy to travel with you to Venta Belgarum after I have had further discussions with my sister and King Aeron. I am the master of their personal guard, so certain arrangements must be made for the ongoing security of the Dobunni lands.'

The courier fumed inwardly, but he had no choice other than to bow perfunctorily and prepare to leave the king's presence. As he turned to go, Pridenow called him back.

'Since you must deliver a detailed report to your master when you return to Venta Belgarum, I insist that you make a thorough search of Corinium with your men. You will be unaccompanied and will be permitted to access any part of the city which interests you. There must be no secrets between Vortigern and King Aeron ... or no more than already exist because of the machinations undertaken by your master. If you permit me to accompany you to your master in Venta Belgarum, I will look forward to hearing your report.'

The courier was left with no choice. Given Pridenow's insistence that the Saxon should carry out a detailed search, it was obvious that his chances of finding the children in this damned town were negligible. But the courier had to go through the motions. His men would be tied up in a fruitless, frustrating search that would take some hours to complete; he felt an overwhelming urge to strike someone's head from their shoulders with his double-sided axe.

Amused by his success in tweaking the courier's tail, Pridenow excused himself from his worried father's presence to pack his few prized possessions and make ready to leave Corinium on the morrow. Grimly, the young man accepted the fact that Severa must be in deadly danger if she had put her name to this impertinent demand for the return of her sons. It was patently obvious to him that he had no way of arranging for the return of the children to Venta Belgarum, even if he had felt an inclination to do so. Paulus had ensured that no one, apart from himself, knew their ultimate destination.

'You can't reveal my plans to anyone, boy, if you don't know where we're going,' Paulus had said to him, while winking down at Pridenow from the deck of *Sea Queen*.

While lying in her bedchamber, Severa's ears were listening for the sound of male footsteps that would inevitably come to shatter her peace. In the four weeks since Vortigern had arrived on her doorstep with his armed mercenaries, she had been unable to sleep alone. In the absence of Dilic, Severa had arranged for one of her remaining maidservants and a companion from her court to sleep on pallets inside her apartments. Her nerves were tautly stretched as she endeavoured to spend as little time as possible in Vortigern's presence – and never when he was alone. In robes that had been hurriedly dyed to a funereal black, she pleaded piety and spent many hours on her knees in the hope that a professed pagan such as Vortigern might have some scruples and would permit her to enjoy the sanctuary of her church.

Inevitably, her absence from the streets of Venta Belgarum and her failure to attend a single court of justice in the King's Hall excited rumours that grew and festered as day followed day. The queen had died of grief; she had been imprisoned by Vortigern's Saxon mercenaries; she was in chains within her own prison and; worst of all, she had fled from her city on the very day that Vortigern had arrived. As the gatekeeper attested, the Vortigern who had returned from Gallia was a cruel man, one who was determined to have his way, regardless of the queen's desires.

While Vortigern was indifferent to the townsfolk's fears and lack of favour, he was concerned that unfavourable gossip was reaching the other kings, especially the ruler of the powerful Dumnonii tribe who was linked to Severa by ironclad treaties that had been negotiated by her father, Magnus Maximus. While most of the southern tribes had been denuded of warriors by Constantine's demands, the Dumnonii king, Cadal, had ensured that many of his warriors remained inside the tribal lands. This practical approach to the security of his tribal interests posed a major problem for Vortigern, although the old man had lost his fighting skills with the onset of age. Still, the memory of Caradoc remained present within the community, so Dumnonii pronouncements were considered favourably by Cadal's neighbours.

Word had come to Vortigern that Cadal's youngest son, Gorlois, named after a relative in Armorica, was already forging a name for himself, despite his tender years. Although barely fourteen years old, the youth was a fire-eater who ensured that brigands avoided the Dumnonii lands. Gorlois had already earned the nomen of the Boar of Cornwall for the courage and crazed bloodlust that settled over him when he was engrossed in the madness of a pitched battle. Vortigern's position in Britannia was still tenuous and he had no intention of incurring the enmity of the rulers of south-western Britannia until he was ready to have himself crowned as the new High King of the Britons. And so, all adverse rumours must be quashed.

But gossip is not so easy to repress. Who can capture the spoken word that is passed from maidservant to citizen behind cupped hands and repeated in hissed whispers? Rumours of death and torture inflicted by Vortigern could only be contradicted by the lady herself, but she was still seated in her own hall and smiling her pale, enigmatic smile. If Vortigern was to consolidate himself within Britannia's hierarchy, he must neutralise Severa's position within her kingdom.

Regardless of his requests to join him in the activities conducted inside the King's Hall, she pleaded weariness, grief and illness in order to thwart his approaches. The Demetae's eyes glowed with an internal light that might have been attractive on some men, but in Vortigern's case was merely sinister.

Eventually, after half a flagon of good Frankish wine, Vortigern lost all patience. The time had come when he must force this bitch to heel, regardless of her milksop excuses and her ability to slip through his fingers like water. He would have enjoyed the chase far more if the sullen faces and sly whispers of the townsfolk hadn't called for an immediate response. Having considered her intransigency, he arrived at a decision.

Vortigern strode through the long corridors of Severa's palace. With a set face and an expression of smouldering resentment, he left none of the servants in any doubt that he was a man on a mission. They pressed their bodies against the walls of the corridors as he stalked past, keeping their heads down, in case he should find some fault in them and vent his fury upon their innocent heads. Maids, stewards, cooks and cleaners shivered and thanked God that they weren't the cause of his rage as the regent passed by them.

When he reached the door of the queen's apartment his fury

caused him to pound on the timber with one fist. Let her cower behind her doors! Let her be afraid! He was the master of this palace and it was time for Severa to resume her duties.

'Who dares to disturb the queen's peace so roughly?' a voice quavered from behind the doors of the apartment.

'It's Vortigern! Open the door immediately!' He had already concluded that Severa must have lowered the wooden latch, which would repel any normal person. But Vortigern wasn't just anyone. He would have the hinges removed if this was the only way to gain entry.

With a sinking heart, Severa faced the truth about Vortigern's likely intentions and she decided to capitulate without offering resistance. She was duty-bound to protect her ladies.

'Wait, Lord Vortigern! The door will be opened for you.'

The regent stepped back from the door, but his rage had become irrational and was feeding on his own frustrations and weaknesses. Years of plotting, of breaking his knees to offer obeisance to lesser men and the scorn that was ever-present in the eyes of less talented aristocrats rose up to taunt him with the prospects of failure. His anger was slow-burning, but the fire in his belly was very hot and it would rise again when fresh air provided the oxygen needed to refuel it. He waited stonily as the latch was raised and a terrified serving woman pulled the heavy door wide open to allow him entry.

Severa was waiting on the far side of the door, her companions cowering behind her.

'Dismiss your serving women,' Vortigern snapped and Severa imagined what this creature would do to them, if she refused to follow his instructions.

'Go, my dears! I shall do quite well under Lord Vortigern's

protection. I will call for you if I have a need for your presence.'

Neither woman wanted to leave their mistress but both were afraid to face the ire of this terrifying man. The maidservant kissed Severa's hand and wept with frustration while the noblewoman pursed her lips and stared at Vortigern with gimlet eyes.

'You'd best tell your friend that she should change her expression or I'll arrange for her to lose an eye,' Vortigern added. His smile was a parody of the courtliness he had pretended at for weeks. The queen held no doubts that he would need little provocation to carry out these threats.

'Please, Dorcas! Vortigern has only come to speak with me, so I can assure you that I will be well.'

The queen presented well in her dark robes and veil of white gauze. In her youth, she had always seemed athletic and wilful, but her appearance was now that of an archetypal daughter of a great Roman father. As she looked at Vortigern from behind her veil, she was every woman he had ever desired, but had been unable to claim.

'It's time you learned that I am the new master of Venta Belgarum,' Vortigern grunted and pushed the door shut with his booted foot. The massive structure slammed hard, but the frame held and Severa trembled at the force of his repressed emotion.

'God help me,' she prayed, much as other women had begged for mercy over the millennia.

As usual, God kept his own counsel.

CHAPTER VII

MEN AND OTHER MONSTERS

Let them hate, as long as they fear.
Oderint, dum metuant.

Allius, *Atteus*

As Paulus helped Ambrosius, Uther and the two maidservants to clamber ashore at a fishing village near the mouth of the Liger River in Gallia, Severa had been forced to capitulate to Vortigern's sexual demands in far-off Venta Belgarum. Without effective protection, she was just a Roman bitch who could be taken, raped and sodomised until her pride was torn to ribbons.

Vortigern had always understood the paths that would lead him to victory, so he accepted that complete domination was required, if further conflict with Severa was to be avoided. Only the queen's abject surrender would be acceptable to the Demetae king, else he would be better off killing her and taking the chance that he could convince the British kings to accept him as the supreme ruler. Both these alternatives boded no good for Severa.

When the bane of her life entered the bedchamber, Severa was under no illusions about the fate that awaited her. Women had suffered such treatment since the days before men learned to speak and reason, for lust and brute strength were always a dangerous combination for any unprotected female.

Determined to have his way, Vortigern ceased to act like a well-born nobleman from the moment the door was closed on the backs of the retreating servants. As a warning of his intentions, the Demetae king cuffed the queen lightly across the mouth, splitting her upper lip and bruising her flesh. Before she could gather her wits, he threw her on to the ornate bed where Constantine had fathered her children, then tore away the elaborate tunic that hid her breasts. The shift beneath it was ripped from its neck to the lower hem in an exercise of sheer brute strength. Winded and gasping for breath, Severa attempted to cover her breasts with the remains of her undergarments.

'Don't struggle, bitch,' Vortigern muttered thickly, for he was aroused by what he had already inflicted on her body. To control Severa was to possess Britannia, a prize worth far more than any Saxon treasure. Without any consideration for the pain he was causing, he kneeled on her thighs and forced her legs apart. Then, with his full weight resting on her body, her breasts were crushed and her breathing was constricted. Constrained as she was, Severa still tried to push his weight away.

'There's no point in struggling, woman, so just accept the inevitable.'

Vortigern paid no attention to the feeble blows she tried to rain on to his back and shoulders as he casually cuffed her across the ears, a buffeting that made her senses blacken for a brief moment.

'What pleasure . . . can there be in forcing a woman on her own bed?' Severa protested from under the weight that was holding her down. Her desperate right hand clawed at her pillow until her fingers fell on to a slim length of sharp iron that she kept within the linen. Calindre! Her knife! She had found the weapon that had been given to her by a wagon driver when she was still a slip of a girl. Since then, the blade, which she treated as an old and valued friend, had only been used in anger on one terrible occasion.

Vortigern's crushing weight lifted from her body as he rose to his feet and removed his mailed coat and undergarments. Under his body armour, his flesh was smooth and hairless and his skin as hard as the marble that it resembled in texture and colour. As he again kneeled over her, Severa was forced to recoil from the smell of a heat that she had never experienced before. The disturbing aroma caused her to gag, even as she lifted Calindre and pressed it against Vortigern's ribs.

'Get away from me, you pig,' she muttered weakly. Vortigern merely laughed.

He raised his left paw to encircle her hand that gripped Calindre with white-knuckled desperation. 'Let me assist you, sweetheart. Come on! Drive your little toy home between my ribs. With luck, you might even pierce my heart.'

Severa pushed upwards on Calindre's hilt. She felt Vortigern's skin split and a small flow of hot blood begin to drip on to her naked belly, but any further aggression was pointless. Her rapist forced her wrist backward before she could drive the blade any deeper into his flesh, breaking some of the small bones in her hand in the process. Snickering, Vortigern ignored the tearing of his own flesh as he twisted her knife-hand until she cried out and released her grip on the hilt. Then, effortlessly, he pulled the knife from his side and threw it into a corner of the room.

'That hurt, bitch!' he said flatly, without any emotion in his voice. 'You'll pay for that little display of independence, although I must admit that I salute your willingness to send me to the shades. But you're wasting your time, Severa.'

At least you're finally using my name, she thought in a moment of pointless triumph. I've made some sort of a mark on you, you bastard!

Vortigern dragged off his heavy leather belt and held it against her bruised face. 'You'll feel the sting of my anger if you continue to struggle against me, Severa. There's no point in resistance, because I'm actually enjoying your puny efforts to stop me. Right, woman! Try to hit me!'

The goading tone in his loathsome voice infuriated the queen and made her long to strike out at him, but she knew she was powerless. She writhed and twisted, but he was too strong and too heavy to dislodge. Tears of frustration and pain ran down her cheeks as she turned her head sharply to avoid the smiling mouth that tried to cover hers in an unwanted kiss.

With a sudden convulsion of impatience, Vortigern pressed down on to her thighs again. This time, he took a firm grip on her shoulders and upper arms, effectively preventing all further resistance. Despite knowing that her struggles were pointless, she continued to fight him, unable to submit to a man who had betrayed her flawed husband.

In an unexpected act of ownership, Vortigern lowered his head and bit her chest where her left breast began to swell away from her sternum. His sharp canines drew blood and she cried out as he sucked on her bleeding flesh as if he was trying to draw her soul out from the wound he had inflicted. Before her travails were over, her body would be covered with similar bites and bruising, for the victor was determined to stamp his spoor over his personal property.

The rape itself was painful, humiliating and brief, but Severa's mind escaped back to her memories of the wild peninsula of Tintagel, the place of her childhood, as Vortigern grunted and growled his victory over her body. Once again, she found herself walking with the old king, Caradoc, who told her stories of her father in those wonderful days before Magnus Maximus became a king and, eventually, an emperor. She could hear Caradoc's measured voice over her rapist's moans of misplaced passion.

'Life can be difficult for well-born girls, little love,' Caradoc had explained. 'There are some men in this wicked world who treat women with cruelty, because they use females to achieve their unholy ambitions. There are flaws in the natures of such men that cause them to abuse their womenfolk. In fact, there is a belief among some of our clergy that men are the chosen sex of God's will and women do not even possess a soul. How can any violence really matter when it is committed against something that God has left without the spark of His spirit?'

'Yes, Grandfather,' Severa had answered, but she hadn't understood the message he was conveying to her. Now, in Vortigern's clutches, she was beginning to.

'Should you ever become a victim of rape, I can only suggest that you close your eyes and submit to the inevitable, frightening though it might be! It's even possible that you won't be hurt if you don't fight against the perpetrator. Ultimately, women are mentally strong creatures. In fact, I believe that women are stronger than men, because they can survive an assault on their bodies as long as they don't allow the man to steal their souls.

'One thing is certain, sweetheart. If such a fate should ever befall you, I'd hope that you weren't crushed by it. You'll grow to become a strong young woman and I'd hope that you'd eventually take your own revenge. Women have revenged themselves on their rapists since the dawn of time.'

As Vortigern forced her on to her stomach, she swore that she would remain alive, if only to cause Vortigern as much inconvenience as she could contrive in the years ahead. She closed her eyes and endured.

'Does this stinking backwater have a name?' Dilic asked fretfully as she eyed the primitive fishing village that was almost identical to the one they had left behind in Britannia.

A small group of fishermen squatted on a hummock of coarse grass as they mended their nets with the same glum attention to detail as their British counterparts. A cluster of small, rounded huts with coarsely thatched roofs, belching smoke, were scattered along the foreshore behind a dry-stone wall, while the drying racks and smokehouses used by the peasants reminded the decurion of every fishing village he had ever seen. At least the farm animals had been penned into neat enclosures, so this community seemed cleaner and better organised than the Roman would have expected from such obvious poverty.

Perhaps Paulus might have been pleasantly influenced by the clear skies and brilliant sun, and the aroma of cooking stew that reached the new arrivals somewhere within the cluster of huts. Unlike Home Village in Britannia, the faces of these fisherfolk were wreathed in smiles of welcome as they gazed at the small group of bedraggled strangers. He felt his spirits lift.

'The river that joins the sea just beyond that headland is called the Liger, although some of the Franks call it the Loire River. We were dumped off here as a result of our captain's spite, God damn the bastard! I'll have to find someone to sell us some horses that will get us to the nearest town. I might even get a chance to have it out with the rogue. He tricked us by assuring me that the village was our ultimate destination. The villain must have intended to abandon us at the first opportunity, because I wasn't to know that Portus Namnetum was further upstream. One of the fishermen told me about Namnetum and confirmed that it's a sizable port where trading vessels visit when they have the opportunity. *Sea Queen*! That vessel should be renamed as the *Sea Whore* as a warning to all honest men, while the bastards who crew her should be branded with the selfsame marks used to denote whoresons and thieves.'

When *Sea Queen*'s captain abandoned the passengers and sailed away, Paulus had been placed in a quandary. As the commander of the mission, his duty was to remain with his charges and ensure their safety. But, because their wagon had been unceremoniously dumped on the beach in calf-deep water and no horses were available to haul the vehicle, the party would be afoot until some means was found to remove the vehicle from the beach. The small boys would be sorely taxed if they had to walk to Portus Namnetum.

The decurion roundly cursed *Sea Queen*'s captain.

Dilic and Paulus were for once in complete agreement, because the maid held grave reservations about their safety if they remained in a strange village during any absence contemplated by Paulus. Left in this alien place, the women would be among strangers who could take advantage of them when the decurion went to find horses or some other form of transport. Dara remained silent and concentrated on playing a complicated game of cat's cradle with Ambrosius.

'I agree with your concerns, Dilic, although the boys might enjoy playing in the sand while we make a decision about our future.' The boys' eyes brightened at the prospect of unexpected playtime, so their nurses took them down to the sand and the pebbles that lay above the high-water mark.

Paulus strode into the village to converse with the village headman and seek some guidance from that elder. The decurion's stride and posture indicated his mood more succinctly than words, and he had no trouble in being directed by a wide-eyed village youth to a stone cottage in the very centre of the walled community. In response to a brisk knock, a greybeard appeared at the doorway.

'I bid you good day, sir. As you've no doubt been told by your people, I've been allotted the task of escorting two small boys and their maids from their grandparents' home in Britannia to the home of their parents in Hispania. The boys must rely on their nurses to attend to their physical needs until such time as we reach our destination in Hispania, while I take care of their personal safety and their travel arrangements.'

Wise to the curiosity of peasants, Paulus decided to speak frankly to the headman, while using just enough respect to satisfy the old man's dignity.

'Unfortunately, I discovered that the captain of *Sea Queen* is an unprincipled rogue, a man who has abandoned us on the doorstep of your village. He dumped our wagon into the shallow waters near the river bank as soon as we were on dry land, so I'm concerned that all the boys' possession are in danger of being washed away on the outgoing tide. If I must, I'll walk to Portus Namnetum, but to do so would require me to leave the women and children undefended in what, to us, is a strange village. You can imagine that I'm reluctant to take such a risk with my charges. One thing is certain, good fellow. I intend to find the captain of *Sea Queen* as soon as I've secured the safety of my women and children, and I'll take my pleasure from his hide for the sins he committed. While I want to find the bastard and tell him that he's earned my displeasure, I am very concerned at leaving my charges unprotected.'

The decurion allowed an open and uncomplicated smile to soften his stern face.

'I don't distrust your people, sir, but I don't know them.' Paulus spread his hands wide and shrugged deprecatingly. 'It's unfortunate, but I can't be in two places at once.'

The two men smiled at each other, causing Paulus to note that the old fisherman's teeth were brown and broken with age.

'I'm prepared to pay a goodly amount of silver to have my charges cared for during my absence. In addition, I'm prepared to reward your villagers if they can remove my wagon from the waters and secure our possessions on the river bank.'

The old man was nobody's fool and he could smell a golden windfall for his village if he assisted this strange Roman who had come into his life. His people barely survived on what bounty came from the sea and the salty soil adjacent to the river bank.

After having Paulus's predicament explained to him, the old man eyed Paulus narrowly, for he was in two minds as to how to approach these problematic strangers who had been visited on his village. Finally, he cleared his throat and bobbed his head like an old tortoise.

'My name is Otto, sir, and I understand your problem only too well. You would have to be a fool to leave your women and children in the hands of people you do not know.'

Otto was speaking in the common tongue, a debased Latin that utilised individual words in the Frank and Goth tongues. As the decurion had spent a lifetime in many places in the Roman world, he had become adept at using a combination of sign language and pertinent words to counteract any gaps in the communication process. Paulus decided to remain silent as the headman launched himself on a long, slow explanation of his intentions. Urging haste would lead him nowhere.

'That bastard from *Sea Queen* cheated us on two previous occasions,' the old man said. 'At that time, we were trading with him for rations and other supplies. Some months later, we forgave him for his earlier misdeeds and allowed him and his crew to spend a night in the village. Then, while the village was asleep, some of the captain's men forced themselves on old Della's daughter. The lass were hit so hard that her wits were rattled. They all had their way with her, but she was only ten at the time. We tried to complain to the mayor and the council in Portus Namnetum, but they weren't interested in our complaints.'

The old man hawked and spat, and then sighed before continuing.

'Life is always difficult for poor fisherfolk.' He rubbed his forefinger and thumb together in the age-old gesture of corruption. 'Bribery always talks, doesn't it? I will help you with your problems, Roman, and my villagers will have your wagon dragged out of the river. We'll place it above the high-tide mark and dry out your supplies. In the meantime, you can keep your coin till you come back – and then we'll do the reckoning.'

'Which is the best way to Portus Namnetum? I haven't been in this region for twenty years,' Paulus asked in a friendly and open tone of voice, although he knew he would probably have to make the journey on foot.

'I reckon you'd have been with one of the legions! True? I thought you had the mark of a legionnaire on you as soon as I saw you come ashore from *Sea Queen*. Rome's good men have that look about them and I've no argument with them. My brother went off with Maximus. He was wild with enthusiasm, but he never came back. His son made his mark with Constantine and he's up on the frontier with the barbarians now. Or he was when I last heard of him! I have a feeling that the captain of *Sea Queen* might have cheated the wrong man this time.'

As in Britannia, few families were without some kinfolk who served in the legions for, more and more, Rome depended on her barbarian allies for the manpower needed to fill the ranks of its armies. Fortunately for Paulus, the headman's brother and nephew had volunteered for service in Rome's legions, rather than serving as reluctant conscripts.

'If you take the track behind the village and follow it into the east, you'll soon reach a bigger road that takes you straight to the port. There are some small farms along the way, so you might be fortunate enough to find a farmer who'll sell you some horses for your wagon. Good luck, young feller, and I'll be pleased if you thump that captain in the eyes for me and my villagers, if you catch up with him.'

'With luck, I might be able to extract some gold from him that might help to pay you for his past misdeeds in your village.

I'll also be looking to remind the captain and his men that he'd be unwise to cheat your people in the future.'

'I thank you, sir.'

Later, after discussing the situation with Dilic and Dara, Paulus joined four young fishermen who strolled down to the river mouth to retrieve the wagon from the encroaching tide. Brute strength and trusty ropes would be essential if the vehicle was to be successfully dragged on to dry land. With these lengths of rope, some primitive winches and the fishermen's muscle, the wagon was hauled up the gently sloping bank and secured on the rough path that ran behind the village.

Dilic swooped on the wagon with a cry of relief. In a trice, she had climbed on to the wheel and flung herself into the dim interior to search noisily through the baskets and packages that were stored in the damp depths.

'I hope the bastards die and their bodies swell till their balls fall off!' Dilic cursed with unwomanly viciousness, while the villagers either winced or smirked at her choice of words. 'They've taken the boys' golden arm-rings and the jewels their mother sent with me! If I catch that captain, I swear I'll tear his lying, cheating heart out with my own fingers!'

'That's torn it!' Paulus responded as he helped her to pry herself from the depths of the wagon. 'You'll have to remain here while I find some horses. There's no other option, short of the wagon growing wings that will help it to fly like a bird.'

'Then go!' Dilic snapped. 'The sooner you get back, the sooner we'll be able to chase after those bastards. We can only hope that the captain intends to spend some days at his berth in the town. We'll never find him if he decides to resume his voyage.'

'Winter will soon be upon us, so the captain will have to find a berth in this part of the world. From what the headman told me, I believe he intends to remain in the port for the next few months. He's a regular visitor to the town and is well known to the local rulers, so I hope to catch up with him there. I'll do my best to get Severa's jewels back, I promise.'

Despite her anger, Dilic realised that Paulus's arrival at the port might put him in some danger, and she tried her best to flash a brief smile at the decurion.

'Keep the boys safe, Dilic,' Paulus said. 'I'm certain you can trust the village headman and he'll help you if you have any troubles.'

Then, with an almost jaunty spring to his step, the decurion began to jog along the muddy path in the mile-devouring stride demanded of legionnaires on the march. He was actually enjoying the sensation of using his muscles after the enforced inactivity of the past month, and he made good progress as he moved along the path that followed the high ground above the river.

Within minutes of reaching the east–west roadway that led to Portus Namnetum, he found a stone and timber structure that indicated a Roman presence at some time in the recent past. But when Paulus reached its gates, they sagged open and he found that grass and weeds had grown between the flagstones used to clad the open paths. As trees had yet to take root and overrun the building, Paulus deduced that it had most likely been a customs house or guard hut that had been abandoned during Constantine's abortive attacks on Rome's forces in Gallia.

He sighed deeply. Was this to be the fate of the all-powerful legions? Would Rome's finest be driven back, mile after mile, until only the City of the Seven Hills remained as a reminder of a lost and glorious empire? He strode on resolutely, his heels striking the solid roadway that was another mark of Rome's recent presence along this largely empty coastline.

Occasional signs of tilled earth, rows of fruit trees along the skyline or dry-stone walls indicated that the land adjacent to the road had been tamed in the recent past. Then, as the decurion strode over the top of a small rise in the road, a rambling, earth-coloured farmhouse came into view atop a small hill at the end of its own private access lane. Paulus swung his legs over a farm stile and started to walk up the rise.

Two shaggy black-and-white dogs greeted him first with half-friendly and half-wary sniffing and waving of tails. He realised that these dogs were bred to protect the master's sheep, so he spoke to them in a friendly tone and kept on walking with an apparent confidence that he was far from feeling. The dogs followed cautiously, but they were close enough to attack this strange visitor if they were so ordered.

As he approached the farmhouse, two peasants armed with hoes suddenly appeared from a copse of fruit trees where they had been working. Taking pains to keep his hands far from his scabbard, Paulus stopped and grinned in a friendly fashion, hoping that his age would allay any suspicions they might have felt.

'Good afternoon, friends. I was told by the headman at the fishing village down the way that a prosperous farmer lives here. I'd like to speak with him on a matter of mutual interest.'

These peasants were obviously unfamiliar with the true Latin tongue that Paulus had used, and this lack was demonstrated in their blank expressions and their hurried, hissed conversation in the local dialect. Paulus could understand most of what the two men were saying, although he tried to look as if he was ignorant of their thinly disguised insults.

'Do we take him to the master, or just smash his head in?'

The younger farm worker's words were accompanied by a supercilious smile that was intended to put Paulus at his ease.

'He might be an old man, but I reckon he know how to use that pig-sticker at his side. We'll let the master decide. And then we'll smash his head in,' the older peasant added, while nodding in Paulus's direction and baring his brown fangs in a parody of a smile.

'Let's go to the master then,' Paulus added in a halting version of their language, while smiling back at them and hoping that his teeth looked clean after weeks at sea. His teeth were a source of personal pride to Paulus, for they were still his own. 'Your master will be pleased when he hears my offer.'

The younger peasant lumbered his way up to the farmhouse with his hoe balanced over his shoulder. Almost the size of a villa, the house was surrounded by fruit and nut trees, and two sturdy barns stood next to it. The older peasant swung into step on Paulus's left side so he could keep a watchful eye on the decurion's weaponry.

The younger peasant disappeared into the barn where the sound of hammer blows on metal suggested that some kind of construction was taking place. With a slight turn of his head, Paulus saw the open-sided building where the blacksmith's forge was blazing merrily away. A tired boy sat beside a huge anvil, close to the large leather bellows that were used to fan the flames. The boy's eyes were closed but, when he felt Paulus's presence, they snapped open and he gaped.

'What do you want of me, Decurion?' a voice asked from the shadows of the building.

Paulus turned his gaze to a short, heavy-set man of some forty summers. The farmer's cheeks were round, his nose was short and snubbed, while his beard was a fiery mass of bright red curls. Such a face was meant for laughter and good cheer, but the farmer's eyes were cold and calculating.

'You've impressed me, sir. Few men would have recognised my rank, especially when I'm retired from the legions and am in the service of new masters. My name is Paulus and I'm the guardian and protector of two young aristocrats and their nurses who are returning to their home in Hispania. They were enjoying a visit to their Roman kin in Britannia when word came that the paterfamilias of their house was dying and wanted to see the boys once more before he entered the shades. We took ship on a vessel bound for the continent, a cesspit called *Sea Queen*.'

Pleased that his tale sounded so plausible, Paulus advanced and extended his hand which, somewhat hesitantly, the farmer took by the wrist in accordance with the Roman custom.

'I've no doubt that your tale would be interesting to some, but I must ask you to get to the point of your interruption. We have horses here that are waiting patiently for shoes,' the farmer explained brusquely in a tone that demonstrated he was accustomed to instant obedience.

'Might I have your name, sir?' Paulus asked blandly, while ignoring the farmer's rude tone of voice. The man coloured hotly.

'Budolf! My name is Budolf Rouge . . . and I was named for my red hair and my beard, or so I've always been told.'

'I am pleased to meet with you, Budolf, and I hope we'll be able to deal together for our mutual benefit,' Paulus responded smoothly, before elaborating on his tale of woe.

'I'm the leader of a small party that travelled across the Litus

Saxonicum on that old trading tub with the grandiose name,' Paulus repeated. 'Unfortunately, the ship's captain stole some of the valuables from our wagon and then dumped us off along the coast. He left our wagon in the river shallows and the fishermen are in the process of winching it ashore. My charges are in the small fishing village that lies a short distance downriver. We are anxious to continue with our journey, so I'm interested in purchasing two horses to haul my wagon plus another animal that I can ride if you have stock that you are prepared to sell. I'll pay in silver for all three if you have suitable horses for sale.'

Paulus grinned toothily.

'And if I come across the captain and crew of *Sea Queen*, I'll be asking for an explanation from them for their treachery.'

'Hummmph!' Budolf snorted his amusement through his nose and ran one of his huge forefingers through his beard. 'I might be able to fill your needs, and I'd be prepared to accept a reasonable price to make a fair sale. Time was when all my spare horses went to the Romans and life for a farmer was very good.' He pointed vaguely in the direction of the fortress. 'But the legions have been gone for five years and I doubt that they'll ever return. You were a serving legionnaire in the past, Decurion. Will they ever come back again?'

'The legions as we knew them are finished, Budolf, especially in the provinces. Oh, the emperors will hang on for a time, but the glory days are dead. Not that I regret their passing! I've had enough of marching for days on end and sleeping on the cold earth. Old age comes to all of us,' Paulus added and paused reflectively. 'Now: about those horses?'

Paulus rode away within the hour, his purse a little lighter and his spirits much improved. The two bay horses followed on a long lead behind the steady grey he had purchased for his own use. The workhorses he selected were both of a breed that was suited to pulling wagons or ploughs, for they were huge, shaggy-maned creatures with garlands of long hair around each ankle. The horse he rode was smaller and leaner, and Paulus could see that it would be perfectly suited to his needs. The farmer agreed to throw in the bridles, a well-worn set of wagon harnesses and a saddle. Paulus was satisfied with the deal they had struck between them.

Once he had thanked the farmer for his courtesy and genero-sity, Paulus rode down the path leading to the farm gate, still followed by the two sheepdogs which stayed at a respectful dis-tance behind him. The two farm labourers were waiting at the entrance to open the gate for the Roman. Their manner was almost sociable.

'Thank you, my friends. I'm sorry you didn't get a chance to smash my head in. I should also tell you that it wouldn't have been an equal contest if there were only the two of you. I would have regretted hurting you, so I wish you better luck the next time we meet.'

On the morning after her ordeal, Severa managed to move her abused and beaten body along the corridor towards the Hall of Justice. Her body ached dully, for the pain of her many wounds were dulled by an infusion of poppy juice. Mercifully, her eyes were almost blank because all her concentration was needed to keep her ravaged body moving towards the throne of her new master. She wasn't afraid, for someone who is partially dead inside isn't really afraid of physical death.

But there are worse punishments.

The night before, when her terrified women returned nervously to her bedchamber, they learned that their mistress had been tied to the bed by one wrist. Her half-naked body had been beaten with a leather belt from the knees to just below her breasts. Blood covered most of her body and stained the fine linen of her bed, but Vortigern had been clever and he had spared her face, except for a small cut on the lower lip and some swelling on her cheekbone. However, the many welts across her back and belly demonstrated the ferocity of his attack.

'Let me call a healer for you, mistress,' her maid begged.

'Old Crisiant will care for me. Explain the situation to her and then ask her to bring sufficient roots and herbs that will heal my hurts during the night. I've been ordered to assist Vortigern when he oversees the citizens' pleas for justice in the King's Hall on the morrow. I must be able to perform my duties by noon, so ensure that she realises the urgency of my need for her.'

As the maid ran out of the queen's bedchamber, one of her ladies untied her pinioned hand and used a strip of material from her mistress's torn shift to cleanse her.

'Thank you, Brisen. Send one of the girls to find the steward. He knows where I keep the old linen, and one of those lengths of fabric would make excellent bandages.'

Brisen tried to stroke the hand that had been blackened with bruises and was leaking blood and serum.

Severa winced. 'I think he's broken the bones in my wrist. There was no need to tie my hand so tightly, because I couldn't have lifted the knife if I had been able to reach it. I suppose he was determined to teach me a lesson.'

'The man's a beast!' Brisen exclaimed. 'I'd challenge him and fight for your honour if I was a male, but the bastard has no sense of decency. He's a coward at heart and he'd avoid fighting anyone who can cause him real harm. I can't imagine what he hopes to gain from all this violence.'

'Can't you see, Brisen? Vortigern is angry with me because I sent the children away out of his reach. He has ambitious plans now that I'm a widow. He intends to marry me and he knows I can't gainsay him after today. Then, regardless of my wishes, he'll claim my husband's throne. I can't stop him, Brisen! I don't believe anyone can, unless the tribal kings are prepared to wage war against him – and such an outcome is unlikely. The tribal kings already look to him for leadership against the Saxons in the spring, so they'll blind themselves to his faults and bow their heads in supplication. Ultimately, they will thank God for giving them a great warrior who can take the place of Constantine.'

Brisen tried to make the queen comfortable in the ruins of her bed until a decrepit old woman entered the bedchamber with Severa's maid. The healer-woman was leaning on a tall staff that had been twisted and carved into the shape of a rearing serpent with gaping jaws, while the maid was laden with a folded length of linen and a basket containing jars of medicinal paste.

'Well, my lovely, why have you called for old Crisiant?'

The old woman moved closer as Brisen folded the sheet back to reveal Severa's battered flesh. With the queen lying on one side to minimise the pain from the welts on her buttocks and belly, Crisiant's myopic eyes assessed her patient through a polished piece of crystal. The queen's women looked at this strange old woman and her peculiar eyeglass with superstitious caution. Everyone knew that old Crisiant was a witch.

'Oh, my! Dear, dear, dear,' Crisiant tut-tutted under her breath as she placed her small paws on the worst wounds on Severa's back, breasts, thighs and belly, then felt the queen's already damp forehead. 'Dear, dear, dear,' she repeated as she issued her orders for Severa's women to boil water and cut the linen fabric into strips for bandages. 'No further need to fret, little one. Old Crisiant's caring for you now, so he can't hurt you any further.'

Somehow, Severa managed to release a dry humourless laugh.

'Put away all thought of trying to protect me, Crisiant. No one can help me and I have no desire to be the cause of your death.'

'I don't plan to attack him, but there are many ways that are known to women that can even the score between us. Rest now, my queen, and we'll talk about it later when you're more comfortable.'

'You don't understand, Crisiant. We'll both suffer if I'm not upright and smiling in the King's Hall at noon tomorrow when Vortigern holds court. The man has the nature of a wolf, but not one who runs with the pack and leads others through his strength and courage. He is a rogue wolf, one who hunts and kills alone. He feels no sense of loyalty towards others and nothing matters to him. Nothing touches his heart!'

'Then he is truly the Wolf of Midnight, the hunter who makes his mark in the dead hours,' Crisiant said vaguely. She shivered, as if a grave had opened up at her feet. Then she shook herself vigorously and returned to the matter at hand.

Her attention was focused on Severa's wrist. 'You mustn't try to use that hand, my dear. I can see that the bones are broken so we shall have to set them back into their true position.'

The healer gave Severa a brief smile of encouragement, then gave instructions to Brisen and the other ladies.

While Severa had been unable to hear Crisiant's orders, she was fretful once the torn garments were eased away from her body. The persistent pains from her wounds had kept her white-lipped throughout the ordeal.

Crisiant took a small vial from her small bag of herbs and the jars filled with ointments. She carefully measured two drops of an oily liquid into some warmed water brought by Brisen. 'Stir this mix well, Brisen, and then give it to your mistress.'

Severa looked at the cup with obvious concern. 'What are you physicking me with, old woman? It looks disgusting!'

'It's just a little poppy juice that will ease the pain when I am resetting your broken wrist,' Crisiant told her. 'If I don't set the bones back into their true position, your hands will become malformed and your arm will be useless for the rest of your life.'

Severa held her breath and downed the water in two long swallows, grimacing at the bitter aftertaste.

As old Crisiant, Brisen and the maidservants bathed the queen, it was as if Crisiant's crystal had formed an invisible wall between Severa's body and the pain. She would have liked to explain to her friends how strange and how comforting this feeling of malaise was, but she was far too tired to allow words to escape from her mouth.

She desperately wanted to sleep and she managed to doze off as soon as her eyes closed.

'Hurry, Brisen! We don't have much time before the poppy juice wears off. You must be ready with the bandage as soon as I've set the bone and we place the splints in position. I'll have to pull the broken pieces of the queen's bones apart and then let them slide back into their usual position. Do you understand what I'm saying, Brisen?'

Brisen nodded, but her eyes were wide and frightened.

'Be brave, Brisen,' the old healer encouraged her.

Then, with astonishing speed for an ancient woman, Crisiant used her sensitive fingers to isolate the dislocated bones in Severa's wrist. She paused, closed her eyes momentarily and then gripped Severa's hand with vice-like fingers. Without hesitation, she pulled the bones apart while manipulating the section of wristbone into its socket with her other hand. Once the bone had slipped back into its original place, Crisiant sighed, thanked the goddess for her kind assistance and then placed the splint into position. The supports that the healer used were no longer than a little finger, but they were thin and very strong. Satisfied with her work, the healer braced the queen's inner forearm while the bandages locked the splints and bones tightly into position.

Next she set to work with a mixture of ointments, pastes and fever root medications to smear the wounds thickly on Severa's back, thighs and stomach. The healer then placed squares of linen over the individual wounds before binding the queen's entire torso with long lengths of linen bandaging. By the time that Crisiant and Brisen had completed their task, Severa looked like a mummified corpse prepared to enter a sarcophagus in ancient Egypt.

The queen's bed was made up with clean linen around her unresponsive body and she was dressed in her softest bed-robe. As well, Crisiant spread a little salve on to her split lip, her swollen ear and the painful bruise on her cheekbone. Finally the healer kissed Severa on the forehead as if the queen was Crisiant's child.

Crisiant and Brisen remained wakeful during the night that followed, while the younger woman pondered whether she should curse Vortigern in her mistress's name.

'Our mistress is a true queen and she has deserved more from men than the pain and suffering that has been laid on her.'

'You're still a young woman, Brisen, and mayhap you'll change your mind in days to come. It's a fact that women have always been the playthings of men, be they rich or poor. It makes little difference to men! We are toys to be thrown away, once our spirits have been broken. Pray to your God that our queen can bear her pain tomorrow, so she can take her place when noon arrives in the King's Hall.'

Stiff and white-faced from pain, Severa made her slow way towards Vortigern and the King's Hall. Crisiant had given her one drop of poppy juice, but the pain still gnawed at her flesh and bones. She could feel a sweaty film on her forehead and she used a length of gauze to wipe it away before it damaged the subtle cosmetics that Brisen had used to create an illusion of health. A delicate white veil seemed to complete the illusion. A long-sleeved gown covered her broken wrist and she avoided using that hand, depending on Brisen's assistance if she was forced to use both hands.

At the door to the King's Hall, Severa turned to face her attendants.

'I am very well, so there will be no worried faces for my sake. I go to preside over the Court of Justice – I am still the queen!'

With a small inclination of her head, Severa recognised the efforts of her attendants who stood tall and smiled as if they had no cares in this wicked world.

Severa, High Queen of the Britons, entered the door leading into the King's Hall and passed into the gloom lit by the banks of candles and lamps that revealed the faces of those men who awaited her.

The men rose as the queen mounted the dais with easy athleticism and seated herself in her chair, her wrist resting in her lap. Then, in a voice that was as clear as a bronze bell, she addressed her ravisher as if nothing had befallen her at his hands.

'Are you ready, Lord Vortigern, to judge the truth of those men who come before us for justice? I believe it is midday!'

CHAPTER VIII

BARGAINS

A man's character is his fate.

Heraditus

With a soldier's cynicism, Paulus surveyed the town of Portus Namnetum from the roadway. The port enjoyed the protection of a wide river near the estuary that led into the open sea and was untouched by the wild winds and high seas of winter. The brackish water and river flats as the river came to the sea were thick with midges and clouds of stinging mosquitos, which made any seaport unpleasant. Now, free from the attacks of insects, yet cooled by sea breezes, Paulus recognised the common sense in siting the wharves upstream where the flood was still wide and deep, but the shoals and sandbanks of the estuary were no longer a danger to moored vessels. Here, few storms could tear at the rigging of the trading vessels that were lined up along the town's wharves like plump ducks.

What a town!

Portus Namnetum had enjoyed the benefits of its prized position near the coast for many years. Not big enough to be a threat to other trading communities, and with berths that weren't quite deep enough for military galleys, the port had set its face determinedly towards trade and had grown rich on the proceeds. At the same time, the fertile farmlands that embraced the river were the grain basket for the newly emerging Frankish kingdoms and a source of wealth for any men who had the wit to pursue trading opportunities beyond the rudimentary walls of their town. Needless to say, the town fathers had fostered the port's trade with Rome, Britannia, Hispania, and would do so with the Devil himself if a good deal was in the offing. Portus Namnetum had grown rich over the centuries.

From a small rise, the decurion could clearly evaluate the town without walking the length of its narrow streets. The area closest to the port, on both sides of the river, wore the dowdy garb of warehouses, storage sheds, cheap inns and rotting houses of ill-repute. Paulus guessed that Portus Namnetum would have more than her fair share of brothels and prostitutes, because returning seamen were notorious for their love of the fleshpots when their pockets were filled with coin.

The higher ground beyond the town's walls bore crowns of greenery and dazzling white, red and yellow houses of significant size. On these prized allotments, the wealthier citizens could capture the sea breezes without the inconvenience of insects, safely removed from the stinking mud and rotting flotsam of the estuary.

With his eyes shaded against the glare, Paulus could make out the shapes of fishing vessels of a larger size than he would have expected among the coracles that were situated beyond the town limits. He could easily imagine the stink of cleaned fish and the pungency of the fishermen's drying racks that were kept at a distance from the sensitive noses of the town fathers.

'Well, Decurion? Is this the place where our erstwhile captain has entrenched himself?' Dilic demanded from the wagon.

'Aye, Dilic! And a very self-satisfied place it appears to be. We'll head towards the centre of the town so we can avoid the port itself. I don't want our friend on *Sea Queen* to catch a glimpse of this wagon. He'll recognise it at a glance if he sees it near the docks.'

'If he's still here,' Dilic muttered sotto voce.

Dilic's face had hardened and with a sense of alarm, Paulus could see signs in her features of an avenger who was set on the worst possible revenge that her mind could devise. The captain of *Sea Queen* would be unable to remember her face – but she would never forget his.

'Women!' Paulus muttered into the ear of his horse. 'If they were a mite stronger, they'd make a meal of us men. Women hate, they plan – and they never forget a slight!'

Paulus was only half joking. He had always possessed a healthy respect for the female sex, probably the main reason he'd refused to venture into the gamble of wedlock. The decurion was fully aware that women's spite could wear down mountains and their grudges were never forgotten but, in the case of the master of *Sea Queen*, he would always applaud any efforts made by Dilic to exact her revenge.

'We'll settle the boys into an inn while I search for *Sea Queen*. I don't suppose we'll need to stay in Portus Namnetum for more than one night, but a sound sleep on a decent pallet will do us all good. We'll also need to purchase supplies for the journey into the south. Burdigala is some distance by cart, so we'll need the bare necessities for survival along the road. You, ladies, can perform these tasks far better than me.'

As Paulus kicked his horse into movement at the very moment he issued his instructions, neither of the women was able to argue with his orders, even if they wished to.

'The boys are in dire need of decent blankets,' Dara observed.

'I agree!' Dilic concurred with a smile. 'Some coarse sailcloth wouldn't go amiss either, so we can warm the earth under them if they have to sleep on the ground. Uther's already showing signs of developing a cold.'

'Perhaps we could afford a sweet treat or two as well,' Dara added hopefully, while Dilic grinned conspiratorially from ear to ear. Although Paulus stared straight ahead at the rutted roadway, he smiled to himself. All women, regardless of their station in life, their wealth or their race, gloried in shopping.

So, in a spirit of accord, the small and diverse party entered the gates of Portus Namnetum and Paulus guided them towards a showy building beside a cobbled square. Several inns faced this administrative structure; Paulus chose the largest and most ostentatious, as he judged the women and children needed at least one night of decent rest before the long journey into Hispania. Once he had paid the eye-wateringly high tariff and seen his charges directed to a generous room with large, shuttered windows, Paulus straightened his travelling clothes, slapped the dust off his legionnaire's cloak and strolled off towards the harbour.

Men and women stared openly at the decurion as he stalked down to the docks with the bearing and determination that proclaimed his ownership of the world around him. All of Rome's legionnaires had this facial mask, worn over commonplace features, from the multitude of years where they stood taller, straighter and prouder than all other men. His red cloak could easily have proclaimed a civilian who was boasting of a military connection, but Paulus's eyes betrayed his origins. Hawk-like, observant and measuring, they swept over pedestrians, riders, shop fronts and the upper windows of buildings as he unconsciously searched for anomalies or dangers after a lifetime of being on constant guard. Paulus could no more change these patterns of behaviour than he could alter his stiffened spine and squared shoulders.

Since the day he had made his escape through the sewers of Arelate, Paulus had refrained from cutting his hair. Perhaps it was an unconscious acceptance that he no longer belonged to the legions after leaving his fellow soldiers to their fates. The reason was immaterial. Slowly and imperceptibly, the decurion's hair had grown and it now curled around the nape of his neck in luxuriant curls. When he accidentally saw his reflection in a puddle or the polished surface of a mirror, Paulus recoiled from the unfamiliar features that looked back at him.

Time had turned Paulus's black hair to dead white, interspersed with the occasional stubborn black streak, so that his hair colouring was reminiscent of the plumage of a carrion bird. Only his newly grown curls now softened this funereal effect. His skin had burned to a rich brown shade with a golden tinge that spoke of his Italic heritage. He was taller than most of his race, though he stood an inch or two shorter than the average Frank or Visigoth, and the thickness of his body and the slabs of visible muscle spoke eloquently of decades of walking, riding and carrying heavy body armour, as well as surviving protracted pitched battles.

The smug citizens of Portus Namnetum stepped aside to let him pass and, even though the decurion had reached the venerable age of fifty, the eyes of matrons and maidens alike followed his muscular frame with unspoken interest.

Once he reached the docks, Paulus turned his attention towards the meanest and dirtiest moorings, having decided that the captain would search for others of his kind while avoiding the payment of exorbitant port fees. This decision took him to the furthest moorings from the warehouses, the most uncomfortable and dilapidated berths, which made him laugh inwardly when he thought of the apprentice lugging heavy items of cargo to the waiting traders.

He could hear the helmsman's curses that manual labour was beneath him, while the tall, laconic seaman hawked, spat and swore inwardly that he'd never again serve on *Sea Queen*.

This captain would never soil his hands with physical effort, as his straining belt attested, while his seamen had struck Paulus as idle, venal and cunning.

Sure enough, Paulus found *Sea Queen* at the furthest end of the wharf where it was loosely tethered to the timbers of the dock. The vessel was filthy and dishevelled, but she was riding much higher in the water, an indication that most of her cargo had been unloaded.

'I'll extract the value from his dirty hide if the boys' treasures have been sold off,' Paulus muttered to himself. 'Better still, I'll hand him over to Dilic to have her way with him.'

This thought pleased Paulus so much that it occupied him all the way to the first cheap wine shop close to *Sea Queen*. Without entering the establishment, he peered through the open window into the smelly, cramped interior and ascertained that the captain had either moved on or had yet to sample the wine that was offered for sale in this stinking tavern. Nor was the captain in any of the next three hovels he visited. The stench of urine offended Paulus's nostrils and, even at this relatively early hour of the afternoon, patrons were either sunk in alcoholic sleep or were looking for trouble with determined belligerence.

The last wine shop in a dim laneway off the main seafront finally revealed the captain seated at a dishevelled table where he was surrounded by the ruins of a large meal. His eyes were glazed and his greasy head swayed loosely to the beat of some personal music that no one else could hear. Boldly, with his tell-tale cloak over the crook of his arm, Paulus stepped up to the bar and ordered a flagon of the host's best Hispanic red.

'That man in the corner, the one with the fat arse and the big nose. Do you know his name?' Paulus asked the barman with a limpid smile.

The barman immediately wished that he was elsewhere.

'Er . . . he's the captain of one of the trading vessels, sir,'

'Aye! I know his status. I was a passenger on *Sea Queen* for some time, but I never learned his name.'

The captain must have made a habit of upsetting his customers, because the barman closed his eyes despairingly for a brief moment before looking beseechingly at the decurion.

'You're not going to break my place up, are you?' the poor man asked and rubbed his grimy hands with a scrap of rag which he had used to soak up spilled food and wine. He stank of sour wine and stale beer.

'No! I'll take him elsewhere private for a private discussion,' Paulus assured him. 'I'm going to ask you one last time. What is his name?'

'His name is Tello!' The barman gulped. 'He calls himself Fulvius Tello! I don't know how he received a Roman nomen, but I believe he's Frankish. At least, he calls himself Tello when he's part-way sober – which isn't often when his vessel is in port.'

Concerned at what might occur between these two unwanted guests, the barman kept his voice down so that none of his drinkers could hear his betrayal of the captain.

'Well said, young man! What of the three sailors who are in his employ?' Paulus's eyes roamed around the room surreptitiously, causing several of the casual drinkers to look away hurriedly and shrink back into the shadows.

'The boy was given a beating and sent away yesterday. The captain refused to pay him his wages, so he bears a lot of malice towards his erstwhile employer. I think the older crewman is called Elgar. He's the deckhand and Tello threw him a handful of coins and got rid of him, at least temporarily. The captain will probably want Elgar back when he's ready to return to the sea, but I don't think Tello will get his wish. The helmsman has a woman in the town, so he usually spends the winter with her. The helmsman has been with the captain for years so I'm certain he'll remain with his master. Good helmsmen are hard to find.'

'Thanks, barkeep! You've earned a silver coin for your assistance, but I'd warn you not to inform Tello that I've been asking after him.'

A small silver coin was quickly moved from the top of the counter to the barman's sleeve and his avaricious eyes narrowed. 'You only have to ask if there are other services I can provide,' he responded with a wink.

Paulus smiled, picked up his flagon and a clean mug, and retreated to a rickety table that was set into the rear of the room.

* * *

Two hours passed in a daze of pain and the gradual return of every small agony as the poppy juice began to wear off and left the queen to sit, ramrod-straight, on her hard wooden throne. When she had first entered the King's Hall, her subjects had cheered spontaneously, although their applause became a little ragged as they saw the pallor of her face, against which her rouged lips stood out like a bleeding wound. The stibium around her eyes that was meant to brighten her complexion simply emphasised the glitter of her illness.

Vortigern had been pleased to see her, although his smile and blank eyes were unreadable. The Demetae ruler had bowed over her hand and pressed her wrist proprietorially, a gesture that was noted by the more observant warriors, servants and citizens who had crowded into the King's Hall. The legal formalities began, but Severa took no part, only smiling benevolently and distantly when Vortigern made crucial decisions about the lives of *her* citizens in *her* town.

No one challenged Vortigern's right to speak in her name. No one dared.

Eventually, just as Severa believed she would faint away, Vortigern shot a sharp glance in her direction and rose to his feet.

'Citizens of Venta Belgarum! I regret to say that the queen is weary and needs to rest! You must excuse us, but I am constrained to cancel the remainder of today's Court. The next sitting day will be announced in good time, but I pray you will leave our queen to mourn her husband's death in the privacy of her home.'

The worthies of Venta Belgarum bowed their heads or

kneeled in apology, for they were eager to wish her good health and assure her of their love. Then, while Vortigern stood silently beside her throne, the citizens filed out of the hall and into the last remains of an autumn afternoon, while the late breezes from the sea sent the fallen leaves dancing over the cobbles of the forecourt. The death of the old year was coming and the signs could be clearly seen in the naked trees and cold skies.

Vortigern offered Severa his arm as soon as the great dragon doors closed. Her hand rested lightly on his forearm as she forced her cramped and bruised muscles to respond, after hours of sitting as still as an effigy. Vortigern gave no sign that he noticed the repairs to her hand, even when her fingers dug sharply into his own arm as she tried to walk. In obvious pain, the queen tottered beside him for half a dozen steps before her iron will failed and her legs began to tremble and buckle. Then Vortigern swept the queen up in one swift action into his arms and strode off in the direction of her apartments.

She tried her best to avoid crying at the agony of his touch. She tried not to wince, but tears continued to fill her eyes. Severa knew she was beaten and her shame knew no bounds.

'I fear you've overtaxed your strength, Severa. You should have told me sooner that you were so ill.'

At first, Severa thought the Demetae king was jesting, but the expression on his satyr's face was so serious that she feared he must be self-deluded and unable to remember the indignities and wounds that he had blazoned upon her body with such sadistic possessiveness. He saw her incredulous expression and his face darkened with anger.

'You don't plan to argue with me again, do you?' Vortigern demanded harshly and Severa was ashamed that, even in his arms, she had flinched as if he had struck her. All she could manage was to shake her head weakly.

With scant regard for ceremony, he banged his fist on her door and Brisen's pale face appeared in the opening.

'Your queen is unwell and must be taken straight to bed,' he snapped and carried Severa to the great bed that had been cleansed of his earlier presence. With almost gentle reverence, he laid her down and then stood over her, shaking his head regretfully.

'I want you to think of those things that you've made me do to you, Severa,' he said in a soft voice that was just loud enough for her to hear. 'From this day forward, it will be up to you to ensure that I don't have to reprimand you at any time in the future. I want you to be a smiling and happy woman, now that I've assumed the role of your guardian and protector.'

Severa wanted to gag but, somehow, she forced her gorge down.

'I'll try to be compliant,' she replied equally quietly, although her mind shrivelled from her craven response. 'I'll be better tomorrow.'

'I hope so, my lady. I want you to show me the least defended parts of Venta Belgarum, so I look forward to hearing that you have returned to good health.'

His smile reflected the usual upturning of a mouth that was always deceptive. She could never be sure how this man really felt, so she feared him even more. Then Vortigern kissed Severa's fingers, turned and left the room.

As soon as the door had closed behind him, Brisen whispered to the queen. Her eyes were fixed firmly on the door in case the Demetae chose to return to the apartments.

'Pridenow has returned and wishes to speak with you, Majesty.'

'Gods, Brisen, I don't want to speak to Pridenow when I'm like this! The boy will want to do something foolish if he discovers what Vortigern has done to me. He mustn't become aware that Vortigern has caused me any harm.'

'How can you possibly hide your condition, Highness? You can scarcely move,' Brisen responded realistically. The queen's face was grey from fatigue and only a blind man could fail to notice her stiff, unresponsive body.

'You can work your magic with your cosmetics before Pridenow comes to see me, Brisen. It should be a simple matter to deceive my brother for a few minutes in half-light. Close the shutters! After I've had a brief discussion with him from the comfort of my bed, I'll plead illness and beg his permission to partake of my sleep.'

Brisen eventually ushered Pridenow into his sister's apartments an hour later. When he entered, he found she was propped up on her pillows, her eyes bright and interested in everything he had to tell her.

'I feared that Vortigern would harm you for spiriting the children away, sister. I was determined to protect you, so I hurried back to protect you.'

Pridenow's earnest sincerity shone from his face. His strange eyes were warm and embracing, while his expression was a blend of fear for his sister's well-being, anticipation of her approval and, over it all, a suspicion that she might well be in serious trouble with the Demetae ruler. She rallied desperately to save her brother from the trials that awaited her, and smiled so lovingly at him that she feared he would sense her anxiety.

He bent over her and kissed her hand, although his sister's

overbright eyes gnawed at his acceptance of her illness. Had her eyes always been so animated?

'As you can see, dear boy, I am very well despite my weariness. But, tell me quickly. What of Paulus and his cargo? Did they sail into the lands of the Picts as we had planned?'

Pridenow realised she was changing the subject, but he permitted her small guile as he gave a complex explanation, using euphemisms and generalities in a totally false story that the boys had taken ship and departed into the north. As he spoke, his eyes scanned the room and the worried faces of the queen's ladies and servants. He lowered himself over her and whispered in her ear.

'Can I assume you trust nobody, not even your women?'

'Anyone can be terrified into disloyalty. Even the most honest of women can be suborned if she is threatened with the loss of her eyes.' Severa's voice was sad and thready, so Pridenow took her in his arms to offer her a semblance of comfort.

In the same instant that he felt the thick bandages, his sister cried out at his touch. Ignoring her fluttering hands, Pridenow carefully bared her body to expose the bites, finger marks, welts and bruises inflicted by Vortigern. Tears ran unchecked down his face as he carefully rebandaged Severa's wounds.

'When has he harmed you?' The request was grim and quietly spoken, so Severa tried to lie by suggesting that she had insulted Vortigern and fought with him, raising his ire against her.

'I'll give you my word, sister, that I will be cool-headed. But by God and his blessed son, I intend to know exactly what the regicide has done.' For the first time, a living pair of lips had voiced that hated word – but Pridenow wouldn't be the last to speak so.

Relieved that she could share the burden of her fears, Severa told her brother of the events that had beset her on the previous day.

Captain Tello had entrenched himself into a corner of the wine shop. Sozzled, he was drinking steadily and growling offensive remarks at other patrons who bumped against his rickety table or spilled the wine from his mug. Paulus watched the man narrowly from his own dark corner, while pretending to quaff a misrepresented red wine that had never seen the sun of Hispania.

Captain Fulvius Tello was an unlovely specimen of masculinity by any yardstick. Bad-tempered and ill-visaged, he brooded away in the dirty corner of a filthy wine shop, a symbol of all that was worst in the far reaches of the empire. Perhaps he had once been Roman or Italic, long ago, but he had traded off that advantage for the doubtful success of cheating the gullible and the needy. Well, Paulus swore silently, he'll soon discover the error of his ways. And it would happen today.

By the time that Paulus had poured most of his wine jug on to the rush- and straw-strewn boards, Tello had obviously drunk his fill. He had eaten his way through a brace of pigs' trotters, so that his face, hands and tunic-front had a new layer of grease over the dregs of the old. With a stumble when his foot caught on the base of his stool, he swore colourfully, and then shoved his way to the makeshift bar where he purchased another flagon of wine to take with him. When he deliberately threw a handful of coins on to the floor and forced the barman to scramble for them amongst the filth, the patient servant set his jaw in a hard line. Paulus watched the barkeep's hands clench so hard that the veins stood out on his forearm like lengths of rope.

'Charming!' the decurion murmured to no one in particular and then drained the last of the wine in his own mug, before coughing as the vinegary lees bit at his tongue. He slammed the mug down on to the stained table top. A drunk lying on an elongated bench seat stirred, muttered, swore and then returned to sleep as Paulus climbed over the man's outstretched legs to make an exit.

Years of honed instinct alerted the decurion to danger, as well as the slightest touch from phantom fingers that were reaching into the pouch where he kept his coin. Paulus's hand gripped the thieving fingers and twisted them backwards until the drunkard fell off his stool with a crash. The villain tried desperately to unsheathe a knife that he'd kept hidden in his sleeve.

'Drop it!' Paulus hissed and continued to twist the filthy fingers to the point of dislocation or breakage. 'I'll really hurt you if you don't release that weapon. Now!'

Paulus had barely raised his voice, for he didn't want to alert the captain to his presence. As soon as the decurion heard the muffled sound of the weapon falling on to the straw, he took a firm grip on the pickpocket's wrist and began to drag him from his darkened corner to a secluded alleyway where the problem could be addressed in secrecy and quiet.

Surprisingly, none of the other patrons bothered to raise their heads from their mugs as the decurion and his prisoner passed out of the wine shop. Perhaps they knew the hooded figure and were aware that, on this occasion, the thief had gone too far by selecting the wrong victim.

Perhaps they were beyond caring.

Once the two men were in the lane-way, Paulus peered into

the darkness and watched Fulvius Tello stagger along the cobbled street leading to the wharf and his nest on *Sea Queen*. Relieved that he could find the captain whenever he wanted him, Paulus turned back to face his captive, who continued to struggle and twist against the decurion's iron grip.

Now that the two men were in the open air, Paulus could make a better assessment of his prisoner. The heavily muffled and hooded figure was of middle height and he possessed a very lean, almost starved figure. The wrist that Paulus was holding was wiry and strong, but he decided that this particular thief was a very clever youth, one whose dexterity was as valuable as the strength exhibited by other men. Assuming the role of a drunkard in a tawdry wine shop was an unusual disguise for a thief who was more gifted with his fingers than his fists.

'Take off your hood and let me see you, laddie,' Paulus snapped, as he pulled the figure closer until he could smell the youth's fear.

'Fuck off!' he responded in a savage hiss. As the lad's voice was unbroken, Paulus reasoned that his captive was trying to bluff his way out of a difficult situation. The fear was visible in his eyes.

'The world isn't kind to orphans, laddie, especially those who try to redress the imbalances by thieving from legionnaires. If Roman law is still used in Portus Namnetum, you could easily find yourself in the galleys or the mines. Is that what you want?'

'Do what you will, you fucker! Just stop talking about it,' the urchin cursed and, for some reason that confused Paulus, the challenge amused him.

'I'll have my way, laddie! It can be easy or hard, so give up before I have to hurt you.' With a swift flick of one leg, Paulus hooked his foot behind the boy's knee and forced the slender figure to the ground. Kneeling on the lad's straining chest, the decurion tore off the hood and scarf that masked his face.

Close-cropped, whitish-blond hair spoke of barbarian blood, as did the high cheekbones, the deep-set blue eyes and a furious, beardless face. As Paulus had thought, this youth couldn't be more than fourteen years, regardless of his height.

'Get off me before you crush me, you Roman fucker! I'll kill you if I get half a chance!'

'You've a filthy mouth for a beardless boy. Where are your parents?'

The boy spat in Paulus's direction and continued to curse with words that would have been appropriate in the most hard-bitten ranks of the Roman army.

'They're dead, thanks to your lot! I make my own way in the world.'

'You're a common thief! Are you so eager to lose one of your hands if you're brought before the town fathers?' Paulus asked roughly as he watched the boy's eyes flinch away from his captor's face.

'Let me go. I'll scarper and you won't get any further trouble.'

'I'm inclined to drag you off to the nearest magistrate and tell him of your feeble attempts at stealing my coin,' Paulus countered.

The boy shrugged. Then, quick as a fleeting thought, he slipped his arms out from the coat that Paulus was grasping in his hand. He took to his heels in a flash, but Paulus was wise to the ways of thieves. He'd half expected such a manoeuvre, so he tackled the boy from behind to bring him down with a sharp crack when his forehead struck the cobblestones.

'Keep still, you little bugger, and you won't get hurt,' Paulus growled as he fished out a length of thin leather thong, one-handed, from the pouch that contained the bag of treasures he kept attached to his belt. Like most professional legionnaires, he had always kept a supply of odds and ends that might become necessities when the legions were on the march.

Now, with the efficiency of long practice in restraining prisoners, Paulus tied the youth's hands together and looped the bound wrists over the framework of a cheap, wooden sign that advertised the wares of a local smithy. On tiptoes and unable to move, the captive was left to hang ludicrously in the dark alleyway, his arms stretched painfully above his head.

Completely immobilised, this position became truly painful if the boy attempted to struggle against his bonds.

'You won't suffer unduly if you stop struggling and don't try to escape. I'll be back shortly to decide what I'm going to do with you. If I think you've been calling out for help or trying to inform on me, you can be sure that I'll hunt you down. Is that understood, laddie?'

'Yes!' The boy spat the word out, but he was no longer struggling against his bonds, having learned that his feet could just reach the slimy ground in the alleyway if he ceased to fight against them. If he remained still, he was able to relieve the pressure on his arms.

'I can't hear you,' Paulus hissed, his temper rising at the youth's recalcitrance.

'Yes! Shit! . . . Sir!'

'That's better. Remember, not a sound! I'll be occupied with finalising a long-overdue business matter of some importance, so it would be foolish of you to put my affairs at risk. Don't cause me any more trouble!'

Like a ghost, Paulus disappeared into the night. A sea fog had risen from the waters of the river and visibility was limited to some four or five arm-lengths. The youth could vaguely make out the dirty-yellow glow of lanterns on the nearer trading vessels, although the ships themselves seemed like grey skeletons in this weird mist. Try as he might, he was unable to see any signs of the dangerous old man and his sharp weapons.

He waited patiently in the darkness, for he knew he had no choice in the matter.

Paulus reached *Sea Queen* without incident. Fulvius Tello had lit the lamp that hung from the single mast, although its swinging, nacreous light did little to alleviate the gloom that embraced the vessel. However, Paulus was an experienced hunter. Thirty-odd years as a legionnaire had taught him to remain perfectly still, use his senses and ascertain any risk before he acted. On this occasion, he realised that Tello was hunched over a wine jug in the open cabin that was located amidships. A series of shutters offered an illusion of privacy, for Tello obviously slept in this small, dirty space. The captain had opened every storm shutter to catch the last of the warm breezes of summer. Paulus could also see that Tello was motionless, as if he had fallen into a drunken daze over a half-empty jug of wine.

The decurion moved on silent feet towards the gangplank and waited until the river current pulled *Sea Queen* close to the wharf. In a moment, Paulus reached the deck and felt his way carefully through any loose rubbish that might warn Tello that an intruder had breached his defences. Blown by the fitful breeze, one of the shutters was slapping intermittently against the wall.

Paulus felt an instant of shock when the captain suddenly burst into a tuneless song. Then, after his breathing settled, he crept from one of the deep shadows and entered the starboard side of the captain's quarters, if the mean and dirty room could be dignified by such a description.

As Paulus listened to a bawdy, waterfront song that was characterised by insults aimed at women, he tried to imagine any female who was so desperate for company that she would permit Tello to paw her with his greasy hands and filthy black nails. Then, as the song trailed off into unintelligible maundering, Paulus moved swiftly into the light and crossed the small area of decking between himself and Tello. He gripped the half-conscious man by the thinning plaits at the back of his head before using his other forearm to cut off Tello's breathing from behind. The captain barely realised he was under attack.

'Whosit? Whatcha doing?' Tello muttered thickly as he belatedly tried to dislodge Paulus, a man who was smaller and lighter-framed, but much stronger than the slothful ship's captain. Paulus tightened his forearm, but released the pressure when Tello's eyes bulged and he began to gasp like a fish out of water.

'Let's begin again, shall we?' Paulus hissed in Tello's ear. 'You are going to return the jewels you stole from my boys and, if you meet my demands, I'll allow you to live. Where's my golden fish?'

'Who? Whosat?' Paulus was almost certain that Tello was foxing, so he tightened his grip as a warning.

'Forget the excuses, Tello. I'm here to have property returned. If necessary, it'll be over your dead body.'

'Someone will come and you'll be hanged as a thief,' Tello muttered thickly. Despite his drunken state, the captain's instinct for survival ensured he was sobering quickly and was aware that a dire fate was staring into his face.

'I don't know who's going to arrest me for theft. If I wanted to complain to the authorities, I have two very angry women and two children who are anxious to revenge themselves on you for stealing the trinkets of my young charges. You're just one man, Tello! You're as nothing, regardless of the fine name you've selected for yourself. My boys come from one of the richest and most powerful families in Hispania, and I'm a Roman who's in their family's service. Who do you think will be believed if I'm stupid enough to let you live beyond the next few minutes?'

Tello swore crudely, while ascribing some impossible physical actions to Paulus, his mother and all his kinfolk. Paulus responded by cuffing him lightly across the face.

'Whoreson!' Tello countered and Paulus released him for a brief length of time, sufficient to sink his fist to the wrist in the captain's belly, an appendage that quivered like jellied eels. Sickened by the sight of Tello as he attempted to catch his breath, Paulus placed him into a headlock once again.

This time, however, the decurion's left hand was firmly gripped around the hilt of his soldier's knife.

'I intend to start with your ears, you bastard. You already know what I want, so you don't need hearing to tell me what I need to know. Your nose will be the next appendage to be removed from your ugly face if you don't give me the response I want. By and large, my ministrations are likely to improve your looks.'

'I don't know what you're talking about, Roman,' Tello rasped, certain that Paulus was bluffing.

As if he was carving a hunk of cheese from a wheel, Paulus sliced Tello's right ear from his skull without the slightest hesitation. After all, the decurion's duties in Rome's legions had made greater demands on his scruples. Paulus remembered

Corinium and Constantine's orders to torture the female brothel-keeper who had been a conspirator in the assassination of a senior Roman officer.

Obeying those orders had been hard, because the woman had done him no personal harm. But Tello was a far easier target, for this man was stinking and villainous. He had stolen from people that Paulus regarded as kinfolk.

The captain would have screamed, but the decurion thrust his scarf into Tello's mouth to silence him.

Paulus carefully dropped the hairy ear on to the deck where Tello could see it. Then he removed the gag with distaste.

'Are you about to change your mind, Tello, or do you need further assistance from my sharp little friend?' The decurion's voice was calm and untroubled, a ploy that added an extra level of menace to his words. Blood was seeping down Tello's head, so Paulus clapped the fouled scarf over the wound to ensure his own clothing was protected from blood spatter.

Tello squealed thinly and nodded his desperation.

'Can I assume you're prepared to return the jewels you've stolen from my boys?'

The captain nodded his head repeatedly, as if he had suffered some sort of fit.

Paulus released his grip on Tello and allowed the captain to scramble his way through a padlocked chest of iron-bound wood that he'd been using as a stool.

Unfortunately for Tello, the locking device was unfastened, so Paulus used his foot to flip the heavy lid open. 'My, my! You are a truly enterprising man, aren't you? I can't believe how much treasure you've been squirrelling away for the winter.'

Tello found a leather pouch which he thrust towards Paulus

with one hand while the other pressed the neck cloth against his wounded ear.

'I want the fish and I want it now!' Paulus demanded, as the rogue checked the contents of his pouch. 'I won't ask you again.'

'Fucking Christians! I hope you rot!' Tello snapped as he returned to his usual state of belligerence. 'Take it and get out.' Then Tello thrust the golden fish at the decurion and resumed his seat on the strongbox.

The decurion took a deep, shuddering breath. Fulvius Tello was a stain on humanity, a man who would never live by the rules of a civilised community. Unable to feel compassion for anyone but himself, he would continue to cheat and abuse anyone who came within his ambit. Quite simply, Fulvius Tello was an irredeemable blight on the human race.

'I don't think so,' Paulus began. 'From the pile of coins, gems and silver in your chest, you must have been cheating your passengers and those around you for years. You're a blot on mankind, Tello, and I believe there's a need to scrub you away.'

Fulvius Tello's eyes narrowed with mingled fear and cunning, alerting Paulus that the captain intended to make a sudden move that would even the score. He might still have have been merciful if Tello had shown any signs of possessing some basic tenets of decency. But the captain was judging Paulus by his own standards.

Later, Paulus would convince himself that Tello had chosen his own death.

He was anticipating an attack from Tello and recognised the gleam that appeared in the captain's eyes as he grasped at a jewelled dagger that he'd found in the strongbox. With a wild, unbalanced swing of his knife arm, Tello attempted to gut the Roman with a single, upwards blow.

Men who are half-drunk and in poor physical condition wouldn't normally be a match for a trained legionnaire, but Paulus's reflexes had slowed with the passing of the years. The blade almost missed its target, but it still sliced through the decurion's leather tunic and the shirt beneath it, scouring a neat slice over his abdomen and breastbone that resulted in an immediate flow of blood.

Paulus's eyes reddened with fury and embarrassment that such an ineffectual man as Tello would be able to wound him. Before he had time to consider his actions, he buried his own knife in Tello's gut. Then, with all the fury he could muster, he twisted the blade.

Finally, despite the weakness that came over him from his own wound, Paulus dragged Tello's dying body on to the deck and threw him overboard.

'Let's see how well you can swim,' he said grimly as Tello's body rose to the surface, along with a growing streak of blood. The captain was trying to flap his arms desperately in a parody of a swimming stroke, but Tello was one of those seamen who chose to tempt the gods by failing to learn the art. With a despairing cry, he sank again, only to re-emerge with water streaming from his mouth. When he sank for the second time, he stayed below the surface, and there was no further trace to indicate that the rogue had ever been on *Sea Queen* at all.

CHAPTER IX

A VERY SUPERIOR TOWN

A man is to be envied if he's been fortunate with his
children and has avoided dire calamities.

Euripides, *Orestes*, l.542

The inn was a hive of activity when Paulus eventually returned
with the struggling young lad in tow, firmly secured by bonds
that encircled his wrists. Several of the patrons stared curiously
at the decurion and his prisoner with sneers of contempt but,
when Paulus looked threateningly in their direction, the citizens
quickly developed an urgent interest in leaving the inn and
returning to their homes and waiting families.

Dragging the reluctant prisoner behind him, Paulus strode up
the stairs to the second floor of the very superior hostelry. The
lad lurched against the stair-rails when he lost his footing and
cried out in sudden pain when his knee struck one of the uprights
with a sickening crunch. With a grimace of guilt, Paulus slowed
momentarily, allowing the youth to regain his footing and stagger

up the few remaining steps unaided, rather than suffering the ignominy of being dragged.

The lad's cry and the clatter of boots on the bare stair-treads drew Dilic from the room that she had rented from the innkeeper. She had waited anxiously for Paulus's return after preparing the children for bed, for she was unwilling to accept the likelihood that the children's jewellery had been lost forever. With only a sweeping and ironic glance at the boy who was leaning on the rails as he tried to catch his breath while massaging his injured knee, Dilic's attention focused on the decurion.

'Well, Paulus! I'd never have thought you'd be a man with an interest in boys.'

'I'm not in the mood for your sarcasm, Dilic. Catch these and put them somewhere safe.'

With a deft underarm throw, Paulus tossed the bag of jewellery in Dilic's direction, causing her to stumble and almost fall as she reached out for it. With his good mood restored by her fumbling and the less than ladylike oath that followed it, Paulus pulled the boy along the landing to the open door.

'Right! You! Get yourself in here so I can have a good look at you,' Paulus ordered in a voice that was so crisp and authoritarian that the tone even surprised Dilic.

The lad sank down on to the rush-covered floor while two sleepy children peered out at him from their pallet bed over a pile of pillows.

He looked across at them with surprise etched on to his smooth urchin's face.

'First question! Who are you, boy? I suggest you don't bother to lie to me because I'll know almost immediately if you try to gull me. I want to know why a beardless youth is wasting his time by stealing from drunken citizens at one of the filthiest inns in this equally filthy town. I wouldn't have thought the profits would have been worth the effort.'

'What I do with my time is none of your business!' the boy replied in a high voice that hadn't yet broken. Paulus noted the boy's daring with amusement.

'You must be lacking in your wits if you don't recognise the trade I've followed for all of my adult life, you young fool. Why would you want to cross swords with someone like me?'

'Are you going to kill me too? I can swim, so you'll have to find some other way of silencing me than throwing me into the river like you did to the captain. The town's soldiers would be eager to learn about your meeting with Tello and what you did to him. They'd probably be so pleased to get their hands on you that they wouldn't be interested in me. Especially when they hear that Tello owned an overfull strongbox.'

Paulus slapped the boy gently with the back of his hand but, even so, he was unprepared for how such a light blow sent the youth flying across the room, to fall in a crumpled heap against the princes' pallet. Two pairs of eyes stared at him in a mixture of admiration and fear.

'Have you killed her?' Ambrosius asked in a shaky voice. 'Mother told me that men weren't allowed to hit girls.'

Ambrosius's pronouncement was greeted with initial incredulity, followed by a dawning suspicion that their prisoner might well be a girl.

The two women examined the addled lad more closely while Paulus stared hard at him for a few seconds before picking him up by the front of his tunic and dragging his slight form over to an oil lamp for a more detailed examination. Surprisingly, the lightly perfumed oil in the hostelry was of a far higher quality than the usual foul-smelling examples of fuel found in most establishments.

'By all the gods,' Paulus hissed, as he realised that the prisoner's skin and throat were quite smooth and there was no trace of an Adam's apple. 'Dilic! Check to see if my little thief is hiding a pair of tits inside her tunic.'

Dara was the first to reach out towards the struggling, spitting boy and surprised the decurion with a ruthless examination of the pickpocket's body. One of her muscular hands clamped on to the boy's groin with a grown woman's experience and lack of shame. The maid tut-tutted under her breath and then pulled up the tunic to reveal a pair of small, but well-shaped breasts that were partially bound with a dirty bandage. After a quick flick of Dara's wrists, the constraint fell away to reveal a young woman who was well past the age for marriage.

'That's enough, Dara,' Paulus said softly. He could see that she would have continued to strip the girl and humiliate her if she wasn't checked.

'Find me something to drink, Dilic! I must think!'

The two children stared pointedly at the young woman through narrowed eyes. They were far too fascinated by the display of female flesh for Paulus's liking. Even as the girl, blushing, covered herself as well as she could with bound hands, the boys examined her with a child's lack of embarrassment.

'It's off to sleep for you, Ambrosius! You too, young Uther! Dilic will turn out the lamp in a moment, and I don't want to hear a word from either of you.'

'I'm not at all sleepy, sir,' Ambrosius responded, while pressing his fists against eyes that were still transfixed by the prisoner's pink nipples.

'Me neither!' Uther added, although his mouth opened in a gigantic yawn.

Dara fussed about in the children's corner of the room and settled them down once more on the solitary bed, kissing them goodnight.

Meanwhile, Dilic had returned the golden fish to the pouch that held their travelling instructions. Then, with a wink in Paulus's direction, she whisked a cloth from over a wooden platter that revealed half a chicken, several crisp radishes and a small bowl of the sticky fish paste that Romans used for flavouring their meals. The final item to tempt Paulus's palate was a large orange. To add to this marvel of fresh food after the insipid meals of dried meat that had been their fare on *Sea Queen*, Dilic produced a large pewter mug filled with freshly brewed beer.

'We've had our differences in the past, Dilic, but you're a woman who understands the things that a man really needs to keep a smile on his face.' Paulus drained half of the mug's contents in one long swallow, then began to drag a cloth bag out of the undershirt beneath his cloak and tunic. The bag had been held in place by Paulus's soldier's belt and its contents were obviously very heavy. It would take a man who was used to carrying a heavy pack to cope with this imposition on his comfort.

'I was forced to deal rather strongly with the captain,' Paulus began. 'I discovered that his name was Fulvius Tello. He'd given himself an impressive nomen, but the fool thought I'd allow him to slice me up the middle with his knife. He took his chance and failed with the only chance he was given. After we'd settled our differences and I'd consigned his body to the river, I decided to confiscate the contents of his strongbox. If I hadn't taken it, the first thug who climbed aboard *Sea Queen* would have discovered the treasure and taken it for himself. I'll convince myself that it's a form of payment for the inconvenience that Tello inflicted on us when he stole our jewellery. When I saw the valuables in his chest, I realised that he was an even bigger thief than we had imagined. He was quite avaricious for a ship's captain.'

Dilic opened the bag containing the jewellery and the contents spilled on to the table top before he'd finished his explanation. A scattering of golden pins, intaglio rings, several small boxes made with exquisite workmanship, a length of rope made from dark-green amber, pearl earrings with long pins to be driven through the ears, scores of golden coins and at least twice that number in silver were winking brightly in the light of the oil lamp. Treasure trove indeed, Dilic thought as her eyes widened in the light from the oil lamps. Dara drew her breath in sharply, while the girl-thief groaned audibly, a response that caught Paulus's attention as he began to nibble on a chicken leg. With some reluctance, he put his meal down and turned his attention back to his young prisoner.

'Now! Enough nonsense from you, young lady. You'll indulge me now and tell me your name. I know you think you might be able to repeat some suspicions to the authorities because of Tello's unfortunate ending, but just one of these golden coins would buy me whatever favours I'd want to purchase from the town magistrate. Don't piss me off, girl!'

The captive was unable to decide whether to spit in his face or to make a dash for the latched door. She compromised.

'Fuck you!'

'You're not very imaginative, girl. You've got one last chance!

Answer the question, or I'll be forced to slap you down and teach you to be polite in front of the children. I'll ask again: What is your name?'

'Etain,' the girl replied, suddenly capitulating to the inevitable. 'My father was a scribe who'd been a priest during his younger days. He aroused the enmity of the church when he met my mother and decided to forsake his vows. Despite this, he made a good living by writing letters and legal documents for wealthy traders, merchants and landowners. He was murdered by rene-gade soldiers who were fleeing from the bastard emperor's army.'

'Which emperor?' Paulus asked, and he could have bitten off his tongue for the revealing echo of annoyance that had entered his voice. But Etain was oblivious to his personal feelings.

'Constantine, the Emperor of the West that was! His armies were destroyed in the south but some of his men escaped and moved into the north, pillaging and raping as they went. They chanced on my parents at the small block of farmland they worked as a protection against poverty. When the soldiers discovered that my father had no secret cache of gold, they used both of my parents before hanging them from the rafters in the barn. I found them when I returned from a visit to the home of my betrothed and his family on the next day.'

Etain's voice sounded crisp and unemotional, but Paulus had heard those flat tones in other victims. Although this girl had been traumatised by what she had seen, he knew from past experience that she would scorn any gestures that could be construed as pity.

'Do you have any kin who could offer you some protection?' he asked.

'No! The soldiers had burned the farmhouse and killed or

carried off my parents' livestock. The soil on the family farm wasn't very good to start off with, so it was of little value to a potential husband. There was no one who could pay the bride price after Father's death, so I became another worthless female with only a modicum of beauty as a bulwark against a life of poverty. My betrothed deserted me and left me to my own devices. So much for love! Then, a week later, a distant cousin of my father arrived unannounced on my doorstep. He immediately declared that, as Father's closest male relative, the farm had become his to do with as he willed. He tried his damnedest to bed me, but I had set a far higher price on my maidenhood than anything that the fat toad could pay. I considered my options and decided I would be well served if I could disguise myself and become a boy.'

'Just like that?' Dilic asked, wide-eyed. She reached out to touch Etain's arm but the girl flinched away from the maid's curious fingers. 'Weren't you afraid?'

'I'm sure you can guess what happens to a girl without male relatives who try to survive in a town such as Portus Namnetum. I was safer with my hair shorn, my breasts bound and attired in stolen boy's clothing. People believe what they think they see and rarely look below the surface of those people who surround them.'

'But why did you become a thief?' Paulus asked.

'What were my choices? A prostitute? A slave? A maid?' Etain's head lifted proudly and Paulus realised he admired her spirit, even if she was likely to become another problem to be solved.

'I'm surprised you weren't caught,' he responded in a more sympathetic voice as he inspected the half-chicken and began to tear it into small pieces. He selected the wing with a large piece of detached meat and offered this treat to Etain. She stared at the offering momentarily and then snatched it from his hand before he could change his mind.

'I'm careful and I work at my trade. I try my best to avoid risks, but you fooled me. I'd decided that the captain was my next mark, but I soon realised that you were watching him and had your own plans for him. To my cost, I thought you were actually drinking from that flagon. The wine shop reeks of wine and food, so I thought you were drunk. I didn't think for a moment that most of your cups were poured on to the floor. You were just another old man.'

After this long explanation, she stuffed her mouth with more chicken meat, ignoring the grease that was staining her lips and fingers.

'You were far too confident, Etain. Sooner or later, your overconfidence would have caught you out.' Paulus snapped his fingers loudly. 'And that would have been the end of you.'

Etain swallowed, paused, and then began to chew reflectively on another piece of chicken offered by Paulus. She was obviously planning some new strategy as she ate.

'I won't say anything to the authorities if you're prepared to let me go,' she promised.

'Do I look stupid?' Paulus responded and turned his attention back to Dilic.

'Escort Etain to the straw in one of the corners, and then bind her legs and arms. We'll keep her trussed up until the morning. You can provide her with water and food if she needs them, but don't trust her. She's been living on her wits since the deaths of her kinfolk, but I believe she'll betray us in an instant if she's caught with her hands in the pockets of one of her victims. A wiser man than I would strangle her immediately, but I admire her spirit and I'm uncomfortable with unnecessary violence. In the meantime, she's a problem and I want to think about her for a while before deciding what we can do with her. If you feel sorry for her, just remember that she'll betray your boys in an instant if she needs to save her own neck from the magistrate's noose.'

Dilic nodded and dragged Etain to her feet. All the fight seemed to have been leached out of the girl, but Dilic still ensured that the knots of her bindings would keep her restrained during the night – just in case. Any threat to the safety of Ambrosius and Uther would always be taken seriously.

As Paulus ate, drank his beer and wondered at the perfidy of the gods who saw fit to mock his plans, the women and children settled down around him and slept. Even the prisoner seemed to be relaxed among the rushes on the floor where she'd been covered with a blanket.

What a coil!

Regardless of the threats he had uttered, the decurion knew he'd never be able to silence a woman to save his own skin. Perhaps he could do so if such an action was necessary to save the boys, but the thought of her slender neck between his hands was repulsive at best. Her death would be a cruel waste.

But what would the young woman do if he released her? How long would she last on the streets before she was unmasked as a criminal? Would Etain make another mistake and try to fleece other men who were more than equal to her trickery? She was on a collision course with disaster and Paulus hated to consider that he might become a part of that small tragedy. To set her free was to put her life at risk.

Should he offer some assistance to the prisoner that would

enable her to escape from the dangers of her present life? She might prove to be a valuable asset if she was prepared to follow his leadership and join the party on their journey into exile. The question wound its serpentine way through his brain until, at last, Paulus surrendered. His head began to sag and he fell asleep.

The party of exiles was on the move before sunrise. Loosely bound now, Etain sat in the bed of the wagon with the boys as they played at cat's cradle with a length of yarn. At the same time, Dara sat with Dilic over the backs of the patient horses, taking turns at the reins while enjoying the last of autumn's warmth on their faces.

In the hour before sunrise, Paulus had surged out of restless sleep to the sounds of children being dressed and prepared for an early-morning departure.

'You've overslept, Paulus,' Dilic sniped at him. Her voice was tinged with sarcasm, but her sunny smile told him that her words were part of the game that they had come to share during this protracted journey. 'Is it possible that the great decurion is becoming old and decrepit?'

'Argggh!' Paulus grumbled in return. He stood and stretched his cramped legs, then noticed that Etain was sitting at the small table with her hands and feet unbound. She still had a mutinous expression on her downcast face.

'Why have you freed our captive, Dilic?'

'Dara and I decided that Etain can't be left in this heathen place without menfolk to keep her out of trouble. If you're agreeable, we'd like her to join us on the journey. Let's face it, Paulus, you'd never have the balls to cut her throat out of hand and she would always be a threat if we left her to her own devices.

We think she can be of some use to us while she makes a decision on how she wants to spend the remainder of her life.'

'Oh? So you arrived at this solution to our problem, did you?' Paulus was none too pleased that the decision had been taken from his hands. 'What do you propose to tell her family if they become aware of her situation and accuse us of abducting the girl?'

'To the best of Etain's knowledge, she has no other family,' Dilic responded with finality.

Paulus stared irritably at Etain, who was glaring back at him.

'I don't want to go to Hispania – or wherever it is that you intend to take me. I like Portus Namnetum and I'd like to stay here. I've learned to hate the countryside since my parents were slaughtered – and none of you has bothered to ask me what I want.'

'And nobody's about to ask you, girl! I'd suggest to you that you should shut up and give your thanks to Dilic. I'd already decided to dump you at the first nunnery we came across, so you've just been spared from spending a lifetime on your knees.'

'See, Dara?' Dilic interrupted. 'I knew Paulus would see sense. She'll be a big help once we're on the road.'

Paulus spluttered and protested that the women hadn't considered the full ramifications of their decision. With some resentment, he tore at his food and fulminated over the disrespect that they'd shown him as he tried to come up with a better solution than the one presented to him, but he was unable to convince his two females that taking Etain under their wing was unwise.

Dara and Dilic stubbornly refused to hear a word he said. With nonchalant expressions, they continued to ready the boys for travel, then picked up all the travelling bags they could carry.

Etain was also given her share of weight and, with Ambrosius and Uther in tow, the party moved to the front of the inn to wait for Paulus. The decurion was left to pay for their expenses, a task he completed with an obvious lack of good humour.

'Women can be the very devil,' Paulus whined to the innkeeper with a grimace of disgust.

'You've more trouble on your hands than I'd like to consider, that's for certain,' the worthy replied with a conspiratorial wink. 'Three to one make for insurmountable odds.'

'Don't I know it!' Paulus replied fervently and made his way out of the inn.

Cart journeys can be tedious for the passengers, so any details of the long, fretful and slow progress along the roads leading into the south were as difficult as Paulus had expected. The horses were large, patient and prepared to walk all day while drawing the heavy wagon behind them, but the boys became petulant with their inactivity and even Etain found that she had no more games of interest that could bring them cheer. The landscape possessed a golden sameness, of bare fields where the grain had been harvested, of rows of grapevines where the fruit had already been picked and the sturdy branches were bare of leaves, skeletons that awaited the chills of winter. This fecund land was frustrating for the boys who longed to run free in the sunshine, but were forced to remain under the covering of their wagon as the steady autumn rain drenched the travellers.

Etain was permitted to glean the grapevines as they lumbered along. Although most of the grape harvest was already in vats and fermenting into the wines that made these fields famous, Etain's sharp eyes found several bunches of ripe fruit that kept the boys busy munching on the sweet, unfamiliar fruit and spitting the seeds at each other. Even Paulus accepted a few handfuls of grapes, a pleasant task which reminded him of home and the happy days of his youth.

'I suppose matters could be worse,' he muttered to himself and made a determined attempt to be more cheerful.

Dilic and Paulus were anything but placid by nature, so the journey involved several weeks of sniping and argument that only ceased when one of the combatants was asleep or Paulus was hunting for game along the margins of the Roman road. Thankfully, the meagre pickings of rabbits and the occasional fat partridge or pheasant provided some relief from the jolting and roughness of the journey.

Paulus's professionalism was appalled at the state of the roads that his party was travelling. He recalled, with some nostalgia, the many times he had commanded construction parties building roads and bridges under the steady, intelligent guidance of Roman engineers. Occasionally, he had participated in the construction of the roads for the sheer joy of using his own muscles, so he knew how solidly and skilfully they were made.

The decurion recalled the warmth of the sun on his shoulders and the slick glaze of sweat on his naked skin. It had been a time in his life when his hair had still been black and his joints moved freely and flexibly. He had set dozens of milestones into the earth that informed travellers how far they must travel on the excellent new roads if they were to reach the next town. Those were the good days, he thought, as he watched the wagon thud its way over a particularly nasty pothole.

It was obvious to the decurion that no one in authority had bothered to keep the arteries of Rome in good condition since the reign of Magnus Maximus had collapsed after his execution. Even the best constructions will eventually deteriorate under the triple assaults of wind, water and wear if their use ignores the need for regular maintenance. Small gaps between cobbles had widened to become large potholes and the wagon swayed and staggered like a drunkard on the damaged portions of the paved surface where flood waters had ravaged the foundations. No remedial work had been carried out for years, or so Paulus thought, when he examined this section of the great communications network that had linked the provinces to Rome.

For ease of travel, and to mislead any pursuit that might have been initiated by Vortigern's agents, Paulus decided to take his party along roads that would take them via a south-easterly diversion that passed through the ancient Roman fortifications at Pictavis before heading back in a south-westerly direction towards Mediolanum Santorum and onwards to Burdigala. Pictavis, their first major staging post, with its grand imperial name, reminded the travellers of its ancient history as a centre inhabited by the Pictones, a Celtic tribe, from where the name came. The inhabitants of the town spoke a bastardised form of their original tongue which, surprisingly, Dilic and Dara could understand with relative ease. This town, which boasted a huge amphitheatre and a public bathing facility, was a clear demonstration that Roman influence wasn't fully lost, although the baths were showing signs of falling into ruin. After much cajoling, Dilic and Dara enjoyed the public baths, and the whole party regretted leaving Pictavis as they headed deeper into Aquitania.

This fertile province had originally been torn from Roman control by the grim-faced Vandals, a tribe who were despised for their ferocity and merciless cruelty during the long march that took these warriors into the north of Africa. The townsfolk of Aquitania, a people who were now a hybrid mix of Celtic, Roman, Gothic and Vandal stock, had barely recovered before, only a decade earlier, the Visigoths had arrived with sword and fire to claim these lands for their own. Eager to take their share of the loot on offer, the Visigoths were assisted by the Franks, an army that had taken the old province of Lugdunensis and was now broadening its sphere of influence. The brief existence of the House of Constantine had been a hiccup in the march of the tribes and the slow decay of civilisation was all too clearly written on the towns that Paulus's small party reached during their journey to Burdigala.

As the party turned towards the south-west, Paulus was beginning to feel like a man who has lived to see the end of everything in life that he prized. Even worse, the loss of certainties that accompanied the centuries of stable Roman rule had begun to leave an aching void in Paulus's world and the earth beneath his half-boots seemed to be staggering under an invisible weight. Towns such as Mediolanum Santorum were little more than grand names now, inhabited by the ghosts of long-dead heroes. This thriving centre had once been the largest city of Aquitania and was noted for the rich army of grapevines that marched up the low hills in well-ordered rows. Though still a vital centre, decay and grime had blurred the indefinable greatness which had once brought wealth and fame to its population. Paulus wasn't able to explain why these towns had changed for the worse, especially as the citizens continued to be tall, healthy and strong, but the invisible ties of order, laws, cleanliness and pride had begun to unravel. He rode in silence for some days, for he was more convinced than ever that he should have chosen to die at Arelate with so many of his kind.

When Mediolanum Santorum was a day behind them, the wagon lumbered up a line of low hills. There, on the windswept crown, and with the Roman road descending gradually away before them, Paulus and his charges once again saw the grey autumn sea. But these chill waters weren't the open seas of the northern shores near Abone in Britannia. Below the party, an elongated gash in the shoreline cut raggedly into the interior, permitting the sea to enter into the land mass where it held the promise of quieter waters that gave protection to shipping.

Gulls screamed overhead, having spied humans who might provide food that their kind cast away wastefully. At first, Ambrosius laughed when he saw them hovering on the sea winds because these raucous creatures were reminders of home, their mother and a life that seemed like a dream of safety and security. But, behind his clenched fists, the little boy was tearful.

Paulus sensed the lad's sorrow and pulled on his horse's mouth so that the cumbersome horse halted, permitting the wagon to draw level with the decurion.

'See, Ambrosius? We'll be following the coastline now until we come to Burdigala, where your mother's friend is waiting for us. I realise this country isn't as rich as your mother's city of Venta Belgarum, but I've been told that many, many hundreds of years ago, before we Romans came to conquer these lands, a tribe called the Bituriges Vivisei came to Burdigala from the far north and settled in this region. I know that the name of this tribe sounds very odd, but when we reach our destination, you'll soon learn to understand the language of its inhabitants. Why do you think we'll be able to understand these people?'

Ambrosius thought hard, because puzzles would always

fill the void of homesickness lurking below the surface of his soul.

Eventually, the boy's face lit up and he grinned in triumph. 'The tribesmen speak Latin and the whole world can understand the language of Rome.'

'That's a good answer, Ambrosius, but these people don't speak Latin as their mother tongue. There's another reason why we are able to understand them.'

Ambrosius's face screwed up as he frowned with concentration. So deeply was the boy lost in thought that he scarcely noticed when the wagon began to move down the long slope.

'Let me know when you work it out, sprog,' Paulus said and rode on ahead, blessing the long-dead engineers who had constructed this particular stretch of road so that the slope was gradual and posed no discernible threat to the party.

Wisely, Ambrosius suspected that there was some trick to this puzzle, so he made several wild guesses, including one that reflected his intelligence. But the answer still eluded him. Once Paulus had called a halt for the evening and the small party had settled into their defensive campsite for the night, Ambrosius could no longer control his curiosity.

'Paulus! Sir! If we can understand the language spoken by the people of Burdigala, this ability must have come to us in some way. I've been taught Latin, of course, but there's no other language that I can think of that would be common to us.'

'What language do the people of Venta Belgarum speak to each other? You can understand them when they're speaking, can't you?'

Ambrosius looked thoroughly flummoxed by the riddle before him. 'I suppose we'd call it the language of Britannia. It's the language given to us by my ancestors on Mother's side of our family. Am I right, Paulus?'

'Of course you are! I've been told that the Bituriges Vivisei, the people of Burdigala, speak the same language as our kinfolk in Britannia. There must have been a time in the past when the present-day Britons belonged to the same tribe,' Paulus explained with a flourish. 'It seems that a group of these tribespeople crossed the strip of water between Gallia and Britannia to reach Dubris. Once there, they moved inland to inhabit the lands in the west of Britannia.'

'My old granny used to tell stories of the ancient days,' Dilic said with a shiver as she peered into the gathering darkness. 'She said that the gods sent our people to Britannia from a faraway land in the north where freezing snow and blue ice prevailed. They fled to the south in search of a better way of life. Some of my people settled in Armorica in Gallia, or so I think the name was, while other tribes took to their coracles and passed through the narrow straits leading to Britannia. Could such tales be true?'

'Your grandmother was probably right, Dilic. I'm just an old warrior who's at the end of his days. I never pretended to any learning during my youth but, by and large, I hope that my knowledge of your language will help me to understand those folk who live in Burdigala. Do you remember our visit to Pictavis? We could almost understand their tongue as well, so there could have been some links between the Britons and those folk too.'

The huge estuary eventually narrowed where the wide, slow-moving river emptied its brown waters into the ocean. And there on the banks of the river was the town and port of Burdigala that straddled the river on two sides. Paulus pulled his cloak around his shoulders and shivered, for he was struck by the town's appearance of pristine beauty.

As a major crossroads for trade routes between the Atlantic Ocean, the Iberian Peninsula, Britannia and the Middle Sea, the Romans had exploited Burdigala's protected location to move wine, grain, lead, tin and other staples from Rome's furthest provinces into the empire's heart. With Burdigala's prosperity came great wealth and prestige, even after the Visigoths had conquered these lands and made the city their own.

Paulus stared at the bend in the Garumna River where the town had been built. The road entered the town walls near the bank on the eastern side of the town. This side of the river was its least salubrious aspect, because any approach from the east was made through a marshy plain dominated by large areas of low-lying land prone to flooding. Paulus swore gently and slapped at the first stinging insects that were arriving with the fading afternoon light.

A rickety bridge over one of the narrower sections of the river permitted crossings by citizens from both communities and had been preserved by the Visigoths and Vandals to ensure rapid communication between the separate sections of the town. Despite the availability of the bridge, a number of small vessels seemed to be ferrying passengers and goods from one bank to the other, with most of the traffic directed towards the western side of the town where a storm of firefly lights was evident within the welter of activity.

From a patch of higher ground above the marshes, Paulus learned that the secret of success for Burdigala's port was the flow of water along the western bank where the main current ran close to the shore. The force of the current had scoured huge amounts of silt from the river bottom to construct a deep-water channel that permitted the entry and exit of ships.

It was clear to him that vessels were assured of a protected mooring with access to superior wharf facilities. He could see that ships of all shapes and sizes were tethered to the wharves, especially in those moorings where the river's flow was more sedate. To Paulus, the vessels seemed like piglets suckling at the dugs of a sow.

Even from this distance, he recognised some of the distinctive metal traders that would have carried cargoes to Burdigala from the western coast of Britannia. From here, the consignments would be trans-shipped to the City of the Seven Hills. The lifeblood of never-ending commerce continued to provide sustenance for Rome's shrinking arteries, but Paulus wondered if Burdigala would perish if the City of Rome lost its way.

Paulus took a deep breath. He was aware that the task he faced in finding one specific ship's captain within this city might be as difficult as finding a single black hair on his own whiskery chin. Still, he had come too far with his charges to doubt Lady Fortuna's generosity.

'Look at what lies before us, Ambrosius,' he called to the eldest of the two charges. 'We've finally reached Burdigala, so you're within spitting distance of your new home.'

Both children responded with watery grins at his choice of words, for they were aware that every passing mile was taking them further and further from their mother in Venta Belgarum. Yet, with a heart that felt more hopeful than it had been for many months, Paulus kicked his horse's hard belly and the travellers made their way into the city.

CHAPTER X

TRAPPED

Odd figures swimming could be seen among the waste of
waters.

Virgil, *Aeneid*, Book 1

A sour taste filled Pridenow's mouth and he hoped that the wine
he'd drunk during the previous evening would remain within
the confines of his stomach. His horse bridled in affront, for
Pridenow rarely used strong heels to urge his mount into greater
efforts, or seesawed the straight bit on his bridle to inflict pain on
the steed's mouth. For the first time in many days, the young
prince looked around him and wondered where his unleashed
fury and deep shame had brought him.

Two days earlier, he had galloped away from the gates of
Venta Belgarum in an uncontrollable killing rage. Since then, he
had ridden his horse blindly and slept on the ground when the
animal had reached the point of exhaustion. Rational now, and
with his anger almost sated, he looked down at his horse's neck,

chest and flanks. A coating of sweat, foam and grime caused by the beast's efforts dulled its distinctive roan colouring. With a surge of guilt, Pridenow dismounted and began to walk his tired charger in a belated search for water.

'I'm sorry, old friend,' he whispered into the horse's ear. 'I've been suffering from a madness inflicted on me by that evil bastard, but I think I've managed to recover my wits. I've done you harm, Red, but I'll do my best to put matters to rights.'

The horse whickered softly in response, as if it could understand its master's confidences.

'Now! Where in Hades are we?'

He could hear the rushing sound of a fast-flowing stream among the tree line adjacent to the road, so he guided his mount towards the source of this noise. The water was clear and icy-cold, as if it had travelled underground for many miles before coming to the surface in this flat valley floor. Light filtered through the trees that grew vigorously in this small area of forest and then danced in the stream, skittering over the washed stones to enhance their varied colours. No human could partake of the waters in this stream and not be refreshed, in both body and spirit.

Once the horse had drunk its fill, Pridenow became conscious of his own hunger and thirst. He hadn't bothered to eat in the days that had elapsed since he stormed out of his sister's palace. At the time, he'd been desperate to kill something – or anyone.

His explosion of rage had been initiated by simple arrogance on the part of the interloper, Vortigern, who was now the undisputed ruler of Venta Belgarum and, increasingly, the one nobleman whose popularity with the citizenry was such that he would soon be endorsed as the next High King of Britannia.

Severa's visible wounds had healed by now, despite the purple scars that could still be clearly seen. Her wrist still needed support and caused her some pain, but the damage to her spirit was deeper and far more permanent. With a wrench of regret, Pridenow had been forced to accept that his fine, brave sister had lost her wellspring of vitality.

Towards the end of her marriage to Constantine, she had learned to mask her feelings for the sake of her sons and those companions that she held in high esteem. It was important to Severa that she should perpetuate the image of a united and dignified royal family, but she was a shell of the woman she had been.

In the few months that had passed since Vortigern's arrival, the Demetae's brutality had eaten away at Severa's hopes for the future. The loss of her sons was an especially hard blow for this strong woman to confront, but Pridenow believed that her wounds went far deeper than the simple absence of her boys or the death of Constantine. She no longer seemed to care if Vortigern usurped her old duties. He had begun to use her personal throne when he made decisions in the Hall of Justice, as well as meeting her charitable concerns and her negotiations with the kings of the various tribes.

Sadly, she refused to speak of her exiled sons, even to her foster-brother, as if she had wiped their memory from all conscious thought. But, thankfully, she had revealed nothing of their whereabouts to Vortigern, who would have made certain that neither child would ever grow to adulthood.

One morning, near to four months after her children had left her side, and as spring came knocking at the gates of Vortigern's house, the queen called her brother to her courtyard, now edged with still unfurled lime-green leaves and a hint of buds on the gnarled rose trees.

'Life will go on, brother, even if our hearts are cold and weighed down by cares and concerns,' Severa said obliquely, while smoothing the folds of her robe with hands and arms that were laden with rings and jewellery. Vortigern insisted that his queen should display her wealth in plain view where it could be assessed by all and sundry.

'We can't defeat the onset of the seasons, sister,' Pridenow had responded in kind, his gaze roving around the small courtyard as if he expected Vortigern to appear unannounced. Since Vortigern's ascension to power, few servants or nobles in the palace were prepared to speak their minds for fear of retribution. Even Pridenow, normally emboldened by birth and his relative youth, restricted his speech to whispers, for everyone knew that Vortigern had eyes and ears throughout the palace – and elsewhere.

Throwing caution to the winds, Pridenow moved close to his sibling and lifted her hand to his lips.

'This poisonous situation can't be permitted to continue. I've said nothing to Mother, but I swear she knows you are having trouble with the Demetae. I've begged her to keep her distance from Venta Belgarum for fear that Vortigern might inflict harm on her, but she won't listen to me forever. Sooner or later, Severa, you must be prepared to make a stand.'

'I cannot do it!'

Pridenow examined her pale face and recognised the fear in her eyes.

'You are the Queen of Britannia, Severa, so he can hardly have you executed. Even Vortigern wouldn't dare to go that far!'

'You're underestimating him, brother. An illness, a fall, any form of accident ... people can die so easily – and so can I. Only those people who are close to me realise that Vortigern almost beat me to death. Frightened men and women only become aware of matters that are politic to their own circumstances. I wouldn't dare to gainsay Vortigern.' She took a deep breath before continuing. 'Please don't antagonise him, Pridenow. I don't believe I have the ability to save my own brother from the Saxon dogs that leap to do his bidding.'

One of the palace servants entered the room as Severa issued this prophetic warning, so the siblings had no further opportunity to continue the conversation.

The unhappy incident that prompted Pridenow's act of defiance had its genesis in a simple matter of little importance, given the punishments that Vortigern had meted out to Severa on previous occasions. On this occasion, the Demetae had ordered the queen to accompany him to an open forecourt near the Hall of Justice where the citizens of Venta Belgarum set up their markets on a regular weekly basis. To Vortigern's mind, such a festive occasion would be a perfect opportunity for the people of Venta Belgarum to observe the newly established ruling family at a time when they were relaxed and enjoying their leisure. Dressed appropriately for the occasion, the queen complied. She was accompanied by an escort of Saxon guardsmen to ensure her safety.

But she had angered the Demetae by begging Pridenow to accompany her during the coming event. With some reluctance, her brother agreed, although he knew in his heart of hearts that Vortigern would be angered by this challenge to his authority.

At first, the queen seemed joyful as she wandered from stall to stall, while passing compliments to the farmers on the quality of their lambs and calves, and offering congratulations on the size and sweetness of their fruit and vegetables. But she became increasingly animated when she examined a display containing lengths of fine wool among the fabrics that had originated in the north of Britannia. She also purchased several lengths of silk ribbon that had survived the long journey from the exotic lands of the distant East.

As she began to speak to the traders with her erstwhile charm and animation, Pridenow began to think that this outing might contribute to his sister's recovery. Farmers and traders clustered around her and, in the process, Vortigern was ignored and would have been jostled, had his guard not formed a tight circle around him.

These momentary feelings of hope on Pridenow's part were quickly dashed when he saw the stony expression on Vortigern's face. The Demetae hadn't expected to be relegated to a minor role by his wife, so Pridenow knew that his sister would pay the price for her successes with the local population. Vortigern's cruel, smiling mouth was pursed now and a deep frown could be seen.

Then the elderly wife of one of the farmers compounded Vortigern's hurt pride when she suddenly kissed Severa's hand while ignoring Vortigern's presence entirely.

Pridenow saw his sister's spine stiffen when Vortigern took her arm in a lover-like clasp. Severa's facial expression changed instantly, as if her animation and interest had been swiped away by an invisible hand. Pridenow wasn't able to see what had caused this rapid change, but he was certain that Vortigern was behind it.

'Unfortunately, the queen is still in mourning after the death of her husband, so the state of her health is such that she tires easily. She's exhausted; please excuse her if we are forced to cut short our visit to your wonderful displays. Perhaps she'll feel a little better next week and we can make a return visit,' Vortigern explained graciously to those stallholders who were in close proximity to the royal party.

The traders' faces fell in disappointment. Not only was Severa a popular ruler, she always spent her coin on their produce with lavish enthusiasm. The farmers bowed and scraped, while pressing gifts and other offerings upon the queen's tight-lipped attendants.

'I'm so very sorry, my friends, but I've been unwell for a long time now,' Severa apologised. 'I had hoped to enjoy your hospitality for the full day, but I'm afraid it wasn't to be.'

Then, before anything more could be said, Vortigern extricated her from the people and led her away, surrounded by her maids and the small squad of Saxon guardsmen who had accompanied them on this brief excursion.

Back in her rooms, Severa sat among the gifts that had been pressed on her by the common people and wept.

'Why do you obey that lout, Severa?' Pridenow sighed deeply and his fists clenched at the thought of his sister's humiliation. 'You were out in the fresh air and it was obvious to me that you were enjoying yourself, so you should have been permitted to continue with your tour of the markets and your shopping.'

'Vortigern's heart is consumed by his ambition, Pridenow. His jealousy is such that he's reluctant to wait for the people to accept his claims to the throne.' She winced as she collected the gifts into a neat pile.

'Show me your arm, Severa,' Pridenow demanded suspiciously.

He had no solid reason for making this request, other than an itch that lay at the back of his mind.

'No, Pridenow! There's no need for you to become involved in these personal matters. Vortigern is a determined man who would destroy you in a moment if he was to see you as a threat to his plans. I don't want to have your death on my conscience. In any event, the pain he inflicted is of little concern to me.'

'Show me your arm!' the young man demanded again. This time, Severa was unable to meet his eyes.

But, when she still refused, Pridenow gripped her by her good arm and recoiled when she cried out in agony.

The prince rolled up the long sleeves of her robe and as he carefully exposed her arm above the elbow, he inhaled sharply through clenched teeth.

'You mustn't hide such bruises from me, Severa. Never! How can we help you if we're ignorant of the harm that the bastard inflicts on you?'

After a careful inspection, Pridenow could even see some red crescents where Vortigern's nails had gripped her arm so tightly that he had marked her, despite the heavy fabric of her robe.

'You must leave him! I'll ask Brisen and the other ladies to make the preparations needed for you to depart from Venta Belgarum, once the palace is asleep. Sooner or later, Vortigern intends to kill you, Severa.'

'I can't leave him,' Severa whispered, as she hugged her body tightly with both arms.

'Of course you can! You aren't a peasant with neither relatives nor wealth to make an escape impossible. Your parents will defend you from harm if we can devise some way of returning you to them. You know that I speak the truth! I have only one concern that must be addressed if I am to assist you. I need to know if you love this man and care for him. It's important that you tell me now so I can leave you in peace.'

'I hate the bastard with all of my heart and passion! I wish him dead whenever he contrives to come near me,' Severa hissed and her mouth twisted into an ugly snarl. 'I can't leave Vortigern, Pridenow, no matter how much I detest the man. I am with child – his child! God help me, but I have tried my best to kill it. Since then, the Lord Jesus came to me in a dream and he has decreed that Vortigern's child must be born.'

Pridenow's jaw dropped. He had never considered the possibility that Vortigern might have impregnated his sister. This was a personal disaster for Severa, because Vortigern would never allow his child to be raised by strangers. Further complications would arise if this child was a male, because any son born to his sister would also be the grandson of Magnus Maximus. Such a child would consolidate Vortigern's claim to the throne of Britannia.

'Sweet Jesus!' Pridenow blasphemed, for he was no longer able to see any solution to Severa's problems with Vortigern's brutality. 'Does he know?'

'Not yet! I don't know how to tell him. I've convinced myself that he'll want to marry me and tie me to him forever. Once I'm securely bound to him, he'll lock me away until the child is born.'

Her eyes reflected her hopelessness and her expression was downcast. 'I have no alternative other than to stay with him. I don't want to lose another child.'

Pridenow took his sister into his arms and tried to console her as best he could.

Perhaps Pridenow could have come to accept the impossible

political situation in which he had become embroiled if he had been able to maintain a low profile when he was within Vortigern's sphere of influence. But Vortigern was aware of the power that Pridenow exerted over the queen, so he missed no opportunity to provoke the young man into taking some form of precipitate action. The Demetae king decided to initiate a confrontation whereby the young man could be executed or, alternatively, he could be banished from the kingdom. The time was on hand whereby Vortigern must redouble his efforts to remove this young prince.

Pridenow was forced to grit his teeth and grin like an idiot when Vortigern cast blatant insults in the young man's direction. Those British warriors who had served under Pridenow's command in the past were aghast at what they saw as cowardly responses to slurs that they would have answered with threats of a sword and shield. But Pridenow was determined to hold his temper for Severa's sake, regardless of the provocations that were placed before him by a determined enemy.

Only two days previously, Vortigern had hosted a small celebration attended by the kings of the Atrebates, the Cantii and the Regni tribes where he announced his impending marriage to the widow of Constantine. The Demetae had deliberately chosen the rulers of the weakest of the tribal clans influenced by their proximity to Venta Belgarum, for this was the region where he would begin his campaign to achieve the Britannic throne. These three sycophants would be easily browbeaten.

Then, when Pridenow realised that he had received a personal invitation by name, the young warrior's heart sank at the potential for ambush and tragedy that could follow from his attendance at this celebration.

Nor were his reservations unfounded.

The feast was little more than an excuse for a night of gorging and drinking, pastimes that held no appeal for Pridenow, who was a temperate young man.

Perhaps the dark gifts associated with the sight made the prince unwilling to relinquish control of his mind to the stupefying effects of alcohol. Any man whose life can be blotted out during trances that aren't of his choice will be wary of what he might say or do when he is in his cups. Perhaps Pridenow simply felt contempt towards those drunkards who had a choice of whether to drink, or not.

Whatever the reason, Pridenow watched intoxicated men lose their inhibitions as wine and beer dulled their brains and robbed them of their coordination. The king of the Regni tribe, a large young man who was prone to fat, spilled as much liquor as he drank from his pewter mug, while his gesticulations became larger and grew clumsier by the minute. One young warrior threw his arm across the shoulders of an older companion and giggled foolishly as the Regni king splashed him with wine. With an unconscious sneer, Pridenow showed his contempt for men who were so unwise as to expose themselves to the ridicule of servants, and the ever-alert green eyes of Vortigern.

For Vortigern missed nothing and would forget nothing of what he saw in an entertainment such as this. Words would be spoken and secrets exposed during the course of the night, much to the cost of those fools who had been seduced by the Demetae's rich food and a river of alcohol.

When Pridenow had eventually arrived at the open courtyard, late and unrepentant, he found that Vortigern's guests were congregated around four massive spits that had been set up in the open to roast two sweet-smelling pigs and a complete steer that the servants had butchered into two separate halves. Servants were standing beside each of the spits to wield the large brushes that would baste the meats with fat, edible oils and salt, while the crackling popped and exploded and sent delicious smells wafting on the breeze. Other, brawnier, servants had been given the task of turning the spit to ensure that the meat roasted evenly. The bodies of these servants were slick with sweat and grease, for they had stripped themselves to the waist to facilitate the preparation of the feast.

Still more servants ran from guest to guest with amphorae of wine and huge jugs of ale. The invited kings and their retinues had already consumed a river of liquor and were boisterous from its effects. Most of the guests were speaking with raised voices and were demonstrating the natural laughter of men who had drunk too much in a very short time. The cacophony of voices was deafening, the jumble of sound almost unintelligible. For all that, Pridenow was still able to discern that Vortigern was considered to be a fine fellow, one who was far more approachable than his predecessor, Constantine, had been. This Demetae was generous with his food and drink, and he took pains to be friendly. More importantly, he never belittled them as the late emperor had done.

Pridenow, grateful that Paulus wasn't able to hear the slurs that were being made against the decurion's erstwhile commander, found a convenient seat, accepted a mug of dark ale and tried to merge his body into the background at the rear of the assembled guests.

But Vortigern saw him immediately and his wolfish eyes gleamed with anticipation.

From certain angles, those distinctive eyes were burning yellow in the firelight and Pridenow was reminded of the sculpture of a satyr he had once seen in the ruins of a villa outside of Corinium. That stone figure had been brightly painted to suit the taste of its Roman owners, but the weather had dulled the black painted fur of the animal's hind legs and glossy hoofs, while its devilish facial features had sneered in Pridenow's direction with the amused yellow eyes that Vortigern's now resembled.

The bastard intends to trap me in front of witnesses, Pridenow thought, while discreetly spilling his beer on to the cobblestones. Survival might rely on keeping his wits intact.

Meanwhile, the noise from the celebrations was increasing in volume. The guests were ushered into the King's Hall and were obviously impressed by the delights that had been prepared and presented on the dining tables. Huge platters of steaming meat; jugs of rich gravy; mounds of roasted vegetables; cascades of stuffed songbirds and candied nuts, as well as cornucopias of heavy pastry filled with fruit glazed with honey and rivers of wine and ales had been placed on view and the guests were only awaiting Vortigern's invitation to commence their attack on the delicacies. The sounds of revelry were rising into the rafters in a cacophony of raised voices as men lost their senses, their manners and their moral boundaries. Pridenow watched their drunken foolishness and felt a shiver of apprehension rise up his spine till it reached the base of his neck. In circumstances such as these, powerful men could be convinced to believe anything and everything if it was presented to them as fact.

What was Vortigern playing at?

Suddenly, the clash of two brass cymbals sounded, and the

guards indicated that the guests should hear Vortigern's address in silence.

'Good fortune to you all!' Vortigern shouted as the room quietened. He raised his cup in his right hand in salute. Then with a wide smile, he bit deeply into a slice of meat that he held in his left hand. The rich juices spurted over his chin and fouled the fine fabric of his outer robe. He masticated the meat voraciously with his all-too-white teeth to demonstrate to his guests that his food was safe to eat and there was no reason for them to fear poisoning. As he chewed with his mouth open, Vortigern's exposed canines gleamed in the light from a dozen oil lamps and the fire pits that banished the last of the cold night air.

'May years of good fortune visit you, Vortigern, for you're a fine fellow,' one of the Atrebates nobles roared, while thumping his empty drinking mug on to the table top beside him.

'You're a lucky bastard, Vortigern,' one of the Regni nobles shouted. 'All this and a beautiful widow lady who'd put a smile on to any man's face! She'd surely add comfort to a man's bed after two years without a man by her side. You're Fortune's Favourite, you dog!'

Vortigern's tousled head snapped back at the retort, and his good mood suddenly evaporated. The young prince shivered. To Pridenow, the pretender to the throne looked like an autumn wolf before its coat began to whiten for the coming winter. His eyes were flat and lupine and Pridenow recalled the words from a prediction that he'd made in those days when he rode with Paulus.

'Beware the Wolf of Midnight.'

Vortigern strode over to the Regni nobleman and stared directly into the man's suddenly sober eyes.

'What did you say, sir? I trust you're simply in your cups and you have no intention of casting slurs on the reputation of the woman who has agreed to become my wife.'

The unfortunate Regni suddenly discovered that the friends who had been clustered around him had shifted away and left him in an empty space that was newly charged with threat.

'I apologise for my foolishness, Lord Vortigern. I meant no disrespect to you or to your queen. I only . . . I wish to extend my congratulations on such excellent tidings. Indeed, Lady Severa is fortunate to have won the affection of a warrior of your status, especially a man who has served the cause of the British people with such loyalty and distinction.'

'You're rambling, Willem, so I'd suggest you close your mouth and remain quiet,' Vortigern snapped, but he smiled vaguely towards the unfortunate man to demonstrate to his guests that no blood would be shed over the Regni's careless words. 'I thank you for your good wishes, Willem, but I would reiterate to everyone here that Lady Severa is the High Queen of the Britons and she is a woman who is beyond price. Queen Severa has given birth to two healthy sons for her dead husband and, subject to God's will, she'll also give me strong and powerful heirs who will serve Britannia in the years to come. For the moment, one thing is certain. The Saxon invasion will resume with the arrival of the spring tides. I can safely predict a Saxon summer where we will all be forced to contribute towards the destruction of their warriors. With the inevitability of their attacks in mind, it is my intention to wed my bride without ceremony. I will then fulfil my duty to her – and to the British people.'

Pridenow barely concealed a groan of despair.

The usurper has just suggested that the rape and his proposed marriage to my sister were carried out to demonstrate his loyalty to the citizens of Britannia. The bastard is devilishly clever and he's put his plans into effect with skill and determination, Pridenow thought despairingly as he watched the other guests nod their support for the Demetae's planned actions.

We are lost!

The only sound that could be heard during Vortigern's speech was a scraping sound when one of the stools was upended by a nervous visitor who wanted to distance himself from his host's notice. The sound of the falling chair was unnaturally loud in the silence. Then, as if eager to fill the void, the king of the Regni tribe raised his mug and offered a toast to Vortigern.

'All hail to Vortigern, High King of the Britons!'

Then the entire gathering took up the call in a roar that shook the rafters.

'*All hail to Vortigern, High King of the Britons!*'

'You aren't drinking, my brother.' Vortigern's voice cut across the enthusiastic cries of praise and congratulations. Once again, his aggressive tone of voice and his wolfish stare left a sudden silence in its wake.

'Queen Severa is my ruler, as well as my sister, Lord Vortigern. She is concerned for my well-being and has instructed me to avoid drinking liquor until I am old enough to control its effects on my person. In accordance with her wishes, I have made certain that I drink sparingly and avoid the embarrassments associated with drunkenness, even at feasts such as yours.'

Pridenow was underestimating Vortigern's persistent malice by offering such tepid praise. The eyes of the usurper glittered lividly and his voice was silky from his obvious anger.

It was only the courage inherited from his noble ancestors

that stopped Pridenow from flinching in panic. He managed to imagine Caradoc, his grandfather, steadying him with a strong hand on his shoulder, which helped him to stare fixedly at Vortigern with a calm expression on his face.

'Regardless of my bride's instructions, young man, I insist that you will drink with my friends on this particular occasion as a mark of respect for the throne of Britannia's ruler.'

Each syllable uttered by Vortigern was clipped short and fell into the unnatural silence, much like a fallen pebble would sound if it was dropped into a deep well.

Sadly, every man in the King's Hall could read the threat that was ever-present in the Demetae's warnings to the young prince.

And so, left without choice, Pridenow raised his mug high into the air.

'You have my congratulations, Lord Vortigern. May you always understand and appreciate the rare, priceless worth of my sister. And may you also protect her from the vicissitudes of the wicked world in which we live.'

Vortigern raised his own cup in acknowledgement, but his eyes were unreadable. 'Severa is the High Queen and I will treasure her in the future as I have always done in the past – both for her beauty and for her worth.'

But Pridenow could almost hear the unspoken words. For the young man, Vortigern's loyalties were obvious.

I will treat her as I've always done, Pridenow, so learn to live with it.

A low hum of conversation began to thread its way through the King's Hall as the drunken guests tried to decipher the cryptic conversation that had taken place between the Demetae king and Severa's foster-brother. Their efforts would be unsuccessful, yet every man present could sense that there had been a threat – and a counter-threat.

But could the boy and the usurper be reconciled without bloodshed?

'I've been told you have an infirmity, lad, a malaise that ensures you are tied to your mother's apron strings. I'm told that this illness was the real reason you weren't prepared to prove your manhood when our warriors were fighting in the hell-holes of Gallia.'

Pridenow drew a deep breath, while ignoring the titters and muffled laughter from those guests surrounding the two protagonists. He knew he must keep a cool head and control his temper when he was in the company of this particular monster, a man who was determined to bait him into an unfortunate course of action. Here, Pridenow would be the only loser in any confrontations that took place.

'I've been cautioned for all of my life by parents who have been bound by a curse that was uttered on the family by my maternal grandmother, a famed seer. Some of your guests will have heard of her deeds as a wise woman. The seer was adamant that those men from King Caradoc's immediate family who possess grey eyes must be forbidden to leave the Britannic lands. She told the king that a man who fitted this description would be required to carry out some task that would be of great importance to the Dumnonii tribe at some time in the future. She warned him that the Mother would inflict a punishment on the tribe if a grey-eyed male from the royal family crossed the waters – although no specifics were given.'

Several of the visiting nobles nodded their heads in agreement, for they were familiar with Pridenow's unusual and distinguished family line and were aware of the curse, which was common knowledge in the far west of Britannia. But their acknowledgement of the tale only served to sharpen Vortigern's tongue.

'This was only a convenient tale designed to relieve you from travelling into danger with your kinsman, Constantine, when he sailed off to Gallia.'

'I was also a callow youth when Constantine made his foray into the wilderness of Gallia, as you well know, my lord. I was less than fourteen at the time. But I was wild to ride with Constantine, as you also know, for you had been given the task of training me to become a warrior. I have now become the warrior and leader that you trained for future command.'

This barb found its mark and Vortigern bit his lip in annoyance.

'But your sister has told me that you suffer from a shameful family ailment. As I'm about to marry into your family, I'm entitled to know what might be expected from your line.'

'Would it not be in your best interests to hold such a discussion in private, my lord?'

'I've already determined that there will be no secrets between myself and my friends and allies who will be in my company. Do you have such illnesses or inadequacies? It may be that my warriors and allies will be forced to fight alongside you during the coming spring and summer. Should they fear to stand in the line with you when we go into battle?'

After much needling, Vortigern could smell blood and his guests were engrossed in the ebb and flow of the conversation, despite understanding little of the battle of wills.

'I have nothing to hide, Lord Vortigern, for I spring from the bloodline of King Caradoc of the Dumnonii tribe, a man whose lineage and courage have never been in question. I have inherited the ability to catch glimpses of the future through the female line of my family. Strangely for one whom the Old Ones have chosen to act on their behalf, I rarely remember anything that I see of the predictions that are given to others through me. I am usually told of the prophecies after the event by those around me. One thing I know for certain is that my gifts have no bearing on my courage or my loyalty to those who deserve it. The one thing that has been of use to me is that I've inherited her ability to recognise the hidden world that exists within men's souls.'

I'm exaggerating my position, Pridenow thought, but we'll see how the bastard handles these pieces of information.

Vortigern had reared back at the young man's response, reminding Pridenow of the aggression of a disturbed snake. The eyes of the usurper were like glittering holes within his features, but Pridenow could sense he was reluctant to discuss matters of superstition.

'This is a strange gift that smacks of witchery! This is a flaw that could prove dangerous to someone with the delicacy of our queen. You've managed to imperil her and frighten her with these gifts of yours, so I will expect you to keep your distance from her in the future. She's been ill in recent times, and I don't want her frightened by imagined threats to her person.'

'My sister has no reason to fear me, for I am her brother. She's quite familiar with those places where dangers to her person reside.'

Pridenow had finally lost his temper and Vortigern swooped on the young man's mistake with ill-disguised malice.

'Do you have the presumption to suggest that I would harm the queen? Your arrogance knows no bounds, young man, if you think you can spread seditious rumours with impunity. Who has suborned you in these matters? And who has encouraged you to cause friction between myself and my friends?'

'I've only answered the questions you have asked, my lord. I was content to sit here and celebrate the announcement of your approaching nuptials.'

'Get out of my sight until I have time to consider what I'm to do with you. You're an unrepentant traitor and, by your own admission, you have unnatural thoughts that pass through your brain. I'm forced to wonder if you have killed the queen's sons!'

An irate Pridenow slammed his mug on to the table with such force that the drinking vessel shattered and the shards scattered on to the floor to join the bones, broken platters and spilled beer that had accumulated at the feet of the revellers.

'You're a barbarian, Pridenow! Offensive gestures such as the one you just made is a disgrace to all civilised Britons. Leave now, before I decide to take more precipitate action.'

Pridenow could barely restrain his rage as he stalked out of the hall with the imprecations of Vortigern following in his wake. The Demetae's eyes were cold, but Pridenow knew better than to turn and look at his nemesis, for he knew that Vortigern had always intended to cause a breach between brother and sister. Both men knew that Severa was easier to control without her brother by her side. For his part, Vortigern knew that the whelp posed no great threat, because he lacked the strength, the wisdom or the methodology to unseat a ruler who was so firmly entrenched.

From this time onward, Queen Severa would be forced to stand alone with only her women for support. In one fell swoop, Vortigern had stripped her of her mainstay while separating her from her adopted parents in Corinium. He had also begun a rumour that Pridenow had assassinated Constantine's young heirs to further his own ambition.

Vortigern drank deeply that evening; and he allowed himself the pleasure of smiles of satisfaction. A buzz of gossip would sizzle through the south-west in the days and weeks that followed, but Pridenow refused to respond to the slurs. He was already travelling into the north.

Severa had anticipated that Vortigern would force Pridenow's departure from the palace, and had said as much to her brother, a warning that caused him to suffer pangs of guilt for his imprudence in matching wits with Vortigern.

'Vortigern is a grown man, a king, and he's well used to connivance and political trickery. You're not yet sixteen, my dear, so how could you possibly expect to best him?'

'I didn't want to react to him. I just wanted to divert his malice. Truly, Severa, I ignored insult after insult from the man. But, eventually, he went too far and I lost my head.'

Severa laughed drily. 'We'll have to hope that this doesn't happen, because Vortigern would be overjoyed if he could easily remove your head from your body. Never mind! At least we know that the boys are alive and we can accept that he fears their continued existence. That's something!'

'I've ruined everything by responding to his taunts! You'll be alone, Severa, truly alone – and it will be my fault.'

'It's of little concern now, brother! The man is a devil and I'm being selfish by trying to keep you close to this man who wouldn't hesitate to have you killed. I'm sorry now for any hasty words of criticism, but it is certain that you must leave Venta Belgarum –

and you must leave immediately if you value your life as much as I do.'

'I'll think of some way to let you know how to send a message to me. Please call for me, Severa, if you ever have need of me. You know that I'll come to your aid, whatever the cost. You know that!'

Then, as he rose to his feet and brushed away a few tears, Severa raised one hand to hold him back for a moment.

'Please promise me that you'll keep in contact with my sons and give them your assistance in the years that lie before us. I'm trapped in Venta Belgarum now, so I'll never be free of Vortigern. But he has made the mistake of setting you loose and not taking your life. He views you as being of so little account that you're not worth the effort of killing. I'm the prize! But even Vortigern makes mistakes and he's fallen into the sin of hubris by under-estimating you. You can serve me in countless ways and, if you're prepared to do so, my hopes and prayers will remain with you for the rest of my life.'

'I'd have hoped that you'd pray for me anyway,' Pridenow replied. The sombre mood was immediately broken when Severa punched her brother on the shoulder. She shook her hand in mock-agony as if she'd hurt herself by striking his hard muscles.

Laughter and tears! Severa thought. We're reduced to such extremes within this house of horrors. But her heart had been set from the moment she realised that Vortigern's child was swelling inside her belly. She wasn't prepared to risk the life of this child, even though it had sprung from Vortigern's seed. She had feared that Ambrosius and Uther would be lost and forgotten, but Vortigern himself had created a new myth about them when he taunted Pridenow over their fate. Severa was confident that anyone who knew Pridenow would never believe that her foster-brother had orchestrated their deaths, and that regular references to them would serve to keep their names with the memories of the people. Somehow, the young man must find a way to save the boys and ensure that they prospered.

Pridenow gave his sister his promise, but his self-loathing and frustrated rage had overwhelmed his mood and his conscious thoughts. Perhaps some intimations of the future were churning inside him and clouding his brain, although no conscious images were forming in his fervent imagination. Once the poisonous atmosphere of Venta Belgarum was receding behind him, however, the dead came swarming back to haunt him.

He had galloped away from Venta Belgarum and ridden along Roman roads that were peopled with the ghosts that existed within his imagination. Night and day, the phantoms in his brain tormented him. Some of these spirits wore the faces of men he remembered from the feast in Venta Belgarum, although they had been hale and hearty when he had last seen them. Others were complete strangers, men who swarmed about his terrified horse and reached out to him with dead, blood-spattered hands.

Did these phantasms come from the future? Or were they spirits from the past? Their numbers included Romans in bloody armour, farmers carrying sharpened hoes in cadaverous hands and even empty-faced Saxons who begged him to save them from this long road that led into nothingness.

Regardless of whether it was the gloom of evening or the sharp clarity of morning, the dead continued to swarm along the endless dusty road. It seemed to Pridenow that this road was the only path they knew, so they were doomed to walk along its cobbled surface while the living ignored their presence. But

Pridenow could see and hear the phantasms now for they were clustered threateningly around him while demanding to be heard as they implored the young man for aid and comfort.

Impotent and shaking, the young prince had ridden his horse to exhaustion and almost caused its death for, by trying to escape from the dead eyes that haunted him, he'd ridden like a madman. But, even at full gallop, Pridenow wasn't able to outrun the hordes of the dead.

The north-west embraced him as an escape route, but he rejected the familiar way to Corinium. His guilt was such that he was reluctant to seek comfort from his mother, so he removed her from his plans.

Silence beckoned as the prince sought an opportunity to gain some peaceful rest.

Perhaps some time spent in the solitude and safety of the deep woods would force the spectral army to leave him be. Perhaps the silence could banish their intemperate hands and transparent faces.

Pridenow fled into the north.

CHAPTER XI

IN THE MOUNTAIN HALLS

Honesty is praised and left to shiver.

Juvenal, *Satires*, 1:74

For no particular reason, other than a need to find a safe place to rest his horse and ease his tired bones, Pridenow led the exhausted animal across the stream and upwards through the light brush until he entered the sparse woodland areas that skirted the base of a line of hills. These ancient escarpments quickly gained his attention, because some rose in green mounds while others revealed evidence of mining that would have enriched Phoenician, Greek and Roman prospectors for years beyond counting.

The undead had finally released him once he moved off the Roman road to follow a lightly used farmers' track, but he could now feel a pressure on his temples as if he had dived into a pond of deep water, so he continued to ride into the hills where he was certain that a peaceful campsite could be found.

The young warrior rested often because his limbs felt weak and his thoughts skittered around and around with thoughts of the disasters of the past few months. Gratefully, his horse cropped the spring grasses that were growing in the glades. In some of these wild places, the feeling of remoteness was such that he could imagine he was the very first man to wander between these ancient trees or drink the clear water from the many springs that came bubbling out of the slopes to trickle their way downwards to join the stream that now snaked through the woods below him.

The afternoon was silent and the forest was cloaked in a quiet that made the hair rise on Pridenow's arms as ancient superstitions stirred within him. Had the gods walked in these woods and drenched this place with the scent of magic? The lad shook his head to banish this foolishness, yet some remnants of past rituals teased his senses. Grimly, he continued to climb.

The vegetation thinned out and those brambles and saplings that were of an advanced age had wrapped their ancient roots around the boulders that anchored the trees along the steeper slopes. Flint and scree made the upward trek more dangerous underfoot and the horse whinnied in complaint. When Pridenow stumbled over the entrance to a disused mine, the steed was quietened when he tethered it to a gorse bush near a patch of long grass that it began to crop.

Evidence of a ruined timber structure adjacent to a dark hole in the rocks suggested that this mine was of Roman construction, as was the still-visible track that wound its way down the easier slopes of the hill. Pridenow climbed into the gaping blackness, although he took the precaution of making a rough torch by wrapping a spare tunic around a length of branch. His saddlebags had revealed a small vial of perfumed oil, a gift from Severa, that he poured all over the cloth to add an accelerant to the fabric and a twist of dry grass. Once he had plied his flints to catch a spark and the torch began to burn, he made a tentative exploration of the mine.

Pridenow possessed a boyish curiosity for dark and secretive underground places. He was still young enough to be excited by the possibility of adventure and he wondered what treasure might have been left behind in the Stygian darkness of the horizontal shaft.

Initially, the passage was wide enough to stand, although taller Britons would have had to bend over to make their way through the shaft. The roof and walls bore the scars from human implements and, with awe, Pridenow noticed that a river of glittering grey-black residue had spilled on to the floor of the shaft from countless barrowloads of galena ore that had been dragged to the mine entrance.

Pridenow had been told of the many ways by which silver and lead were extracted from the galena ore, a commodity that was highly prized by the Romans, and Roman miners had been engaged in this trade in the early years of their conquest of Britain. Many of these mines were under water now, but, so far, this particular mine was dry and dusty.

The veins of ore were still visible by the fitful light from Pridenow's torch and he could see traces of metal that appeared like a silvery-black leviathan stretching into the darkness. Grey crystals caught the light like small stars and Pridenow was charmed and fascinated by these wonders. Occasionally, a discarded wooden handle from some ancient tool was lying among the dust of ages to mutely explain that the decision to abandon this mine had been hurriedly made. The young warrior was teased with many questions. Why had this mine been deserted? What disaster had befallen the slaves who had laboured for so long beneath the earth?

Even in this underground vault, Pridenow could still hear the voices from the lost, but these ghosts were speaking in whispers and they were using languages he wasn't able to understand. His rational mind told him that he was alone in the mine shaft, and that these spectral voices belonged to long-dead slaves who had laboured out of the light to bring wealth to their Roman masters.

Besides, like most adventurous young men, he had a fascination for the magic that was still evident in this ancient place. Somewhere, far below him, he could hear the sound of rushing waters, and he wondered if some of the tunnels that had been cut into the bowels of these hills had been flooded by underground rivers. He had no doubts that some distant cataracts flowed, moved and regularly changed course as they made their way through the hills. Their dark song could be clearly discerned through the echoes sounding in this dry tunnel that enclosed Pridenow in its dusty arms.

The main shaft led to a number of other tunnels that branched off to the left, to the right and, occasionally, downwards. In several cases, these shafts had collapsed over time and the serpentine passages were completely blocked by rubble. Yet more yawned open to the prince's wondering eyes, because his torch was the first light to intrude into this silent gravesite for many years. With a thrill of anticipation, he entered one of the larger tunnels and brought the light from his torch on to the rich seams of galena that seemed to permeate these hills like arteries filled with black blood.

He found the rusted remnants of broken manacles and felt a frisson of horror when his fingers touched these relics of the past. A man had struggled to work and walk with his ankles bound with a long chain of linked bracelets of iron. Had the wearer died here, far from the cleansing light of the sun? Or had he managed to experience a brief period of freedom before the guards had hammered new shackles that would bind him to this mine forever?

The tunnel narrowed and Pridenow was forced to crawl on hands and knees. For the first time, he sensed the weight of the hill pressing down on him, but he felt no terror. This passageway enfolded him, like the arms of a mother who protected him with her whole body from the pain and dangers inflicted by a vicious and demanding world. He found himself curling into a foetal ball as if the hill was charming him to rest here forever as the child of these ancient places. With an enormous mental effort, he broke free from the hill's glamour and forced his leaden limbs to crawl onwards.

Suddenly, after following the tunnel on hands and knees as it rose gradually in front of him, he came to a section of the tunnel where thread-like roots from a variety of trees were growing down from the roof of the shaft.

'I must be close to the surface,' Pridenow said to himself in a low voice, for the passage was silent and oppressive. He felt a faint draught of cool air and decided that a tree had forced some opening to appear in the roof of the tunnel above him. He manoeuvred his body through a network of fibrous roots that curtained half the passage until his questing hand fell on something smooth and peculiar, something that had no place in this world of rock and rubble that was living proof of nature's endless power.

His hand recoiled as he edged forward, for his fingers had traced the outline of a skull.

A full skeleton was caught upright in the trailing roots of the tree as if the corpse could still stand. The smooth, yellowed skull had black holes where Pridenow knew there once had been eyes and a nose, while the shrivelled body seemed only an eye-blink away from life.

The bones belonged to the corpse of a young woman.

Rags of ancient, earth-coloured clothing still covered the curves of the ribcage and held the delicate bones of the legs and feet in position. The female clothing had been bound together by the curling tendrils of underground tree roots. This woman had been young, Pridenow decided immediately, because her upper jaw was still in place and the mouth contained a full complement of teeth. He found the lower jaw on the floor of the shaft and a mass of reddish hair at the skeleton's feet, where it had fallen. With a sigh, Pridenow noted that a knotted length of rope was tied around the neck and vertebrae of the pathetic remains.

'She must have been strangled,' Pridenow whispered, for he was unwilling to break the unnatural silence that held sway in the shaft, despite longing for the sound of a human voice. Even as he realised the woman's fate, his foot felt something solid on the floor of the tunnel. He fumbled after the object as he reached down among the fallen bones to pick it up.

The torch was beginning to burn up the last of the accelerant, but sufficient light remained to pick out an earring with crimson stones that caught the fitful flame like drops of blood. In only a moment, he had found its pair, as well as a crucifix that hung around the skeleton's neck. When he snapped the chain to release the necklace, the skeleton broke free from its supporting nest of roots and crumpled into a jumble of disconnected bones on the passage floor, as if this body had only remained upright until a stranger came to set the corpse free from her tomb.

A puff of dust and rotting cloth caused Pridenow to cough uncontrollably and, as the light from the torch began to gutter, the young man saw that the tunnel ended abruptly a few feet beyond the fallen pile of stained bones.

Pridenow crossed himself, partly out of superstition and partly in relief. Whoever the young woman might have been, her soul would have long departed and no wraith remained in the dark tomb to trouble any living explorer.

Pridenow scrambled from the main tunnel in a choking, still-coughing panic, but with the almost-dead torch, the earrings and the crucifix grasped firmly in his hands. When the torch began to die, Pridenow had almost decided to retrace his steps and return to the entrance. It was patently obvious to the young man that he could become lost and he would be trapped underground until his own body became a skeleton that was bound into a trap of tree roots. Grateful at making good his escape, he collapsed on to the sharp blades of grass and stared at the dying sun through a red and orange sky.

His horse nuzzled his face with its soft black lips.

As his pulse settled and his breathing returned to normal, the young man laid the mine's treasure on to a rock so he could examine the jewels in the last of the day's light.

'She was young and she must have been wealthy,' he said aloud for comfort. 'The gems and the gold settings are too fine to have come from British artisans.'

The earrings had thick shanks that were inserted through holes driven through the ear lobes and then locked into place. They would have hung down to an adult woman's collarbone and the pieces must have been very heavy.

She'd only have worn these jewels on special occasions, Pridenow decided, when he lifted one to check its weight. She must have been trying to look her very best on the day she died, or she was trying to impress the man who killed her. Four large cabochon rubies glinted inside their gold settings with a deep fire that was brought to life by the ambient light. The other precious objects, including some tiny seed pearls that had been attached to the chain holding the crucifix, glowed softly. The pearls shivered from the warmth of his hands.

When he'd snatched the necklace from the corpse, he'd also dislodged some of the rotting rope that had become entangled in the chain. The knot in the garrotte was still in place around her neck, but the rope had frayed away with age, leaving a grisly record of this unknown woman's death.

Something about that simple garrotte sparked a fleeting memory that refused to come to life inside Pridenow's conscious mind. Something hideous was gnawing at him – a vague memory of a memory. Perhaps it was an old woman's tale of the early days, a time when human sacrifices were made to appease angry gods. But why here? The bones in that shaft weren't so old that they could be classed as ancient. Pridenow struck his forehead with the palm of his hand to vent his frustration.

But the memory he was trying to recall wouldn't solidify within his mind.

Suddenly hungry, the young man searched through his saddle-bags for something that could be eaten, but he must have devoured all his supplies during his headlong dash from Venta Belgarum. Also hungry, his horse whickered softly, as if to remind his master that he too needed water and a comfortable stable. Convinced that there was no reason to remain here, Pridenow used the last of the light to return to the Roman road. To his surprise, the dead-straight carriageway was deserted. Not a single ghost, wraith or spirit was attempting to stagger, caper or run towards him. The long stretch of road was empty under the rising white disc of a full moon.

'It's time to go to Aquae Sulis, Red. There'll be lots of oats there that'll be certain to fill your belly,' Pridenow said into his horse's ear. Then he swung into the saddle with the energetic flexibility of youth before riding away into the developing night.

The ceols loomed out of the mist, while the rowers dug into their reserves of strength to send the awkward, broad-waisted vessels ploughing through the rippling water and up the gritty sand to come to a halt at the high-water mark. With two warriors left to guard the boat, the rest of the crew lowered the single sail, tossed their oars into the hull and then used muscle-power to drag the ceols to safety along the line of dried black seaweed. Once the vessels were secured, the Saxon warriors took their weapons and strode through the dunes to vanish into the wind-scoured brush that edged the cove.

Behind them, other ceols followed. These craft might have been squat and ugly, but they were deadly in their unprepossessing functionality. The men who came ashore were like their boats, for they were large and bulky; they wore heavy furs and had stiff hair and beards that darkened their natural colouring. Had any Britons been present to watch this landing, they would have noticed the smell of these raiders first, for they reeked of the bear fat, unwashed wool and body odour that the wind would have brought ashore to the Britons' nostrils. Despite the long journey from Jutland or Saxony, these seafarers rarely immersed their bodies in water.

The northern raiders might have been unclean pagans, but they held physical advantages over the Cantii and Regni warriors who had been forced to oppose them during the four years that had passed since Constantine had abandoned them and left them to fight under their own auspices. To a man, they were superb physical specimens.

Furthermore, the lands to the north of the raiders' homelands had experienced severe weather conditions and regular famines for many years, resulting in a massive migration of northern refugees who were seeking a better life by usurping the lands of their neighbours. Landless, angry and desperate for a better way of life, there was no dearth of skilled warriors who were prepared to infiltrate their number into the British homelands.

The average northern raider was well over six feet tall and was armed with fighting axes, spears and fighting swords, weaponry well suited to his superior reach. Although their reputation in battle was second to none, the few Romans who remained in Britannia were even shorter than the British tribal warriors, so they were forfeiting as much as ten inches in reach to the invaders. Under their heavy furs and woollen cloaks, the Saxons were heavy-boned, broad-chested and muscular, whereas the tribal warriors at Vortigern's disposal were young, slighter in build and, more importantly, inexperienced.

And so, with the arrival of spring, the Saxons landed on Britannia's shores with their brutally effective ceols. Here, they would rape, steal and terrorise the local population into submission so that few of the local lords would raise a hand in protest.

Britannia was under attack and, so far, the Britons were mostly ignorant of the intentions of these fur-clad giants who were searching for a new homeland that would be far removed from the snow-covered wastelands of the frozen north.

A week after the Saxon raiders had settled into their new encampment, a dim moon washed over a fully provisioned encampment in the small cove. The Saxon flotilla had managed to avoid detection, because the cove was too small for use as a port by British fishermen and the difficult landscape of swampy ground and patchy woodlands rendered agriculture impractical.

The leader of this particular raid was a thane whose home was in the lands that bordered Frisia. Herkeld Black-Tooth's name had been derived from a large, black tooth that dominated his fearsome smile, the result of a blow from an axe handle that killed the tooth's root.

Herkeld was driven by old resentments, the greatest of which was the loss of his clan's broad acres when he was a young man. Unable to recover his heritage, he preyed on the sheep of Britannia in his middle years, stripping these lands bare in the spring and summer, before sailing back to the barren lands that he had taken by force from a weaker thane.

Herkeld's pickings in the Cantii lands had been lucrative and easily harvested. In the previous season, his raiders had sacked the town of Portus Lemanis and then extended their influence inland to Durovernum and up the coast to Rutupiae. Lightning-fast raids had won gold and silver plate from British churches, as well as a groaning chests of coins, jewellery and artefacts that were sent back to the palisades that protected his wealth in Frisia. But nothing could fill the void in Herkeld's breast, for he could never forget the wife and children who'd been slaughtered when he had been driven from his homeland a decade earlier by raiders who attacked Frisia from the northern wastelands.

Once the ceols had disgorged their cargoes of men, supplies and weaponry, and the Saxon encampment had been secured behind a rough, circular wall of sharpened tree trunks, Herkeld called his captains together for a council of war. While pouring their mugs of native lager, Herkeld began to issue his orders.

'Roganvaldar, my friend, you'll have forty men in your command and I want you to reconnoitre the lands near the village of Anderida. There's a wide Roman road on the western margins of this port, so any traffic that is moving along the road should be easy to intercept. We need supplies for the spring and summer and any gold or silver that you find will never go amiss. Can you carry out this task for me?'

Roganvaldar White-Hair was a tall man with whitish-blond hair, tanned features and broad muscular shoulders. Unfortunately, the Jute had been struck across the face with some form of weapon that left him with a puckered scar that started on his right cheekbone, stretched across his nose and finished on his opposite jaw where the cicatrix was a finger-width across. The smile he directed towards his comrade appeared as a ferocious scowl and his open mouth revealed that this old wound had also knocked a number of teeth from his mouth.

'I can swear by the life of my son that there'll be no movement along that road without the full payment of your taxes, my lord.'

Behind Roganvaldar, a blond-haired youth of extraordinary beauty was deeply engrossed in his allotted task of cleaning and polishing his father's armour. The similarities were such that there could be no doubt that this boy was Roganvaldar's son and heir.

'This is good, but as difficult as my orders might be, I have one further hard task that will be allotted to Torcuil Red-Beard. I require him to carry out a scouting mission that might place him in some danger, but it will have the effect of luring British resistance towards a prearranged ambush on the edge of the swamps outside Portus Lemanis. With luck, we'll be able to intercept any force that is mounted by the British and dispose of their warriors in one battle. If we're successful, we can take what we will for the remainder of the summer.'

'I am honoured, Thane Herkeld,' Torcuil responded. 'I'll carry out any task that is asked of me. My men are eager to prove that they are worthy of your praise.'

Torcuil brushed back his stiff grey hair that still possessed hints of redness in the occasional wayward strand. His blunt, grimy hands were heavily calloused from years of sword-work and from decades of rowing at the oars of innumerable ceols.

'Aren't you going to ask what I will be demanding of you?' Herkeld asked Torcuil as he gazed directly into the hooded eyes of the oldest of his captains.

'No, Thane! You need only point the way and I will happily carry out whatever task is expected of me,' Torcuil replied. His words hushed the odd snigger of amusement from his companions for the power of his honesty, for few men among the Saxon raiders stood so straight and true as Torcuil Red-Beard.

Roganvaldar grinned, displaying his ruined smile without

embarrassment. 'I'm afraid there's not much redness left in your hair, old friend.'

'Age comes to all of us in the end. I'm grateful that each spring I can still pull my share on the oars and carry out the bidding of my thane.'

'It pains me that I'm forced to send you into great danger, old friend, but we must entice these timid Britons to come out into the open, now that they've come to know us so well. Still, much will depend on Durobrivae, which is many miles from here and is closer to Londinium than our palisades. Durobrivae is well defended, so I don't expect you to take this town – but I do want you to sack any villages of note, as well as stripping the countryside bare and closing off the Roman roads to traffic. As with the Britons who'll be facing the wrath of Roganvaldar, I expect the merchants who come to your attentions will be heavily laden at this time of the year.'

'I'll put a sting in their tails, master! They'll be screaming, loud and long, when their goods are confiscated and their prosperity is threatened.'

'Excellent, Torcuil! The trick will be for you to avoid capture until you arrive at our palisades. You must maintain contact with the Britons and keep them moving closer to our forces, because the whole plan goes for naught if you should outstrip these weaklings.' Herkeld spoke quietly, but his officers sensed the concern in his voice. 'The spring sailings have just begun, but I intend to take our share of Roman trade goods as payment for those years of privation that were meted out to us by the legions who waged war against our people.'

Herkeld grinned like a hulking bear that was advancing for the kill. His black tooth was a mark that the superstitious often believed to be the sign of a chaos monster, an insult that amused Herkeld whenever he saw the eyes of Christians as they became riveted on his mouth and prayed over their crucifixes in a lather of terror.

'Sumarlieia, my cousin, I need your sharp eyes and your fleet feet to warn me of any threats that are approaching me from the west. You'll take a small detachment to the forests that are known to the local citizens as Anderida Silva. There's a network of roads that run to the trading centres from the island of Vectis to Calleva Atrebatum. Fuck me – but these Roman names always leave a shitty taste in my mouth! If any opportunity should arise where you can sort some of those buggers out without endangering your mission, you have my permission to take it. I hate those fuckers with a passion, so I look forward to the day when some lucky bastard burns Rome to the ground. That cesspit would surely possess spoils worth risking your life for.'

'Yes, Thane! As you wish!'

'You can carry out raids if you consider the spoils are worth it, but don't take any unnecessary risks. The main object of your missions is to lure the Britons into my trap. I'd expect that any real threat would come from Venta Belgarum or Durobrivae, but since that idiot, Constantine, sailed off to attack Rome, there's been no one with the balls to protect the towns and farms.'

Herkeld spat a glob of phlegm into the fire where it sizzled away.

'If these lands were mine, no man would ever wrest them from my hands! But these fools seem to chase bigger dreams than I possess. It's a good thing for us that they do! We'll make these lands bleed before we're done ... and then we'll take all of Britannia, whether the Britons like it or not.'

Herkeld's face was set in rigid lines of scornful determination and his eyes were red in the firelight from his great hatred. His captains took heart from their thane's controlled fury, knowing that he'd lead them to plunder, ripe young women and enough grain to feed their families throughout the next winter.

The captains drank their beer and laid their mugs down on a campaign table under the woollen tent that was Herkeld's only concession to the luxury that his position demanded. Then they bowed to show their respect, before slipping through the tent flaps to see to their men and the defences of the palisade.

Only Roganvaldar, Torcuil and Sumarlieia remained behind, to be given their thane's advice and good wishes. Night had barely set over marshland, forest and palisades but the Saxons were already on the move, for they were determined to carve a bloody wound into Britannia's flanks. Herkeld believed that no one remained to halt the Saxon force in its ruinous intent but, cautious by nature, he hoped to flush out any potential British leader who might rally the local citizens to mount a defence against his warriors.

He smelled the air like a grizzled hunting dog and breathed in the scent of growth, life and wealth. Good soils, regular rain and a warm climate in the summer were godsends that these cowardly Britons never appreciated until Herkeld, or another of his kind, came out of the mists to wrest these fields from their fat and lazy fingers.

'But the day will come when these Britons will be forced to learn,' he vowed, as his three captains walked into the night to prepare for their departure. Herkeld looked up into a sky that was lit by thousands of stars and wondered how that same sky looked down on his barren acres in the north of Saxony.

'They'll learn the sound and taste of my name before I'm finished with them,' Herkeld added. Then he permitted the tent flap to fall and close the entrance as he padded off to his sleeping furs.

The night was quiet. Herkeld could almost believe he was a young man again, safe in his wife's warm arms, before the evils of fate tore his life to ribbons.

THE SAXON AMBUSH OF
THE TRADING CARAVAN

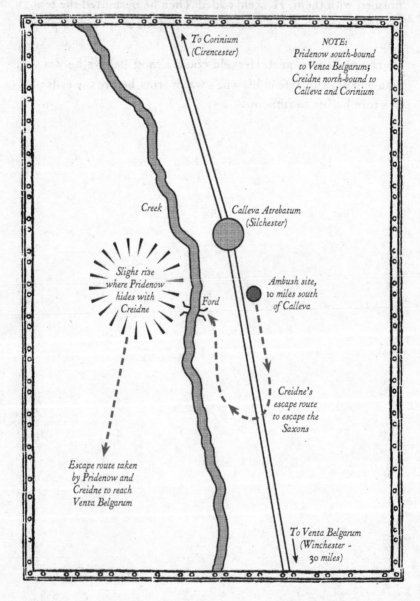

To Corinium
(Cirencester)

NOTE:
Pridenow south-bound
to Venta Belgarum;
Creidne north-bound to
Calleva and Corinium

Creek

Calleva Atrebatum
(Silchester)

Slight rise
where Pridenow
hides with
Creidne

Ford

Ambush site,
10 miles south
of Calleva

Creidne's
escape route
to escape the
Saxons

Escape route taken
by Pridenow and
Creidne to reach
Venta Belgarum

To Venta Belgarum
(Winchester –
30 miles)

CHAPTER XII

INTERLUDE

Travel light and you can sing in the robber's face.

Juvenal, *Satires*, 10:22

The road stretched out before Pridenow's careful gaze. The thoroughfare seemed blank, featureless and empty of threat, but the hair at the back of his neck was standing on end. Something in the air around this remote road was telling the young prince that something was terribly wrong and dangerous situations were lying in wait for him. He rarely experienced any *conscious* forebodings of future happenings, because portents of danger usually manifested themselves through dreams. But this long road, punctuated by patches of woodland and carpeted with vigorous growth from underground springs, had caused his senses to quiver with alarm. The sky was mostly clear, except for a smattering of fluffy clouds, so bad weather wasn't threatening his journey from Calleva Atrebatum to Venta Belgarum. Yet, in the back of his skull, important concerns were skittering and chirruping as they clamoured for his attention.

'I can almost swear that there's trouble in the air, Red. Despite my good health, old friend, I must still be in the world of the crazed.'

The horse whinnied companionably and continued to amble along the roadway, its mind fixated on fresh grass, clean water and the possibility of a nosebag filled with oats at one of the stables that occasionally appeared at day's end. Pridenow wondered whether life as a horse could amount to anything other than mating, drinking, piddling huge streams of urine and enjoying a good canter through deep, green grass without his rider.

'Probably not!' Pridenow decided as the horse pricked its ears at the sound of its master's voice. 'Still, it's damned quiet for a fresh spring morning. Even the birds are still abed.'

Despite his inability to find a rational explanation for the strained nerves that were clawing at his senses, the prince's every sense remained alert. Pridenow's strange ability that sometimes warned him of future events often complicated the mundane events that occurred in his daily activities.

He was also concerned over other matters, particularly the chain, crucifix and jewellery that were resting inside his pack. These ugly relics from the mine shaft had touched a chord inside his mind, because he was certain that they would be of importance to the victim's family. While their intrinsic value was limited, their history, whatever that was, would surely be of importance to some unknown family members.

Meanwhile, Pridenow was anxious to contact Severa and make her aware that Queen Endellion was in poor health. Worse still, the ageing queen had been beset by strange prophetic warnings in recent times, dreams that spoke of impending disasters in the immediate future.

His instincts shouted the message that this innocuous Roman road, a carriageway which was devoid of any sign of life, was taking him on another journey into the south – and danger.

Suddenly, a long finger of black smoke plumed above the roadway ahead of him. Pridenow reacted immediately and sank the heels of his boots into Red's flanks. The beast launched itself into a gallop and thundered across a fallow field filled with shrubbery and long grass until horse and rider were ensconced within a stand of oak trees and heavy underbrush.

In the minutes before making this headlong rush into the thicket of trees and its relative safety, Red's flaring eyes had already revealed his eagerness to leave the road at the earliest opportunity. It was almost as if the destrier sensed the presence of dangers that were beyond human sight or hearing. The beast finally came to a skittish halt on a small, tree-covered hillock that shielded the horse and its rider while still permitting Pridenow to have an unimpeded view of any activity that took place along the road.

A labouring horse came into view on the road below Pridenow's vantage point. The beast was limping, but its rider was prostrated over the beast's neck and back. Pridenow barely had time to register the animal's intrusion into the bucolic peace of the road when a cluster of running warriors appeared in the horse's wake. It was obvious from their harried backward glances that these men were fleeing from something and their fears had lent wings to their feet. Without any thought for the safety of their comrades, the five men in the group were strung out along the roadway as they struggled to escape from some unknown horror.

The pursuit was so frightening that every man was out to save his own person – regardless of what happened to his friends.

From their body armour, Pridenow decided that these men must be former warriors, who were hired to guard merchants and churchmen when these worthies made dangerous journeys along poorly protected roads. Since Constantine had lost his throne, isolated bands of brigands had become an unfortunate new problem for wealthy travellers but there were any number of landless and masterless survivors from the wars in Gallia who were prepared to trade their muscle, fighting skills and lives for coin. Pridenow was almost certain that these men were such mercenaries.

Instinctively, the Dobunni prince readied himself to ride to the assistance of the foundering horse and its rider. But the extra sense gifted to him screamed at him to remain in hiding and to wait, before making decisions that could prove to be irreversible.

As the horse drew abreast of his place of concealment, Pridenow could see that a massive blow had sliced open the horse's chest to expose muscles and flesh. The wound was seeping blood at every step. Brave to the end, the horse was making a valiant attempt to keep moving, even as its lifeblood was leaking on to the cobbles of the road.

What nameless horror could so frighten a horse that it should attempt to make good its escape while carrying such ugly wounds? Every step must have been agonising.

Meanwhile, exhaustion had brought the running men to a halt and they formed a ragged circle, as if to create a collective defence that might give them some protection.

Unable to see the pursuers, Pridenow admired the defensive

skills displayed by these tired men and their desperate resistance against an unknown foe.

The air was deathly still – far too still – and Pridenow realised he was holding his breath. Even from a distance, he could imagine the tensed bodies, straining muscles and the breathless silence of the surrounding landscape.

But the road remained silent. Nothing stirred in the eerie stillness, and Pridenow imagined that the shades were approaching to harvest their portion of souls.

He kept his eyes fixed on the road in the far distance where the road emerged from a stand of thick woodland and his extra sense howled out an urgent warning of impending threat. Something fearsome was coming through that narrow gap in the trees, and the humble creatures of the woodlands were hiding themselves until it had passed.

The first warning that the pursuit had arrived was a swirl of dust raised with the approach of the chasers. The passage of running feet disturbed the loose soil and created a small dust cloud that was moving along at an earth-devouring pace. Then, as the formless shapes came closer, Pridenow was able to see that eight hulking men were running as a disciplined pack at a measured rate. The men's size, their heavy furs and their obvious self-confidence told him that these warriors were aliens who had been born far to the north of Britannia's shores.

It was clear to the prince that the pursuit was fixated on one goal – the destruction of those men within the small defensive circle who were waiting to meet their fate. Such was the pursuers' resolve that their pace remained headlong as they brought their swords and axes to the ready and fell on the doomed men like a tidal wave. During his recent travels, Pridenow had seen the great tidal surge that came in from Sabrina Aest to drown the mudflats in an unstoppable flood. He could spot similarities between the remarkable display of God's power and the bone-shuddering clash as muscles, armour and weapons met on this remote Roman road.

The outcome was never in doubt. Fear weakened the defenders' muscles and their swords trembled in nervous hands. Like attack dogs, the pursuers set about the grisly business of destroying their prey and swept the defenders out of their path with minimal effort. Out of desperation, the last man standing eventually took to his heels and ran from the fur-clad northerners in a vain attempt to escape from the inevitability of violent death. When one of the shaggy warriors pointed at the fleeing man, three of his confederates immediately took off after him. The fugitive was caught, cut down by an axe and left to die on the verge of the road.

'They must be Saxons,' Pridenow said quietly into Red's ear, grateful that he was far enough from the carnage to be spared the reek of battle and the possibility of discovery. 'Who else would use axes to such ghastly effect?'

Pridenow was no coward, but he was no fool either. He knew that trained warriors with the skills of these men would defeat him before he could mount an effective attack, so he could do nothing but view the slaughter with a growing sense of shame.

From his safe vantage point, the young prince watched as the Saxon leader gave an inaudible command to his men to remove all traces of the attack. Although he was too far removed from the thane to hear the barked instructions, they could be easily interpreted. The warriors used their axes and shields as makeshift shovels to scoop out an eroded area where rains and flowing water had carved a scar into the edge of the field. The burial site was far enough from the edge of the road to disguise the inevitable smell of corruption that would reveal evidence that a slaughter had taken place. One by one, the corpses of the victims were searched for items of value, tumbled into the makeshift grave and then covered with loose soil, rocks and sod. Then, once the victims had been interred, the thane inspected the mass grave. He nodded his satisfaction before sending three of his warriors in pursuit of the bleeding horse that had continued to make its slow way along the road.

Careful to avoid being seen or heard, Pridenow dismounted and led his horse through the trees, while avoiding fallen branches or obstacles that could reveal his presence. His caution was well founded for, when the young prince reached the far side of the copse, he was surprised to find one of the Saxons had made his way into the field adjacent to his hiding place. This fur-clad man was little more than a stone's throw from Pridenow's place of concealment.

The warrior raised his head and seemed to sniff at the air like a hunting dog. His movements were only a blur, even to Pridenow's healthy young eyes, but the warrior stood very still as he listened intently for a revealing sound to be carried to him on the wind. In that moment when the hunter was seeking its prey, Pridenow controlled his breathing and placed one hand across Red's soft lips to still any betraying sound. Satisfied, the alien warrior shook his head dismissively, stared once more at the copse of trees that had drawn his suspicions and then loped away to rejoin his fellows.

At the edge of a ford that crossed a shallow stream, the Saxon warriors eventually stumbled over the carcass of the dead horse that had finally collapsed and died from its massive blood loss. The northerners searched through the thick tangle of saplings, brambles and bushes that lipped the banks of the watercourse, but could find no trace of the rider who had been perched over the horse's back and neck. The rider had disappeared.

Severa's advancing confinement gave her little joy. Her marriage to Vortigern had been hastily arranged to give their union some sense of propriety, although none of the tribal kings would have dared to make derogatory comments that might cause her embarrassment. Vortigern would have given short shrift to the authors of any such rumours.

Despite the cautious acquiescence of his peers, the Demetae was conscious that the queen was open to sniggers of amusement from some tribal notables who might be prepared to risk Vortigern's ire, especially those citizens who lived in far-flung places that were beyond his sphere of influence. The hive-like fortress at Tintagel was one kingdom that was unlikely to accept his right to rule over Britannia. The Dumnonii aristocracy, especially Caradoc the Wise, had acted as regents for the Roman rulers of Britannia for centuries, so their stiff-necked pride was such that they'd never accept the ascendancy of an unknown minor king.

Years earlier, a younger Vortigern had visited Tintagel at a time when he'd been a tribal hostage in the service of the Roman commander, Constantine. He had seen, at first hand, how the ancient builders had constructed an impregnable citadel that could never be taken by force of arms. While the mature Vortigern had gritted his teeth in fury when the Dumnonii king refused his invitation to come to Venta Belgarum, he knew there was no way he could force old Cadal to leave the safety of his fortress.

Severa felt the weight of this particular pregnancy far more heavily and painfully than her earlier confinements. This child was large and restive, attributes that gave promise of a difficult delivery; the prospect of bearing this unwanted child terrified her. Childbirth killed one out of every three women and the benefits of wealth, good birth and prayers couldn't protect them from the probability of death. Foreboding rose in her stomach like a tidal surge whenever the child kicked at the insides of her belly.

More and more, Vortigern chose to invade her privacy in this place of women, for he was fascinated by the growth of his seed in her body and was proprietorial about her now that she would soon be the mother of his son. As with his favourite hound, a beast that was also swelling with young, he took every action possible to ensure that his child was kept safe. Despite Severa's belief that he had little personal regard for her, the Demetae king ensured that she received the best food and was attended by servants of her own choosing and, best of all, he made no sexual demands upon her person.

Only the elderly Crisiant, with her herbal potions, and Brisen, the body-servant, were able to offer Severa some surcease from the state of anxiety that Vortigern engendered in her, even though common sense told her that she could die in the coming childbirth and might never see her beloved children again.

No normal woman would have forgiven Vortigern for the violence he had inflicted on her during his initial rape, but Severa had been trained from childhood to understand and accept the pragmatic nature of an aristocratic marriage. Still, she might yet have forgiven the Demetae for his many sins if he had shown a trace of kindness or affection. But he equated softness with weakness, so her marriage was doomed to remain a lonely travesty, regardless of how many children she was prepared to carry for him.

Her favourite window looked out over the north of the town and extended beyond the stout Roman walls that gave it a sense of security. Patches of mist clung to the hills in the distance and softened the angles of the landscape. Like so much of the sweet southern fields of Britannia, her lands promised bounty, but a man, a citizen or a king must always be prepared to wrest the prevailing riches from the earth by force of arms and the strength of his will. With her elbows on the sill and her palms supporting her chin, Severa decided that Vortigern was the one man who was most suited to be the High King of Britannia during these difficult times.

As her thoughts drifted back to her first husband, Constantine, she accepted that he had lacked any ingrained links with this new land, a flaw which had precluded him from giving the British people his total devotion.

Her own father, Maximus, hadn't loved Britannia either. An overambitious man, this Roman had bled these lands dry in a constant search for warriors and wealth before leaving Britannia to undertake his fatal gamble with Fortuna and destiny.

Severa often wondered why she loved these lands so deeply. Being half-Roman, many of her British subjects were reluctant to accord her any respect or love. Yet she was devoted to each and every one of them.

As her thoughts returned to the present and her likely future, Severa decided that Vortigern loved the throne itself, its power and the land, in that descending order. But one thing was certain. Her new husband's avarice was such that he would fight to the death to hold on to what he owned and loved.

Severa looked into the blue-grey distance and thought of her brother's eyes. Where was he now? Would she ever see him again in this lifetime? Something in his eyes suggested that Pridenow had an important future, one that was as imposing as those foretold for the greatest persons in the land. She had been aware of the ancient prophecy that bound him within the shores of Britannia as she was growing to adulthood, so she often wondered what God planned for her mercurial foster-brother.

One thing was certain: Vortigern had no idea that Pridenow might be important to the future of Britannia, or else he would have arranged for the lad to be quietly assassinated. Severa vowed that Vortigern would learn nothing of Pridenow from her lips.

Wearying now, she allowed Brisen to help her to her feet and lead her back to her marital bed. She sighed with resignation. Perhaps God had turned his face away from her. Concerned, she fell to her knees, regardless of the sharp lances of pain that flashed through her joints.

Then she began to pray.

The three Saxon warriors had searched for the corpse of the missing rider until darkness began to creep over the roadway. Long fingers of charcoal slid across the sky as the clouds bled the last redness of daylight along their underbellies. Although his own mouth was desert-dry, Pridenow remained in his position of relative safety. He gave his horse the last of his water by pouring it into his helmet. Better that the horse should drink than to have his presence revealed to the three men who continued their diligent search along the river banks. The smell of running water close at hand could make a thirsty horse restive and noisy.

The leader of the Saxon raiders finally strolled down the road and joined the three warriors beside the stiffening corpse of the dead horse. Then, using a long knife that he kept in a scabbard attached to his belt, the leader proceeded to butcher the beast's hindquarters, wrapping the large chunks of meat in fresh grass and then loading them into cloth bags that he hung around his neck. His confederates followed his lead, until a goodly supply of meat was prepared and ready for future consumption. Then the horse's butchered remains were dragged into the vegetation bordering the river, effectively returning the road to its peaceful self.

As the four Saxons loped away in the long, easy strides of superbly fit men who were well used to running, Pridenow's mind continued to circle and spin as he tried to understand the events he had just seen.

These Saxons had embedded themselves into the landscape like parasites and were established in positions that were close to Venta Belgarum and the Roman road. Most importantly, they were determined to keep their presence secret, as was attested by the labour they had expended to hide all traces of the ambush and its associated carnage. How many warriors were in this party? The young prince could see that their presence posed a threat to Venta Belgarum itself, and wondered if Vortigern realised that his lands were under attack from a force that could make itself invisible within Britannia's landscape?

Once full darkness had fallen, Pridenow moved further away from the thoroughfare and began to search for a comfortable site that could be defended in the event that the Saxons should return. Suddenly, like the answer to a prayer, a waist-high stone wall loomed out of the darkness. Once he had surveyed this hideaway, he knew he could risk a small fire without any danger of revealing his presence.

But before he could consider his own needs, his horse needed his urgent attention.

After lighting the fire and tending it till the logs were ablaze, Pridenow took Red down to the stream where the animal could drink its fill. Spring was well advanced now, but Pridenow noted that the water was still icy. It reminded him that his boots would need drying, and that he was filthy from his travels along the road and his efforts at concealing his presence from the aggressive northerners.

Once he had completed his ablutions, the prince filled his water containers with fresh water and climbed up the steep bank of the watercourse. He had just begun the return journey to the campfire when a slight movement caught his attention. Something, or someone, was hiding in the long grass just behind him. But the stalker was beyond his vision.

Pridenow allowed Red to plod towards the wall, the fire and the long grasses that were waiting for him. For his part, the young prince was careful not to make any sudden movements that would reveal to the watcher that he knew he was under observation.

There! Pridenow heard the sound of grass crackling as someone followed him just beyond the range of his night vision. He sniffed unobtrusively at the air and swore he could recognise a scent of fear that was as potent as the reek of sour wine. But when he turned his head to survey the darkness around him, the night seemed empty of any threat.

At the campfire, Pridenow brushed the horse's coat and attached belled hobbles on to its front legs, tasks that always settled Pridenow's racing brain. Although well trained, the destrier was a greedy eater and would search for food whenever he had the chance. Pridenow was prepared to gamble that the Saxon raiders would be miles away by now and any survivor of their attack would find that Red was a one-owner mount if they tried to remove the reluctant horse from its hobbles. Any attempt to steal the animal from under Pridenow's nose would probably result in pain for the thief.

Opening one of his saddlebags, Pridenow found a small cooking pot and some dried meat, wilting vegetables and enough of his small salt supply to meet the needs of two hungry men. Well-practised at preparing meals in the field, Pridenow concocted a stew that was allowed to simmer over the open fire before carefully removing his knife from its sheath and concealing the weapon in the long grass beside his thigh. Fully prepared to confront his stalker, the young prince sat back against the stone wall, and waited.

Nothing happened.

As the moon rose and shed a gentle radiance over the scene, Pridenow stirred his stew and continued to wait. Red had wandered away from the firelight to fill his belly with the choicest nettles, so the sweet tinkle of bells on the hobbles was the only sound to compete with the peace and quiet of the night.

The thin rags of high-level cloud in the stratosphere seemed to embrace the moon in a diaphanous robe. Its brightness had dimmed a little as Pridenow removed the stew from the fire and prepared his meal for eating. The coals from the fire were already beginning to die as the flames devoured themselves and its comforting heat abated. Then, while staring into the grey ash inside his makeshift fireplace, Pridenow devoured his share of the stew.

With his prized silver spoon in hand, he finished his meal quickly. But he left half of the stew in the pot that was still sitting above the dying coals. Satisfied with his repast, he rinsed his spoon with water from his canteen and rinsed out his mouth. The last of the ale in his saddlebag quenched his thirst, so he settled back against the wall with one hand resting on the handle of his blade.

The night was so quiet that the crickets and insects inhabiting the margins of the stream provided a melody of sorts, one so repetitive and soporific that Pridenow's eyelids began to droop.

He was almost asleep when Red whinnied in alarm. The animal reared indignantly and its hoofs beat at the air and earth before it shied away from some invisible danger. Although he had been expecting an attack, the prince had dozed off, so the ensuing cacophony of noise caused him to leap to his feet with a startled oath. Following the sound of jangled bells from the hobbles, Pridenow slipped barefoot into the darkness.

Pridenow had now become the hunter.

With an animal's instinct for self-preservation, Red was always reluctant to wander away from his master during the hours of darkness. On this occasion, he had found a stand of wild grain that came to his attention when a small human suddenly appeared at his feet. Red reared with alarm, but his whinnying hadn't frightened off whoever was attempting to remain clear of his iron-shod hoofs, so he was placated when his master loomed out of the darkness to grip the figure by one shoulder. Sweating profusely from its frightening experience, the trembling horse

watched wide-eyed as his master struggled to control the interloper who had almost come to grief under its giant hoofs.

Neither master nor horse expected the resistance put up by
the horse thief who struggled in Pridenow's grip. Sharp teeth had
reached the flesh of Pridenow's thumb and bit hard until blood
ran, but he clouted the thief around the ears until the small
creature went limp.

As he rose to his full height, Pridenow discovered that he had
good reason to curse. Blood was running down his fingers and he
was forced to tear away the hem of his second-best tunic to bind
the wound and stem the flow of blood. Other cuts on his neck
that had been inflicted by the horse thief's sharp nails were also
bleeding sluggishly. Considering the obvious weight and height
advantages that Pridenow enjoyed, the horse thief had acquitted
himself well. But Pridenow still regretted the loss of a tunic that
his mother had sewn for him.

He swore again, using the most blasphemous words he knew,
for bites and scratches from a human were extremely dangerous
and regularly resulted in poisonous infections.

With this knowledge in mind, Pridenow was inclined to be
rough when he dragged the thief to his feet and slung him over
his shoulder with the thief's head dangling down his back. With
a horse's wisdom, Red followed his master with the curious gait
of a hobbled animal.

When he reached the fire, Pridenow allowed his captive to
drop to the ground with no concern for the man's well-being, a
contempt that allowed one of the thief's hands to fall on to the
dying coals of the fire. Despite his unconscious state, the captive
cried out in a voice that roused Pridenow's suspicions that the
prisoner might even be a child.

Almost as an afterthought, the prince swore and kicked the stalker's hand out of the fire.

Then, regretting his lack of concern for the prisoner, Pridenow inspected the scorched hand carefully and noted the clean, clipped nails and the softness of white fingers that had never known hard work. He guessed that this youth must have been a part of the group of traders who had been ambushed by the Saxons, an experience that must have been horrific for a gently raised young man. All things considered, this horse thief had done extremely well to evade his pursuers before he had eventually found an effective hiding place. The courage and determination needed to steal a horse from a trained warrior was laudable, so Pridenow's anger at the small, crumpled form began to evaporate.

Despite being close to the fire, the thief's hand was relatively free of damage.

Now that Pridenow had the leisure to examine his prisoner, he soon discovered that the delicacy of bone and the high cheeks of the face indicated that the captive was a boy or a young woman.

He soon realised that his prisoner was a female.

The young girl had clad herself in male clothing by tying her skirt around her waist and concealing the excess material under an extremely wide belt. She had also donned a pair of boy's trews made from much-scuffed leather to protect her modesty. Turning his attention to her head, he found that the knitted cap over her brow was hiding a mane of long, red curls. In the residual light from the fire, Pridenow imagined sparks flying from this mane, as if the locks of hair had been energised by a strange, supernatural force.

Her hair colour would convince superstitious men that this

girl was a child of the Otherworld, perhaps a changeling who had been left in a cradle to replace a human child stolen away in the night by a mischievous spirit. However, given the grey of his eyes and the suspicions that surrounded the young prince as a result of his own trances, Pridenow was unlikely to make judgements about anyone based on appearance alone. As he considered the plight of his prisoner by the dying light of the fire, he sucked away at the wound on his hand and spat out the globules of blood that were drawn to the surface. He knew it was important to cleanse these bites if he was to avoid any mouth poisons.

The girl moved and groaned automatically, while clutching at a short length of firewood with her left hand. Many Britons believed that left-handedness, the use of the *hand sinister*, indicated a person who was in league with the Devil, but Pridenow wasn't so superstitious that he permitted rank ignorance to influence him. Even so, a combination of red hair and left-handedness was a powerful curse for any person who was so afflicted.

With her eyes closed, the girl seemed angelic.

Pridenow tried to wake her with a gentle cuff to the side of her face.

'Wake up, girl! Come on, wake up! Wake up!'

She remained prone with her eyes closed, although a groan escaped from her lips. Pridenow splashed a good cupful of liquid on to her face.

Spluttering and cursing, the girl sat up and lashed out at Pridenow with both hands.

All mental comparisons with angels vanished from the young prince's mind.

'Keep quiet while I ask you some questions. Whether you're a girl or boy makes no difference to me! I want to know why you tried to steal my horse.'

'I have to get word to Calleva Atrebatum! There's no time to waste, you dolt! Good people will die while you stare off into nothingness . . . and . . . and . . . drool.'

Having delivered her worst possible insults, the girl rose shakily to her feet and was suddenly aware that her legs were exposed. She hastily began to pull her skirt and shift free from the constraints of the wide belt. Pridenow noticed that she had green eyes that complemented her red hair, and her white complexion was scattered with freckles across her nose.

'What's your name, girl? I suggest you give me the truth because you won't be going anywhere until I find out what's happening here. That's one thing I *can* promise you!'

Once again, the girl scowled her way through a flurry of nasty insults, without realising that her choice of words would hardly win this man over. 'Many men have already died out on the road – I was lucky to make my escape when they fell on us, and you keep maundering on like a useless blatherskite. You'll be well paid for it, so give me your horse!'

As the girl was shouting in his face, Pridenow pushed her backwards and she landed on her tailbone with an audible thump.

'Your name, young lady? I'm beginning to lose patience with you and I'll have to tie your wrists and ankles together, if you don't come up with a good reason for me to listen to you.'

'You're a brute!' she hissed, 'and I'll see you hanged before I'm done. My name is Creidne, the daughter of Cael ap Cynog, the trader. You'd be wise not to raise the ire of my father, or of any members of his clan, if Father has been killed by those savages who attacked us on the road. My uncle, Cynfab, or my aunt, Olwyn, will pay whatever ransom you care to ask for my safe-keeping, but they'll exact their revenge if you attempt to ravish me. My kin will hunt you down like a mongrel dog if you attempt to steal my maidenhead – or my life.'

When Creidne paused for breath, her small breasts rose and fell interestingly within the tight confines of her bodice. Pridenow executed an ironic bow with impeccable timing, an action that momentarily stilled her tongue.

'My, my, my, young lady! Greatness is surely embodied in your flesh. It's a great pity that I have the power to have you killed out of hand for horse-stealing.'

'I'd have sent him back to you after I was finished with him,' she retorted piously.

'Of course you would! You'd have returned my property as a matter of course, because you're so far above me that it would be shameful to steal from me. You know my name, my tribe and my township, don't you? You can find me, can't you?'

'I'd have used my kin to find you,' she snapped defensively.

Pridenow simply laughed.

'Forest trees have been known to talk, my lady! I'm sure you'd have tried to find me – for a heartbeat, perhaps! Meanwhile, my favourite horse would have been given to others to be overworked, beaten, abused or even eaten as horsemeat, in much the same way as your horse is being eaten by the Saxons who ambushed your father's caravan.'

'No! No! I wouldn't have done that . . .' she said softly before her voice trailed off into silence. This strange man with the cold, peculiar eyes was probably correct in his assessment, making her feel like a fool who had been caught out in an obvious lie.

'Now, Creidne, it's time that you told me what your family is doing on this godforsaken road with neither maids, manservants nor a personal guard to keep you safe.'

With the first sign of tears beginning to shine in her eyes, she decided to speak.

'My father, Cael ap Cynog, purchased a number of excellent river pearls from beyond the Wall. These jewels were very large in size and were of the highest quality. He had also traded successfully for fine gold, silver and electrum ornaments made in Deva, as well as bales of wool, mountain salt, a store of food items and another collection of gems that had been purchased from the mines of Cymru. Our caravan was very large and it was well guarded, so we had no difficulty in reaching Venta Belgarum some three weeks ago. I've made this journey with my father on several occasions now, so his wishes . . .' Her voice faded away and she grimaced as her tears spilled over. 'He had just told me that he wanted to have me married to a suitable husband, so this journey was a way to show me off and find an acceptable spouse who would become a part of our family.'

'I wish you good luck with that plan.' Vortigern would have taken you for his own purposes if he was given the opportunity to see you! But please continue.'

'I've already had the misfortune of meeting that unpleasant man. He actually licked his lips when he was introduced to me. I wanted to sink into the earth, but my embarrassment is immaterial. My father sold all his trade goods and purchased a cache of fine Egyptian and Middle Sea cloth for his clients in Deva. Since we decided to leave Venta Belgarum quickly, when Father made his calculations for the journey he decided he would only need twenty guards and five of his wagons to accompany us on the return journey to our home.'

Pridenow could imagine the progress of the small caravan as the wagons moved ponderously along the Roman road. The merchants would have been careless of any impending danger, right up to the time they were ambushed.

'I'm certain that those Saxons were waiting for you and yours,' the young prince stated flatly. His facial features were set in a grim stare. 'Your caravan would have been too large to ambush when you were on your initial journey down to Venta Belgarum, so they let you pass. But they waited and attacked you on the return journey.'

'Aye! The Saxons tied a length of rope across the road and this unseated my father when he rode his horse into it. The warriors leaped out from their places of concealment and there were so many of the brutes that Cael doubted his ability to protect our caravan. He slapped my horse across the rump and told me to ride like the wind to Venta Belgarum.'

'Your father appears to be a brave man who has a surfeit of good sense,' Pridenow said quietly, as he tried to hide the pity in his eyes. 'By sending you away, he gave you a chance of survival. Like him, it's my belief that the Saxons intended to murder your entire party.'

'Can you see why I have to ride to Calleva Atrebatum? One of those Saxon monsters slashed at my horse, but I rode the bastard down. I hope I killed the son of a whore.'

'You're a bloodthirsty little bitch, aren't you?' He grinned, for he was trying to divert her attention away from the fate that had befallen her father. 'I watched a large group of Saxons dispatch five of your guards after they chased them down the road. They made sure that they hid the bodies and removed all traces of their presence. How did you manage to make your escape after your horse died under you?'

Creidne stared fixedly at her hands that were stained with mud, grass and blood.

'My mare foundered when we reached the stream. She was in terrible pain, so I forced myself to cut her throat and put her out of her misery. I knew that killing her would tell the Saxons that I was still alive, but I couldn't let the mare suffer. Then I ran through the water to disguise my tracks. I ran as far downstream as I dared before I climbed out on the far bank. I hid in the long grass several fields away from the water's edge and half buried myself in dirt. The ruse worked, so . . .'

'So you decided to steal my horse after the sun had set, and you'd watched when I was lighting my fire,' Pridenow finished for her.

She nodded with a numb expression on her face.

'I'm making my way to Venta Belgarum on a matter of some urgency, Creidne, but I now have further reasons to take issue with Vortigern. I'm afraid that I can't afford the time to return you to your family, which means you'll have to accompany me to Venta Belgarum. No, young lady! Don't bother to complain! I'll be doing what you require of me.'

'But we'll be caught . . . and you're only one sword against twenty Saxons. They'll kill us!' Her voice was plaintive without being self-pitying, which made Pridenow's opinion of her courage increase.

'I don't plan to ride down the road to meet up with them, if that's what you expect. No, we'll reach Venta Belgarum by journeying through a less-frequented route and I'll place you into the care of my sister, Queen Severa.'

Creidne looked at Pridenow with a deadpan expression, although her eyes told him how rapidly her brain had absorbed the information he had provided.

'Since you haven't asked, Creidne, my name is Pridenow ap Aeron of the Dobunni tribe. While I'm a prince in my own right, Vortigern and I have not endeared ourselves towards each other, and as a result he'll take any action he can to stop me from exerting any influence within Britannia.'

The young man's sincerity impressed Creidne, who relaxed when she absorbed the information.

'Now that Vortigern is the High King of Britannia, he must be made aware that a band of Saxons are deeply embedded into the countryside and they have been active within a stone's throw of Venta Belgarum. Regardless of his many sins, Vortigern is a fierce warrior and a clever strategist. I've no doubt that he'll search for the Saxons who attacked your caravan and root them out of their stronghold.'

Creidne looked doubtful; Pridenow redoubled his efforts to convince her that he could guarantee her safety.

'Queen Severa is my sister, so I can assure you that she'll protect you from harm. She is Vortigern's wife, but I'd feel more comfortable if you were in Venta Belgarum where my sister can support you till we return you to your family. For her part, she needs a friend and she won't allow you to be bullied by her husband. Trust me, Creidne! I'll do my best to find your father, living or dead, and I'll return you to your household myself – whatever happens.'

Creidne eventually nodded in agreement, unable to trust her voice to be steady enough to answer this earnest young man.

'Now, girl, I want you to eat some of this stew that I prepared for your eventual arrival at my campsite. It's cold, but it will give you strength for the morrow.'

Creidne nodded dumbly as she examined the fine silver spoon that Pridenow polished on his shirt before passing it to her. Even as she marvelled at the richness of his possessions, her mind was awhirl with wonders and misery.

'Tomorrow, child, we'll carry out a discreet search to discover what the Saxons have done with your father before we leave this place and make our way to Venta Belgarum.'

CHAPTER XIII

LOVERS AND OTHER STRANGERS

Would that the Roman people had but one neck. Caligula.

Suetonius, *The Lives of the Twelve Caesars*

Having arrived in Burdigala at the very worst time of the year for sea travel, Paulus decided that further haste was pointless. In addition, the travellers were badly in need of rest, because the children were worn out after weeks on the road.

'A place to rest and recuperate must be our first priority,' Paulus said bluntly to his travelling companions as they were entering the port.

Dilic, in contrast, was determined that Paulus should hunt up Severa's sea captain at the earliest opportunity, in order that the travellers could make their arrangements for the journey into Hispania. Because it would be difficult to find a single seaman in a major trading port filled with sailors, this task should be their first priority if they were to protect Severa's boys. As far as Dilic was concerned, the party should depart for Hispania at the earliest opportunity.

The maidservant's face flushed bright-red with anger as she shouted her opinions at the decurion, while ignoring the faces of those casual pedestrians who were listening as they passed by. With a face that was white with his own repressed emotion, Paulus led the party towards a recommended inn with attached stables that enjoyed a favourable position on one of the main thoroughfares.

Under the lash of Dilic's shrewish tongue, Paulus decided that he'd heard enough. He dismounted from his horse with his mouth set in a thin line that seemed to be stitched to his face.

'Look to the children, woman.' He rasped out this command to the maidservant, who obeyed out of pure habit.

'Ambrosius is attempting to act like a little man, but he's lost far too much weight in recent weeks and he can hardly keep his eyes open. What's the point in dragging these children to safety if we kill them in the process? See sense, woman! As for Uther, a nasty cold hasn't improved his temper in the slightest. Despite her inner strength, Dara can barely walk for the pain in her spine that's been caused by the countless weeks she's spent in that sodding wagon. She doesn't complain, but she's been in need of rest for a long time. Just because you're hale, doesn't mean the rest of us are in good health.'

'Excuses, Paulus! You're just too old and too tired to be bothered with finding our man as soon as possible.'

Dilic was feeling cross and she was frustrated, so her argumentative side was swamping her common sense and her sturdy peasant practicality.

'You can insult me as much as you like, you little shrew, but I'm not dropping everything and putting the children at risk to find a man with a common name in the stews of a trading city. Stamp your feet, spit at me or promise to cut my throat when I'm sleeping – whatever you feel is warranted! I don't care! And – since your mouth is open to argue further – I don't give a fuck what you think. Do your worst, Dilic!'

'I hope your balls fall off, you old fart.' Dilic screamed loudly enough to cause several of the citizens who were examining heads of cabbage in a small roadside market to look at these new arrivals in surprise. She cast her eyes downwards and surreptitiously wiped away several tired tears.

Paulus felt no particular guilt. Dilic was just as exhausted as the rest of the party. In fact she was probably more tired than the others, because she took on some of the heavy work that Etain, the young traveller, would normally have carried out. But Paulus reasoned that Etain might feel an urge to escape if she was left unsupervised, so he kept her close to the wagon and ensured that the unwilling captive was restrained during the hours of darkness.

With these extra responsibilities, Dilic's workload had almost doubled. Her duties now included the onerous task of collecting firewood and chopping it into usable lengths on those occasions when Paulus wasn't available.

Dilic sulked, swore, argued and pleaded as they crossed the bridge and entered the more salubrious quarter of Burdigala. Mindful of their store of coins, Paulus ignored her last outbursts and chose a modest inn near the river which was likely to be cooler and cleaner than most of its competitors. Here, the sea winds scoured away the sour smells of too many people living in close proximity to each other.

Although the innkeeper looked at the small group of road-weary travellers with some doubt, Paulus explained that he was the children's maternal grandfather who was escorting three of his daughters to the home of their kin who now resided in Hispania. As the stable boy reported the spirit, if not the subject, of Dilic's tirade towards Paulus, the innkeeper sighed with satisfaction because he had already given them the large room in the attic of the hostelry. His religious propriety had been disturbed by thoughts of one depraved man with three servant girls and two young children. But he still felt unease for these three women, supposedly sisters, who looked so dissimilar.

Fortunately for the innkeeper, Paulus couldn't read his mind. Had he been aware of the innkeeper's doubts, Paulus would have been tempted to remove the inquisitive nose that was thrust into his business. Although the decurion was unlikely to admit it, he was almost at the end of his own strength and was beginning to wish he had never set foot in Venta Belgarum.

The room allocated to the party was hardly palatial, having been used for the storage of broken furniture, useless baggage left behind by absconding guests and even some worn-out harness from the stables. The servants of the hostelry had stacked all the rubbish into the furthest and darkest corners of the attic and swept up the most obvious of the garbage, but Dara looked at the corners of the large space with real concern.

Etain was blunt. 'There'll be rats in there, so we'll need to watch the children.'

'There are always rats in hostelries,' Dilic replied. 'Open the shutters and let some air in, and we can only hope we don't have to spend the winter in here,' she added with a grimace.

'We can cross that bridge when we come to it,' Paulus retorted. 'But for now, we need pallets and some things that will make this place bearable.'

The ensuing discussion between the Roman decurion and the innkeeper was brief and to the point. A combination of threats and the promise of good silver galvanised the staff into a flurry of cleaning and they belatedly found furniture and accoutrements that made the space habitable. Paulus's martial gaze conveyed all the icy command of a lifetime of giving orders, so mine host was truly relieved when the old soldier eventually pronounced himself satisfied with the final arrangements.

Two days slid by with none of the party interested in setting foot outside their attic, except to eat or cater to their bodily needs. In the intervening time, Dilic decided that the inn's latrines were tolerable, while Etain sang the praises of the cooks who manned the kitchens.

'But you'll eat anything that's put in front of you,' Dara argued, surprising Paulus by her contribution to the conversation. Dara usually accepted fate with silent acquiescence, including the harsh conditions they had endured during their travels.

'The food is fresh and nourishing, and it's adequate for our needs. Uther eats it, and that boy's an absolute pain if he's given food he doesn't like,' Dilic stated firmly. After this the conversation was allowed to lapse.

At noon on the third day, the boys begged to leave the strictures of the attic room, for they had finally caught up on their sleep and rested themselves back to good health. The room, which had seemed so large and echoing when they first arrived, was far too small now to cater to the needs of two vigorous little balls of unspent energy. To use up some of their stores of excess vitality, Dilic volunteered to take the boys to the river bank where they could play in the long grass and deep mud, for it was low tide and the late autumn sun was unusually warm.

Left with little else to occupy his time, Paulus donned his scarlet cloak to repel any possible chills and decided that he should finally begin the search for the sea captain, an ex-legionnaire called Daire. As this name wasn't particularly unusual, Paulus was gratified that he'd been given the name of the man's vessel, *Neptune's Kiss*.

'Urrrgh! More water, and more damned boats!' Paulus muttered grumpily under his breath. Having voiced his dissatisfaction, he found the amulet that would prove his credentials to Daire before setting off into the brisk morning light to find his man.

Burdigala was a beautiful town that still bore the remnants of its Roman past with self-conscious honesty. A small forum had felt the brunt of tribal conflicts during the recent wars, so some of the columns of veined green marble raised their broken capitals like shattered teeth. Paulus noted that a small Roman theatre was still operational in the slopes that led down to the river bank. This concave area utilised the shape of the hill to create the stone seating that overlooked the central stage at the base of the hillock. Although this open-air structure was small, Paulus could clearly hear two peasant boys arguing with perfect clarity over a cockerel at the rear of the stage. Long-dead Roman engineers of yesteryear created the acoustics for these theatres, and Paulus felt a thrill of pride in those of his ancestors who had travelled so far and had built so high.

The port straggled along the southern bank of the river before it met the protected waters where the shipping was moored.

Warehouses, inns, stables and industrial buildings crowded the foreshore and a busy throng of citizens moved purposefully in hasty, disciplined groups. Noise seemed to fill every enclosed space and Paulus could hear almost every conceivable language as men shouted, barked out orders or carried out their particular business. Yet he could understand most of the conversations, for they were cobbled together with Latin, the language of trade and the lifeblood of this teeming marketplace. Satisfied, Paulus also heard snippets of the local language and discovered that, like the tongue of Britannia, it shared common words and cadence because of the shared tribal root of both lands. His women would be able to stop and speak with the locals. He strode towards the Garumna River, knowing that he would eventually find his sea captain in this small, commercial world devoted to endless trade.

A cold wind was blowing in from the sea as Paulus observed the full vista of Burdigala's resources from an elevated vantage point. He noted that the river widened at its mouth, where the brown, silted waters were pumped into the blue bay in a large stain. Beyond the river mouth, the landlocked sea was filled with vessels of all sizes, some anchored safely for the winter and others moving towards the open waters to skitter along the bay on short journeys to nearby towns along the coast of Aquitania. These smaller craft carried humble trade items that were offered for sale, as well as providing a fast means of transport for itinerant passengers who had the required amount of coin to pay for their journeys. For them, the winter gales were merely an irritation because the foul weather did not pen them into berths for months at a stretch. Coast-hugging, broad-beamed and low-drafted, they were able to find temporary shelter behind headlands where they could survive the worst excesses of the Oceanus Atlanticus. If *Neptune's Kiss* was one of these coastal traders, then Paulus might find himself on a wild goose chase.

Like any intelligent huntsman, the decurion began his search in those premises where sailors were most likely to congregate – those inns and hostelries that were closest to the wharves. After spending a few base coins, Paulus learned that Daire was a well-known man of doubtful temperament, albeit possessing an impeccable reputation, who could be found somewhere in the port. One particularly clean, well-patronised hostelry, which Paulus still described to himself as a hole-in-the-wall, served a rich-smelling rabbit stew and he paused long enough to devour two bowlsful. After this hearty repast and some hunks of sandy bread, the old soldier was given the address of a widow called Mavourna, the warm friend with whom Daire spent the winter months.

Paulus, tearing at some bread he had taken away with him after his meal, ambled along the unfamiliar alleyways of the old town above the water as he searched for Mavourna's house. The wintry sun produced sufficient heat to warm his face and the slight wind from the ocean was perfumed with weed, sea salt and the persistent odour of fish, which was quite pleasant when it was compared with the combined smells of a large, close-living community. Burdigala was a clean, well-administered town, but the most hygienic cities still had vermin, stored rubbish and the sour stink of human flesh. Even buildings that had stood for a long time carried the unforgettable reek of rot, of long summer rainfalls and the ice of winter that ate away at all building materials and made them brittle and sour. After many weeks on the road, though, Paulus's nostrils smelled this combination of perfumes and sucked in the nature of human occupation in this large city with a modicum of pleasure.

The other citizens on the streets of Old Burdigala gave Paulus a wide berth, a circumstance so familiar to him that he scarcely thought about it. His scarlet cloak warned any lurking bully-boy that this particular old man might bite back at them, while his upright stance and easy swagger pronounced him a man with an ex-military background at the very least. Something about the way his heels struck the pavement first with sharp warning thuds spoke of a life of discipline, order and confidence. When Paulus noticed passers-by looking at him, he smiled pleasantly and nodded as those citizens dropped their eyes and scuttled away.

As he searched for Mavourna's house on the Street of Dolphins, the worst obstacle that Paulus was forced to contend with was a persistent attack by a large seagull whose beady black eyes were fixated on the last hunk of bread in Paulus's hand. The bird flared its wings majestically as it swept past Paulus's head in the vain hope that he would drop his appetising morsel. Then, when Paulus refused to surrender the hunk of bread, the seagull swelled his wings to their largest size and screamed a vain series of curses.

Paulus was amused by its determination.

As the seagull continued to abuse and insult him, he tossed a small piece of bread in its direction. Then, as other gulls appeared like magic to demand their share of the booty, Paulus gave the original gull the last of his bread with an apology for teasing it for such a long time. He watched as the bird took to its wings with its prize, followed by a small detachment of other gulls eager to befriend their companion.

'You shouldn't feed them vermin. They'll be demanding food

from all of us if you do,' a shaky old voice admonished him from the shadows.

Paulus shaded his eyes and peered into the darkly shadowed recess in front of a partially open door. The mud-brick dwelling was very narrow and seemed to lack any windows, an omission which probably accounted for the gloom. An old woman was sitting on a stool on the stoop, swathed in many layers of black and grey fabric topped with a face as wrinkled as a raisin.

Paulus bowed respectfully towards her.

'I shall bow to your local knowledge and ensure that I'll never repeat this mistake again. I must say in my own defence that I found the bird to be an implacable enemy that was determined to deprive me of my bread. He was very brave!'

'He's a lice-ridden, flying rat,' the old woman answered bluntly. 'The bastards live on garbage, so their only purpose is to clean up our filth. Them that live around here leave rubbish everywhere to feed them buggers.'

She delivered her opinion of her neighbours with a defiant toss of her shrivelled head. Her scarf slipped to reveal some sparse grey plaits; she returned it to its place with a hand that was misshapen from swollen knuckles and twisted joints. Deciding that persistent pain might be responsible for her bad temper, Paulus turned to move away, but then asked the old harridan for directions to reach the Street of the Dolphins.

'You're in it. And I can see you're a fighting man as well. The Roman soldiers have all gone now, so I suppose you're retired.'

To cut her short, Paulus asked where he might find the house of the widow, Mavourna. He was surprised when his request was greeted with a cackle of spiteful laughter.

'Her? So you be another one who's been hanging about since

her old man died at sea. Well, you're out of luck. She's got a new fool to pay for her fancy shawls and her useless children. You be far too late, old man!'

Paulus smiled lazily as he ran his eyes up and down the old besom with a soldier's insolence.

'I'd be careful if I were in your shoes, mother, else you might cut yourself with your own tongue. Your age would matter little to the city fathers if this widow Mavourna chooses to take her revenge for the claims you're making against her. I, for one, would have to agree that you've been very unkind to her.'

The old woman bridled like a nervous horse, rose to her feet far faster than Paulus would have expected and scuttled back into her house. The door was slammed behind her with enough force to shake the frame.

Another passing child pointed out the widow's house and Paulus found himself standing on the clean step in front of a freshly whitewashed wall and door. A cracked cooking pot that contained a healthy red geranium had been placed on the edge of the step.

'At least this woman keeps a reasonably clean house,' Paulus said quietly to himself. But before he could knock on the door, it swung open to reveal a tiny, plump woman with humorous green eyes and a cloud of blue-black curls. Lost for words by the suddenness of her arrival at the door, Paulus began to stammer.

'Never mind the nice words, laddie! I was watching through the window and I saw you upset old Beara. Anyone who can annoy that old bitch deserves a mug of cider or a taste of my best wine. Come in! I can see that rain's a-coming.'

With this proffered greeting, the woman turned and plunged

into the cool of the room without bothering to close the door behind her. Confused, and at a loss as to what was expected of him, Paulus followed her into a large open space that was filled with light and colour.

The decurion stood, shame-faced, in the familiar homeliness of a peasant kitchen. He was forced to give a mental apology to the widow, for he'd expected this to be the home of a slattern, but care and pride gleamed from every piece of polished brass and sand-scoured wood. The widow smiled up at him as she helped him to remove his scarlet cloak. She marvelled at the weight of it as, with housewifely care, she brushed a splatter of dried mud from its folds.

'What can I be doing for you, you darling man?' she chirruped, looking up into his time-worn face with frank admiration.

'I'm here to speak to your man, Daire, and to ask him to take a small party of six passengers on a short voyage. I know it's well past sailing weather, but I need to deliver my charges to a destination in Hispania. I was given Daire's name by mutual friends, along with a letter that explains my credentials.'

Mavourna felt Paulus's strength as if she had known him for many years. Man and woman stood close to each other, suddenly intimate in the old attraction of the sexes.

She touched his arm hesitantly and, with a coquettish, sideways glance, she offered him a mug of the local red wine. Paulus accepted with an open grin that reminded Mavourna that Roman legionnaires had never been gullible.

Paulus swallowed the wine with a hasty toss of the head, for he expected the harsh, vinegary draught that legionnaires could usually afford. To his surprise, Mavourna kept a decent vintage, one that was deep-red and smooth. He accepted another mugful enthusiastically and settled down beside the fire to stretch out his legs.

'I'm sorry, lord, but Daire is about the town where, no doubt, he'll be drinking all his savings. I've hidden some of his coin for a time when he needs it next, although the bastard won't thank me for it. I'll tell him you're in need of him, and why, if you'll excuse my impertinence. If you can tell me where your party is housed, I'll make sure that Daire will call on you at a convenient time.'

Paulus grinned. Certain that Daire would be drinking away the contents of his purse, the Roman knew that he wouldn't see the ship's captain during the coming evening. He raised his mug to toast Mavourna with a soldierly gallantry.

'Daire's a fool to leave a fine woman like you to waste his time in the fleshpots. If I were in his boots, I'd be staying close to home to enjoy . . . er . . . more than wine with you.'

Mavourna simpered at his compliments, so Paulus lifted one soft paw to kiss her wrist. She shivered at his touch and automatically leaned towards him. Paulus needed no further invitation. If he had learned one thing in the thirty years he had followed the Eagles into battle, it was the need to take advantage of chances that were offered. Since Mavourna was ripe for the plucking, who was Paulus to disappoint the lady?

Mavourna was totally lost to reason and invited him into her bed without hesitation. Enclosed in the warmth of her arms and affectionate nature, Paulus quickly forgot his duty and his charges. After all, he had travelled a long way during the journey from Venta Belgarum.

As the pain deepened, Severa suddenly screamed and drew in a long, shuddering breath.

Around the room, the midwives, nurses and maids were clustered in small groups, like plump chickens disturbed in the roost. Hours had passed as the queen's screams grew louder and her strength ebbed away like straw in the wind. Severa was weakening, and all their potions, prayers and experience could not force the unborn child to come into the world.

Vortigern had come to the birthing room earlier, but the low moans, the smell of sweat and the fresh blood of Severa's labour had brought him to a halt at the doorway. Embarrassed by his weakness, he had angrily informed the queen's women that their deaths would be protracted and painful if his child should die in the birthing. He didn't mention the likely fate of the queen.

When the boy-child finally capitulated, he was born in a welter of blood. One of the midwives lifted the babe jubilantly and he cried lustily at the cold air in the queen's quarters. Angry and demanding, Vortigern's offspring continued to cry desultorily.

The older midwife immediately began to pack Severa's womb with strips of cloth, to help staunch the bleeding.

The queen's personal maid carried the babe, swaddled in a bloodstained cloth, to Vortigern's apartments.

She approached the door timidly and found Vortigern in his rooms.

'Your son is born, my lord.'

Bowing low, she held up the child for Vortigern's inspection. At first, the king recoiled from this newly born babe whose small feet were trying to kick vigorously into the air.

He looked at the squirming, red-faced infant for a brief moment and a strange expression of softness blurred his features. Ashamed of these tender emotions, his attention turned back to the servant.

'Look to your mistress, for I'd rather she survives this night. Give her this small token of my esteem and tell her that I'll join her shortly.'

Vortigern tore a heavy gold ring from his thumb and handed it to the woman. Surprised, she almost dropped the ornament in confusion before she bolted to the door and made good her escape.

Safely inside the queen's rooms, the maid inspected the birth-gift in the dim light provided by a sconce on the wall. An ugly piece of onyx, beryl and rich gold blinked balefully at her so, without the slightest trace of feminine envy, she thrust the ring into the hands of the young midwife.

'Give this to my lady. I'll be glad to be shot of the hellish thing.'

The midwife at the queen's bedside, noting with satisfaction that the flow of blood from the queen's genitals had slowed to a trickle, proclaimed that Severa would live.

'But she'll be poorly for many months,' she stated softly, while the maids crossed themselves with superstitious fear. When this old crone made her pronouncements, all sensible persons listened carefully.

The ring lay in Severa's breast like a grotesque parasite; regardless of its value, none among those present would care to own such an ugly jewel.

'This trifle is a poor birth-gift if it's been offered as proof of the master's love,' the midwife muttered.

'Get on with you, you old besom,' one of the maids retorted. 'You'd be happy to take it for your own if a man was prepared to gift such a jewel to you.'

'There's blood and death in that damned stone,' the old woman went on, with none of her usual malice.

'Then the master be the bringer of misfortune into his house,' Severa's maid interrupted sullenly. 'Now, don't you lot be bickering and gossiping about your betters. You could find yourself without your hands if I was disposed to inform the master of this conversation. Be quick now! Lord Vortigern is coming and your hides will be beaten raw if this room isn't put to rights.'

Severa lay on her fine bed like one dead. Ashen-faced from blood loss, the queen turned her face away from the sleeping infant.

'I'll suckle this poor little babe because he is an innocent, but I'll never love him as a mother should, no matter what his sire demands,' Severa confided to her women. 'The babe is a child of pain, and he'll never be free of the taint of poisoned blood. This lad will have trouble enough before he goes to the shades, so I pray to God that I'll not be alive to see it.'

Midnight came to Venta Belgarum and, with it, a deathly silence. In the empty streets below the palace walls, all honest folk were abed. The deep stillness was only broken by the ominous cry of a hunting owl, an omen that something warm and living was about to die.

The world waited as Fortuna spun her wheel. A boy-child had been born within the fortress, and this infant would carry destruction, chaos and death with him until such time as the Dragon was come.

And Fortuna laughed at the displays of hubris from these insignificant mortals.

CHAPTER XIV

ACROSS THE BOILING SEA

Travel light and you can sing in the robber's face.
Canabit vacuus coram larrone vinter.

Juvenal, *Satires*, 10

Paulus woke with a start in the early morning. Old soldier that he was, he usually came immediately to full consciousness but this time he looked around the tiny feminine space and felt the odd dislocation that comes from sleeping in a strange bed. With a surge of his still-powerful leg muscles, he rose from the soft bedding and stood to attention, naked and confused, for just a heartbeat.

Mavourna laughed with a sound like tinkling bells and Paulus felt his loins stir. 'I have an excellent loaf of bread and a slab of bacon, so you'll be able to break your fast with a strong meal in your belly. A man like you needs meat to thicken your blood after heavy exercise.'

Mavourna grinned at him engagingly and Paulus felt his

cheeks flush under her cool gaze.

'You're a witch, woman, but you make an old man feel like he's still a boy.'

Paulus dressed with renewed vigour and sprang down the single step that separated the sleeping space from the kitchen. Mavourna was standing over a hot skillet that was sizzling aromatically over the fire. As she lifted out a thick slab of bacon from which fat was oozing the Roman felt his mouth begin to salivate.

'Daire came home during the night and he's sleeping his head off in my garden.'

'I hope I haven't brought you trouble with your man by spending the night with you,' Paulus apologised with a guilty glance towards the rear of the cottage.

'Daire!' Mavourna exclaimed. 'Don't worry yourself about him! He doesn't own me or this snug little cottage. I'm the mistress here, so I can invite who I choose. Daire be damned!'

Paulus felt distinctly uncomfortable. Daire had obviously upset the lady of the house; Paulus was glad that he himself hadn't drawn Mavourna's ire.

'The silly bugger arrived home at midnight and promptly spewed his guts all over my doorstep. I'll be scrubbing it for a week.' Paulus winced. 'Sit yourself down now and taste this piglet. I raised him myself, so the meat's as sweet as any pork can be.'

Paulus obeyed and, with his mouth already tasting the rich meat, he tore off a piece of bread from the newly baked loaf and set about the meal with gusto.

Suddenly, as he was sopping up the last traces of pig-fat from the platter, a dishevelled man staggered through the rear entry and stumbled over the step. He fell headlong at the decurion's feet.

'That creature is Daire, Roman. He might be a master seaman, but he's an all-round sot,' Mavourna said acidly.

The object of her fury got to his feet and peered owlishly at the decurion.

'Do I know you?' he asked.

Mavourna pushed her face close to Daire's mouth, while wrinkling her nose at the sour smell of stale wine and vomit.

'The Roman wants you to take him into Hispania at the first possible sailing. He says he'll pay you well, but he has five others with him – three females and two children.'

'Women be bad luck at sea and I've no mind to go out at this time of the year. I'd be risking me boat and that's one thing that I won't do without a good reason.'

Paulus found his cloak and drew out Aeron's missive from its capacious depths.

With little comprehension, Daire stared at the tattered scrap of vellum.

'He can't read,' Mavourna said sardonically as her man grinned up at her without a hint of embarrassment. After all, most Gallic citizens were illiterate. With a brief apology, Paulus explained the instructions penned by Aeron.

Daire stood a little straighter and Paulus could see traces of the legionnaire that Daire had once been.

'My British friends need my help and I have an oath to consider. 'Tis true that I owe Constantinus's kin and there's no mistake. I'm oath-bound to answer any plea that King Aeron might ask of me, but at this time of year? It's no joke sailing into open waters at times when the storms are upon us. *Neptune's Kiss* is like to founder if the worst of the winter gales hit us.'

'If I was concerned for myself I wouldn't ask you to take to the open seas in winter,' Paulus said, casting one eye towards the open door where isolated patches of sunshine had replaced the rain clouds of the previous evening. 'But I have young children to consider.'

The decurion paused, for he could see that Daire was considering his options.

'The longer my boys remain in one place, especially when we might be within the reach of Vortigern's assassins, the greater is the danger in which they are placed,' Paulus said hesitantly. 'I believe our journey would take some three days, or less, and we should be able to follow the coastline during our journey into Hispania.'

Daire sank down on to a nearby stool in front of the open fireplace and stared vacantly into the coals. Paulus could tell that the seaman was weighing up the possibilities of putting to sea in the inclement weather that prevailed at this time of year.

'It'll be a risk, mind you! It's one that I wouldn't normally take, but I am tied for life to the men of the legions. Your master and I stood side by side in far-flung places and he saved my skin on many occasions. I owe him my life and we have a kinship between us that will last forever. I'm a fool to risk my boat, but *Neptune's Kiss* has been lucky. Let's see if our trust in her good fortune will continue to hold true.'

Paulus looked across at Daire with the respect and admiration that he held for other men of the legions who were placed in difficult situations.

'I'll see that you're set up for life for any risks you take on our behalf. King Aeron has been generous to those of us who are carrying out this duty and I fully understand the risk you are taking by agreeing to put to sea during the storm season.'

Paulus clapped Daire on the back with a soldier's heartiness, while Mavourna watched this display of camaraderie with female disgust. She moved to Daire's side with a sullen swish of her skirt.

'If you've finished congratulating yourselves, I'll get your sea kit packed. I imagine you'll be gone for several weeks.'

Daire realised that she was upset, so he picked her up in his arms and squeezed her ample buttocks.

'I'll miss you, darlin', but gold will always override my concerns over bad weather.'

While Mavourna sulked, she helped her man find his heavy fur-lined coat and a tight-fitting tunic that had been liberally soaked in waterproofing tar. This garment might have been dirty and greasy but, happily, it would remain waterproof when the weather was foul.

The sea boiled like a pot on hot coals and Paulus could feel the gorge rising in his throat with every crazy slide into the steeply sloped troughs. Once again, the decurion was reminded of how much he detested the sea.

The ragtag party had seen the dark bruising clouds in the sky that spoke of approaching storms in the hours before they departed from Burdigala. Daire was confident that he could sail his vessel across the face of the approaching squalls and outrun their worst effects, but luck didn't favour *Neptune's Kiss*. The gales began to bite into the flesh of the travellers with small, penetrating knives, and they knew they were about to experience the sea god's anger.

The severe weather had hit the vessel just as *Neptune's Kiss* reached open water and took up a southerly heading that would parallel the coast of Gallia. Daire swore with a legionnaire's imagination and lashed the rudder into place as soon as he felt the sea buck under the keel of the boat like a live thing. Then, as the boat climbed to the crest of each wave, Daire could only see water around his vessel, so the comforting sight of land was lost from view.

'Yer won't kill me, Sea Witch!' Daire laughed with a wild shake of his wet, shaggy hair. 'I'll be damned if I put any blood on yer altar, you bitch, even in this kind of weather. Sweeten up, yer pile of old weed and dead things, for I'll not put up with yer tantrums.'

Dilic crossed herself like a good Christian and prayed that God would forgive Daire for his blasphemy. Under the doubtful shelter of a canvas awning, the three women and two children had lashed themselves to the ship's mast. Dara was forced to hold Ambrosius's head as paroxysms of seasickness overcame the child.

Dilic yearned for the stillness and calm of the boats that were moored among the wharves in Burdigala. Her limited knowledge of the sea told her that *Neptune's Kiss* could easily be driven far from their original course by this fierce tempest, even with their solitary sail lowered. She almost cheered when Daire turned the rudder hard to the right and the bow of the boat reacted immediately as it turned into the wind and waves. The boat speed slowed perceptibly.

Meanwhile, Paulus found a length of light mooring rope that he used to tie himself to the mast. With little confidence in its quality, he prayed to God that he might live to see another day.

Having lost all visual reference to the mainland that lay to the east and the south, Daire was fully aware of how perilous their situation had become. All he knew for certain was that their small vessel was being driven towards the south-west.

Despite having her bows pointed into the oncoming sea and with her sail lowered, Daire knew that he must slow the ship's progress to ensure it wasn't blown further on to a lee shore on the northern coast of Hispania. The vessel was being blown inexorably in a south-westerly direction before an ever-freshening winter gale. Daire could see that the ropes were freezing as the cold increased, while the rigging also froze and creaked as if it was in pain. A thin coating of rime ice was beginning to form on the decks of the waterlogged vessel.

'The self-bailers aren't getting rid of all the water, so you'll have to help me with the bailing,' Daire yelled at Paulus over the sound of the growling mast and the oncoming wind.

Paulus used an old bucket in an attempt to scoop water from the scuppers, while Uther tried to supplement the Roman's efforts by using the decurion's helmet as a makeshift bailer.

It was time to release the sea anchor, the drogue that would keep the ship's bow into the wind and ensure that the vessel remained upright.

'Make your way back to the stern, Paulus. There's a large basket filled with rocks that is tied to a long length of rope. The other end is tied to the ship's stern. I want you to play out the length of rope until it is trailing out behind us. Once it is all played out, use your knife to cut the bindings that tie the basket to the stern. Once it's in the water, it'll slow us down and keep us safe till the storm blows itself out.'

Unwillingly, Paulus complied, although he had no real understanding of the seacraft that the bedraggled Daire exhibited with every instruction.

Paulus's efforts quickly bore fruit and *Neptune's Kiss* was soon riding higher in the water with its bow directly into the wind. The yawing and sideways movement stopped and, within minutes, the boat's motion was confined to fore and aft pitching without any obvious roll.

'Dilic!' Daire screamed. 'Your eyes are better than mine. Look for a landfall when we are at the top of each crest! Look to your left, yer silly cow, or even the back of the boat! Those are the only directions where the land can possibly be found.'

Paulus held his breath and prayed that they hadn't been blown too far off course. The Oceanus Atlanticus was wide and dangerous, and Daire had no real idea where they were, although he would never admit it.

Shaking and blue from the cold, Dilic peered owlishly into the distance whenever the boat crested each wave. Irritated by the failing light, she clambered to the top of a small area of elevated decking and gazed into the far distance.

Then, off to the left, and slightly behind the stern of the vessel, she saw some dimly glowing sparks of light that sent a dirty yellow glow through the gloom. A number of small, blinking glimmers suggested that a fishing village lay just beyond a thick area of darkness.

'There's a small village to our left. I think it's some sort of a settlement,' Dilic bellowed as she clutched at her fragile perch with straining fingers.

'How big is it?' Daire shouted. His response was interrupted by several curses when he lost his footing on the icy deck and slipped into the scuppers.

Paulus gripped Daire by his tunic so that, for a brief moment, the seaman hung over the sea and the dangerous swell. 'Best watch your footing, man. We'll get nowhere if we lose our captain,' Paulus snapped in a voice that was marred by the chattering of his teeth.

Daire grinned.

'If it isn't Donostia and there are more than three or four houses in the settlement, it'll have to be the fishing village at Simpliae. We've been lucky, because it seems that the storm blew *Neptune's Kiss* towards the border of Hispania and Gallia. Either way, it's of no account because both places have sandy foreshores where we can run the boat up on to the beach.'

'All I know is that my children are freezing,' Dilic interrupted. 'We need to make a landfall so they can be warmed and fed,' she ordered in a combative voice. Daire and Paulus looked at each other with trepidation.

Daire moved carefully to the rear of the vessel and freed the large rudder that he had lashed into position before the storm struck. Then, with his razor-sharp seaman's knife, he cut away the rope that tied the sea anchor to the stern of the vessel.

Freed from her restraints, *Neptune's Kiss* leaped at the waves and Paulus imagined that, like a joyous young woman, his vessel was plunging into the sea swell for the sheer pleasure of pitting her muscles against the strength of Father Sea. Paulus watched Daire's control of the rudder with growing respect. The greasy-haired, unshaven sailor might look unprepossessing, but he understood the sea and those men who seduced her for personal gain.

Then, as Paulus strained his old eyes, he saw that their vessel was nearing a headland.

'By the gods!' Daire muttered. 'I do believe that this is Simpliae, so La Concha Bay and Donostia are just a few miles down the coast. With the luck of fools, we've managed to chance on to our destination. I've sailed these waters before, and I recognise the shape of that headland.'

Paulus looked at the detritus from the storm that had scattered the possessions of the women into an unholy mess in the scuppers of *Neptune's Kiss*. The footwear and clothing would dry, and even Paulus's cloak would survive this rough treatment, but several scrolls that Paulus had carried with him, including details of his military service, had been pounded into a solid mass of sludge.

'Most of our things will dry, but what doesn't isn't of any real importance.'

Paulus looked at his large calloused palms and felt a twinge of regret. Still, his charges had survived the storm without a loss of life, so his responsibilities had not been compromised.

'Look to the children, Dilic, and see if you can warm them up. I'm almost frozen solid, so the little ones must be suffering cruelly from this damning cold.'

For once, Dilic didn't question Paulus's authority and she obeyed him without query.

For some little time, Daire was busy with the sails and the rudder as he endeavoured to slow the boat's progress to a crawl while manoeuvring his vessel in the moonlight. Gradually, *Neptune's Kiss* came about and, groaning from every board, the vessel was forced to follow her master's directions to avoid a rocky shoal that appeared suddenly on their right. From his adroit handling of the rudder, Paulus could tell that Daire had indeed sailed through these waters before and understood the hidden network of reefs and barnacled stone that lay in wait for novice seafarers. With the skill of a true seaman, Daire had avoided the pitfalls.

'We'll be making our landfall soon, Dilic,' Paulus called. 'Once the vessel is moored, I'll go ashore to find us an inn where the boys can get warm. Make haste with your packing! If I know Daire, he'll want to head off to the fleshpots, so it'll be up to you to keep him on the boat until our possessions are taken to whatever lodgings I can find.'

To Daire's disappointment and Dilic's grim enjoyment, the sea captain was forced to dance to the servant's authoritarian tune as Paulus climbed down on to a low and shaky wharf before strolling off into the village. In the distance, he could still hear the maidservant berating the sea captain with her usual shrewish refrain.

Darkness had fallen and the hour was late when Pridenow and the merchant's daughter entered Venta Belgarum on his exhausted warhorse. Red had done his very best and Pridenow could find no fault with his mount, but the demands on the horse had been such that the prince had been forced to sleep during the day to rest both humans and the beast.

'How long will it take us to reach Venta Belgarum?' Creidne asked in a strident tone that made Pridenow's hackles rise. The girl was obviously used to issuing orders, but she sensed the stiffness that had come over his body. Wisely, she attempted to make amends at once. 'I'm anxious to gain some redress through the offices of the king.'

Pridenow was forced to bite his tongue, so he didn't make an insulting reference to Vortigern. Instead, with a honeyed smile, he left Creidne in no doubt that Vortigern had no place in their regard.

'As far as I know,' Creidne said sardonically as the city gates came into view, 'Vortigern has yet to win the approval of the tribal kings, least of all the common men of Britannia. They will fight to preserve their own lands, but too many of their kin spilled their blood in Constantine's wars. They don't lack courage, but they are weary of the self-seeking games that rulers play. Until he is confirmed and crowned as the High King, Vortigern will need to prove himself before the British people will accept him.'

Pridenow examined the young woman with an emotion very close to admiration. In a few succinct words, Creidne had summed up the tangled skeins of life in Vortigern's palace.

'Then let us hope that Vortigern is ready to fight, else I'll be without my head. I've been banished from the kingdom and only the most urgent of reasons should bring me back to my sister's halls.'

The gates of Venta Belgarum were firmly shut, forcing Pridenow to batter on the entrance gate that allowed travellers on foot to enter the town. After several lamps were lit and complaints rose in the evening like startled birds, the gatekeeper's hutch swung open and a small man peered up at the prince.

'Who be there to upset my peace? All good souls should be abed by this time. Be quick and answer me, or I will set the guard after you for trying to break into the fortress.'

'Let me in, you oaf. I am Lord Pridenow, the queen's brother, and I bring urgent messages to Lord Vortigern concerning Britannia's safety.'

A snarl revealed the gatekeeper's black teeth and nasty demeanour. 'You be that prince, the one what is banished. Stop yer caterwauling before I call out the guard.'

Pridenow realised that the gatekeeper had been misshapen by an accident of birth that raised one shoulder above the other, so he moderated his tone and treated the gruff little creature with respect.

'You're right to protect your mistress, gatekeeper. I wouldn't be here if the Saxons weren't abroad. The bastards are killing and thieving at will, and Lord Vortigern must be warned of their presence if there is to be any Britannia left for him to rule. Let me in, man, and I'll take my chances.'

The little man took two paces backwards and struggled to move the large crossbeam that held the gate in place. The black slabs of oak, still marked with the footprints of the adzes that shaped them, gradually swung open with much groaning and creaking. With a shout to Creidne to run behind him, Pridenow spurred Red forward so that the horse breasted the partially opened gates as if they were a simple timber fence.

Having lithely dismounted, Creidne pursued the horse and its rider on foot. She sprang nimbly over piles of refuse, while praying that she could keep pace with the warhorse and her benefactor.

For good or ill, Pridenow had returned to his sister's side. Only time would tell if Fortuna would smile upon him, or lead him to ruin.

The maidservant came running, her bare feet slapping on the mosaic tiles.

Severa looked up from her weaving with a small cry of alarm. Beside her, the infant lay swaddled in a woollen blanket to protect him from any wayward chill.

'It's your brother, mistress, and he's come from the north with a message for the master. Prince Pridenow is like to be chained like a common felon unless you come quickly.'

'My brother is here? Why has he come? He knows that Vortigern intends to kill him out of hand if he returns to Venta Belgarum.'

Severa rose to her feet without her usual grace. Only two weeks had passed since the arrival of her son, Vortimer, since when she had been prone to bloody fluxes and debilitating pains. At least her illness was keeping her husband out of her bedchamber.

She made her painful way down the stairs, crossed the mosaics and entered the King's Hall where her brother was standing between two huge warriors. Behind Pridenow, she noticed a small, angry girl. It was obvious to Severa that Vortigern had upset another young female who had come within his ambit, although, now that she examined the girl more closely, Severa remembered the young daughter of a merchant who had caused some disruption in the peace of Venta Belgarum. At the time, Vortigern had belittled the merchant's complaints and it had been left to Severa to calm what might have become an unpleasant situation.

The Demetae king was sitting on Constantine's throne with a thunderous expression on his face and a goblet of Falernian wine held casually in his clenched fist. The object of the High King's fury was standing unrepentantly before his master, staring fearlessly at him.

A shard of light from the sconces caught something from Pridenow's russet hair as he turned to face Severa. With a pang of presentiment, she saw her foster-brother crowned in bloody light, and only his shark-grey eyes showed any trace of the young man who she had loved so well.

Pridenow had changed. The world had altered and Severa realised that her part in this small drama had almost come to an end. But there were still some challenges that needed to be faced before her part in Britannia's history was complete.

'You've had the gall to return to my lands in contravention of my expressed commands, boy,' Vortigern said in a voice that sounded harsher than usual. 'Well, Pridenow? Do you hold any doubts that I can order your execution? If you do, you are very much mistaken.'

Against all common sense, Creidne pushed her way through the mass of warriors until she was standing alongside Pridenow.

'Pridenow came to your court because he took the time to save me from an attack by Saxon invaders, Your Highness. I'm the one who insisted that he come to warn you of their presence in your kingdom. If anyone should be punished, then it should be me.'

'You haven't been invited to speak, girl,' Vortigern interrupted, his sickly smile distorting his venomous face. 'You mustn't make promises you can't keep.'

Creidne paled visibly, but she stood her ground and stared the Demetae down. Vortigern grinned and his wolfish likeness deepened as he licked his lips and tasted the young woman's fear.

Pridenow interrupted the nasty little tableau by trying to draw Vortigern's attention away from Creidne.

'Sire, I've returned to your city out of a great need to tell you, and our people, that a large party of Saxon raiders is abroad and in control of a large parcel of Roman road some days' distance from here. No merchant or legitimate traveller can pass through their area of influence with safety, as this harmless girl can attest. Her father and his hired warriors were killed and she would seem to be the only survivor. Their caravan, along with all their trade goods, was taken and despoiled by these Saxon invaders who are sufficiently numerous to threaten the roads that lie between here and Calleva Atrebatum. It was beholden on me to warn you of their presence. The tribes must be gathered and we must smash their onslaught before a trickle of raiders becomes a flood. I believe our enemies landed at some place in the vicinity of Anderida and have spread out through the south. They have the ability to sack all the settlements that lie ahead of them, even to places as far north as Venta Belgarum.'

Vortigern could tell that Pridenow was in deadly earnest and the young man's warnings were well-meant. The seasoned warrior in Vortigern came to the fore and he sat a little straighter, while the wolf pelt that he wore as an affectation began to slide from his shoulder to fall on to the floor like a puddle of molten silver.

'Tell me your thoughts then, Prince,' Vortigern snarled, while impaling Pridenow with a basilisk stare. 'I need to know everything that you know or can assume from what you've seen and experienced during your travels.'

With occasional embellishments from Creidne, Pridenow recounted the misfortunes they had experienced on the road leading to the north. Vortigern listened carefully and, when he smiled, Pridenow knew that his orders wouldn't be particularly pleasant.

'Alert my guard and the leaders of my force of tribal warriors,' Vortigern ordered one of the grizzled officers who were standing in the open space adjacent to the imperial throne. 'At the same time, you can send appropriate messages to the Dumnonii tribe and that beehive of traitors who hide themselves away in Tintagel. We'll probably need all the warriors we can get, so don't accept any excuses.'

The grizzled veteran nodded briefly and backed away from

the king, his armour clanging as metal rubbed against metal. The sound grated on Pridenow's nerves and sent his pulse racing.

'Those warriors who are presently in Venta Belgarum will be the backbone of a force which I shall lead personally,' Vortigern added. 'You, young Pridenow, will act as my scout and you shall keep me informed of the disposition of my enemies. Is there any reason why you might feel unable to fulfil these duties?'

Severa drew in a sharp breath. She knew that Vortigern would sacrifice Pridenow at the earliest opportunity; if her husband had his way, Pridenow would die on a Saxon sword. Alternatively, he would disgrace himself in battle and be open to fabricated charges of treason. Either way, Vortigern would win. Then reason began to override her fears, for Pridenow had a strong sense of self-preservation. More importantly, Vortigern now had a need for her foster-brother's services.

But Vortigern will lie and manipulate circumstances, a quiet voice whispered in Severa's ear. He'll do whatever he can to destroy Pridenow because he's fully aware that the prophecies have spoken of the boy's importance to Britannia's future. To Vortigern, Pridenow's demise was the ultimate challenge, something he must bring about if he was to achieve his own ambitions.

Vortigern looked directly at Severa. His eyes were as flat as wet river stones with no trace of emotion to indicate that he understood her fears. Rather, he was daring Severa to question his authority. Both knew that Pridenow would be the only one who would suffer if she protested, so Severa closed her mouth and bit back any argument she might otherwise have made.

Pridenow was boyishly excited at the prospect of returning to the scene of the ambush and facing the Saxon invaders. Unblooded and not yet a seasoned warrior, he was eager to pit his strength against a vicious and implacable enemy. Besides, there would be spoils available to the victors and, as a scout for Vortigern's force, he would be given free rein to roam at will through the broad fields of southern Britannia. A landless youth, Pridenow now had an opportunity to establish himself as a man and profit from whatever fortune came his way.

For his part, Vortigern was energised at the prospect of facing an enemy in battle. This was a perfect opportunity to legitimise his rule by destroying the traditional enemies of the Britons. When he rose to his feet, his hair seemed to crackle with energy and his features held a wolfish hunger that told his followers that he was eager to do battle. The other British warriors took heart from his obvious enthusiasm, even those who knew that their numbers and resources were limited. Britannia's warriors might be fewer in number without the trained soldiers who had perished in Gallia, but Vortigern believed that those who remained, along with volunteers from the Dumnonii and levies from Tintagel, could put his enemies to the sword.

As he strode from the King's Hall, Vortigern's officers fell into step behind him.

'You see this as an opportunity to consolidate your rule, you bastard, but how many of your warriors will still be alive when the snows come,' Severa whispered to herself.

Other than her loyal nurse, Brisen, no one heard the queen's words. This worthy held her arms wide and hugged her mistress in consolation. Then, with the babe safely held against her breast, Severa could forget that Death had come to the isles and wouldn't leave till it had eaten its fill.

CHAPTER XV

FINDING A HAVEN

To understand the true quality of people, you must look
into their minds and examine their pursuits and aversions.

Marcus Aurelius

The village's main thoroughfare snaked its way to the summit of
a low hill that dominated the surrounding landscape. The cobbles
that had been so carefully placed into the road paving were slick
and wet from passing rain squalls and Paulus could feel the wind
as it sliced through him with all the force of a Hispanic winter on
its chill breath.

Having almost reached Donostia, his destination, Paulus's
demeanour was nonchalant and relieved when he strode upwards to a dimly lit timber structure at the top of the hill. His
cloak, still waterlogged from the sea-journey in *Neptune's Kiss*,
was flapping irritatingly around his legs. Still, with all the confidence of a seasoned Roman soldier, Paulus knew that this
unprepossessing building was a hostelry that would offer a

temporary haven and security to weary travellers.

As he halted outside the ramshackle buildings, he realised that horse stables, inexpertly constructed from coarsely hewn timber, were the source of the open light. Even in the darkness of the night, he could see that attempts had been made to repair the sagging structure and even traces of mud-daub and willow-lath indicated to Paulus that these stables had once been part of a larger and more substantial property. Unfortunately, the entire building had a decided inwards lean, and it was in danger of toppling during periods of strong, gusty wind.

The decurion was surprised to find that the inn itself was in total darkness.

Then, as Paulus stood at the open doorway of the stables, a drowsy stable boy stumbled to his feet from his makeshift straw bedding and hailed the Roman with a look of surprise and trepidation on his face.

'What do you be wanting?' the boy asked through his chattering teeth. Paulus was surprised to see that, despite the lad sleeping in a bed of hay, he was only wearing a thin tunic to stave off the icy cold of winter. Paulus obligingly pulled the stable door closed behind him.

The gloom in this large, open space was almost Stygian. The stable had sufficient accommodation for four horses, including mangers for their feed, while the narrow spaces above the feeding-boxes served as storage areas for supplies of hay, a few bags of grain and the inn's winter store of root vegetables. The timber shelving was so old and brittle that Paulus hoped he wouldn't be required to climb into any of the narrow recesses. Instead, he turned his attention back to the shivering stable boy.

'Is the inn open?' Paulus asked the young lad with all the patience he could muster.

The boy quailed with nervous fear.

'I be Rhun, the stable boy of this place. The master keeps some rooms in the inn for passing folk, but all honest travellers are abed by now. He won't want to talk with you!'

'My companions and I were hoping to arrive before dusk, but we've been delayed by storms,' Paulus responded crisply. 'I need a good-sized room to house three women and two children, not to mention a corner where I can lay down my own head. Find your master for me.'

The boy stared nervously at the decurion, and noted that his visitor was wearing the red coat of a legionnaire. He fully understood its significance and the power that came with the uniform, for no one in the Roman sphere of influence would be ignorant of the meaning of legionnaire's scarlet. Rhun feared that he might well rue the day that a Roman soldier came knocking at the stable door.

As Rhun ran towards the ramshackle inn, the lad prayed with all his heart that the innkeeper would spare his rear end from the beatings he regularly endured, whether he earned them or not.

When the boy left the stables, he pulled the door closed and plunged the deeper recesses of the building into darkness. Then, in his haste, he slipped on the wet paving and fell into the small plot of late vegetables that had been grown by the innkeeper's wife. Terrified, Rhun heard the terracotta pots break into large shards.

'I'm for it now,' the boy whispered to himself as he pounded the shoddy timbers of the inn with both hands. 'Hergel won't be satisfied with any excuses.'

From inside the inn, Rhun heard an angry oath from Hergel and the shrill, piping sounds made by the innkeeper's wife. After a few minutes, the splintered, sagging door swung inwards.

'What in Hades are you after, you young fool? You'd better have a damned good reason for waking me at this ungodly hour of the night or I'll beat your hide till you're black and blue.'

The latch swung open and revealed a thick-set man with a greasy pate of grey hair and a solemn expression on his ugly face. Rhun flinched away from his master's fists as if he had been struck.

'There's a Roman soldier at the stables, master, and he wants to know what rooms you have. He says he'll pay good coin for whatever shelter you can give him, but he's soaking wet. He's said he has three women and two young children with him, so he must have come from the sea. He wants to speak to you and he won't take no for an answer.'

'You're an idiot, Rhun! What would a Roman soldier be doing in this flea-bitten village? No boats have arrived today, so you've misheard him.'

Shifting his weight from foot to foot, Rhun glanced up towards the stables where Paulus was waiting. 'The Roman is a soldier and he's ever so fierce, master. You should hurry!'

Once again, Rhun shot a frightened glance in the direction of the stables as if he expected this frightening soldier to materialise beside him. Then, as the innkeeper moved towards him, Rhun flinched. He tried to step away from his master's path, only to slip on the icy steps.

Hergel was in a foul mood by now, for the coldness in the outside air had bitten into his rolls of fat and left him gasping in pain from a severe tightening in his chest.

When he reached the stable door, he thrust it open with a bad-tempered oath.

'Who is it that rouses me out of my warm bed?'

Paulus moved out from the shadows but all that the innkeeper could clearly see of the red-coated stranger was the light that flashed out of his glittering eyes and the scarlet of his woollen cloak. Hergel was no fool. Even though he professed to have no interest in affairs outside of Simpliae, he realised that the man standing before him was, indeed, a Roman officer. Hergel shivered, plastered a sycophantic smile on to his greasy features and stepped forward to curry favour with his visitor.

'I'd have hastened to meet with you if this buffoon had told me that you were a Roman officer. What can our small inn do for you, my lord? We are a remote village, but you can be sure that your every wish will be met if it's within my power to serve you.'

Hergel glanced at the hapless Rhun with venomous intent then, making the boy quail as he tried to fade into the background.

In the short time that he had been left to his own devices when Rhun had run off to find his master, Paulus had investigated the stables and discovered the presence of two shaggy-coated horses that had been housed inside the building. One of the beasts whickered in the darkness and, with some relief, Rhun hastened to settle the nervous beasts.

'I require accommodation in which I can house my party for a night or two. Our boat was blown off course in a storm as we were travelling to Donostia so the women and children need to recuperate. You appear to possess the only sizable accommodations in your village.'

The flaring of the decurion's nostrils and the arrogant tilt of his head were indicative of the contempt he felt for Hergel's hostelry and the man's malodorous presence. The innkeeper reeked of unwashed flesh.

'Beggars can't be choosers and I need a place where three women servants, two young children, and myself, can rest for the remainder of the night. I'll have to conduct some business in the village on the morrow, meaning it's probable that we'll also stay here for one more night. We'll need meals for the whole party. You'll be paid in good coin, subject to negotiating a fair price for your services. I'm also interested in purchasing two horses and a serviceable cart so that we can continue our journey by road.'

Hergel rubbed his grimy palms together. Fortuna had delivered a rich prize into his ambit, and the greedy streak in him intended to milk his good fortune for all that it was worth.

'I do have a large single room that could meet your needs, but I'll have to reorganise my hostelry to accommodate your requirements. You can be sure that I'll calculate an acceptable price. My wife can cook for all of your party, my good sir, and I dare say that I'll be able to find a local farmer who'd be prepared to part with a serviceable cart that would meet your needs. In the meantime, I have two well-bred horses that are stabled directly behind you. They are family favourites, sir, and I'd hate to lose these beauties. However, I'm prepared to sell them if you make an offer that makes the transaction worth my while.'

Paulus had assessed Hergel's character by this time and he decided that he didn't like this sycophantic innkeeper; in fact he distrusted the man's every word. The tone of his voice became clipped and his manner was harsher than would otherwise have been his habit. As a widely travelled and worldly man, Paulus was wise to the cheating ways that were practised by purveyors of liquor and accommodation. He insisted on inspecting the inn's horses for himself.

Rhun leaped to obey as soon as Hergel jerked his head in the direction of the stalls where the beasts were stabled.

'They be fine animals, sir, as you'll see when daylight comes,' Hergel informed him. 'I'm certain that I could sell them for twice the price I'm prepared to accept from you, but I've always assisted the legions when it's in my power to do so.'

Paulus inspected the two animals with a sense of derision.

Neither of the beasts was young, as he discovered when he examined their teeth. But they were sturdy animals and, as far as he could judge by the light of an oil lamp that Rhun had set down outside of the stalls, they seemed healthy enough. Their coats needed brushing, but someone had taken good care of their hoofs and ensured that they fed on quality grain. Paulus guessed that the stable boy had used his initiative by assuming responsibility for their care.

Satisfied, Paulus made a non-negotiable offer for the accommodation and food that would be provided for his party during the two days and nights that he expected to remain in Simpliae. Left with little room to negotiate, Hergel accepted the offer, but he was determined to receive a good price for the two horses.

Paulus, however, had already decided that he would be prepared to pay a premium price for these animals. The decurion's need for comfortable transport for his people was great, so he made an offer that was eye-wateringly generous. However, the agreement came with a proviso. Hergel would have to locate a suitable cart from one of the neighbouring farmers that could be purchased in Paulus's name.

With minimal reluctance, the two men struck their bargain.

Paulus retraced his steps down the hill until he reached the dilapidated wharf where *Neptune's Kiss* had been tied. Daire was impatient to find a satisfying drop of wine, and he was cheered at the prospect of spending the night in a hostelry. He was easily persuaded to carry Ambrosius up the hill to Hergel's inn while Dilic took Uther by the hand. The difficult child had refused to rest until Paulus had returned.

Then, as they climbed the hill, Daire reassessed his intentions to imbibe the local wines and decided to spend the night on *Neptune's Kiss*, just in case. A single glance at the inn had changed the sailor's mind.

'There's men here who'll steal the eyes out of a needle if I give them half a chance, so it'd be best if I spend the hours of darkness on board the boat. I'll make me way back to Burdigala in the early morning. Perhaps we can settle our accounts before I set sail.'

Daire shot a regretful glance towards the doubtful comforts of the village's inn, before turning and looking at the decurion with reckless eyes.

'I tell yer, Paulus. You be a good man and I'll be sorry to hear if you've been cheated blind by these thieves in Simpliae. Take care, my friend, and I'll see you in the morning.'

With Paulus's usual efficiency, the party made its way up to the inn. Dilic examined the filthy floors and cobweb-veiled ceilings with a jaundiced eye, but for once she kept her tongue between her teeth. Grateful that he had been spared her usual diatribe, Paulus assisted the women to bed the children down on a verminous pallet that had seen better days. The bedding had never experienced the benefits obtained from soap and water.

Too tired to think, the women and the children fell asleep. Paulus, however, knew that he'd never be able to sleep in the limited space that was available to him. After propping a broken chair against the door frame, the Roman made his way down the steep stairs and returned to the stables in order to sleep there. The chair, the decurion's makeshift warning system, would wake the women if the innkeeper tried to enter their room.

Ensconced in the stables and comfortable on the relatively clean straw, Paulus began to wonder if he would ever be free and unencumbered again. The children were heavy weights that would always hang around his neck and he doubted that his responsibilities would ease in the months and years that lay ahead of him. 'I'm a damned fool!' he upbraided himself. 'I was a silly old goat to accept the task in the first place.'

An owl shrieked in the darkness outside and Paulus could hear the coughing of a fox. He guessed that hungry predators were abroad and some unwary victim would die before first light. He patted his gladius for reassurance.

'We're safe enough for now,' Paulus informed the soughing wind. And then, despite his efforts to remain awake, he fell into a deep and dreamless sleep.

Midway through the following morning, Paulus was pleasantly surprised when a farmer's cart trundled up the hill and halted outside the stables. The ageing vehicle was in surprisingly good condition and met all of Paulus's requirements, so the decurion accepted the purchase of the wagon and a complete set of harness leathers without hesitation.

'It's on to Donostia, young Uther,' Paulus told the boy. 'With a little luck, we'll be there in a few days – and then we can rest easily.'

Uther grinned companionably at him from his perch on the

back of the wagon. Since the storm, the boy was developing a peculiar companionship with the Roman.

'You'll see, Uther. Everything will work out once we've reached our destination.'

Pridenow drew his borrowed stallion to a halt by pulling firmly on the reins. His normal mount, Red, was resting among the reserve horses in Vortigern's camp after weeks of hard riding, and the prince had felt oddly disconnected when he began to ride this strange horse. Fortunately, the bay was well trained and it responded immediately to his touch.

The road stretched out before him like a long silver cord. Pale moonlight glinted off the regular milestones that informed the young man of his nearness to Calleva Atrebatum and the British garrison that had set up camp inside the city walls. During his month-long wanderings, he had found evidence that the Saxon raiders had penetrated deeply into Britannia's countryside, proving conclusively that Vortigern must call on the other British kings to send men, gold and equipment to this industrial city where he intended to make a stand against the Saxon invaders. Here, the smiths were already hard at work, forging weapons that would be used during the approaching Saxon summer, although the last vestiges of winter could still be found in those farmlands that were still white with rime frost. Meanwhile, reinforcements sent by the reluctant rulers of Britannia's tribes had been slowly drifting towards his encampment.

The Britons hated Vortigern to a man, but they feared the Saxon warriors more. The northern infiltrators, with their torcs of yellow gold around their throats, were toweringly tall and heavily muscled. Few Britons had the physical attributes to stand

315

against these northerners who had come to Britannia's shores in search of plunder, meaning that success for Vortigern's forces would only be achieved if he carried out a well-planned, disciplined attack that utilised all of his slender resources. Fortunately, Vortigern possessed strategic acumen and a dogged determination that had been bequeathed to him by Constantine's forces during the emperor's foray into Gallia.

Vortigern had one further talent. He used his personal aura of cruelty and barbarism to inspire respect from the hearts of the Saxon thanes, leaders who were far less sophisticated than their British peers. In his wolf pelt, Vortigern was a fearful figure, for he understood the power of symbolism on untutored, super-stitious minds. The Demetae's cold reasoning and a callous disregard for everyone, except for himself, enhanced the power of his short form.

Pridenow sighed deeply. Vortigern's forces were massing behind Calleva Atrebatum's defences and the prince could see that Vortigern intended to use the shanty town that clung to the city approaches as the centrepiece in his line of defence. Even at this early stage of preparation, the forges inside the town glowed with white and blood-red heat as weapons were made or repaired as part of the British preparations for the coming conflagration.

Vortigern had chosen his ground carefully. To the north and west of the city, a rivulet had carved its way into the marshy lowlands before the city gates, a geographical advantage that ensured that attack from these quarters was extremely unlikely. Meanwhile, the flotsam who had lived and flourished on the dregs of the city's wealth had packed up everything that could be stolen and headed, with their wagons, towards Corinium. At first, the road had been choked with these fleeing peasants, but the flood had been reduced to a trickle as the last of the non-combatant populace left the area of conflict. Even the camp followers who usually attached themselves to standing armies had been encouraged to decamp and, with their possessions in handcarts, leave their hovels in the shanty town. The Demetae king had been given an opportunity to mobilise Calleva Atrebatum's defences and entice his Saxon adversaries into a trap of his choosing.

As a result, despite Pridenow's natural suspicion of the Demetae's motives and sincerity, he could find little fault with the strategic acumen that was evident in Vortigern's plan of attack. The Saxon commanders believed their warriors were invincible when engaged in pitched battles, but Vortigern intended to take full advantage of their self-confidence.

Pridenow was fully aware that the northern invaders preferred to attack their enemies as individuals although, traditionally, they obeyed their thane to the letter. For these giant warriors, life was a constant search for individual fame and glory; like the Demetae king, Pridenow accepted that this could be the Saxons' greatest weakness. Vortigern intended to present his enemies with a battlefield scenario that would be decidedly favourable to Saxon battle plans and strategies. But, in truth, he intended to add his own twist to the scenario once his British warriors were committed to hand-to-hand combat in the shanty town that had grown like a giant mushroom outside the city walls.

Against all common sense, Vortigern planned to send a large number of his British warriors out of Calleva Atrebatum to make a frontal attack on the Saxons as the northerners were approaching the shanty town and were committed to the coming conflict. The suicidal attack by Vortigern's force would result in many casualties, although more than half of his total force would be kept in reserve within the city walls. The loss of life would be dreadful as Vortigern's warriors retreated towards the city gates, but the Saxons would pursue the survivors of the frontal attack remorselessly as they tried to capitalise on what they would see as British stupidity.

Then, when reason suggested that the British defence was failing, the mean streets of the shanty town would be set alight behind the flanks of the Saxon attackers. If this portion of the plan was successful, the front ranks of the Saxon attackers would be trapped before the gates of Calleva Atrebatum. They would be caught with the advancing flames behind them and a force of reinvigorated British troops in front of them. The remnants of Vortigern's reserve troops would man the defences along the wall, raining down large rocks, flaming arrows and gourds of boiling oil on the Saxons from the ramparts.

This line of defenders would be more devastating than a mass of reinforcements.

The Saxons would be trapped if Vortigern could wait until his enemies were at the gates of the city. But his plan would only work if the Demetae king could hold his nerve until the very last moment. Only then would his fresh troops inside the city be unleashed to begin their attack on the tiring Saxons, warriors who would soon become the hunted.

With the shanty town ablaze and blocking any enemy retreat, Vortigern's fresh warriors from within the city might well win the day. But did the Britons have the nerve to face these giant warriors from the north? Would they be prepared to die so that the trap could be sprung? If the Demetae's expectations were met, many of the combatants inside the area of conflict, both Saxon and Briton, would be consumed by the flames.

Vortigern's plan was both callous and dangerous, because its success depended on perfect timing by the commander and a smile from Fortuna when the trap was sprung. Not even Vortigern, for all his experience, could guarantee that events would occur in accordance with his predictions. He would be gambling everything on one roll of the dice.

Ruthless as he was, Vortigern intended to use this parlous conflict as a means of furthering his own ends. Pridenow's small force had been given the difficult and potentially fatal task of holding the line in the shanty town. As the battle grew in complexity and ferocity, the tawdry streets would be alive with overconfident Saxons, men who would be glorying in their early successes. Pridenow's force must fight their way through the shanty town and maintain pressure on the Saxon rear. Pridenow was aware that his force was expendable, his warriors probably to be sacrificed in the execution of Vortigern's feint. But, for Vortigern, this was of little account. He would have achieved his ends and Pridenow would no longer be an alternative claimant to the throne of High King.

When Vortigern had elaborated on his strategic thinking at a meeting with his subordinates, he gave the assembled officers a sanitised assessment of his strategy and tactical expectations. Young Gorlois, as the leader of the Tintagel forces, had felt an immediate shiver of fear as the Demetae explained the likely sequence of events. Although he was still a tyro in military matters, Gorlois accepted that he would be used as a tool in Vortigern's duplicity. Like Pridenow, he had never participated in a pitched battle but his fellow prince had seen the stamina and strength of the barbarian warriors, although only at a distance. At the very least, Pridenow could make a reasonable assessment of their abilities.

Both of these young men accepted instinctively that a significant number of the British force would be butchered and sacrificed on the altar of Vortigern's ambition. And so, once the Demetae was satisfied that the victory over the Saxon force was within his grasp, the princes would be ordered to turn the shanty town outside Calleva Atrebatum into a fireball.

Gorlois had arrived in Calleva Atrebatum at the head of a column of Dumnonii troops from Tintagel. He had prevailed on his father to allow him to take part in the very first battle of the current Saxon season. Committed to the treaty that united the southern kings of Britannia, the time had arrived for Gorlois to earn his spurs in defence of his father's kingdom.

Now, the young man looked out at the countryside around Calleva Atrebatum and marvelled at the risks that Vortigern was taking with his army of Britons. Something of the dread he was feeling must have been obvious on the Dumnonii's face, because Pridenow gripped him by the shoulder and flashed him a wink.

'I can see that you've worked out the intricacies of Vortigern's nasty little plan. Yes, he rather hopes that I will perish during this mad attack on a vastly superior force. It's sad, but I've seen the Saxons in action. They are very good at what they do, so there is an excellent chance that you and I will die once battle is joined.'

'You're very calm about it,' Gorlois responded. 'I thought I'd piss myself when I realised that we're about to be sacrificed in furtherance of Vortigern's ambitions. Because my father warned me not to trust the Demetae, I wasn't really surprised when you were volunteered to hold the line and block off any Saxons who might want to escape during the final stages of the battle. But I didn't think I'd done anything that could have offended him.'

Pridenow grinned at his friend who, for all his youth, was powerfully built and square with a good seat on a horse and an ever-present glint of excitement in his eyes. 'He can't have a high opinion of you if he's sending you into a battle at my side. What have you done that's brought you to his attention?'

'It doesn't take much to upset the Demetae wolf,' Gorlois replied.

'I've heard that he hates your kinfolk for imagined slights against the Demetae people during the time of Macsen Wledig – that's Magnus Maximus to you, my friend – so it would seem that you've been selected for a fiery end, just like me,' Pridenow added with a glimmer of reckless humour. 'I haven't discussed the matter with anyone, but I intend to stay alive and make the Demetae whoreson rue the day he was born. He has under-estimated the fighting spirit of our warriors, and I believe we'll win the day rather than surrender to the Saxon invaders. Since our people have more to lose than the Saxons, I'm convinced we can protect our own acres from the barbarians. Vortigern has forgotten how desperate peasants can make supreme sacrifices when the odds seem impossible.'

'If I'm to die, then so be it,' Gorlois said with a smile that matched Pridenow's own clear-headed courage. 'As the Saxon poets have said, *tomorrow might well be a good day to die.*'

CHAPTER XVI

A GOOD DAY TO DIE

When you arise in the morning, think of what a precious
privilege it is to be alive – to breathe, to think, to enjoy and
to love.

Marcus Aurelius

The night before the battle for Calleva Atrebatum commenced, Pridenow admitted to himself that he felt nervous about its outcome. When he closed his eyes and slept, a Saxon warrior of enormous size seemed to be hovering above him. Gigantic, brutal and flecked with dried flakes of blood, the abnormally tall figure seemed to block out the stars with its huge bulk. One hand held an iron axe and, when Pridenow tried to flee, the firm earth under his feet turned into quicksand and threatened to swallow him whole. The axe began the descent that would dash out his brains and Pridenow woke, in a lather of sweat, to find that he had torn his pallet to pieces in his imagined struggle with the barbarian.

'You're a fool, Pridenow! Look at what you've done now,' Pridenow hissed at his calloused hands. 'You're afraid that you'll prove to be a coward on the morrow.'

Even more than death, the young man feared cowardice. It wasn't as if he was afraid to die but he was terrified that he might not distinguish himself as a leader of men, a task for which he had been training from birth. The thought of not fulfilling his duties with distinction made his mouth so dry that he could barely swallow.

A muffled curse from the mound of leaves to his right told him that Gorlois was also awake, but Pridenow could barely make out his friend's nervous face, features that were lit by a fitful moon in the near-full darkness. In his dream state, the bones of Gorlois's facial features entered his vision, and it seemed as if the young man's body had been decapitated. Pridenow shivered at this strange presentiment and forced himself to push aside his sickened imaginings. He might have been spared from prophetic dreams during the past few months, but the shadow of his earlier imaginings made his stomach roil from nervous tension.

The prophetic dreams had been very clear and the prince realised he had been watching an older Gorlois who was in the company of a particularly beautiful woman. Her hair had fallen in long coils that almost brushed the earth when she moved, and her face and form were so perfect that her beauty took Pridenow's breath away.

As he watched, Pridenow imagined that an older Gorlois had brushed some welling tears from the woman's face before opening his arms and allowing the woman to slip into his embrace. Like shadows or ghosts, two little girls appeared at his feet and looked up at Gorlois with adoring eyes. As if by magic, a dragon suddenly entered this scene of domestic peace and its flaming breath burned Gorlois into black embers, before the beast coiled itself possessively around the feet of the fair woman.

In the thrall of his dream, Pridenow tried to assist his friend, but the heat had driven him back. He could only watch helplessly as the beast scoured Britannia with its fiery breath.

In that dislocation that occurs between dreaming and wakefulness, Pridenow returned to full consciousness. He immediately recognised the prosaic actuality of those men who had been trying to sleep on the hard earth, while other warriors on picket duty moved along the perimeter of Vortigern's encampment to the sound of the bells that tinkled on their horses' harness.

'Are you still awake, Pridenow?' Gorlois asked, his voice muffled by the blanket that had kept his sturdy bones off the cold earth.

'I'm awake, my friend. It seems that I haven't been able to rest properly.'

'I wish I were in your boots, Pridenow,' Gorlois continued as he turned over in his leafy pallet and tried to find a more comfortable resting position. 'You've carried out the duties of a warrior on many occasions and you've proved yourself as a leader. I'm still terrified that I'll make a fool of myself during a time of great need.'

'You aren't the only one, my friend,' Pridenow answered. 'I've been sleeping badly and I spend my days worrying about that selfsame thing. I suppose all warriors feel this way before a battle. After all, any man who isn't terrified by thoughts of violent death is either a fool or a liar – or both!'

Gorlois was placated by Pridenow's careful words, but the Dobunni prince was unable to allay his own nervousness. His extra sense had told him that he would survive this battle, but only a credulous fool would put too much faith in superstition. Pridenow knew that the odds were still stacked against his survival, especially if Vortigern had any say in the matter.

Pridenow remained wakeful until the sky was stained sanguine in the east and the birds had woken with their customary cheer-fulness, regardless of the activities of man. The horses stamped their hoofs and whickered to remind their handlers that they must be fed and watered. The camp came alive then with the sounds of men cleaning their armour and braiding their long hair, as well as the bustle and hurry of those warriors who wanted to quell their fears by distracting themselves with the everyday duties that are carried out by all soldiers.

Pridenow and Gorlois took turns to braid each other's locks which were then packed inside their iron helmets, a device by which their brains might be given some protection if they should receive a glancing blow from an enemy sword.

Gorlois's armour was shiny with newness and his broad shield made of bull-hide and brass had been decorated with the figure of a great boar. The young man had already become known by the nomen the Boar of the South, as a tribute to his hunting prowess.

By comparison, Pridenow's armour was plain and was of Roman construction. However, the prince carried a stylised portrait of a woman on his shield in recognition of Saraid, his famed ancestor. As well, Creidne had shyly placed the sole remaining piece of material from her father's trade goods, a short length of precious, flame-red silk, into the young man's hands. He attached this strip of scarlet cloth to the crest of his helmet in a barely understood tribute to the young maiden.

Once their armour was gleaming from their vigorous polishing and their weapons had been thoroughly sharpened and oiled, the pair made their way to Vortigern's tent to receive their final instructions from their commander. They were given orders to ride out to the east of the city for some distance and wait in a concealed position until the Saxons were committed to their attack on the defensive line at the city's wall. The bulk of the British defensive force, levies dispatched by the king of the Brigante tribe, would stay close to the city walls to bear the brunt of the initial attack by the advancing northerners.

As yet, the road beyond the city remained empty of all life. The air had that peculiar stillness that embraces warriors before the commencement of a battle. Even the birds were silent, as if the dumb creatures of the air were waiting expectantly for the carnage to begin.

The Brigante tribesmen, noted for their aggressive military skills, had come down to the south in response to Vortigern's call for reinforcements. This ferocious tribe, who were wont to meddle in affairs of state, presented some difficulty to Vortigern in that they might oppose any future claims on Maximus's throne if they felt disenfranchised. But, in the meantime, they would make an extremely effective defence before they were sacrificed at the gates of Calleva Atrebatum. They would happily fight, and die, to prove their prowess. Pridenow allowed himself a cynical smile as the Brigante warriors lined up in their formations, for these men were willing and ready to block any Saxon advance that was forthcoming.

'Brigante tribesmen are very brave and they'll never run from a battlefield. Father told me that their pride is such that they always fight to the very end, regardless of the reputation of their enemies,' Pridenow explained to the younger man. 'You can see that these Brigante are already prepared to take part in the coming battle, even though the Saxons aren't even in sight.'

From behind the walls of Calleva Atrebatum, Pridenow could hear the sound of the two Roman siege machines as their buckets were loaded with large rocks, pieces of twisted metal and small lengths of timber. When these missiles were catapulted over the wall and out on to bare Saxon heads, the ensuing carnage would be terrifying. Both men could hear the creaking of the heavy ropes as the huge throwing-arms were winched into their firing positions.

'These machines might be effective,' Pridenow said knowledgably, 'but they take far too long to reload once they've catapulted their missiles. It's time-consuming work to collect and prepare the rubble that fills their baskets of death. They might be a useful attacking weapon during a prolonged siege, but I see little value for them as defensive weapons when time is of the essence.'

'All these infernal weapons are unsporting,' Gorlois muttered when Pridenow teased the younger man over his scruples.

'We're at war with these Saxon bastards, my friend,' Pridenow responded. 'Their warriors are twice the size of our men and that's not fair either. With luck, these Roman siege machines will even the scores a little – if they work! These examples were built during the days of Maximus, so the timbers, ropes and mechanisms are old, rusted and decaying.'

As if on cue, one of the large timber sections on one of the machines began to groan and shake ominously in rejection of the demands being made on it. Fortunately, one of the Roman-trained engineers pounded at the machine's base with a heavy maul hammer to free the mechanism. The ancient oak timbers on the catapult shivered and groaned in protest, but they managed to hold without splitting.

Then, as Pridenow gazed along the roadway and off towards the horizon, his young eyes made out an approaching cloud of dust. He pointed one arm towards this strange manifestation and hissed at one of the scouts: 'Tell Vortigern's officers that the Saxons are coming. They always run into battle, but it's only a ploy that tells weaker men that the northerners are stronger and more determined than their enemies.'

Gorlois stared at the plume of dust and shivered. 'The bastards aren't human if they can run for hours and still fight a pitched battle at the end of it all.'

'They are physically strong, Gorlois, so we shouldn't underestimate them. The shortest of them stands a head taller than you or I, but I'm convinced they can still be beaten.'

Pridenow's small force watched the approaching Saxons from a vantage point on a low hill to the west of the shanty town, a site that was removed from the Saxon line of approach. Below Pridenow's force, and at the shanty town's edge, the Brigante warriors waited expectantly with the spears and shields that would protect them from the lumbering attackers.

'Sweet Jesus, Pridenow, they're fast,' Gorlois breathed as he yanked on the reins that controlled his horse's head. The affronted animal shrieked shrilly until Gorlois released his pressure on the reins and it quietened. The two leaders and their thirty-strong force rode down to the edge of the shanty town, where they could be hidden from Saxon eyes while still able to maintain a clear view of the Saxon line of attack. On reaching the dilapidated buildings, the warriors hobbled their horses and released them.

The beasts would be useless in the hand-to-hand combat that was about to begin, so they must wait among the slatternly tangle of empty wine shops and deserted food stores until the Brigante line broke, as it surely must. Then, Pridenow's complement would set fire to the gimcrack buildings and charge into the rear of the confident Saxons. His fresh troops, while few in number, would assist the advancing fire to herd their overconfident enemy towards the killing zone near the city gates.

The air was as still as death. The only real movement was that of a few mongrel dogs who were searching patiently through the filthy streets for food scraps that might have been left behind when the non-combatants fled. Time stretched out and, with it, the young men's nerves were taut with expectation. Pridenow was almost relieved when he heard the thud of hard, calloused feet on the roadway and the shouted responses from the Brigante warriors as they braced themselves for the Saxon attack.

'These buggers are huge,' Gorlois remarked to no one in particular. 'Our Brigante defenders can't possibly stop them.'

'The Brigante might be smaller but they make up for it in cunning. Look! They're about to loose some fire arrows.'

Whatever the Brigante strategy might have been, the Saxons ignored the rain of arrows, although several of their number had fallen. Some flaming arrow-shafts were burning sluggishly in enemy flesh, but the northerners' sheer weight of numbers and their greater size had pushed the Brigante back by several spear lengths. As the battle was now clearly joined, the Saxons settled into their usual patterns of combat.

Their longer reach gave the northerners a decided advantage, but the Brigante warriors were faster and more agile on their feet. Many of the Saxons found themselves hamstrung by lithe, black-haired men who barely reached their shoulders.

Still, yard by yard, the Britons were driven backwards, leaving trampled earth behind them that had been turned to the colour of rust by blood, entrails and the messy detritus of war. Many of the warriors slipped on the wet cobbles that were slick with the blood of their companions. Yet, for all their disadvantages, the Brigante tribesmen made the Saxons pay dearly for each foot of earth that was won. But the scales of war, that turning point in time when the Saxons could claim victory, were beginning to tilt.

'It's almost time for us to play our part in this battle,' Pridenow said. 'Vortigern must be ready to fire off the signal arrow from atop the city wall. That arrow will tell us when to join the battle.'

'Can the Brigante hold for much longer?' Gorlois asked, his knuckles stretched to a taut, bone-white sheen on the hilt of his sword.

'Over there! See? Vortigern's signal,' Pridenow said calmly as a lit fire arrow arced over the stone and timber ramparts of the old city.

Pridenow gripped his friend's wrist in that age-old gesture of camaraderie that exists between soldiers who are about to enter the battlefield. 'We'll have something special to tell our own sons if we are still living at the end of this adventure. I'm beginning to believe that Mithras wants us to survive this battle, if only to annoy Vortigern and punish him for his hubris.'

'I'll be perfectly happy if the sun rises over both of us on the morrow,' Gorlois added, his face set and determined under the shadow of his helmet.

Pridenow bent over and grasped a burning flare that one of the warriors had carried to the top of the hill.

'Light your torches from Leith's flare and we'll set this fleapit ablaze,' Pridenow shouted as all thirty of his men began to obey him. He stared out over the waiting buildings. 'Gorlois!' he continued. 'Take half the men and light this side of the town. Burn everything! The rest of the men will take care of the right flank, and may God grant us the day over these heathen savages!'

'Amen to that!' Gorlois responded, for the time for hiding had passed. With their practised tribal battle cries echoing through the town, the small British detachment began to run through the first line of shanties, setting fire to the brittle, paper-dry buildings as they went about their destructive business.

'Today is a good day to die!' Pridenow shouted above the roar of flames that lent a ruddy colour to his helmet and shield. A refrain went up from thirty young throats that gave heart to those Brigante who had survived the Saxon advance. The doomed defenders redoubled their efforts, for they could see the tendrils of smoke and flames beginning to appear.

'Let's see if these bastards have the same stomach for carnage when the blood of their own warriors is staining our swords. Will they be eager for death when the metal of our swords is accompanied by missiles from the catapults and fire from the burning shanty town?'

The more superstitious of the Saxon warriors shivered a little when the rallying cry went up from stern British throats and, for a brief moment, their attack faltered. But then, when the northerners took heed of the shouted orders from their thane, they took heart from his reckless courage and returned to the business of killing with even more ferocity.

Creidne stared out towards the northern sky with anxious eyes. No word had come from Calleva Atrebatum since a solitary messenger had returned to the palace and informed the queen that a major battle was about to be joined. Creidne felt ill at the very thought of this confrontation.

She had lain awake for several nights as she assessed her situation. Her father was dead and her only surviving relative was an uncle who lived in Glevum.

To all intents and purposes, she was truly alone. Without a dominant male to give her shelter and protect her, she was dependent on the queen to save her from any male who saw fit to use her for his own pleasure and purposes. In the process, she had become fond of Severa and ran any errands and carried out every task that the queen desired of her. For her part, Severa was cheered by Creidne's boundless enthusiasm and her love for Vortimer, the babe whom the queen could barely force herself to hold. And so Creidne had built herself a safe little nest, no matter how temporary, until such time as Pridenow returned. She barely dared to think of what would happen to her if Pridenow should perish in the coming battles.

With her usual good humour and excellent common sense, Creidne focused on making the queen as happy and as comfortable as possible. Still, the nagging thought of Pridenow's death in battle persisted in the back of her mind.

Creidne had tried, unsuccessfully, to understand why the young prince had risen so high in her esteem. She recalled how, when she was a nine-year-old girl, she had cherished a childish passion for one of her father's guards. But she realised now, with all the hindsight of her sixteen years, that this early attachment had been the romantic dream of a child. She had no accurate yardstick by which she could measure her attachment for Pridenow.

Creidne missed the young friend who had entered her life during the ambush of her father's caravan. She barely knew him, even now, but he had become an important part of her life. When Severa spoke of her foster-brother, the girl flushed hotly. For her part, the queen smiled knowingly and treated the orphaned girl as if she was a treasured guest.

'Creidne,' the queen called from the small courtyard where she was working on her loom with her ladies. Beautiful red roses bloomed here, whose fallen petals lay like drops of blood on the flagstones.

'Can you ask my steward if he can find the basket of new wool we've been spinning into yarn?' Severa asked her. 'One of the traders brought some new supplies to the palace and I've been itching to try them to weave a shirt for Pridenow.'

Creidne hurried to find the steward who took her to the room where the wool had been stored. Then, with her arms piled high, she hurried back to the courtyard.

'Do you think my brother will like these colours?' Severa asked, her hands plucking at the unspun lengths of fleece in shades of red and orange.

Creidne assured the queen that Pridenow would love anything that was made with his sister's own hands.

'I'm afraid that Vortigern intends to have my brother killed during these battles with our Saxon enemies,' Severa said with soulful eyes. 'I can only hope that Pridenow remains careful.'

'Surely the king isn't that treacherous,' Creidne answered. Yet, even as she denied the possibility, Creidne knew, with a sick certainty, that the queen was judging the situation truly. 'Pridenow is a brave and competent warrior, so it would be strange if the king decided to waste his services out of petty spite.'

But Creidne knew in her heart that Vortigern would kill any person who stood in his way. Her stomach felt hollow from fear.

'My foster-brother is a hard man to kill, as Vortigern has learned. It might be difficult to believe, but a famed seer made a prophecy many years ago in which she told King Caradoc of Tintagel that one of his descendants, a grey-eyed member of the family line, would sire a son who was destined to become the greatest king in all of Britannia. No sanction for non-compliance was recorded at the time of the prophecy, but the seer insisted that any such grey-eyed children must be forbidden from leaving the shores of Britannia. Pridenow is the first of Caradoc's descendants to have grey eyes, so my brother may not leave the shores of Britannia, regardless of his wishes. He has remained in our lands to this day.'

Creidne was slightly discomforted, but recent disasters in her family situation had taught her that little reliance should be placed on vague expectations. The daughter of a trader, she had more than her share of common sense and was loath to accept the ramblings of a seer's prophecy.

'I wish he'd send word to us. At the very least, we'd know that he's among the living.'

'It's sad, Creidne, but the lot of women is to wait and receive scant comfort when our loved ones die. In fact, we are fortunate if we have a body to bury.'

Severa spoke with unusual harshness, and with a pang Creidne remembered that nothing remained of Severa's former husband, Constantine, and her father, Magnus Maximus, men who died in failed quests for glory in lands that were far removed from Britannia.

She had been left with nothing to bury.

'I'm feeling unwell, girl,' the queen said hesitantly. 'I'm aware that I might well die of my ailment before my son, Vortimer, has grown to manhood. Whatever happens, Creidne, I desire that you marry my brother. Pridenow must remain in Britannia at all costs, but he must spend the remainder of his life in some remote part of our lands where my husband will allow him to live without harassment. It's possible that Glevum could be such a place and you do have kin there, so I believe you'd have the wit to keep my brother safe.'

'But he may not wish to marry me,' Creidne yelped in surprise. 'He's never shown any partiality towards me.'

'Pridenow has to marry someone and he normally follows my advice,' Severa replied with a sly grin. 'You'll have to trust me, Creidne, if you intend to win his heart.'

Pridenow wiped his arm across his blackened brow and discovered, with some surprise, that his hand was stained thick with clotted blood when it came away from his face. At that moment, when he realised he was bleeding, his head hurt from a gash along his scalp that was caused by a glancing blow from an axe. In the sudden stillness before another Saxon came at him with reddened, angry eyes, he took in the whole scope of the battle with unnatural clarity.

The Brigante defenders had been forced back against the city walls by now. Sensing victory, the hulking Saxons pressed forward with their attack.

Pridenow's troops swooped down on the flanks of the Saxon line and attacked individual warriors who had been mopping up the Brigante wounded and isolated pockets of Vortigern's defenders with grim, methodical efficiency. In that moment of stillness when the northerners' attack became more and more confused, Pridenow saw the Brigante leader and a comrade force their way out from the protection of the wall to make a small, ineffective counterattack against their enemies. The Saxons before them gave some ground and this, in turn, gave a little heart to the struggling Britons who were close to exhaustion.

'Kill the bastards! They're on the run!' Gorlois screamed out his encouragement and Pridenow saw that the Dumnonii prince was covered in blood. Fortunately, it was Saxon blood.

Pridenow threw himself back into the fray and eviscerated a wounded Saxon who was using his axe to pound out his anger against the gate. He heard the infernal whistling sound of a projectile flying through the air, so he threw himself behind a pile of tangled corpses. Large clumps of rock and stone, various sizes and shapes of metal and varying lengths of timber hurtled on to the standing Saxons, cutting them down in a swathe of dead and wounded warriors.

The old Roman catapults were still working.

In the chaos that followed, Pridenow knew that some time would elapse before the ancient machines were reloaded. Then, as he looked up from his supine position on the ground, he realised that the Saxons were still a viable fighting force. As a group of anger-filled warriors staggered towards him, he saw that many of them bore superficial wounds, but they were far from dead – or even immobilised.

He rolled away from the Saxon line of approach and scrambled to his feet. Then, as he heard agitated yells from the ramparts above him, Pridenow hurried away from the protection of the city wall, while shouting urgent words of alarm to the British warriors around him.

'Move your arses!' the prince screamed as containers of hot oil, pitch and other flammable liquids rained down from the ramparts of Calleva Atrebatum's southern wall. 'Hot oil! Get away! Run for your lives! There'll be fire arrows coming! Keep away from the gates!'

Pridenow again hurled himself into a place of relative safety behind a pile of corpses in time to look up and see liquid fire rain down on friend and foe alike, setting fire to men, corpses and the detritus of war without fear or favour. The British warriors cooked like torches within their armour, while the Saxons experienced the horrors of burning flesh and flaming furs when the oil poured down on unprotected flesh in a molten stream.

Meanwhile, Gorlois had dug a depression with his bare hands to avoid being splashed with flaming liquid. Even so, he could smell the sweet, sickly odour of burning flesh and human excrement as he plastered his injured arms and open body areas with soil to dowse any liquid that might splash on him. Luck stayed with him, so his burns were minor and relatively pain-free.

Further containers of oil followed that first barrage and Pridenow watched in sickened horror as one of the Saxons ran past him to disappear into the burning shanty town. With his body wreathed in fire, the warrior collapsed in a tangle of burning fur and blazing flesh.

Pridenow shouted at the Britons to press forward with a counterattack and, in the small hell of dying men, the Saxons weakened and began to retreat.

Then, above the sound of the flames and the continuing battle, Pridenow heard the distinctive sound of the catapult buckets being winched back into their firing position.

The Britons threw themselves into hollows in the ground or

hid behind piles of bodies in an attempt to protect themselves from the hail of rubble that was about to fall on them. Less familiar with the danger above, many of the Saxons were cut down by the missiles once again, but the more intelligent warriors were warned by the noise of the winches that the catapult was being prepared for firing. Like Pridenow, they took advantage of whatever cover they could find.

Pridenow rose to his feet and returned to the affray. After their initial retreat, the Saxons redoubled their efforts and made a desperate attempt to reach the relative safety of the wall. With a sick feeling in the pit of his stomach, Pridenow saw that the British warriors were still losing this battle. As he cut down an already-wounded man before him, it was clear to the young Briton that there were just too many Saxons involved in this conflict.

Meanwhile, from the ramparts, Vortigern made a huge wager against Fortuna and his fate.

One of the rules of warfare accepted by commanders was the basic truism that the gates to a city should never be opened during a siege, lest an enemy should gain access to the city during this manoeuvre. Undeterred by these strictures, Vortigern ordered the gatekeepers to swing open the great, iron-studded gates on the southern wall so that fresh troops could pour out of the city and enter the open space outside the city walls. Here, they would confront the last of the tiring Saxon attackers. In normal circumstances, a commander would never leave the relative safety of stone walls to try his luck in the open, but the Roman-trained strategist that was Vortigern was prepared to gamble with the lives of his warriors and the entire population of the city in an attempt to catch these hulking savages off-guard.

Pridenow was slashing at the knees of a very determined, but severely burned and wounded, enemy when Vortigern's gamble began. He only realised what was taking place with the gates when he heard the creaking of the old hinges and gate mechanisms. The southern gate of the city, rarely wide open, exposed the British to a Saxon counterattack but, with tribal yells and sheer enthusiasm, the reserves poured out through the gates. As the gap in the gates widened, the British reserves pushed aside the Saxons with the sheer weight of the number of warriors who were exiting the city.

With this mad gamble, the British defenders took heart and forced the Saxons to move away from the gate. As they retreated, the Saxons found that while the fire in the shanty town was behind them the fresh British troops were ahead of them, and they became confused. To compound the situation, several of their thanes had perished during the battle and the two leaders who had survived knew that they were about to taste the sour acid of defeat.

The Saxon line began to falter. Like a chicken without a head, the beast that was the Saxon force ground onwards towards an inevitable failure. Vortigern had proved to be a canny tactician but he knew, all too well, the smell of defeat could easily have been gifted by Fortuna to the Britons. The Saxons were gradually pushed back towards the flames. Here, those warriors who chose to live elected to bolt and run for cover, while the nobler souls among them chose to die rather than yield to their enemy.

The decimation of the remaining Saxon invaders had begun.

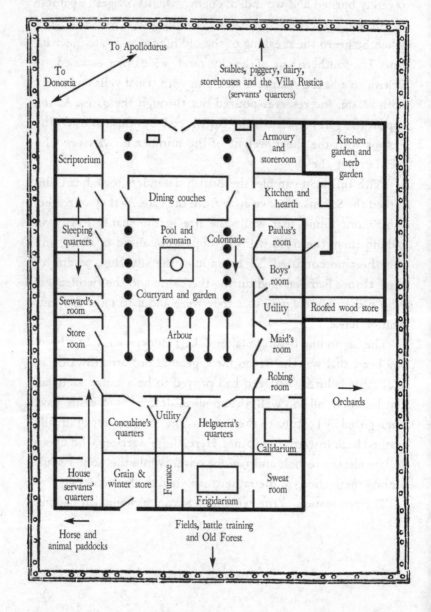

FLOOR PLAN OF THE
VILLA AFRICANUS

To Apollodurus

To
Donostia

Stables, piggery, dairy,
storehouses and the Villa Rustica
(servants' quarters)

Kitchen
garden and
herb
garden

Scriptorium

Armoury
and
storeroom

Dining couches

Kitchen and
hearth

Sleeping
quarters

Pool and
fountain

Colonnade

Paulus's
room

Boys'
room

Steward's
room

Courtyard and garden

Utility

Roofed wood store

Store
room

Arbour

Maid's
room

Robing
room

Orchards

Concubine's
quarters

Utility

Helguerra's
quarters

Calidarium

House
servants'
quarters

Grain &
winter store

Furnace

Sweat
room

Frigidarium

Horse and
animal paddocks

Fields, battle training
and Old Forest

CHAPTER XVII

A NEW BEGINNING

Never let the future disturb you. You will meet it, if you
have to, with the same weapons of reason which today arm
you against the present.

Marcus Aurelius, *Meditations*

Donostia proved to be a place of relative comfort compared to
the privations suffered during the rest of the children's journey
into exile. When Paulus finally drove his wagon into its rutted,
dusty streets, he breathed a sigh of relief in the knowledge that
their travels were almost over.

Donostia was a city of some size, one that had been garrisoned
by a detachment of Romans who had served in Maximus's army.
Because the local population still retained the sound of Britannia
on their tongues, Paulus, the servant girls, and even Etain, could
understand the language used in the bustling marketplace by the
inhabitants of the town. Paulus was able to ask directions that
took him to a suitable inn and, with a profound sense of relief, he

was able to sleep in clean and comfortable surroundings.

The town still retained a blend of Roman and Armorican culture so, when he woke after a long sleep that lasted till well past sunrise, the decurion asked his host whether the comforts of Donostia included the luxury of a public bathhouse. He was cheered to discover that a Roman bathing facility had survived Hispania's colonisation by the Goths and learned that this amenity still provided cleanliness for an ever-shrinking clientele. As his flared nostrils assured him, Paulus discovered that few persons in Donostia shared his passion for hygiene and the populace rarely noticed the stink of their unwashed human flesh.

Within the marketplace, the reek was strong enough to make Paulus's stomach clench, but the grime-encrusted stallholders and their clients seemed impervious to the potent aroma in this crowded space. The traders hawked their wares, spat globules of phlegm on to the dusty earth and waved live chickens, sides of meat, basketloads of cabbages and numerous examples of the strange fruits that proliferated in the countryside.

Even the smell of newly baked bread was spoiled by the market's proximity to the town's latrines, a facility that spread the powerful aroma of urine and excrement through the crowded alleyways.

As a seasoned traveller, Paulus had seen and experienced many things but, after mixing for some years with his betters, he expected higher standards of hygiene and etiquette than those accepted by the inhabitants of this border town.

Somewhere in this prosperous place, the decurion would find Helguerra, the man who would be asked to give his protection and hospitality to Paulus's small group of travellers. The Roman prayed that Helguerra would feel the same obligation that inspired Daire to ferry his party from Burdigala to Donostia in the midst of winter. Paulus was fearful that a comfortably situated civilian would be very nervous when confronted by an armed Roman officer, three female servants and two exiled children who were about to be foisted on him.

After washing his body in the public baths and using his knife to scrape off the worst of the stubble on his chin and head, Paulus finally felt clean. The many days of wandering on land and sailing through the briny waters of the open sea had caked the decurion with a thin film of grime. Now, with his shining head and his red cloak brushed clean of clinging mud, he set off to find the Hispanic landowner who would hold the fate of Severa's children in his hands.

Helguerra conducted most of his business from a house in Donostia. Paulus had discovered, by making discreet inquiries with the innkeeper, that Helguerra owned a large estate in Apollodorus where he spent the winter months. But, for most of the year, Helguerra could be found at his house and place of business on the outskirts of Donostia.

Paulus hoped that Aeron had made a correct assessment of Helguerra's character, for the man would be asked to provide care and security for two young boys over a period of time that might stretch out to fifteen or more years. The decurion understood that his request for assistance could be seen as an imposition; after all, Helguerra was being asked to act as a foster-parent for the sons of an emperor.

And so, Paulus found himself pounding on the stout door of a well-maintained Roman house on the outskirts of Donostia. After a few genteel knocks, he attacked the stout timbers with the hilt of his sword. The door finally swung open to reveal a wizened man with sharp blackcurrant eyes and a reddened nose that twitched like the nostrils of a rat.

'And who would you be wanting?' the little creature asked as he took in the red cloak that Paulus was wearing. 'State your business, sir. However, I must tell you that my master doesn't believe in charity or the distribution of bread to beggars, not even for old soldiers.'

Paulus felt his face suffuse with colour and he spoke with more brusqueness than usual. 'I am Paulus, decurion to two emperors and protector of the two sons of Queen Severa of Britannia. I've been dispatched to speak to your master by King Aeron of the Dobunni tribe in Britannia. I believe Master Helguerra will become angry if you fail to admit me to his presence. Given the importance of my message, I suggest that you inform your master that I am here.'

The old retainer stretched out his scrawny neck like a tortoise and his eyes reflected his anger and the dislike he felt towards his visitor.

'Wait on the seat under the apple tree while I convey your message to my master,' he said disdainfully, while pointing towards a gnarled old tree by a fishpond that cooled the courtyard outside the gates leading to the house. Angry that he had been dismissed out of hand like a junior lackey, Paulus ignored the servant and sauntered over to a long marble bench that was obviously used as a resting place for important visitors.

After waiting for some minutes for his benefactor to appear, Paulus returned to the spreading apple tree, which had been bared of leaves during the winter months. He sat at his ease and stretched his legs out in the sunshine.

'If this is Helguerra's idea of hospitality, I shudder to think what he'd do if he disapproved of a visitor,' Paulus told the empty air and watched as an undernourished squirrel started to descend the trunk of the apple tree in a hopeful search for nuts that might have been missed by other visitors

With a sigh, Paulus looked across the garden towards a sun-dappled street. Provident women had strung freshly dyed cloth and some pieces of faded linen on lines that crossed the paved surface below. Meanwhile, the strong sunshine playing over his outstretched legs warmed his skin and almost lulled him into sleep.

The decurion woke with a start when the doors of the house suddenly creaked open. As he struggled to regain his feet, a portly man of middle years hurried across the portal with outstretched arms.

'I believe you are the Roman officer whom my steward, Cletus, brought to my notice. The name of King Aeron of Corinium and Queen Severa of Venta Belgarum take me back a long way into the past. You'd hardly believe me, good sir, but I was once a cavalryman. I was a fine figure of a man in those long-gone days, but any horse I ride now will groan under the burden of my weight.'

The huge man patted his paunch affectionately and seemed pleased with the extra weight he carried around his waist and hips. With the enthusiasm of most men from Hispania, he gripped Paulus by the forearms and hugged him with gusto.

Paulus was taken aback by this outward display of affection but he remained silent and took the man's proffered hand in a nervous demonstration of respect.

'I believe you answer to the name of Paulus,' Helguerra said. 'I can tell you without hesitation that I would do much to assist the children of Constantine. I owe the life of my own son to the intervention of the emperor whom I served with in those long-gone days, years ago, when he was still a humble young officer who was serving in Hispania and Gallia.'

Helguerra paused and Paulus could see that the memories were flooding back into the old man's brain.

'My son faced death when he played his part in one of Maximus's ill-fated battles with the Roman emperor. Constantine protected my boy after he was sorely wounded by a barbarian warrior. After the battle, my friend arranged for his wounds to be treated and his efforts ensured that my boy survived. Yes, Paulus, I owe Constantine the greatest of debts and these are equally payable to all of his kin, both Queen Severa and the children. I am honour-bound to assist you with your quest.'

Paulus looked across at the chubby man and, suddenly, Helguerra ceased to be a ridiculous figure. Under the extra flesh that came to the Hispanic from good living, Paulus recognised the ruthless determination that was serving Helguerra so well as a merchant prince.

'The boys are very young,' Paulus began. 'The eldest lad, Ambrosius, is barely six years old, but both are sturdy children who are likely to bring good luck and profit to any family who takes them in. They are the children of an emperor and they're the direct descendants of Emperor Maximus and a British tribal queen. Their lineage is impeccable.'

'I don't give a toss about their lineage. All that matters to me is that the boys are protected and my duty to the past is done.'

The Hispanic's jaw set under his fleshy jowls and Paulus decided that this particular merchant would be a very bad enemy. He looked at the plump businessman with growing respect.

'I believe that your boys would benefit from some clean country air,' Helguerra said, while rubbing his forefinger along the side of his nose before sinking into deep thought. 'I have a country estate near Apollodorus where the climate is pleasant and my fine Hispanic horses are trained. I also grow grapes and olives there, crops that provide me with a tidy profit.'

Helguerra grinned like a mischievous child who was playing a forbidden game.

'The sons of Constantine will grow tall and healthy from the plain fare, plentiful water and clean air that makes my estate such a pleasant place in which to live. There are other children on nearby estates, so the boys will also have access to tutors who can conduct their education. I assume that you and your servants will remain on the estate with the boys to further their knowledge and prepare them for their future, whatever it might be. Is that your intention?'

Paulus tried to express his gratitude but Helguerra brushed away any fulsome praise that was on offer.

'Apollodorus is a day's travel away, so I'll organise transport and an escort that will take your party to my estate. Now, are there any other matters that require my direct attention?'

Paulus thought for a brief moment.

'I do have one other matter of concern. It's of little moment, but I'd appreciate your advice on it. I picked up an orphaned girl when we were passing through Portus Namnetum. I could hardly abandon her as she was in a great deal of moral danger at the time. It was likely that she'd have found herself on the streets of the city. I thought she might be useful to me, but she has proved to be a total nuisance. I can say on her behalf that she was gently raised in a Roman household. It's sad, but Fortuna has turned her face away from this child and her entire family was slaughtered. I'd rather not take her with us, because she really needs to serve in the household of a firm woman.'

Helguerra looked a trifle bemused but promised to relieve Paulus of this problem by placing Etain in his household in Donostia. Here, she could learn a trade, preferably one that was better suited to her than theft. The other two women, servants in the employ of Queen Severa, would remain with Paulus and the two children.

Happy with the morning's work and buoyed by the chagrin of Cletus, Paulus retraced his steps to the inn. When his charges were told of the fate that was in store for them, Ambrosius was thrilled at the thought of having horses to play with, while Uther insisted that lessons in swordplay should begin immediately. With some difficulty, Paulus managed to deflect the boy's enthusiasm for weapons and bloodletting with a promise that these skills would be imparted to him in the fullness of time.

Dilic and Dara were ecstatic that their long journey was almost over and they could anticipate a well-earned rest.

On the other hand, Etain was far from enthusiastic at the prospect of gaining honest employment in an unknown household. She sulked and swore by turn and threatened to run away until Paulus was forced to incapacitate her by tying her hands together. In this atmosphere of anger and mistrust, Paulus's good humour evaporated and even Dilic was forced to upbraid the girl for her lack of gratitude. Somehow, Paulus was certain that Etain would never become a useful and trustworthy servant.

Creidne paced around Severa's courtyard like a caged animal. Meanwhile, the other ladies in Severa's circle tried to appear casual in the face of the girl's obvious concern.

Severa's friends knew that she was desperately ill, and her health was deteriorating. The queen had been poorly since the birth of Vortimer, even though her son had thrived.

'How goes my lady?' the queen's nursemaid asked Brisen. 'The master won't react well if he returns to the palace and finds that Queen Severa's health has deteriorated.'

'The queen has been ill for a long time now, and she still bleeds intermittently. If I had my way, word would have been sent to her husband to seek out a truly competent healer who can assist the queen to return to health. But no one listens to me.'

'Has there been any word of Pridenow's fate on the battlefield?' the nursemaid asked as her hands flashed busily over the yarn she was spinning. 'My lady dotes on her brother, and she's truly happy whenever he's in residence at the palace.'

'He'll never return to Venta Belgarum if Lord Vortigern has his way,' one of the younger courtiers said softly.

Brisen confronted the maid, face to face. 'Our master isn't stupid! He knows that the queen is beloved in her lands, so he won't do anything that will cause her physical harm.'

The girl, Caitlin, shrugged her shoulders and cheekily poked her tongue out.

'I suppose you hope to take her place in Vortigern's bed,' Brisen responded. 'I can assure you, you little fool, that Lord Vortigern will devour you whole. By the time he is finished with you, there'll be nothing left of you to remind him that you even existed.'

'He'd never think of looking in your direction, you old crone. You're just jealous over something you can't ever hope to have.'

Brisen would have struck the girl across the face but her

common sense prevailed. Everyone in Vortigern's hall knew that he was charmed by a well-turned ankle and was always interested in biddable females.

The sound of a great hubbub arose from the antechamber outside the Queen's Hall. 'A courier from the King is approaching,' one of the queen's women called after she ran to the open shutters and craned her neck to see who or what had disturbed the peace.

The queen was almost running as she raced towards her bedchamber with Creidne hard on her heels. Brisen brought up the rear, a few paces behind them.

'Hurry, Creidne! A courier has come from the master, and he'll have some word of my brother. Quickly, girl! Help me to dress so I can learn if Pridenow still lives.'

Caitlin gazed smugly at the remaining women and smiled. Her expression was gloating and triumphant.

'The queen should be concerned for her husband rather than championing a landless youth who can't be counted among her true kin. When a woman marries, she becomes her husband's vassal and can be treated as he wills! I, for one, would never disrespect him as Severa has just done.'

Brisen heard the remarks and turned back from the open doorway.

'You're nothing more than a passing fancy, you little slut. Queen Severa will still be here when you become big-bellied and cease to be of use to our master. Severa holds the kingship of the West in her bloodlines, and Vortigern would never leave her for a trollop such as you.'

Severa re-entered the hall with Creidne at her side. An obviously exhausted courier was escorted into her presence. Pausing only to bow towards the queen, he began to recite Vortigern's message.

'My lady, I bring a message from Lord Vortigern that is certain to lift your spirits. Today, a great battle was fought outside the walls of Calleva Atrebatum. God heard the prayers of the Britons and delivered the heathen Saxons into our hands.'

'You bear great news, courier,' the queen answered through her chattering teeth. 'What of Pridenow? What became of my brother?'

'Lord Pridenow held the line in the skirmish that took place before the city walls. He fought in the vanguard. The battle was fierce in the vicinity of the gate and many Britons lost their lives during the early part of the conflict. I cannot tell you what happened to your brother, my queen, for I was waiting with the reserves and Lord Vortigern. I didn't see Lord Pridenow, either living or dead.'

'I'm pleased and reassured that my husband still lives and that our warriors have prevailed over their enemies. But what has become of Pridenow?'

Then, as she mulled over her lack of information, one of Severa's stewards came to her side. In an almost inaudible voice, he told his mistress that a second courier had just arrived and this warrior would join her in the hall in the next few minutes.

When he entered the hall, the second courier genuflected and moved close to the queen. In a soft voice, he explained the reason for his presence as he kissed her hand.

'Lord Pridenow lives and is in good health, mistress. I've been given a missive to deliver to you in person.'

Then, after surreptitiously slipping a strip of parchment into her hand, he spoke loudly so that all of the listening onlookers could hear his words, but would be deceived as to his true actions.

'My lady, I've been sent by Gorlois of Cornwall who asks that you send word of his survival in the battle at Calleva Atrebatum to his mother. Lord Vortigern gave his approval for my journey out of concern that one single courier, unaccompanied, might have been compromised and failed to complete his duty and the task for which he was selected. Our master wanted to reassure you of the outcome of the battle with the Saxon invaders.'

The queen concealed the strip of vellum within her voluminous skirts. With luck, no one would have seen the exchange when it took place, so neatly was it conducted.

She felt so ill from nervous anticipation that she was barely able to control her shaking hands when she eventually reached the privacy of her rooms.

Mindful of her duty as the queen, Severa had barely been able to wait through the extended period of congratulation given by her courtiers and the gracious thanks that must be given to the couriers who had made such a hurried journey through unknown dangers. The missive seemed to burn a hole through her skirts and her flesh until she had an opportunity to open the scroll and read it properly.

The vellum was lying on the bed like a live thing when she picked it up; she felt tempted to cast it away out of fear that it might contain bad news from the battlefield. Fortunately, a streak of common sense asserted itself. Only Pridenow would have had the wit to send word to her with such subterfuge. At the very worst he might have been injured, but at least he was far from dead.

The actions of the second courier made no sense otherwise.

She inserted a fingernail under the wax that held the scroll together.

The missive fell open and Severa could almost hear the beating of her heart.

Dear Sister

I write to you in haste and I intend to send this message in the hands of one of my men who has no truck with your husband. It is sad, but my dislike is such that I cannot even write down the bastard's name.

Your husband tried to hasten my departure from this earth by placing me in harm's way throughout the battle that has taken place at Calleva Atrebatum. Strangely, I don't really blame the man for his treachery. Had I not been chosen for this dangerous mission, another warrior would have been forced to risk life and limb in my stead. Blind Fortuna, or God, or Mithras, protected me from harm, so I now have an opportunity to send this message and can assure you that I suffered no hurt. The Saxons have been routed and our troops will harry their surviving warriors all the way to Anderida or whatever place they used to make their landfall in Britannia.

With luck, they won't attempt another invasion for some time.

Meanwhile, I ask that you take special care of Creidne. I speak truthfully when I say that no woman is safe around Vortigern. He will attempt to force himself on her if he can, if only to cause me pain. Perhaps the girl should be sent to a place of safety.

This missive is overlong and it has consumed the last of my supply of vellum, but I wanted to allay your fears and console little Creidne.

I expect I shall be sent into the south-west under the pretext of chastising those British kings who did not answer Vortigern's call to arms, so I take this opportunity to wish you good health.

*Send word to Mother and Father that I am in good health and
assure them that I received no wounds in the recent battle.*

Farewell, Sister,

By the hand of Pridenow in Calleva Atrebatum.

After reading Pridenow's missive, the queen wept fat tears of
gratitude that fell on to the vellum. 'Pridenow is alive,' she sobbed.
'Nothing else matters, as long as he survived Vortigern's treachery.'

Severa accepted that she must take the future into her own
hands if the prophecy that foretold Pridenow's destiny was to
come to pass. Pridenow must be encouraged to marry Creidne, if
only to ensure that the young couple could be spirited away from
Venta Belgarum and the major centres of the south. But, as yet,
there was no indication of a binding love between the two young
people, despite the mutual respect and admiration they held for
each other.

'Fetch Creidne for me, Brisen,' the queen addressed Brisen in
the quiet of the empty room. 'I have an important matter that I
want to discuss with that young lady and I've just decided that
there's no time like the present. Oh! One further thing! Don't
mention any of my meetings to anyone – especially Caitlin. She's
a hungry little vixen, and she intends to dance on my grave – and
take my place in Vortigern's bed.'

As Brisen hastened to do her mistress's bidding, Fortuna's
wheel stuttered to a stop. For one brief moment, the fate of
Britannia hung in the balance, and then, slowly and steadily, the
wheel started to move and began a totally new pattern of rotation.

So it is that lives are irrevocably changed by decisions made
in desperation.

* * *

With the exception of Paulus, the Hispanic lands and culture were new experiences for the travellers. For his part, the decurion had served time in Gallia and Hispania some twenty years earlier when he had been a junior officer in Rome's legions. Now, as the small party trundled along the empty road leading to Apollodorus, he reflected on the pleasures of a legionnaire's life and the conscientious soldier he had been. His heart stuttered with surprise as the memories slowly returned to haunt him.

The inexorable march of time mocked his memories and made him feel like a foolish old man.

'Look!' Uther called excitedly from his seat on the back of the wagon. He pointed towards an open field where a herd of sturdy ponies were cropping grass in the sunshine. The large stallion which ruled the herd raised his head as if he had heard the boy's shrill exclamation. The animal pranced nervously before leading his mares away at a brisk canter.

Uther watched them run off with regret.

'Can I have a horse, Paulus?' Uther asked the decurion. 'I'd really like to ride on one!'

Paulus examined the excited boy with understanding and some wariness. Good humour from this boy usually indicated that he wanted something.

'You'll get your first pony when you've shown me that you're worthy of that privilege. You'll have to convince me that you're prepared to curry his coat, brush him thoroughly, feed and water him and, finally, to take responsibility for him. Can you do these things, Uther?'

The child looked mutinous and Paulus waited for the inevitable explosion of bad temper that usually followed any thwarting of the boy's requests. However, at bottom, Uther was an honest child and he looked at his benefactor with soulful eyes.

'I can do some of them, but I've never been near a horse before. Mother wouldn't let me look after a pony and she told me they were very dangerous. But I know I can learn to do all the things you've suggested.'

Paulus tousled the boy's hair, more to reward Uther's sincerity than for any other reason. 'I'll speak to Helguerra when we reach Apollodorus, and I'll ask him to include lessons in horsemanship among your other studies. But you can be certain that this will only happen if you are very, very good.'

The light in Hispania was clean and bright and the travellers enjoyed excellent visibility that extended to the far horizon. The dark hills in the distance seemed closer than they really were and the grass was a vivid shade of green in the hollows where the intermittent rain showers had left small pools of water in their wake. Paulus could feel the promise of heat and dust in the brisk spring breeze and he sensed that a true Hispanic summer would soon be upon them.

These lands were very rich, although they could become dry and arid for months at a time. Paulus gazed out over the grapevines where the fruit was already beginning to droop from the gnarled branches. This part of Hispania was famed for its wines, the sunshine in these provinces a gift from nature that ensured superb vintages.

In the higher parts of the countryside where the earth was dry and thick with shale, peasants grew olive trees in swathes of grey foliage. Paulus had tasted the olives produced in this region, so he knew that these fruits were among the finest grown in the Roman Empire.

And so, as the travellers moved ever closer to the small town of Apollodorus, he felt his spirits rise.

'What a perfect place to raise children,' he said as a smile wreathed his craggy face.

The boys scampered down from their wagon to play at a childish game where they ran between freshly ploughed furrows of earth. They picked up rich dark clods that they hurled at each other and, within minutes, their feet and hands were splattered with soil. Dilic and Dara also felt carefree in this fecund countryside.

A tearful Etain had been left behind in Donostia, where she had been apprenticed to a pastrycook in Helguerra's employ. Paulus hoped that the girl could resist the impulse to run away, but the cynic in him anticipated that Etain was too independent and too imperious to become a baker, or any type of servant-girl. Though pleased to see the last of her, Paulus wished the young girl well.

'Who knows? She'll probably come to a bad ending, but she might even find her future as the wife of a merchant prince,' he reflected.

And so, with amity and hope, the travellers finally reached their destination. From a distance, the town seemed pleasant and well kept.

Apollodorus was a smallish town that retained some of its Roman flavour, although the local bathhouse no longer functioned and the marketplace teemed with a population that was more Goth or Hispanic than Roman. A small theatre housed a colourful welter of vegetables, livestock, bright cloth and gimcrack jewellery. Dilic proclaimed that they could have been at their homes in Britannia.

Paulus, however, realised that there were subtle differences in the buyers and sellers who clustered around the saffron stalls. The trade goods here were a little more exotic than those of British markets, for Apollodorus was on a trading route that came into the north from Massilia on the Middle Sea. For their part, the townsfolk were shorter and their complexions darker than those of their counterparts in Britannia and the familiar checks that had been woven into the tribal clothing of the Britons was altogether absent from the clothing that could be seen in Apollodorus. Even the vegetables were different.

Dilic and Dara were starved of the infinite variety of goods that could be found in marketplaces, but Paulus was so stern and so determined to reach Helguerra's farm before nightfall that he refused to entertain any pauses in their journey. Without a single backward glance, he led the women out of the town and back into the countryside.

Now, with the afternoon stretching on towards evening and the first bite of cold overtaking the warmth of the day, the countryside lacked the excitement of the earlier hours. For their part, the children were fretful and the women wanted nothing more than to arrive at a suitable place where they could lay down their heads in safety.

The Helguerra villa, when it finally appeared from out of a gathering dusk, seemed as insubstantial as a dream. A long, winding road stretched its meandering way up to the top of a small hill and a series of paddocks that were separated by wooden fences. As well, low fieldstone walls defined the grazing lands that were allocated to the various breeds of farm animals. After a long day on the road, this rustic vista looked quite idyllic.

The villa itself was surrounded by trees that seemed to anchor it to the gardens and Paulus could see that the outbuildings, stables and orchards were well maintained. Beyond the stables, the main villa towered over the other buildings in tones of terracotta and gold. The buildings had been constructed around a central courtyard and Paulus was certain that he could hear the sound of a fountain as it tinkled pleasantly in the atrium at the centre of the structure.

Then, as the carts were almost at the apex of the hill, a man on horseback approached the newcomers.

'Identify yourselves, sir. I have already received word from the master that guests will be arriving at the villa but his courier had very little information about you and your party.'

Paulus dismounted from his horse and spread both hands wide so that the thick-set man at the head of a small group of servants could see that his sword had not been drawn.

'I am Paulus, late of the Dracos Legion and, in recent times, I have been appointed as the protector of two Britannic princes. I came from Donostia after being given a promise from your master that the children and my servants will be given sanctuary in the villa. The boys are the sons of an emperor and the grandsons of Maximus, another emperor. They must be treated with respect. I have been assured by your master that my charges will be staying with you as valued guests and they will be raised in ways that are appropriate to their station.'

The man looked suitably impressed and Paulus felt his spirits lift.

'Of course, sir. The courier from my master told me that a small party with children would soon be arriving but he gave me no indication of when you might appear on my doorstep – or why! My name is Petrus and I am the steward of the Villa

Africanus. This is an ancient Roman estate which my master purchased from a previous owner who was the last of his line. I can tell you these things because we follow the old Roman ways here, as my name implies.

'Come up to the villa now and my servants will direct you to your rooms. You will find that the Villa Africanus rivals the better country estates that exist in the Roman world.' The steward pointed to the buildings behind him with some pride.

Paulus took in the glowing beauty of the Villa Africanus and felt a thrill of precognition.

The soil of this villa would cradle his bones when he went into the shades. He knew with certainty that this place marked the end of his wandering.

He had finally found a home.

CHAPTER XVIII

THE CROWNING
OF A KING

All that is valuable in human society depends on the
opportunity for development accorded to the individual.

Albert Einstein

The day that Severa died was as grey as the hearts of the men and
women who loved her. The queen had grown dreadfully thin, as
if something was devouring the flesh from her bones. Some
unknown force had eaten away at her vitality and left the husk
behind.

The queen was fearful for the safety of Endellion and
Pridenow, and she was determined to see them on one last
occasion before death overtook her. She instructed Brisen to
send couriers to Corinium to alert Endellion to her plight, while
others were dispatched to Isca Dumnoniorum, the ancient
garrison town on the southern coast of Britannia where Pridenow

was carrying out a mission for Vortigern. Endellion and Pridenow were informed that the queen's health was failing and their presence was required in Venta Belgarum.

Brisen knew that Pridenow would be gambling with fate if he returned to the wolf's lair but the maid feared to leave the prince in ignorance of the queen's parlous state of health, knowing as she did that Severa was beginning her irreversible journey into the shadows.

Fortunately for Pridenow, Vortigern had continued with his plan to exterminate the remnants of the Saxon invasion force and was shoring up the faith and finances of the cities and towns that lay between Londinium and Corinium. Uninterested in Severa's state of health, the king refused to budge from his base at Calleva Atrebatum, a place where he was revered with godlike respect.

Meanwhile, Venta Belgarum was silent and the customary rattle and clatter of trade had been stilled out of respect for the queen's illness. Severa had tried to carry out her duties in the King's Hall, but those petitioners who saw her were shocked by her gaunt appearance and feverish eyes. To a man, Venta Belgarum's petitioners chose to defer their litigation once they realised that their queen was close to death.

The streets of Venta Belgarum were unnaturally still and silent when Pridenow arrived in the town, so he hurried towards the Hall of Justice with a feeling of dread. The guards would normally have stopped him from entering the Hall's anteroom, but one look at his blazing eyes and rigid shoulders told them that this young man was holding his emotions on a tight leash. He handed his weapons to the guards and followed the steward into the hall where the queen was waiting.

Pridenow scarcely recognised the shrunken creature who sat like an effigy on Constantine's imposing throne. The queen was swallowed in its vastness, and dwarfed by the wolf pelt and woollen garments that surrounded her.

Pridenow was walking, cat-footed, as he approached the queen's throne, but she heard his approach and turned towards him.

'Oh, it's you who approaches, Pridenow! Is it truly you? Have you come to see your sister? Vortigern is absent, as always, so I don't have to concern myself with hiding you away from his gaze. I've hungered to see you and, recently, I've wondered if you'd heard anything of my boys. They'd be taller by now, because children grow so quickly. I made the right decision when I chose to send them away, but my heart aches for them. Vortigern has sunk his fangs into the flesh of Britannia and he won't let go until he's devoured everything that is good and true in our lands.'

Pridenow tried to help her sit up, but his assistance was ineffective. Every action he took failed to ease the fading woman's pain.

The prince tried to hide his feelings of pity, but something of his emotions must have been visible. Belatedly, Pridenow wondered if his sister had sent for a priest. Undeterred by his concerns, Severa held out one hand to stroke his forearm and reassure her foster-brother. She could feel the tension in his body, her heart touched by this young man who had been forced to grow to maturity before his allotted time.

'I'm dying, Pridenow, and I have no patience with those of my ladies who've been trying to dress up my illness with kind words. I sent for you because I'll shortly enter the lands from whence no one ever returns, that place where I'll rejoin my Constantine.

You mustn't weep for me, dear boy, because my pain is as nothing when it's compared to the troubles I suffered in those days when Constantine became High King of the Britons. I began my final descent towards death when he began to covet the throne of Rome, so this final illness has been a blessing of sorts.'

Pridenow grasped her hand and would have protested that she was surrendering to death without resistance, but she shook her head gently and stilled his words by pressing a skeletal hand over his mouth.

'Don't speak false, my boy. I can tell from the servant's eyes that Death is waiting for me in the corner of the room and he's growing impatient. I've kept him at bay so I can see you once more.'

'I'm not a fool, and I know that you've given up on your life. Please, my dear girl, fight to live. What will I do without my big sister? Who will I turn to when all appears to be lost?'

Pridenow buried his face in her furs and sobbed like a child. There had always been a special bond between the young man who was afflicted with strange dreams and the wife and mother who still had room in her heart for a foster-brother. Severa had poured out her own passions into a brotherly relationship with Pridenow when Constantine finally became a distant excuse for a husband. Pridenow had been her champion and, in return, she had become his protector.

'There is one last boon that I must ask of you, Pridenow. It would be a great undertaking, and it's a request that mightn't be to your liking. I'd rest easier when I enter the shades if I could convince you to enter a marriage with Creidne. She is orphaned and has no place in this hive of wickedness that is Vortigern's city. Even if you should marry her, Vortigern will still try to have her, so you'll be forced to flee to some remote place in Britannia where both of you will be safe.'

Pridenow blenched and would have protested, but Severa stopped him.

'A marriage between yourself and Creidne would be in your best interest, and it is a matter that must be addressed. Creidne may not have the blood of the British kings flowing through her veins, but she is well born. You'll never need to feel ashamed of her, for she is kind and naturally generous. She'll know what you need and will fight to keep you safe with all of her strength. I couldn't select a more suitable spouse if I were to live for several lifetimes.'

'But what will I do if Creidne doesn't want to marry me? I am a younger son, and I'm a man who is burdened with strange, prophetic dreams. I have also attracted the enmity of Vortigern, and this curse is likely to be the death of me. These are impediments that will be difficult to overcome.'

Severa looked earnestly into her brother's mutinous eyes. For all his seeming reluctance, she was cheered to see that he had not refused her plan directly.

'The peasants expect Vortigern to take Constantine's place as the High King of Britannia before the snows of winter are among us. If these rumours came to fruition, any wife of mine would be living with the constant fear of Vortigern and his grasping reach. I wouldn't blame Creidne if she refused such a doubtful honour.'

'Creidne will do what is best for both of you,' Severa responded. 'She listens to my advice and I have found her to be a very biddable girl who has looked to my comfort at the expense of her own.'

'I don't want a wife who will accede to my demands without

question. Creidne is young and beautiful, and she deserves better than a landless man like me.'

'Creidne will make the final decision! All that is required from you is agreement with my suggestion – and then leave the rest to me.'

With the certain knowledge that he had been manoeuvred into a trap, albeit one made from silk, Pridenow was happy to accept her offer.

Winter gave way to spring in an explosion of growth as, with the slow turning of the seasons, the boys grew taller at the Villa Africanus. Both Ambrosius and Uther learned to ride under the stern and watchful eye of Paulus. Life in the villa was relatively simple and comfortable, so servants and guests accepted that Apollodorus was their entire world.

The boys had been running about the villa like wild things when a messenger on horseback made his way up the long avenue of trees that marked the northern boundary of the villa. The rider was dusty and weary after a long sea voyage and an even longer land journey through the countryside of Hispania as he searched for Paulus and the exiled sons of Queen Severa.

The arrival of the courier caused some little consternation and Paulus ordered the two children to remain within the relative safety of a crowd of servants. Uther, as always, took no notice. Paulus started to walk down the pathway when he felt the boy tug at the sleeve of his tunic. Practical and bloody-minded, Uther had offered his own small knife to the decurion as an added protection against the unknown stranger.

Before the saddle-sore messenger had reached the top of the hill, Paulus had already drawn his weapon from its sheath and was waiting to greet the newcomer. Always the commander, he was mentally prepared either for an attack from an antagonist or, hopefully, some beneficial information from the outside world.

'Who are you, stranger?' Paulus's voice rasped out, and his naked weapon was a clear threat. The two boys came running to join Paulus, and the Roman noticed that the ever-ready Ambrosius had grasped a hoe that was taller than he was.

'I mean no harm to yourself or the children of Constantine, good sir, but I need to know if you are Paulus, the old legionnaire who stood with Constantine when he fought against the armies of Rome?'

'I am Paulus, but you'll discover how old I am if you take one step closer. State your business now, or I'll be unleashing the villa's workers to harry you away from here.'

The messenger spread his arms wide to show that his weapon was still sheathed. Slowly, and with one eye firmly fixed on Paulus's sword, the messenger unbuckled his gladius and allowed it to fall on the ground.

'As I said, I've come to speak with Paulus, the legionnaire. Send me on my way if you aren't the man I seek, for I'm weary of searching for this elusive Roman.'

By this time, even more slaves and servants had come running from the buildings to protect Paulus from the strange visitor who had arrived at the villa. Most of the workers were armed with whatever tools had come to hand, and they encircled the messenger with a ring of iron.

'I am Paulus! You may state your business with me, but do it clearly. I would hate for innocent blood to be spilled because of a misunderstanding between us.'

'I bring tidings from King Aeron of the Dobunni tribe in

Britannia. My master bade me to speak directly to Paulus – and only to him! I bring sad news of events in Venta Belgarum.'

'Speak then, stranger! I suggest that you speak truthfully, for I have no interest in subterfuge. You won't be harmed for the messages you bring, regardless of events that have taken place in our homeland.'

'Vortigern has seized the throne and has been crowned as the High King of the Britons. As well, Queen Severa has died after a series of illnesses. Her state of health worsened when Vortigern outlawed her brother, Pridenow. These are bad tidings for the people of Britannia.'

The messenger spoke in an angry voice and his eyes betrayed the contempt he felt for Vortigern. Paulus relaxed a little and his body straightened from the knife-fighter's stance he had adopted when he first challenged the unknown stranger.

'Speak no more of this matter while the children are in earshot. Meanwhile, we'll find somewhere comfortable where you can rest and drink some of our excellent brewed beer that will wash the dust from your throat. Once we are comfortably settled, you may tell me the balance of your news. There's no need to spare me the nastier details.'

Paulus turned to the two boys who were staring balefully at this stranger who had mentioned the names of their mother and uncle.

'Uther! Ambrosius! We have a guest! Run to the kitchens and bring beer and cheese to the scriptorium. Our friend needs refreshments.'

The children sprang into action as Paulus led a very bemused messenger into the heart of the Villa Africanus.

* * *

Paulus stared out at the darkening sky and recalled the last time he had seen Queen Severa. She had seemed far older than her thirty years and Paulus had felt a pang of grief for a young widow who was being forced to relinquish her children.

The Roman continued to stare at the cold white stars and dwelled on his memories of the queen and her husband, Constantine. Both of these fine people had gone into the shadows now and Paulus must find the words to tell the children that their mother was dead.

The messenger had left Corinium nearly a year earlier, so the tidings he carried to Paulus were close to a year old. Much could have taken place in the interim. Paulus was considering everything that the courier had told him during the two hours they had spent in the scriptorium and, now that the messenger had taken himself off to his pallet for some well-earned rest, the decurion could mull over the import of his tidings and what these snippets meant for Constantine's sons and the island of Britannia.

It seemed that Severa had taken the best part of a year to die, but she had steadfastly refused to send word of her health to her sons. She had assumed that Vortigern's spies would intercept the courier and use the information to ascertain the whereabouts of the children.

'Happily for the queen, one of her last acts had been to preside over the marriage of Pridenow and Creidne. Although she had difficulty standing, her face had been wreathed in smiles and the few people who attended the subsequent feast believed that she had experienced a brief day of happiness.

'The queen lived for a bare sennight after her mother arrived at Venta Belgarum. Severa's foster-father, King Aeron, ordered me to find you, although his directions were difficult to follow and those men you met on your journey to Hispania were reluctant to assist me.'

The messenger sighed as he sipped on a mug of the excellent ale before him.

'I've doubted sometimes whether King Aeron trusted me, but only a fool would have complete faith in other men in Vortigern's Britannia. In my own way, I'm an honest man and my hatred for Vortigern runs deep and hot, but I'm not prepared to show my feelings openly. I'd do harm to Vortigern if I could, so, when Lord Aeron asked me to convey this message to you, I agreed to undertake the task. I wanted to strike out at the king without risking my own hide.'

Some of Paulus's scorn must have registered with the messenger, because the visitor hastened to explain away his earlier words.

'Lord Vortigern sacrificed my two brothers and my own self during the Battle of Calleva Atrebatum. The very name of that place makes me want to vomit, for I can still hear my youngest brother's screams when he was drenched in burning oil. He was blazing like a torch when he died. Vortigern would have killed us all if it would have won the throne for him and he sits in Constantine's place and dispenses justice! Justice! The Demetae doesn't know the meaning of the word. He kills every high-born man who stands against him under the guise that they are Saxon sympathisers. Despite this, Vortigern continues to employ Saxon guards who will gladly do his bidding, no matter how repellent his orders are. Saxon sympathisers! I'd rather trust the Saxons than that wolf in sheep's clothing.'

Some of the messenger's tale had been extrapolated by Paulus.

The old warrior could imagine Vortigern sitting in state on the dragon throne, at his ease and indolently dispensing his wishes and demands to the sycophants who were clustered at his feet. The courier had gone on to describe the bleakness of the queen's funeral service, and how Vortigern had chosen a brief Christian burial ceremony rather than the cremation that the Romans and Celts reserved for their kings. The Christian priests had made little of Severa's history, for they were fearful of Vortigern's wrath if they offended him.

Severa was lowered into a hole in the ground on a wet day when the earth was easily turned to mud. Vortigern was determined to defile Severa's memory and kill her for a second time now that he was about to become the High King. He no longer needed her name or her lineage. Paulus's stomach tightened with rage that a woman such as Severa should be sent into the shades with scant honour or fanfare. She would soon become a faded memory as Vortigern introduced other women into his bed.

'I tried, Lady Severa! I failed to save you, but your children grow strong in these Hispanic lands. Meanwhile, I'll teach them about you and yours, and I'll turn them into aggressive weaponry that will strike out at Vortigern's heart in days to come.'

The old man remembered Severa as a frightened girl, many years earlier, when she had been forced to flee from an avaricious uncle and his minions. She had shown her bravery and her aim had been true when she killed her kinsman rather than be used to steal the throne of Britannia. But, now that Constantine was dead, Severa and her sons might soon be forgotten.

Paulus told the boys the truth about the death of their mother. Both boys still had some faint memories of Severa, and they felt the loss, but they were angry rather than miserable. Uther, in particular, swore to exact his revenge on Vortigern if he ever had the chance.

Paulus approved of the young boy's arrogant rage, but he was already aware of the violent streaks that flared up whenever Uther was thwarted. He discovered that Severa's youngest child had strung a straw-filled effigy of Vortigern into a tree, only to kill it repeatedly with his small knife until the elements blew the stuffing away on the breeze.

Such fits of anger did not bode well for Uther's future.

Days turned to years, and the seasons changed in their regular cycle. Hispania's climate stimulated the boys' physical development and they grew straight and tall, especially Uther, who inherited his lofty height from Magnus Maximus, the long-forgotten memory of glory and destruction.

Paulus instructed Ambrosius and Uther in political strategy and military tactics and taught them everything he knew, including vast amounts of trickery that the Roman legions had perfected over the centuries. The two boys learned their lessons well. Perhaps they might have become stewards for their benefactor, Helguerra, and remained in the safety of the Villa Africanus for the remainder of their lives, but Fortuna is neither kind nor fair.

Paulus understood how the old gods could punish Fortuna's favourites on a whim. Fate decided to knock at the gates of the Villa Africanus, and Paulus's comfortable life was about to change.

Vortigern was blazingly angry. He had been thwarted by the Ordovice and Brigante rulers who distrusted the High King on principle. The Brigante warriors loathed Vortigern with a passion, for they still remembered the carnage that had taken place outside the gates of Calleva Atrebatum. Having heard the tales of what had taken place in the battle with the Saxon invaders, few of the British kings trusted the High King and most of the British rulers were slow to respond to Vortigern's demands for men and supplies. On this particular occasion, he had demanded troops that could man the defences of the fortress at Canovium, near the Island of Mona. The local population had been decimated after regular incursions by the northern Picts and their leaders had petitioned the High King for assistance.

Unfortunately, the fortress at Canovium was situated on the north-western coast where freezing winds blew in from the Oceanus Atlanticus. Because warriors were reluctant to serve in this barren place, Vortigern had been forced to coerce the tribal kings by holding their sons to ransom, an action that ensured their obedience – if not their complete loyalty.

Most of the tribal kings in the north were discontented with some aspects of Vortigern's administration. For their part, the Deceangli were furious with the High King over his never-ending demands for men and supplies, while the Ordovice were enraged by his constant meddling in their political affairs. Similarly, the Brigante tribe viewed his manoeuvres along their borders as a territorial threat. Eventually, he had been forced to abandon the fortress and make a strategic withdrawal from Canovium. Vortigern was furious.

To compound this setback, Vortigern viewed the latest information from Gallia with a very jaundiced eye when the latest courier to arrive in Venta Belgarum spoke of the emergence of two dangerous young men who claimed to be the sons of Constantine.

Their military successes against murderous brigands who paralysed the trade routes and a number of victories over the avaricious criminals who caused significant chaos in the eastern parts of Cantabria had eventually brought the young men to the attention of the Hispanic authorities. The Goth kings who held sway over these lands had rewarded the young men with red gold for their assistance, while the Roman magistrates along the coast were grateful to these young men who helped them to shore up their control over their flagging population centres.

Vortigern realised the significance of the re-emergence of the children immediately and his angry response frightened the servants and his current favourite, Caitlin, who had risen from being a lowly maidservant to the heady heights of a concubine. Now, as she suckled their new-born son, Katigern, she tried to calm her lord as his excess of temper made the servants quail and the infant cry.

'I wish that Severa was still alive so I could inflict a particularly nasty death on her,' Vortigern snarled. 'I should have known that the bitch would have left her sons behind as potent weapons that could be used to strike at me.'

'These boys can cause you little harm, my lord,' Caitlin said softly. 'They are landless men and a great sea lies between them and us. Regardless of this, they can be no older than fourteen or fifteen years and they have no armies at their backs.'

'You're a stupid woman, Caitlin.' Vortigern's face flushed scarlet. The woman flinched away from his fists, for he had beaten her into a bloody mess in the past when he had no one else to blame after his plans had come to nothing.

'You have no understanding of how men think, so you'd best be quiet if you don't want to feel my fists. Those boys have the blood of two emperors in them and their lineage could be used against me by any number of British traitors. I should have tortured that bitch and her whole fucking family when she sent them away. I had my chance to discover where they were and I was too soft on her. It's easier to kill a sapling than it is to cut down a tree. Constantine's seed would surely harbour ill-will towards me, and the throne of Britannia could well be at stake.'

'They can't do anything, lord,' Caitlin said soothingly. She could usually tease Vortigern back from his insane rages but, on this occasion, all her coaxing and flattery counted for nothing.

'That bitch, Severa, was trouble from the first day I met her. She was a fitting match for Constantine, a man who caused disasters in Britannia before he was executed. But I won't allow him to harm me or mine, even though he speaks from the shadows.'

'Send men to remove them. You've eliminated other threats – so there isn't a problem!'

'It would be best if you stayed out of affairs of state, Caitlin, and amused yourself with raising my children. Your little bastard and Vortimer are my bulwarks against fortune's folly.'

Caitlin stared fixedly at her infant child in her lap. She was already plotting to elevate him over Vortigern's milksop son, Vortimer. If the High King had known that she was planning the death of his first-born child, he would have been horrified to find that treason could exist within his own household from a source in which he had complete trust.

The boys treated Paulus like a father or a grandfather and steadfastly refused to entertain any mention of his great age. Fortuna had been generous to the old decurion as, with creaking joints, he had gone with his boys on their military forays into Gallia. For his part, Paulus feared his death, not out of cowardice, but because his boys would react badly when the wellspring of their life was plucked away by time.

The boys were practising their swordplay and moving through the basic manoeuvres that Paulus had taught them as youngsters. But, after all these years, the youths had turned into fine specimens as they approached manhood.

Ambrosius was the shorter of the two boys, but he was sturdily built. He had cut his locks in the Roman style and kept it militarily short, like that of Paulus, his mentor. Ambrosius was even-tempered and very much attuned to the feelings of others. The lad also possessed a wisdom that exceeded his fourteen years. He never acted without conscious thought and Paulus was very proud of Constantine's heir.

By contrast, thirteen-year-old Uther was completely different. His emotions ran hot and cold by turn, but once he had decided that any person within his sphere of influence was flawed, he would neither forgive nor forget. Uther was exceptionally tall and powerfully built. His curling hair fell down his back and almost reached his waist.

As the two boys exercised under the Hispanic sunshine, the younger man's curls seemed to be shining like spirals of brass. Constantine's second son was a handsome boy and the pert serving-girls at the villa vied for his attention. Sadly, Uther saw these women as playthings to be cast aside when some newer beauty came along. His sense of loyalty was strong, but it was focused on Paulus and Ambrosius to the exclusion of all others.

Unlike his brother, Uther often acted before he thought, although Paulus had done his best to break the lad of this bad habit. Despite this, Paulus feared for both of them, because their height, their colouring and their military talents had already won a certain amount of attention in the north of Hispania. Paulus sensed that Vortigern would eventually learn of their whereabouts and take steps to have them assassinated.

Then, as Paulus watched the swordplay, Ambrosius tricked Uther into overreaching and the younger, stronger boy ended up on his backside with Ambrosius's gladius at his throat.

'Shite, brother! You've tricked me – again!'

'You shouldn't use your added bulk to force me to capitulate, Uther,' Ambrosius said good-naturedly. 'If you're not careful, you'll lose an arm or even your life. You can ask Paulus if you don't believe me.'

Uther stared at the trampled sod of their practice arena and scowled at his brother.

Paulus knew that an explosion was imminent, because Uther always attempted to shine when he was in the decurion's presence.

'Ambrosius has shown us that a good swordsman can use the momentum of an opponent's rush to trip him up. No man can expect to win a bout if he's thrashing about and falling. Ambrosius has been outthinking you, Uther, despite the fact that you're bigger and stronger than he is. I'll say without hesitation that you'll eventually become a formidable warrior – but only when you're capable of defeating your brother in a fair contest.'

The expected tantrum died on Uther's lips, and he looked at Paulus with eager affection.

'Do you think so, Paulus? Could I really become a formidable warrior?'

The naked hope and love in Uther's eyes made Paulus stutter

over his words of praise, for such adoration from one such as this young prince placed a high demand on the recipient.

'Yes, Uther! You can be far better than your father, or any other man I've served with, but you must learn to think before you act.'

'I'll try, Paulus! I swear I will!'

Paulus pulled a small circlet of brass from his wrist and handed it to the young man.

'I've worn this armlet for as long as I can remember. Take it, Uther! In those times when you must make a decision, or before your temper explodes, perhaps you might look at it and remember the advice that I've just passed on to you.'

The old man stared up the hill and spied Dilic approaching from the direction of the villa. Her entire body was screaming disapproval.

'What do you think you're about, boys? The sun is far too hot and there's too little shade here for the decurion. Help him to his feet and take him back to the courtyard.'

Since they had settled into life at the Villa Africanus, Dilic's attitude towards Paulus had completely changed. Where once she had been highly critical of Paulus, she now saw herself as his protector; a minder who saved him from his worst excesses.

Like any tyrant, she drove him demented by her solicitude. Now, with a furrowed brow, Paulus was forced to bite back on his anger.

'I'm old enough and ugly enough to move without assistance. The day I have to use a stick will be the last day that I'll want to live.' Dilic would have helped him to his feet but he brushed her hand away angrily.

'Damn it, woman, I'm not in my dotage yet!' He turned back to the boys. 'Help me to the courtyard, Uther, and we'll have no more fuss.

'Think about what I've been saying, Uther, because we'll be working on your archery tomorrow.'

The young man tried to protest, but Paulus had an explanation to hand.

'I know that aristocrats don't use bows for anything but hunting, but your father was always prepared to use any weapon that was to hand when the need arose. I expect you to become proficient with the bow at the end of the next sennight. No! Don't bother to argue with me, boy – just do what I say!'

The young men obediently strung their bows and began firing at a target that had been set up some distance from the exercise yard. Then, when the servants ran off to collect the loosed arrows, Ambrosius grasped Uther by the arm to gain his attention.

'Paulus is beginning to fail, brother. Can't you tell? He is walking with great pain and, while his brain remains sharp, his body is like an old shoe that is fast wearing out.'

Uther responded angrily and bared his teeth at his brother.

'Paulus still has years before he must go to the shades. Don't talk such nonsense!'

'Wishing doesn't make something so, and we can't hold back time. Every step he takes causes him pain. I don't want Paulus to leave us, but we must face facts.'

Uther argued with his brother all the way back to the villa. The very thought that Paulus might soon leave them caused him to register an emotion akin to panic.

Perceiving this feeling as a weakness, Uther became more and more angry, and his fury remained cold and obdurate for some weeks.

The day that Paulus died was fine and sunny, and even the animals in the field seemed imbued with newly found joy and vitality. The decurion had never been a man to cause any fuss, so the end of his life was as simple and as uncomplicated as his entire existence had been.

He was found in his bed at daybreak, and there was no evidence that he had fought the approach of his oldest enemy. Lying on his side, he seemed to be resting under the woollen shawl that Dilic had woven for him. His eyes were closed and he looked so peaceful that the boys who were summoned to his room believed he was merely sleeping. The unnatural chill of his flesh was the only indication that Paulus's spirit had flown.

Dilic wailed like a professional mourner and tore at her flesh with her nails, leaving no one who saw her in her grief in any doubt of the love she felt for this Roman officer.

The boys were hamstrung by their masculinity and were robbed of any physical expression of their loss, but Uther became quiet and withdrawn. Meanwhile, Ambrosius pulled unconsciously at the hem of his tunic until the fabric was shredded and useless.

'Paulus must be sent to the gods with all ceremony,' Uther said passionately. 'We must tell our people that he was a giant among men.'

On the other side of their mentor's body, Ambrosius concurred.

'I don't know what god Paulus believed in, so I suggest we

dedicate him to Mithras, the soldier's god. Paulus was a true Roman legionnaire.'

'We must have a feast, with the master's wine and a libation to the gods,' Uther added.

'I'd have chosen to send Paulus's old horse into death with him, but he wouldn't have liked that,' Ambrosius decided. 'Instead, we'll use blood from one of the Hispanic bulls in the ceremony to speed him on his way to the shades.'

The two young men planned the ad hoc ceremony as they stood over Paulus's corpse. Both used the ceremony as a means of keeping busy and would have helped Dilic and the other women to prepare Paulus's husk for cremation if they had received the ladies' approval.

Then, with scant regard for their benefactor's property, Constantine's sons stripped dozens of trees for timber as the funeral pyres were prepared for burning. Unlike the cremation of other men of Paulus's station, the decurion's corpse was consigned to the underworld atop a pyre constructed from pine timbers that had been liberally laced with the best oils that the villa possessed. The servants added their gifts to the tall structure and, amid floods of tears, Paulus was prepared for burning.

As a final tribute, Uther climbed into the pyre and spread Paulus's red legionnaire's cloak over the body, which now seemed more like an effigy than a once-living man.

Ultimately, the boys agreed that Ambrosius would speak on Paulus's behalf, while Uther was granted the privilege of setting the funeral pyre alight.

'Paulus was a father to us and he was our teacher. He was also our protection from enemies who sought our deaths. Without pay or compensation, he dedicated near to half of his life to keeping us safe from harm. I remember no father, other than Paulus, and I cannot conceive of a better man. He wore his Roman cloak with pride, so we will send it into the funeral pyre with him. He made men of Uther and me, and the best of us was Paulus himself. Goodbye, dear friend, for your long duty is finally complete. *Vale!*'

The crowd roared out their refrain, *Vale*, while Uther plunged his torch into the heart of the timbers. Within seconds, the flames rose until Paulus's cremation fire was blazing so fiercely that distant villagers saw the rising smoke and wondered what disasters had come to plague the inhabitants of the Villa Africanus.

Long after the servants had returned to the courtyard to enjoy the funerary feast, and long after the corpse had turned to ash, Ambrosius and Uther were standing in respectful silence. Only when the last vestiges of the funerary pyre had collapsed in a great explosion of sparks did the brothers return to the villa.

And, from her tear-soaked pillow, Dilic could have sworn that she could hear Paulus's laughter.

CHAPTER XIX

THE WOLF'S LAIR

The journey of a thousand miles begins with a single step.

Lao Tzu

The sun was very hot, far too hot for the fair skin of the Briton who had near killed his horse to reach the Villa Africanus. The courier ignored the small knot of slaves who tried to bar his way as he forced his suffering horse up the avenue that led to the main buildings. Alerted by a cry from the steward, Ambrosius and Uther followed the steward out of the courtyard and into the tiled area adjacent to the atrium.

'Alert the servants and make them ready, Uther. That horseman is pushing that animal too hard for my comfort. Something might be amiss with him.'

'He's obviously set on reaching the villa, and he's ignoring the slaves,' Uther added.

When the horseman reached the small knot of servants, he pulled back on his reins and brought his beast to an ungainly

383

halt. Brushing aside several servants who would have stopped him, the courier spoke directly to the two young princes.

'I'm searching for the sons of Constantine. Are you the men I seek?'

Ambrosius nodded.

'I come to you from my friend, Daire, who lives in Burdigala. He sends his greetings and a warning that you must leave this sanctuary before Vortigern's assassins find you and attempt to kill you.'

Daire's messenger was a middle-aged man who had obviously ridden hard and fast to reach the villa. His tunic was dark with sweat and his whole person was covered with a fine patina of dust that spoke eloquently of a journey that had taken some weeks to complete.

After he issued his words of warning, the messenger slid down from his horse and tried to stand on legs that had been sorely weakened from his long stint of riding.

'I bear a belated message from my adopted home in Burdigala where I was promised a tidy sum by your seaman friend to deliver his message. Daire assured me that I would be rewarded for my efforts. He wanted to be certain that you've been warned of dangers that surround you. A party of five men have come from Britannia and they are seeking your whereabouts from people in and around Burdigala. They are offering good coin for information on your movements and Daire believes that their purpose is to ensure that neither of you sees out another year. I've been told that the wolf king, whoever that might be, has offered to pay well for proof of your deaths.'

Uther looked thunderstruck, but Ambrosius seemed far more thoughtful and decisive. The two were familiar both with the details of their initial flight from Britannia and with Daire, the mad seaman who had gained status in the telling of their escape from Britannia. But the boys had never expected to hear from the man who had taken them to Apollodorus in his small boat.

Ambrosius was the first to gather his addled wits and come to a decision.

'We'll prepare ourselves for a journey to Burdigala, brother, and we'll destroy Vortigern's assassins of our own volition,' Ambrosius announced. 'They won't expect us to come looking for them and make a direct attack on five fully trained warriors who are at the height of their powers. We'll surprise them by placing ourselves into harm's way to destroy them. I, for one, don't like the prospect of having to guard my back for the rest of my life. It would be far better for us if we confront these men on ground of our own choosing.'

Uther shook his head, as if to move cobwebs from his brain.

'As you wish, but will we take men with us? The odds aren't in our favour.'

Ambrosius smiled in a way that was totally foreign to his usual genial self.

'Better we don't involve our patron, Helguerra, or any of his servants, lest Vortigern seeks revenge on our friends for their sins, either real or perceived. Paulus always said Vortigern had a very long reach, so let's cut off some of his arms. It's time to lay our plans, brother, for we should make our way to the port as soon as we can. We'll need dried food for at least a few weeks, spare horses, and we'll have to see to our arms. It will be important to our success that we surprise these murderous animals. If we can kill them swiftly and silently, Vortigern can fume to his heart's content while never knowing what happened to his assassins.'

'They'll be the very first of Vortigern's minions who feed my revenge if I have my way,' Uther retorted with a vicious twist of his lips. 'Vortigern owes us for the death of our mother and I haven't forgiven him for a single moment of the pain he inflicted on her.'

'How can we find these men of whom you speak?' Ambrosius asked the messenger who was trying not to hear the plans being concocted.

The courier had belatedly realised that he might have been wise to ignore the silver coins offered by Daire to find these elusive lads. They would never have known the details of his perfidy if he'd failed to warn them of the danger in which they had been placed. While Daire would have had his suspicions, it would have been too late once the boys had met their fates.

But the expression in the younger brother's eyes suddenly made the messenger feel quite ill. He had seen Vortigern's assassins from a distance in a wine shop in Burdigala. They were hard and dangerous men, seasoned by battle and brutal by inclination. He had initially thought that the two lads would be easy prey for the assassins but one glance at Uther changed this mood. He had seen men like Uther before and knew that he would mature into a cold and calculated killer.

The gleam of madness in Uther's eyes signified an insane passion for destruction. With his own eyes, he had seen some of the Goth warriors who became so maddened during a battle that they had been known to kill ferociously even after suffering terrible, incapacitating wounds. If he had not seen such ferocity for himself, he would never have believed it was possible.

The youths moved quickly once they had decided on their course of action. Servants were sent scurrying to find packhorses, their own steeds, their weapons and sufficient supplies for a journey of several weeks.

And then, in this sudden flurry of activity, Dilic and Dara sought the boys out.

'Don't think for a moment that you're going anywhere without us,' Dilic said pugnaciously. 'My dead mistress would turn in her grave if she thought for a moment that her sons would go into a place of danger without me to protect them.'

'You needn't think that I'd stay here when you boys might never return,' Dara interrupted, and her voice was made courageous by the necessity to convey her message. 'There's little to keep us here in Apollodorus now that Paulus has gone to the shades. We're of a mind to return to Britannia, dangerous though it might be.'

'But no carthorse could keep up with our animals,' Uther replied imperiously.

Dilic's mouth set into a mulish line.

'If we pay our courier friend to escort us back to Burdigala with a carthorse and our possessions, we could meet you at Daire's dwelling-house when we arrive,' Dilic countered. 'You'll be able to find us once you've dealt with the assassins. When we've finalised our business in Burdigala, we can take ship for one of the ports in southern Britannia. From there, we'll have to find a place of refuge in our homeland, but I've no doubt that such places exist, especially along the coast to the north-west and north-east of Britannia.'

Ambrosius capitulated.

* * *

With the lightning responses that would, in the future, mark the brothers' strategic brilliance, Ambrosius and Uther were ready to make their departure at first light on the morning of the following day.

A missive was sent to Helguerra to explain their hasty departure, and to thank their benefactor for the many years of sanctuary he had given to the boys without any hope for recompense. Helguerra had remained true and, in doing so, he had repaid an old debt that many men would have ignored. Ambrosius explained to his brother that a personal visit to Helguerra's townhouse would only serve to ignite Vortigern's enmity towards their benefactor if their relationship became the subject of common gossip.

Another letter was sent to Daire in Burdigala with one of the estate's best horsemen whom the two princes co-opted as a courier. His message was simple. The sons of Severa were about to leave their refuge in Apollodorus and were bound for Burdigala. The seaman should avoid all contact with the men from Britannia.

Every detail of their planned course of action had been checked and re-checked to Ambrosius's satisfaction so, at dawn, the two youths set off on horseback with their supply horses in train. They were followed by a lumbering wagon carrying Daire's messenger and the two women who had nurtured the boys for so long. Slower by far, the second party was left behind in the dust raised by the stallions ridden by Ambrosius and Uther. These horses were the best that the Villa Africanus could muster, and they were fine animals indeed.

Even though the two were moving at a fast clip, they still contrived to move stealthily through the landscape for they were alert to the possibility that the assassins might be carrying out a systematic search of the district. The boys knew that Paulus would have been angry with them, even from the shades, if they had been foolish enough to be captured by murderous enemies while blundering along without a plan.

'It'd be best if we kept off the road and travelled parallel to it. It would slow us down, but we'll be difficult to see if we can remain hidden by the tree line. I'm of the belief that Vortigern's assassins consider us to be safely ensconced in some place of safety, and therefore they would never expect to meet up with us on the open road. They are scouting for information from the local population, so they're probably becoming careless. If we ensure that we see them before they see us, we might be able to ambush them. In any event, we should try to hunt down any rumours of strangers who are prowling about in the district.'

This suggestion was so sensible that Uther stilled his impatience and agreed to ride ahead to gather whatever information might be elicited from the local peasantry. With a silent prayer that Uther could control his temper and wouldn't alienate the local farm folk, Ambrosius agreed to his brother's course of action.

With Paulus's instruction to treat poor farmers with respect ringing in his ears, Uther turned off the road and headed inland for a short distance. While remaining within the tree-cover while keeping the road under observation, it would be fairly easy to see travellers before they became aware of his presence. Each evening, he'd return to his brother's campsite and advise Ambrosius of any intelligence he had gained.

For more than a week, Uther fumed at the wastefulness of his self-appointed task – and the absence of any information about his quarry.

Then, on the ninth day, Uther was travelling along a low valley and was thinking of nothing in particular when a herdsman with a flock of goats hove into view. On a whim, and with no expectation of success, Uther urged his horse up an incline in a spray of shale and frightened the boy witless with his questions. After so many blank faces and negative responses from other travellers during the last few days, Uther's jaw dropped when the pimply-faced youth blurted out a sighting of the five men.

'I've seen 'em, but I weren't able to help 'em,' the herdsman answered when Uther asked the usual questions. 'They weren't good men, I could tell from the way they treated their horses. Cruel, they were! And one of them would've ridden down my best goat if I hadn't stood my ground. If you want news of them, and you don't like them, I wouldn't have to think much on it. I wouldn't do them bastards any good turns – not if my life depended on it.'

Uther grinned and the goatherd suddenly felt a thrill of surprise – and fear.

'I'll not be doing them any good turns at all,' Uther snarled. 'I can promise you that they won't be scaring any more goatherds like yourself – not unless there are goats in Hades.'

The boy responded with a doubtful smile.

'Tell me what you can remember about these men, and where you saw them. You were right to be frightened of them, because they are assassins who are paid to kill people – mostly innocents. Sadly for them, however, they might have outreached themselves on this occasion.'

The goatherd told the frightening young man everything he knew, while keeping one eye on the tall young man's sharp sword, which was nearly as tall as the goatherd himself.

The assassins had crossed paths with the boy a day earlier as he was guiding his goats across the Roman road. By the lad's reckoning, the assassins had returned along the road leading back to Burdigala after finding no trace of Ambrosius and Uther along this particular stretch. The five men had been travelling slowly and the boy estimated they would be a half-day's travel from where they met him. Well-trained and experienced, these assassins were also travelling using the Roman road to maximise their search efforts.

After tossing a copper coin to the boy, Uther headed back towards a fold in the hills where he expected Ambrosius would be setting up their camp for the night. As he rode, he swore colourfully because the assassins had only missed Ambrosius by some lucky chance. His brother must be warned of the dangers they faced before another coincidence could warn the assassins that their intended victims were close to hand. By sheer chance, these murderous men could have stumbled over the women's wagon if they had continued along the Roman road. Such an event would have been an unmitigated disaster for the young princes, so Uther quickened his pace.

Despite his eagerness to test his swordsmanship on warriors who made their living from killing, Uther could still feel a knife-edge of panic that was scraping away at his nerve endings. Fortuna may have favoured the young men, but Uther could still remember Paulus's words: *'It's not enough to be lucky, because a sensible man will always prepare for the worst possible mischance.'*

Once Uther told Ambrosius of his discussion with the goatherd, the elder brother also realised that a disaster had narrowly been averted. While Dilic and Dara would have made a brave effort to mount some sort of defence, any assassins worth their salt would have extracted a great deal of information from the two women.

Uther wondered what Paulus would have done in a similar situation. The young man would soon get a chance to prove his mettle, but he remained fearful of failure during the physical confrontation that was about to occur.

'We'll have to catch these assassins napping, brother,' Ambrosius said. 'Five against two are very poor odds!'

Uther grimaced and the ferocity of his expression turned his face into an ugly and twisted mask. For one short moment, Ambrosius was afraid of his brother, but the moment passed and Uther returned to his usual taciturn self.

The boys plotted the downfall of their enemies and, just before dusk, they stumbled on traces of the assassins' passage through the scrub. They soon realised they were actually within bowshot of the warriors' camp.

They dismounted and tethered their horses some distance away from the camp where a copse of trees would hide them from scrutiny. Then, to allow some time to pass before they made their attack in full darkness, the youths set about the grisly task of determining how two relative tyros could kill five experienced warriors. While Ambrosius and Uther had the advantage of surprise, their opponents would not die easily. The young men could only hope that the assassins would underestimate the lads' skills and, hopefully, make some basic mistakes.

The young men's strategy was simple. Isolate those warriors who were on guard and kill them silently while the others were sleeping. If the guards were dozing, Ambrosius and Uther might be able to make one-on-one attacks and cut their throats before they could wake their friends. The two young men could then turn their attention to the rest.

The twilight was still lit by the last shards of daylight. With difficulty, Ambrosius stilled the pounding of his heart, which was threatening to leap out of his chest. Spread-eagled in a patch of long grass on a slight rise overlooking the assassins' camp, the elder prince wondered if the comfort of this mundane resting place would be one of the last pleasurable experiences in his short life. Uther seemed so very calm that Ambrosius felt shamed by his fears.

The two princes were too inexperienced to understand how many factors could go awry with their plan, but Fortuna sometimes favours fools and true men of courage. They gazed at the camp and their spirits rose.

'They're far more confident than I would have expected,' Ambrosius murmured. 'They've only placed one man on guard duty and he looks like he'll fall asleep in a trice. The other four are already sleeping, so the man on guard duty will have to be our first victim.'

'Good!' Uther snapped. 'The careless bastards deserve to die!'

The huddled shapes were black mounds around the dying fire. What light the ashes gave off revealed four blanket-wrapped bundles and the young men could make out, among the hobbled horses, the extra man who had been given the task of guard duty.

On hands and knees, Ambrosius slipped past the sleeping guard who had wrapped himself in a blanket and curled himself into a ball near the picket line. Uther moved to the man's right initially, before turning and approaching him from one side. Then, with his razor-sharp blade, he almost decapitated the man with a slash across the throat. The assassin never knew what hit him. Uther left him to drown in his own blood and continued to slink towards the fire where the other assassins were sleeping.

With the animal cunning of a born scout, Ambrosius was almost on top of his first victim when his sword-blade sliced through the assassin's greasy tunic and entered the man's windpipe. This assassin never took another breath, but his noisy death roused the other sleepers.

Trained warriors, the remaining three woke immediately and scrambled to their feet, but the third man in the group was slow to retrieve his weapon which had become entangled in the folds of his blanket. He became Uther's second victim when the young man's sword disembowelled him with a vicious slash. The assassin's strangled scream sent the last two scrambling towards the safety of an old tree trunk behind the banking fireplace.

'Who the shite are you?' one of the two remaining men bellowed as he evaded a wild swing from Uther, who slipped on fresh blood and almost lost his footing.

'I'm one of the men you are seeking,' Uther snarled through his gritted teeth as he made another wild swing with the sword. The young man's awkward blow missed, and served to convince the warrior that Uther was a tyro.

Uther should have died then, for he deserved to have been impaled on the sword of this seasoned professional, but Ambrosius leaped over the banking fire and drove his knife deep into the man's side. The man fell to his knees and blood began to pour from his mouth.

The last assassin was inclined to run, for he could tell that the tide of combat had turned. But Ambrosius stepped away from the man he had just killed and moved closer to the last survivor who was standing with his back against the old oak tree that blocked his escape.

The man dropped his weapon on to the ground in an act of surrender.

But Ambrosius wasn't inclined to be generous, so he held his knife against the man's throat until his own bloodlust cooled and his wits had returned to normal.

'Who sent you?' Ambrosius snapped, while Uther had to be restrained from killing him out of hand. 'If you don't reply, I'll let my brother cut the answer out of your balls. He's nowhere near as civilised as I am!'

The man was terrified. He knew that his chances of survival were negligible, but his current master had only a limited claim on his loyalty. Perhaps this youth with the nasty gleam in his eyes might let him live. At worst, cooperation might earn him a quick death.

'We were paid by one of the tribal kings in Britannia but we knew from the start that we were carrying out the wishes of King Vortigern. We were told that we had to find two boys and kill them, but we were never told how old the intended victims were. I didn't sign up with Vortigern to attack two fully grown warriors who knew we were searching for them.'

Ambrosius nodded at the compliments and Uther allowed himself a confident smile. He was still smiling when he embedded his knife in the assassin's belly and gave the weapon a vicious twist.

'My brother is a youth of fourteen years,' Ambrosius told the man who was kneeling before him with blood seeping from between his fingers. 'I'm a youth of fifteen years! King Vortigern may have employed you as warriors, but he sent you to kill two tyros. Unfortunately for you, my brother and I were trained by Paulus, the Roman decurion, so overconfident fools like you have become easy prey for us. I hope Vortigern paid you well, and that your widows will inherit something of use from this sad business.'

'But you let me think you wouldn't kill me,' the man muttered as he looked from one adamant face to the other, and his gaze lowered to the blood that was soaking through his fingers and dripping on to the soft earth.

'I lied!' Ambrosius retorted with a careless shrug.

Uther thrust his knife into the man's back to give him the boon of a faster death.

'Strip the bodies of valuables and dump them in the thicket,' Ambrosius ordered.

'Why bother?' Uther asked, but habit forced him to obey his brother's command.

'The last thing we need is for more strangers to enter the search for the children of Constantine,' Ambrosius told him. 'We don't want Vortigern to know that we've been in the district, so let's keep our problems, both real and imagined, to a minimum.'

The assassin's campsite was cleansed of any traces that five men had lived and died here. Several pools of blood were shining in the moonlight that could have betrayed the boys' red work but, by morning, this blood would congeal before being diluted in the next rain shower.

The bodies had been stripped of everything of value when the corpses were eventually discovered by itinerant travellers, but Vortigern never received any news of the grisly fate that had befallen his team of murderers. On occasion, he might wonder at the men's silence but, uncaring, he eventually lost interest in them and their mission.

But, in the late-night darkness, his wakeful mind conjured up visions of the two sons of Constantine. To his horror, they wore crowns but had no faces. Shaking and afraid, he woke from these night terrors and sleep would elude him for the remainder of the night.

Pridenow watched his sleeping wife, who was curled up on her pallet like a frightened child. Creidne's red curls were matted with sweat and she moaned quietly in her sleep. The young man smiled, for he knew every line of her body, as well as the sweet curve of her mouth and the determined pugnaciousness of her chin. Creidne always slept deeply, because she was constantly being woken by their restless son. Cadoc was often fretful for a child who had still to survive his first year, but remained the apple of his mother's eye.

Yet Pridenow had been gifted with a prophetic dream in which he sired a girl-child whose name would be remembered long after Vortigern and all his kind had turned to dust. Creidne was already pregnant for the second time, and Pridenow had been given a further dream that a woman with a sword was abed in their sleeping chamber with his wife – as if to protect her.

In the oddness of nightmares, the dream-woman had opened her arms wide and blood-red roses had fallen from them in a sudden splash of scarlet. Then, when Pridenow stooped to pick up one of the thorny blossoms, it had shrieked and transformed itself into a death-mask of Severa's face. The long thorns had pierced his skin repeatedly until he cried out in pain and alarm.

Pridenow understood that Creidne could easily be the mother of the girl in the dream, but the symbol of the sword escaped him. Was Creidne, or their daughter, fated to bring death and destruction into Britannia? Though fearful of the answer that might be forthcoming, he knew that Fortuna made her own decisions.

The reference to red roses in the dream made him think of the long-dead Severa, the last queen of the Britons, and her personal rose gardens. But what link was there between Severa's ancestry and his? What trick of fate would mingle his blood with the line of the emperor, Magnus Maximus? With a shiver, Pridenow remembered that two fearsome old men had come to him in a waking dream. He had known neither of these men, but they had mocked his ignorance before introducing themselves as the shades of Magnus Maximus, co-emperor of the Roman Empire, and Caradoc, the ancient king of the Dumnonii tribe. What the long-dead pair had to do with his kin was beyond his feeble imagination.

'We made him the King of the Britons,' the Roman figure stated proudly.

'He runs through our veins and he's succoured by history,' Caradoc added cryptically.

But the woman with the sword forced them both away so all that was left for Pridenow to see were her glowing eyes.

The dream left Pridenow feeling dislocated, as if he had forgotten something that might be of importance to the safety of his son. Breathlessly, he left his sleeping chamber and prowled through his house in Glevum.

Pridenow's villa was small but exquisite, and it incorporated every attractive element he required from a Roman building. The atrium was larger than usual and was fully half the size of the house. A fountain, shaped like a cheeky satyr, sprayed water over the ornamental cabbages and other colourful vegetables that grew around a tall peach tree. Pridenow chose not to dine in the Roman fashion, so the divans had been removed, to be replaced by chairs that were almost barbarian in style. The entire house was so well designed that no individual part of the décor had been permitted to overshadow any other.

The floors were constructed of fine mosaics which included tiles of gold, depicting the sea creatures that made their way on to the dining tables of his house. Pridenow felt his spirits lift, as they always did when he was within the confines of this refuge.

The scriptorium in the villa was small, but it was beautifully appointed, with numerous racks for scrolls, maps and Aeron's memoirs of the years that had been served in Gallia with Magnus Maximus. The king had also gifted Pridenow with a generous supply of scrolls that included some love poems that made Pridenow blush. Though never one to read voraciously, Pridenow valued the gifts of the lives of the Caesars and the writings of the Roman philosophers. Even the famed *Iliad*, by the ancient Homer, nestled within its own vellum box.

More to Pridenow's taste was the small room situated near the heavily barred entryway where Pridenow kept his weapons and a goodly store of the deadly tools that were used in the killing trade. These weapons would always be close to hand if the villa came under attack.

Pridenow took great pleasure in prowling through the villa's corridors at night. The furniture was old and highly polished, while inlays of brass and exotic timbers gave each item a rare and valuable beauty. Creidne's loom had been set up near the atrium and she had spent many happy hours with the women in her household as they spun long skeins of wool. Pridenow never tired of praising her skills to any visitors who came to the villa.

Now, at midnight, that time when the human blood ebbs and flows at its weakest, Pridenow examined all that he had built with a sense of pride. Endellion had gone to the shades only three seasons earlier and all Britannia had mourned her passing. Throughout the south-west, citizens had remembered her even-handed justice and her care of the common people who served her so well. Vortigern was furious at the praise that had been heaped on her.

Aeron had lived but a single month longer, for life without his lover was too terrible to contemplate for this sensitive and caring man. The invisible springs in his heart simply stopped working and the king died without fanfare or tears. His eldest son, Selwyn, took his place in the Council of Kings and all things followed as Aeron and Endellion would have wished.

Most of the British lands remained silent and peaceful for four long years, although the borders of Vortigern's kingdom were always in a state of flux. Vortigern was kept busy harrying the Saxons who came spilling up the River Thamesis in Londinium, a part of Britannia where the High King had little influence. Their squat ceols breasted the waves like ugly ducks, but the warriors who landed were savages intent on forming beachheads where they could confront the Britons. Meanwhile, occasional rumours reached Britannia from Gallia that the sons of Constantine had risen from the ashes of their sire's dreams, as with the tale of the phoenix, and they were amassing a quantity of gold, supplies and loyal warriors for an insurgency that threatened to overwhelm Vortigern himself.

During these long years of constant conflict, Uther had chafed at the delays in returning to their homeland as Ambrosius sold their expertise to the highest bidder. Their journey back to Britannia might have been overlong in the planning, but the canny Ambrosius reasoned that the name of the great Constantine was as nothing unless it was backed up with sufficient gold, coin and warriors to remove the British crown from Vortigern's head.

And so they developed their military skills in Gallia while their war chest continued to swell. Inevitably, word reached them that Vortigern was aware of their gradual rise to power and influence. They had received regular reports from Britannia. Word came to the two princes that Vortigern, against all logic, had invited an influential family of Saxons from the tribe of Hengist to take up land to the south of Londinium. This betrayal of everything that Britons held dear caused a muted fury to erupt within the ranks of the tribal kings. Yet no one dared to openly gainsay the tyrant. Vortigern was increasingly subject to fits of violence and demonstrated such ungovernable fury that he could, and did, order the execution of entire towns of recalcitrant citizenry. This insane behaviour stopped all treasonous talk, but the hatred that was directed at Vortigern was deep-seated and unrelenting.

This festering sore on the flesh of Britannia grew rapidly until the whole country was poisoned by it. So, convinced that the time was ripe for their return, Ambrosius and Uther took ship for Britannia – and home.

CHAPTER XX

THE NAKED SWORD

Whoever fights monsters should see to it that he
doesn't become a monster in the process.

Friedrich Nietzsche

The shingle on the pebbled beach crunched under Ambrosius's
feet as he leaped over the side of the fishing vessel and set foot on
the south-eastern shore of Britannia. Uther followed, and, as
soon as he reached the beach, he bent over and grabbed two
handsful of gritty sand which he raised high above his head
before emitting a defiant scream.

'May the gods bear witness that I'll never leave Britannia
again,' the young man yelled at the top of his voice. He permitted
the damp sand to fall through his fingers while the mica crystals
among the grit caught the sunlight like tiny jewels.

To the north of their landing point, Ambrosius could see that
the chalky cliffs were shining whitely in the glare of the sun as
the huge formations were slowly gnawed away by weather and

the ever-encroaching sea. 'We're creatures of sunlight and shadow,' Ambrosius mused to himself as he gazed into the distance and the darkness of the sands and the whiteness of the chalk seared his eyes.

During the last four years of their wanderings, Ambrosius had become more and more aware of his brother's qualities – both good and ill.

Fortunately, Paulus had insisted that the elder brother should see his sibling's better qualities with clarity, but he must always remain cognisant of Uther's weaknesses.

Ambrosius knew that Uther was a natural leader of men who gloried in his physical prowess, determination and sense of duty. But the elder brother also knew, all too well, that his sibling's only true loves were his elder brother and the British throne. All else meant nothing to Uther, so his leadership qualities would only be valuable for as long as the younger man could be forced to resist the lure of untrammelled power. Left to his own devices, Uther would revert to the rage and violence that seethed below the surface. While Ambrosius kept Uther's excesses penned, the younger brother had no need to exercise self-control and he only obeyed his older sibling out of a deep, filial love. In the darkness of the night, Ambrosius wondered what would happen if Uther was unleashed to do his worst.

Ambrosius had assembled a small force of one hundred committed mercenaries who would cross the Litus Saxonicum and make their landfall to the south of Dubris. Boats at the embarkation point in Gesoriacum were in short supply, so Ambrosius decided to move his warriors, along with their horses, equipment and supplies, in a series of crossings that would take some days to complete.

The clamour of frightened horses, the shouted orders of warriors and the harsh metallic rattle of weaponry turned the first crossing into a cacophony of military might. With a sense of relief, the first draft of invaders saw the shelving beach as it grew closer to the bows of their craft. Fortunately, the weather had been kind and Fortuna had blessed them. The seas in the Litus Saxonicum were smooth and their vessel's crossing had been uneventful.

The brothers, as well as the other mounted warriors who were part of Ambrosius's command, had refused to part with the magnificent horseflesh that had been bred by Helguerra at his estate in Apollodorus and schooled by the lordling's personal horse-trainers. No competent horseman would have willingly parted themselves from such noble beasts.

The horses' mettle was obvious when Ambrosius and Uther forced their animals, after making their landfall, to leap from their boat into shallow water where their footing was uncertain. The horses reluctantly complied, but Uther chose to use his quirt across the back of his stallion when the animal balked. Its blood-red nostrils spoke mutely of its fear.

The warriors had disembarked from their boat, along with their animals, supplies and weaponry. Then, once the vessel had been emptied of men and cargo, the boat returned to Gesoriacum to prepare for its next voyage. Meanwhile, the brothers and their bodyguard had moved their supplies to higher ground where a strong defensive position was being prepared.

For month after month, Ambrosius and Uther had pored over pieces of vellum on which primitive maps of Britannia had been drawn. Ambrosius knew that one hundred men could never hope to take the isles and only an appeal to the heroics of the brothers' noble past and the legendary figures of Maximus and Constantine could hope to sway the selfish, self-interested kings of Britannia.

The strategy and tactics for their crossing of the Litus Saxonicum had been developed over some months, for Ambrosius and Uther had come to the conclusion that the time to foment a rebellion against Vortigern had arrived. The two young men had gained a reputation for their military accomplishments and professionalism throughout Gallia. There, in that violent and war-ravaged part of the world, they had earned the gratitude and dedication of a number of Gallic noblemen and warriors who were landless in a society that valued property above all else. These men formed the nucleus of the small force that the two young princes were taking to Britannia. For some of these men, this was the first time they had set foot on the shores of Britannia and they would have to feel their way. Those who had some knowledge of the Britons would become the spearhead of the brothers' battle plan, but the bulk of Ambrosius's army would be drawn from those dissidents who chafed against Vortigern's rule in the tribal kingdoms. The British warriors would be encouraged to throw their swords behind the standard of the two young princes. So, with the use of cajolery, force and even trickery, an army must be raised to stand against the usurper of Constantine's throne.

Meanwhile, the balance of Ambrosius's command would disembark from their vessels at the landing point on the Cantii coast and, once safely ashore, they would rendezvous with their fellow warriors at the Red Horse, a hostelry that served a shady clientele in a village to the south-west of Dubris.

Ambrosius was aware that Vortigern's spies would take word

to the High King that the sons of Constantine had landed in the south-east of Britannia with a large mercenary force. Aware of Vortigern's propensity for violence, the young man hoped that he would respond angrily when he received word of the young men's return to their homeland. All things being equal, Vortigern would wait until the brothers revealed their plans before making any response. But, once satisfied that the odds were in his favour, he would attempt to nip the rebellion in the bud. Ambrosius could only hope that Vortigern's response would facilitate his own plans.

The brothers knew that speed was of the essence.

Ambrosius, a born strategist, planned to split his force into two columns. The first would ride along the southern coast of Britannia and proceed to Tintagel in Cornwall, gathering men, horses and gold from the tribal leaders in the lands through which they would be passing. Ambrosius would lead this column himself, and he would seek out those rulers in the south of Britannia who would give a positive response to his call to arms. Constantine, Severa and old Caradoc had left a legacy of sorts in these lands, so Ambrosius intended to manipulate this advantage to achieve his own ends.

The second column would cross Britannia from east to west and would pass through the tribal lands to the north of Corinium and Venta Belgarum with Uther in command. Again, the tribal rulers would be asked to fund the princes' campaign against the High King, while pledging them reinforcements and supplies. Naturally, the rulers would be nervous about the princes' requests and would be as skittish as young horses until a rational and disciplined hand convinced them to make an agreeable response. Ambrosius, however, was certain that his army could win their loyalty through his skilful use of diplomacy, governance and military strategy.

The lords of the Dobunni tribe were sympathetic to the kin of Endellion and Severa, but they were also pragmatists who understood the importance of trade. Vortigern, for his part, had always been contemptuous of commerce and the merchants who were Corinium's lifeblood.

The two brothers talked late into the night as they quaffed a flagon of rough red wine. The Red Horse had an evil reputation and sold bitter wine, but its large, single room was dark, and very private. The few old patrons, gap-toothed and whiskery, minded their own business and were naturally nervous of the two young men with their hot, passionate eyes.

'It's time to make our final decisions on how our separate columns will travel to Corinium,' Ambrosius said softly as he turned his empty wine cup over a spill of red liquid on the dirty table. With his heightened imagination, the young man pictured the spilled wine as a gout of fresh blood. 'I expect that the balance of our troops, along with their equipment and supplies, will have arrived in Dubris by tomorrow afternoon. We should commence our separate journeys at first light on the following day.

'When I leave Dubris, I'll pass through the Cantii and Regni lands,' Ambrosius continued. 'I'll confront both kings on my arrival and thrust the new order in their faces, but I don't expect much in a practical sense from them. These tribal kings lack courage and I'm aware that Maximus and Constantine had to coerce them into providing aid to their forces. I don't expect any change in their manner, because their citizens have borne the brunt of the Saxon invasions. But I do want their moral support. Nay, I'll demand it!

'I'll continue along the southern coast at best speed until I reach Tintagel Fortress. Along the way, I'll beard the kings of the Belgae, Durotriges and Dumnonii tribes on their own thrones and demand their unreserved loyalty. My fifty warriors should be sufficient to enforce any demands I make, but I intend to order our new allies to hold their troops and supplies in reserve until we issue our call to arms. Any plans for troop movements must be fully coordinated, Uther. I have to keep you informed of my plans, brother, because at least one other person must know and understand them. That person can only be you! The last thing I want is to have loosely coordinated troop movements that criss-cross the land and cause confusion before I know what forces are beholden to Vortigern and which are loyal to myself.

'Once I've secured the support of the newly crowned King Cardell in Tintagel, I'll proceed to Corinium where I'll meet up with you. Tintagel's complement of troops and supplies will be at my back when I arrive. I anticipate that the total time for my journey to Corinium will be less than twelve days, unless some catastrophe occurs.

'If I haven't arrived in Corinium by the morning after the fifteenth day, you are to assume that I've met with some form of disaster. In this event, brother, you'll assume command of our rebellion and I'd urge you to pursue it to a satisfactory conclusion. The lives and aspirations of many people will be depending on you.'

Ambrosius stabbed his brother with his gaze. Uther was certain that these instructions were vital to the success of the rebellion that was soon to begin, so he schooled his face into an expression of sincere admiration and determination.

'You, Uther, are required to carry out a special task which I will soon explain to you. This task is in addition to those I have already outlined for you.

'The small port and township of Anderida is situated on the southern coast just a few miles from here. It's little more than a name, but Anderida's strategic importance to our plans cannot be underestimated. Anderida will be your first test of strength! I must have this port, because it's the gateway into the south-west and it's Vortigern's underbelly. It's also a perfect jump-off port if I want to send couriers or agents into Gallia or Hispania.

'You are to proceed with your column to Anderida Silva on the south coast before you start your own journey through the British tribal lands. Once established on the northern outskirts of the woods, I want you to leave forty of your men in an encampment while you pay a visit to the port of Anderida with your ten remaining warriors.

'Inside the town, you'll be entrusted with an important mission where your use of tact and diplomacy will be of equal importance to the strength that lies in your arms. Aye, brother! Your task is to turn Anderida's good citizens against Vortigern and Venta Belgarum. You'll use tact initially, just as a favour to me. But, if they argue the point, you'll punish those who talk the loudest and warn the rest that those who stand against me will share the same fate.

'No mercy, Uther! You mustn't waste too much time here, because Vortigern will act against us as soon as he learns that his enemies are arming against him.'

'But I don't understand!' Uther interrupted. 'Vortigern won't come out and fight you if he thinks that you're raising an army in the south-west that is likely to best him. I wouldn't, and the Demetae's far wiser than I am. God rot his black soul!'

'Don't blaspheme, Uther! Like Mother, Paulus would have clipped your ears if either heard you using such language.' Uther looked embarrassed, so Ambrosius let the mistake pass.

'I apologise, brother,' Uther whispered contritely. 'You're right! I remember little of Mother after all this time – but I do know she prayed. I can remember seeing her on her knees, and I still recall the sweet smell of her hair.'

For a moment, Ambrosius looked at Uther and saw the confused face of his younger brother as a child.

'Once your business in Anderida is satisfactorily concluded, you will leave the port and collect the balance of your command from their camp in Anderida Silva. You'll then begin a long journey that will take you through the lands of the Trinovantes, Catuvellauni, Coritani, Cornovii, Deceangli, Ordovice and the Silures tribes. Finally, you will proceed to Corinium and the Dobunni tribe where we will meet again.'

Ambrosius's blunt hands were lying on the table top amid the spilled wine. He rubbed at his sticky fingers where the congealed liquid had formed a crust. Then, absent-mindedly and lost in thought, he drew circles on the table until he felt his brother's eyes upon him.

'I anticipate that your journey will also take some twelve days. If you haven't arrived by the morning after the fifteenth day, I'll assume that you have suffered some catastrophic event. If that should happen, I'll continue with the rebellion in accordance with our plans.

'Your column will have a greater distance to travel than mine, but I expect you to move at far greater speeds when you are travelling along the Roman roads. These carriageways will enable you to move faster and this will be to your advantage. Conversely, you might well encounter other travellers who aren't to your liking. If this occurs, you must exercise your own judgement. You can also infer from my instructions that your column is to avoid the Atrebates lands. Vortigern doesn't hold much sway with the citizens in the lands that you will be visiting, but he does have some loyal groups within the Atrebates tribe. We can always exact retribution from those Atrebates who oppose us at some future time of our choosing.'

'Fuck me, brother! You take on the safe solutions every time, when the only way to convince these dogs is to kill a few, and then knock the others around their snouts until they obey you. These southern kings are all talk and fuck-all action.'

'You're probably right,' Ambrosius replied, his brows deeply furrowed from concentration. 'But I'd rather sweet-talk them first. If we can't win the kings' acquiescence using common sense and blandishments, we'll teach them what their fate will be if they oppose us.'

Ambrosius smiled. Uther's ferocity was far too useful for Ambrosius to further punish him, so he made an irrevocable decision to overlook his brother's excesses. It was time to unleash Uther from the chains that bound him.

'When you leave Anderida, harry all the towns of the south as you pass through them, brother. I know you can maintain your speed and I know you can be cruel, so you must be prepared to scare Hades out of any tardy kings as you move inexorably towards Corinium. Pridenow dwells in Corinium. The last time you were in his company, you barely reached his waist. You must always defer to that young man, because it's been said that he was speaking of you when he described the man who would father a great king who will come to rule over our lands.'

Ambrosius paused to allow his instructions to sink in.

'Once you've completed your negotiations with the tribes to the north and west of Venta Belgarum, you'll join me at Corinium. I'm confident you'll do well when you learn to negotiate with other rulers and convince them of our needs.'

'God help them then, brother!' Uther replied with a boyish grin. Somehow Uther was always happier when his sibling trusted and depended on him.

Ambrosius slapped his back with affection. 'You're the strong right arm of this enterprise, Uther. In fact, you're of far more use to me than a century of trained Roman soldiery. Paulus should be commended, for he gave us the heart and the skills that turned us into leaders of men,' he added. 'Between brains and brawn, I'm confident we'll be driving Vortigern into a trap. Especially if we have God and Paulus on our side! That stony-hearted bastard will learn to regret that he killed our mother.'

Ambrosius watched as Uther's face caught fire, spurred into an outpouring of passion and idealism that he rarely felt.

Uther will do those things that I lack the stomach for, the cold part of Ambrosius's mind whispered silently – and he'll never consider shame or retreat. Perhaps I'm doing a wicked thing, but the search for a crown makes monsters out of otherwise good men.

Uther departed Dubris in a thick cowl of dust. The roads criss-crossing Britannia were well maintained and still bore witness to the road-building skills of long-dead Roman engineers. The excellent road surface ensured that Uther's cavalrymen could maintain a tight arrowhead formation as they swept the miles behind them like a spool of thread. None of the warriors wore badges of rank or the tartans of their tribes, for Uther's officers had decided that the men should wear neutral-shaded, woven clothes over their breastplates as a precaution against unit identification. They had also insisted that the men should cover all burnished metal and chain mail to disguise their origins, but Uther had made a personal decision to wear Paulus's scarlet cloak when he was in open view. This worn fragment of Roman military pride not only stiffened his personal resolve but that of his warriors too, who knew that cloaks such as this had seen many campaigns and experienced many brutal sunrises. Paulus had worn this cloak when he campaigned with Constantine in Gallia, so it had come to represent all that was noble and military in the brothers' shared history.

The prince chose to remain visible to his officers and men at all times.

When Ambrosius had left his brother to make his way to the Cantii and Regni halls, he had considered Uther's use of Paulus's cloak with some misgivings. Then, when Uther had explained that Paulus's spirit might stiffen his spine during the disconcerting tasks that would confront him at Anderida, he had admitted his fears and concerns in a shame-faced fashion. The fact that he had chosen to speak at all convinced Ambrosius that Uther was suffering from a profound case of nervousness. Ambrosius opted to hold his tongue and comply with his sibling's wishes.

Now, resplendent in his faded scarlet cloak and mounted on a wonderful black stallion, Uther felt as if he was finally equal to the task that Ambrosius had entrusted to him.

'Every soul in this town will suffer if Anderida attempts to interfere with my brother's plans. I will not fail!' Uther asserted decisively. With such violent thoughts running through his brain, he considered the details in Ambrosius's plan that could possibly go awry.

When the horsemen reached Anderida Silva and the ancient dark woods, Uther ordered the bulk of his men to set up a defensive camp at the edge of the primeval forest. Several of the younger hotheads protested that they were being left behind, but Uther quelled their protests with a single glance. Chastised, the men vacated the roadway and began to build an overnight camp in the deep shadows beneath the trees.

Once the column had been divided, Uther drove his small detachment onwards at a withering pace. The horses were just beginning to founder when Anderida appeared in the distance, lapped at by a grey sea and surrounded by viridian-green swamplands along the shoreline. Coarse grasses and tussocks of vegetation blurred the outline of solid earth.

Uther accepted that his troop movements would soon be common knowledge, not only to the citizens of Anderida, but also to those farmers who populated the surrounding district. One of Vortigern's spies would be sure to have already left the town with a message for their master that a small troop of armed Romans had arrived at Anderida's gates. The young prince knew it was important that he ride hard and fast if he didn't want to be caught in a rathole such as Anderida.

Perhaps stealth and diplomacy would have been the most sensible manner of gaining access to the town, but Uther was always impatient. Let the citizens of Anderida know that the new British order had come to their little town to shatter their peace. The use of war cries, once so prevalent in these lands, was Uther's means of defying the Fates. Let Anderida shiver by its warm hearths and let the merchants hide their gold. Let the town's women thrust their unwed daughters into places of concealment. Uther was making his approach to the people who lived in this hamlet in the same way he meant to finish it: with speed and aggression.

Uther's small troop of armed men galloped directly to the western gate.

Use of the eastern gate would have implied that the swamplands and quicksand flats on that side of the town didn't pose a dangerous threat. Now, in a slow arc, Uther approached the gate that remained stubbornly closed.

In an open show of force, Uther led his men towards the worn timber. Then, using the pommel of his sword and with one eye raised above his head to see any missiles that might be cast down over him, he announced his presence to the citizens of Anderida.

'What do you want?' a surly voice demanded from above the ramparts. 'Be on your way, or you'll feel the heel of my boot.'

'I've come with a message from the High King,' Uther answered without shame at the lie he was telling. 'You'll open this door immediately, or you'll feel the heel of *my* boot.'

The few merchants, town officials and traders might have looked askance at Uther's Roman dress but, as Vortigern was known to favour the use of mercenaries among his guardsmen, these hard-eyed young men could easily have come from Vortigern's court. With much forelock-tugging and apologies, the citizens of Anderida opened the gate and Uther gained entrance to the town.

Anderida was small, even by British standards, so barely a

dozen dwellings and a similar number of shanties filled its untidy streets. With a sense of amazement, Uther wondered at the political importance of the township into which he had been admitted with such cursory inquiries. He was especially interested in the road network which provided Anderida's sole link with the rest of the world of Britannia. Then, as soon as he saw the eastern road that led to a wide, shingled beach, he understood why this flyblown part of the isles was of such importance to Britons – and to invasion forces.

The men who held Anderida under their control secured the two sets of flimsy gates and the walls that surrounded the township. These fools had allowed him, along with his warriors, to enter their town with only minimal questioning, Uther thought with amazement. Vortigern must be supremely confident that he held total control over the vast network of roads that were the arteries of these lands if he allowed such abysmal security to exist in this strategic hamlet.

Some of the unwashed citizens stared, gape-mouthed, at Uther and his troops as they headed for the only elevated structure in the village. This crude building was small, filthy and several pigs had been allowed to foul the old Roman mosaics that had once beautified the floor.

With an exclamation of disgust, Uther dismounted and kicked away a piglet that had taken up residence on the hall's threshold. The disgusting smell consisted of several layers of filth, pig dung and unwashed human flesh as well as the rotting food, spilled drink and large dogs that had been allowed to litter the building.

Resisting an impulse to cover his nose, Uther entered the dim wooden structure and peered into the gloom. Several chickens squawked loudly as his feet almost dislodged them from the perches near a wall sconce. The old Roman lighting hadn't been used for years; there were signs of neglect at every turn.

He had barely taken five steps when a voice stopped him near the dusty dais that had once graced the hall.

'Who are you to disturb my peace?' a querulous old voice demanded. Uther peered into the darkness and saw a very small man who was perched precariously on what had once been a throne. 'Answer me quickly, or I'll turn the townsfolk on you.'

Uther was forced to suppress a snort of amusement. 'Who am I addressing?' he asked in a vaguely mocking tone.

'I am Scoular, headman of the village, and I demand to know the nature of your business.'

Uther drew himself up to his full height and looked down his long Roman nose at the headman who was forced, to his chagrin, to look upwards at his visitor.

'I require all of your horses and two serviceable wagons,' Uther said in a firm voice. 'If this flea-trap has any gold, it will be confiscated. You needn't think of hiding it from me, for my men are adept at winkling out valuables that have been squirrelled away.'

The little man seemed to puff himself up to twice his normal size.

'We don't give our coin to thieves. There are still some men among us who are prepared to fight against theft, even if you are a sodding Roman.'

Uther smiled and Ambrosius would have warned Scoular that his sibling hated to be thwarted. Even in the dimness of the hall, Uther's eyes seemed like chips of ice.

'If you should make any effort to raise your hands against me or my brother, I will burn Anderida to the ground and execute your entire population. This will take place without any hesitation. Call for your citizens now, so they too can see that I speak in deadly earnest.'

With an unnatural turn of speed, Scoular sprang down from his perch, causing the chickens to squawk and flap themselves away. The headman reached the threshold of the hall, where Uther could see the whole population of Anderida drawn up.

The small courtyard was filled with citizens and most of them were carrying farm implements of some kind that they presented as makeshift weaponry. The men among them seemed to be surprised at their own temerity and, as Uther's men fanned out to protect each other, the local citizens seemed ready to bolt to safety at the slightest provocation.

Only two plucky individuals, both fishermen, displayed the courage that told Uther they intended to stand their ground.

The prince gazed directly at the two men who seemed to be the only effective opposition to the edicts that he was about to impose on Anderida. Remembering his brother's warning to remain conciliatory, Uther forbore to unsheathe his sword. Instead, he decided to ignore Scoular and keep his attention fixed on the two fishermen who were his only threat.

'I am Uther, second son of Emperor Constantine, who was the last ruler to be anointed as the High King of the Britons. My elder brother, Ambrosius, has returned to these isles to wrest the crown back from the tyrant, Vortigern, whose impious hands have usurped the British throne. We intend to restore a descendant of Magnus Maximus on to the throne of the High King.'

Uther kept his gaze on the faces of the two fishermen.

'You must decide, women and men of Anderida, whether to throw your weight behind my brother, Ambrosius, who is the true king of these lands, or face his wrath. Should you fail to obey us, you will be put to the sword. The choice is yours!'

One of the fishermen stood fast and thrust out his jaw towards Uther. His hand toyed nervously with a fishing knife that was attached to a belt on his waist.

'Them's only empty words! That's all you've given us! How are we to know if you're speaking the truth? You could be a liar . . . or a madman . . . for all that we know. Beware we don't send you out of here with your tails between your legs.'

Uther realised he was pleased that this fisherman would refuse to accept his demands. The prince would be given a chance to draw this man's blood. He had always understood that it would only be the threat of violence and overt reprisals that would ensure Anderida's cooperation.

Two of the veterans who had fought with Uther in Gallia stepped forward to acknowledge a flick from Uther's hands. The closest fisherman died before he could make a sound and the second was impaled on the same warrior's gladius before he could gasp out a word of complaint.

'Ambrosius brings both prosperity and the sword. The choice will be yours! Like Ambrosius, I am one of the brood of Magnus Maximus and what I say will not be gainsaid – and certainly not by you. You will obey, or you will die.'

The wounded fisherman writhed in the mud and blood and gazed up at Uther as if his assailant had the power to save him. When Uther's red cloak flapped wildly after a sudden gust of wind caught it, the dying man whispered through a bubble of blood:

'Pendragon is here! The Dragon has come!'

* * *

The warriors rode fast and hard as they swept like wildfire through the south-west and north-west and north of Britannia. Ambrosius spoke with a honeyed tongue, so that those rulers who heard whispers about the younger brother listened with relief and gratitude to Ambrosius; convinced that the devil had chosen some other route. In the great halls of the south, men squirmed as they listened to Constantine's eldest son, and wished that they had been born in earlier, less dangerous times. Many of the southern kings were swayed by Ambrosius's passion, but most prayed to their gods that Uther Pendragon would never set his eyes on their halls.

In slow dribbles, the gold and supplies sought by Ambrosius were promised and accepted; the prince issued an edict that these levies should be sent to King Cardell in Tintagel.

'Don't choose to promise your gold and then withhold it! King Cardell will keep a good accounting of who has sent men, supplies and metal. You can be certain that I'll send my brother to enforce any agreements that are made between us if you make a promise and then renege on your bargain.'

The threat of Uther was usually sufficient to ensure the kings' compliance. Word had spread, like a cancer, of his treatment of those kings who spoke and lied during the early days of this campaign.

'In Glevum, the young prince came like the Wild Hunt and few men dared to stand against him. His warriors tore into the old town and demanded fealty from the old king who was slow to respond. Uther's answer was immediate. He spared the children of the tribal king but the king's women and mature sons were punished for his tardiness. The women were raped repeatedly, and the sons were taken as hostages. Perhaps they still live, but only a fool would rely on Uther's innate decency.'

Willem, the grandfather who had spoken these intemperate words, had served with Constantine and held a faint memory of Macsen Wledig. With an internal shudder, the old man turned towards the other men who made up the tribal council.

'Let's pray to God that this Uther never sets his eyes on us,' he continued. 'Our king has promised gold so we can expect to be spared, especially when young Creidne and the warrior, Pridenow, spoke on our behalf and reminded Uther that he had escorted the young princes away from Vortigern's assassins when they were little more than babes-in-arms. I was told that Uther blushed when he was told of the lifelong debt that he owes to Pridenow and his kin. Still, we were little more than a hair's breadth away from that madman's retribution. Thank God that the dragon remembers his debts ... and honours them as much as a man like him can do so.'

'I'd still be happier if that young man stayed away from Glevum,' Willem's companion replied. 'The only person he trusts is his brother, and he's the only person who can stay his hand.'

'I've sent my own son to Venta Silurum and I can only trust that Uther won't want to make war on the lands that are ruled by the Deceangli – his own tribe!'

The old men nodded wisely towards their cronies and turned the conversation to less dangerous subjects.

Ambrosius had arrived in Tintagel with all the fanfare of a returning emperor. He was clad in burnished breastplate and chain mail of such intricate design that Tintagel's armourers marvelled at its strength and beauty.

'I purchased this coat in Apollodorus from one of my patron's best suppliers. The merchant assured me that the armour came from one of the best artisans in Rome, but I have no way of proving it,' Ambrosius had explained to Cardell, the newly crowned king of Tintagel.

'This material is marvellously light, yet I believe it will turn aside all but the heaviest of blades,' Cardell said thoughtfully. 'The man who wears this mail shirt is doubly blessed.'

Ambrosius had first seen the magnificent fortress at Tintagel from the landside and had been struck dumb by its wonder. Enamoured, he had galloped down the sloping road that led down to the causeway like the wind that scoured the cliffs of the citadel. Darkness had begun to fall, so the sloping roadway had been afire with flint sparks and the fitful light provided by the great metal sconces.

The night had been heavy and humid after the summer heat and, from far off over the ocean, great knots of lightning sent down portents of coming storms to terrify the watchers. Occasional gusts of wind tore the grasses on the island into long green rags while the sea below the causeway boiled with a vicious tidal flow. Ambrosius's hair, cropped as it was, fell in fey locks around his engrossed features. He had never seen Tintagel before. Then, as he reached the causeway, a single seabird hovered over the darkening sky and screamed loudly, either in warning or in recognition, as it rode on the thermals.

Beneath his heels, Ambrosius could feel the strength and certainty of this citadel to the men who lived here. This fortress would turn a bleak and unforgiving face to the viewer when the drums and trumpets of war came.

He found it easy to believe that this fortress had never fallen in battle. Even the sandals of the unbeatable Romans had never left angry footmarks on its stonework. The entire citadel is a miracle, he thought with wonder in his heart. The ancients must have worked long and hard, using the highest-quality flints, to wrest this fortress from Tintagel's flesh.

Ambrosius felt a little light-headed, for he was totally smitten by this ancient and wondrous place. Some dormant part of his soul rejoiced with pride that he shared some lineage with the long-dead artisans and warriors of yesteryear. Cardell looked up at Ambrosius with eyes that were alight with something of the same fervour that was illuminating Ambrosius's face.

'We've done our best to construct the walls of our citadel from material that will endure forever,' Cardell told him with pride, but much of his voice was blown away by the rage of the angry winds. Even Cardell was struck anew by the wild beauty of his home.

'I can understand why the old Romans let your fortification be,' Ambrosius replied. 'In all seriousness, I never saw a finer stone structure during my years in Armorica, the place where the Giant's Dance filled the sky. There, in that Gallic land, they built great mounds of stone for their dead kings and green swards cover the resting places of their ancient heroes. Yet Tintagel outshines them all.'

Ambrosius looked thoughtful as he compared the marvels he had seen.

'In all my wanderings, I've never beheld a stranger place than this. Here, the stone appears to speak and it's a place where men know immediately that they are small and insignificant competitors who try to survive within nature's domain.'

Some part of him realised that Tintagel would always reject

him. Kings meant nothing here! Only the stone, the sea and the great forces of nature had any chance of touching Tintagel's inner spirit. Regretfully, Ambrosius shook his head and began the business of gaining an ally for his cause.

'We've heard how your brother persuades fractious kings,' Cardell said. 'Don't bother to offer me the choice of standing with you or dying. If you do, you'll soon discover what the Romans learned when they tried to best the defenders of fortress Tintagel.'

'I confess that Uther is sometimes overzealous, but he is always loyal to me and to Britannia where our mother, Severa, took her last breath, and where Constantine and Magnus Maximus both wore the Grass Crown of the Roman legions. Our blood is entangled with the fate lines of these lands, so we have come to save our people from Vortigern, the wolf king.'

Ambrosius's face grew paler until the bones of his forehead and jaw shone like polished ivory.

'My mother's shade calls to me from the earth at Venta Belgarum. Vortigern crushed her spirit until she no longer had the strength to live. He murdered Constans most foully and betrayed my father, before running away from the Romans who would have killed him out of hand. His perfidy is so deep that I wonder that the earth doesn't refuse to bear his weight. I will swear to you, Cardell, that the time will come when Vortigern turns his eyes on your possessions and you, too, might need the assistance of others. Vortigern is all lust and hunger, so he is eaten from within by his own avarice. He'll knock at Tintagel's doors and he'll take your soft lands. If this happens, you'll be left with this fortress to provide you with a semblance of safety and security.'

Ambrosius took a deep breath and even Cardell, who hadn't been inclined to believe the other man, was unable to doubt his sincerity.

'Vortigern will take, kill or poison everything else, for he knows no other way. He has come to take our lands, and only a man who is graced by God can stop him. I am convinced that I was born for this purpose. God saved me from Vortigern so I could persuade you on this day to remove him from the throne and reject his mad rule.'

The two young men continued to speak into the night as Ambrosius cajoled, begged and threatened until, finally, the king of Tintagel was convinced.

The impregnable fortress had fallen!

CHAPTER XXI

A BARGAIN WITH
THE DEVIL

The hardest hit, as everywhere, are those who have no
choice.

Theodor Adorno

Pridenow stared down the long, empty road before him and
wished he was at home in his own bed. But needs must, so
Britannia's torment was increasing as the kings chose sides for
the conflict that was about to commence. The rulers jostled for
prominence within the new social structure and, while each
intended to be on the winning side, they intended to suffer
minimal inconvenience.

Creidne was close to term, so Pridenow was struggling with
his own guilt and his concerns for the safety of his wife. The
young woman carried children easily, but she was too narrow in
the hips to give birth without incident. One infant son had

already died because she had been overlong in labour. Pridenow recalled that terrible night of waiting when everyone believed that she, too, would probably die. By some miracle of chance, Creidne had survived, but her midwives were terrified that this child of sunlight might perish and be dragged down into the world of the shades.

Corinium's warriors loved their master, Pridenow, who served the Dobunni king, his brother, by protecting the trade routes that lay to the north and south of the provincial centre. The Roman roads were always under attack by vagabonds, bandits, escaped felons and countless adventurers, because the road was a source of wealth for Britannia. Corinium was one of the major trade centres patronised by merchants and traders who carried manufactured goods from the south and exchanged them for raw materials obtained from the mines and farmsteads of the north. Like great pulsing arteries, the roads carried the commercial lifeblood through central Britannia; the task of seeing to the health and safety of these crucial networks had been left in Pridenow's capable hands.

Pridenow's son was a curly-haired, loquacious boy who smiled often and complained rarely. Pridenow watched him grow with a feeling of proprietary pride. This lad would be a fitting heir to the Dobunni throne, although the prince still hoped that his elder brother, who had five daughters, might yet father sons and release his own son from the crushing responsibility of kingship.

On the other hand, Pridenow longed for a daughter. He clearly remembered the many prophecies that promised a daughter who would become an ancestor of the greatest-ever ruler of Britannia. But Pridenow refused to burden any child of his with such responsibility. Again and again, his sleep had conjured up a dream-woman and her drawn sword until the imagery had been burned into his brain. He could no longer pretend that the gifts of prophecy did not trouble him.

This pregnancy had been a burden for his wife, for the babe grew large and kicked so vigorously that Creidne stated in all seriousness that this unborn infant was almost certainly a male: 'For what little girl would use such force against her own mother?'

He preferred the softness and sweetness of little girls. Creidne frequently laughed at his choice, pointing out that most men desired sons and that his wishes were almost unnatural. Still, when Pridenow padded silently through his villa in the dark places of the night, the weight of his responsibilities left him sleepless.

Word had come to Corinium that Vortigern was prowling through the sweet lands beyond Calleva Atrebatum. These rumours had made Pridenow's patrolling task more difficult now, because Vortigern was also blocking the trade routes in an attempt to restrict the brothers' access to gold, supplies and the fresh warriors needed to flesh out Ambrosius's army. Pridenow knew that Ambrosius planned to rendezvous with Uther and the tribal lords at the ford to the south of Corinium, so Pridenow must sweep through these open spaces and clean out any attempts at infiltration by Vortigern's Saxons. Behind him, Pridenow led a tight band of fifty Dobunni warriors who had been trained to facilitate troop movements. So far, these rangers had met with little opposition but, surprisingly, Vortigern had issued a call for volunteers to rendezvous with the High King's forces on the verges of the Forest of Dean. This strategy would demonstrate their loyalty to the High King's cause.

Of course, some of the smaller tribes had been reluctant to

provoke the wolf king into taking retribution. Like jackals confronted by a wolf, they prostrated themselves and assured Vortigern of their fealty while promising the same to Ambrosius.

The prince, who had expected such hypocrisy, tended to use Uther's aggressive spirit to bring these nervous kings to heel. Uther's methods of gaining acquiescence were often extreme, and always dramatic. Eventually, the tribal kings learned to refuse Vortigern's demands with whatever excuses would placate Uther while still giving respite from Vortigern's rages.

The tribal kings were walking an impossibly difficult tightrope.

As was expected, the Demetae tribe had thrown their support behind Vortigern, while the population to the west of the Forest of Dean had also shown approval for the High King's cause. Those envoys sent to the local rulers by Uther under flags of truce were promptly returned to Ambrosius in neatly arranged pieces. The Forest of Dean had become a natural border, although Vortigern tried to press westward in an attempt to shatter the will of Ambrosius's allies.

When Pridenow considered the huge advantage in men and materiel held by Vortigern's force and the Demetae's strategic and tactical expertise, he was quick to realise that the onus was on him to keep the roads clear and open. There would be scant time for the young man to dally with a pregnant wife, even when the babe had almost reached the time of birthing.

On one of the few occasions when Pridenow could absent his forces from their continuous patrols, a courier galloped through the ford and climbed the short rise to where Pridenow and his men were resting in the shadows of some great oaks. The horseman seemed careworn and was shrouded in dust when he flung himself out of the saddle to recite his memorised message.

'"Greetings from Uther, Brother of the true High King, Ambrosius the Great.

'"The usurper has massed his troops to the north of Glevum, thinking to wrest all of Cymru and the lands to the south of the Forest of Dean from our hands. Battle will soon be joined, and all men of good faith who suffer under the reign of the wolf king are called to ride to the lands near Glevum at the headwaters of Sabrina Aest. Our enemy boasts that he will drive Ambrosius and all his supporters into the sea.

'"Ambrosius has made his call! True Britons must make a start to send the usurper back to whatever lair he has selected to live out the rest of his life."'

Pridenow nodded to tell the courier that he understood the crux of the message. 'Did your master tell you how long Prince Ambrosius would wait for the final gathering of his troops?' Pridenow asked.

'All glory to those warriors who fight with Ambrosius and Uther. Uther instructed me to tell you that his army should be assembled within fourteen days.'

'Excellent! I'll place my warriors on total alert,' Pridenow said. 'Alas, man! I can see now just how spent you must be. Have you been pursued during your travels?'

'Aye, lord! My companions and I have been harried by Vortigern's Saxons for these last seven days. They picked up our trail near Tintagel and the bastards have followed me continuously. They run like the wind! I thought I'd managed to throw them off when I carried my master's message through the fringes of the Atrebates' lands and continued into the realms of the Regni and Cantii kings.'

The young man paused and regained his composure.

'I was mistaken! Four of us left Tintagel, but I'm the only messenger who remains alive. Vortigern's assassins didn't hesitate to use ambush as a means of stopping our couriers.'

The messenger spoke baldly, as if the loss of these young men was commonplace. Pridenow was concerned at the thought of losing such promising young lives. He couldn't help but note the messenger's grey complexion, as well as the condition of his horses that were obviously exhausted.

'You'll go no further if you don't get some rest,' Pridenow advised him. 'My horse-master will provide you with two new steeds and this pair can be released to run wild in the open. They've earned their freedom!'

'What will happen if the rest of Uther's messages don't reach their destinations?' Pridenow then asked.

'My last stop is meant to be in the Dobunni lands. I'm heading for Corinium and I hope to be free to take my rest before joining Ambrosius's army in the final battle against Vortigern's Saxons. I don't know exactly where this conflict is meant to take place for Lord Ambrosius keeps this to himself. All I know for certain is that all men of good will must stand together at some place to the south of Glevum. From there, Ambrosius intends to drive the black-hearted usurper back into the seas off Cymru.'

After instructing the courier to take his rest, Pridenow promised the young man that he would personally ensure that his messages would be carried to their final destination. Not yet fully informed of current events, the Ordovice, the Silures and the Deceangli tribes had warriors among them who were avowed enemies of the wolf king. As well, the Brigante tribe still nourished a hatred for Vortigern that had lasted from the time he had spent the lives of his warriors so casually at the Battle of

Calleva Atrebatum. Vortigern, deeming his Brigante warriors to be expendable, had used them as fodder for his cause. The Demetae's name was still hissed at in the hearths of the Brigante women.

Pridenow acted with all of his usual economy of movement and speed. Four warriors were sent to the kings of the north and north-western tribes but Pridenow decided that any messages sent to the Demetae tribe would be pointless. The other kings were likely to see Ambrosius's call favourably, but the young messengers were ordered to avoid Vortigern's clutch of likely allies.

Pridenow finally turned the balance of his command towards Corinium and, ultimately, towards Glevum. His warriors would be given a single night with their wives and sweethearts before they would ride to Glevum to take up their positions in Ambrosius's offensive line.

Pridenow's young warriors were stoic and stern as each man confronted the possibility of meeting his death during the coming battle. Pridenow spoke plainly but his message stirred the men's blood and made any waverers think twice. His message was simple.

'We in the north rarely feel the hot breath of the wolf king at our throats. Nor do we have to lock our daughters away, so they are freed of Vortigern's lasciviousness. His taxes barely inconvenience us and he rarely troubles to meddle in our affairs. Yet we have seen the worst of his excesses! When he comes into our lands, the Demetae brings death and suffering, for he takes what isn't his to take. Yet we rarely feel the full force of his anger.

'But he needs us now!

'He would use our youth to batter at the great cities of the south, while keeping his own troops far from the lines of combat. He would then turn his warriors against us and force our kings to be his vassals. But it won't happen this time.

'The heir to these lands has come! He's the true claimant to the throne of Magnus Maximus and Constantine, and no man living has a greater claim to this honour than Ambrosius the Fair. The prince has come out of Gallia and he's eager to take back what is rightfully his, so Vortigern will be forced to do everything in his power to smash the son of Constantine. Do we choose to follow the wolf king blindly, and do we choose to justify Vortigern's use of Saxon warriors to bolster his regime? Do we turn our eyes aside while Britannia is stolen away from us?

'Do we permit Vortigern's Saxons to prosper and breed on our soil? Much of the wolf king's army was born in Saxony, across the narrow sea and far from our homeland. Vortigern has given them land to protect his own interests and he offers gold and power to these savages if they will bolster his rule. Is this wolf king worth dying for?'

Like hounds moving in for the kill, the young men growled from deep in their throats. Their eyes burned with a new passion and, for the first time, they thought of Britannia as a living force, something great that was deserving of respect and loyalty.

The young men unsheathed their swords. If any of Vortigern's warriors had been close to hand, they would have been slain in these first flushes of patriotism.

Pridenow permitted himself a small smile of triumph; for his oratory had demonstrated to the young prince how easy it was to inflame the senses of simple citizens. Why should it be that otherwise sensible men were willing to fight and die for a cause about which they knew little?

The warriors in Pridenow's column were superbly trained and eager for action.

Even the long ride that would take them back to Corinium failed to placate their growing resentment towards Vortigern and his cause. Every man was familiar with occurrences where renegades and Saxon infiltrators had penetrated into the lands populated by Vortigern's allies and these miscreants had demeaned those Britons who would normally have cast their lot in with Ambrosius's troops. Fortunately, the British warriors were aware of Vortigern's subversion, so their anger grew as they absorbed Pridenow's message and the long road scrolled past them.

The longer that the warriors pondered over Pridenow's words, the more their anger grew. Whatever the cost, Vortigern must fail.

Creidne's labour had commenced, but she was struggling to slow her birth pains until Pridenow returned from his patrols. When the prince finally reached the gates of Corinium, she heaved a great sigh of relief and stopped fighting against them.

Nature took its course on this occasion, and the child was born quickly.

The midwife looked at the infant's face with horror when she saw that a caul of flesh covered the upper section of the girl's face. Hastily, she grasped a cutting implement and removed the flap of skin.

'You will not speak of this morning's work to anyone, anyone at all, about the afflictions you have seen on this infant,' she ordered. 'The babe will be treated poorly if superstitious people heard rumours of a facial caul, so it must remain our secret.'

The women in the room twittered like nervous birds but Creidne had heard the protestations made by the midwife, so she demanded to inspect the child for herself.

The midwife handed the infant back to Creidne without explanation of what had happened, and she examined every inch of the infant's body.

'She's perfect!' Creidne whispered.

The child was indeed perfect. Without the caul, the child's skin was rosy with good health. She took hold of Creidne's hand in one little fist and tried to suck on her mother's fingers.

'It's time for her wet-nurse to do some work. We can't keep this pretty little thing waiting for her first meal, can we?'

Tired but triumphant, Creidne stared upward at the ladies who were ranged above her. She had provided the daughter that her husband longed for.

'Has the master returned to Corinium yet? I'd hoped that he would be here to meet with his daughter,' Creidne asked. After such a long and anxious wait, she was keen to present him with the long-awaited girl-child.

'We have just received word that the master was seen approaching the city walls, my lady. He sent a message by courier that he wouldn't come to you until he'd removed the dust and grime of the road. He will be with you as soon as he's clean.'

Creidne closed her eyes for a moment and only opened them when her husband settled his length along the bed and embraced her. Initially, the child protested at her father's nearness but some spark seemed to pass from the large eyes of the infant to Pridenow's slate-grey irises. With the babe's hand resting lightly on his, Pridenow felt a jolt of force pass from her into his veins. Then, in a waking dream, he saw the same child running in a

435

wide stand of daffodils and strewn wildflowers as she collected great armfuls of the flora in a blaze of yellow sunlight. The dream-child opened her mouth and Pridenow heard the words she uttered as if the phantasm was real.

'*I must be married to a man who will cherish me, for my life will be long and I shall be fraught with troubles in the marriage bed. A great man will want to possess me, but I will be forced to flee from him. I will be the mother of kings but will hold them in my arms but once, before the shades finally take me into their care.*

'*Marry me to a strong man who can bear the weight of the portents that surround us. You must choose well, for I will lack your wisdom when you eventually pass into the shades. You are entitled to pride, my father, for your seed has been chosen to present Britannia with a great king – one who will bear your eyes to prove his mettle.*'

The lady's form began to fade and her substance became long shreds of cobwebs. Then, as Pridenow desperately reached out with one hand to catch at her skirts, the woman laughed and turned to smoke.

'Don't fail me, Father!' she whispered from the thin air that had surrounded her. 'Your grandson that is to be will depend on the steadfastness that lies within your heart!'

Pridenow began to waken as two ashen-faced women snatched the babe from his arms. He'd been holding his daughter with such force that they were fearful for her life.

Then, as he came to his senses, Pridenow heard his wife's frightened voice. But he was still in a fog and unable to understand her meaning. He fell into an unconscious state at his wife's feet and knew no more until the sun had set and risen again.

* * *

Creidne was terrified. In her snug bedchamber, warmed underfoot by the magic of Roman engineering, she tried to remember everything that her husband had uttered during his latest bout of fitting.

Later, he had sworn that he remembered nothing of the prediction, but Creidne had stared fixedly into the depths of those grey eyes that trapped the light within her warm room.

Urged on by a terror of the unknown, Creidne had instructed her women to repeat every word of her husband's predictions to a scribe who would collate their remembrances and copy them into a missive describing everything that had taken place during the event. Even now, Creidne could feel a series of chill winds on the nape of her neck, as if some vast and indescribable god-like figure had entered her apartment to suck at her child's essence.

'I want to be woken as soon as Pridenow recovers so I can see to his needs before he makes his departure on the morrow. Our little one must be named and blessed before he leaves the palace walls.'

She looked around her room to ensure that her women understood her instructions.

'The bishop must be informed immediately to ensure that the child is baptised in the morning. Her soul would wander for eternity if she should die before she was consecrated and given to the baby Jesus.'

When Pridenow eventually woke, he found himself in the eye of a storm. Around him were dozens of women whose husbands, sons and lovers would leave at midday on this latest campaign. As they hurried to prepare the warm cloaks, polish armour and package dry food, a cacophony of cries, snapped arguments, raised voices and shrill complaints rose like the angry squawking of geese. Pridenow attempted to close his ears to the din, but he quickly realised that he had little more than a single hour to say his farewells to his wife before he must leave Corinium and lead his column to the rendezvous with Ambrosius. He had barely forced his shaking legs to stand upright when Creidne entered the room with her daughter in her arms. She immediately issued her commands to the waiting maidservants.

'You're awake, my love,' she said as she smiled across at Pridenow. 'I was fearful for you during the night, but I can tell from your eyes that you're well now. Meanwhile, I've instructed my maids to prepare some food for you, and you aren't to move from your seat till the whole repast is finished. No! Don't argue! You have sufficient time, so your warriors will wait until such time as I decide that you are ready.'

Pridenow knew that his wife was right. He sat on an available stool and began to partake of a hearty meal while Creidne watched him with arms akimbo, her ears sharp to any sound from the sleeping child. Pridenow, noticing that his daughter was decked out in unusually good finery, assumed that the child would be baptised now that the head of the family had returned to his senses.

The demands of good military leadership force commanders to exercise ruthless control over their troops for the sake of the common good. Pridenow knew he had to balance the needs of his warriors and his debt to the rulers of Corinium against the many small tasks that are asked of a husband and father. Finally, with Creidne dragging him along by the arm, he found himself led into the wattle and mud hut that the churchmen of Corinium used for their religious ceremonies. Some splendour was given to this stark and empty place by a tall bronze candle holder and an altar cloth woven and intertwined with gold and silver thread.

In the gloom of the small dark space, the bishop was standing in the finely woven fabric that befitted his station.

He stepped forward and Pridenow caught the smell of incense as the thurible spread its aroma throughout the cramped space.

'This child is an innocent, a little girl who has been born into the taxing times in which we live. Let us pray that God will spare her – and her parents – from the trials and tribulations that are about to visit these lands.'

Under the light thrown out by the brass wall sconces, the priest's skull was as pale as bone and Pridenow was reminded of his many dreams of the pale woman and her sword. Driving back any fears of the phantasm, Pridenow realised that the priest had almost completed the catechism of Latin words that the Church used for the baptism ceremony.

As he repeated all the necessary responses to the priest's offerings, Pridenow wondered if God was really aware of the multitudes who worshipped him. The prince had never been particularly religious, despite having done his best to live up to the standards taught to him by Severa. The weight of his responsibilities might have crushed him then, but he knew he would do anything and suffer any privations if his efforts and sacrifices contributed to the safety of this beautiful daughter.

The ceremony was soon completed and the babe was whisked away with the exquisite name of Ygerne. Her very name told Pridenow that his daughter would become a beautiful woman, but he was unsure if he wished such great physical loveliness on her. All the truly lovely women he had ever known were either saints who had no knowledge of their own worth or women who used their beauty as weapons. Pridenow hoped that his daughter would suffer neither such fate.

The incense had barely guttered in the wall sconces before Pridenow and his men were blessed with holy oil and prayed over for their continued safety.

As a man who had seen violent death on many occasions, Pridenow's calculating brain had long told him that no prayer could turn aside a Saxon axe or stop a sword thrust from the hand of a trained warrior. However, he had one last task to perform in case he didn't survive the coming battle and failed to return to his family in Corinium.

He would never allow his wife and children to be set adrift on the cold seas of charity.

Pridenow had secreted away a small vellum purse which held the gems he had discovered deep inside the mine shaft that he had chanced on during his journey into the mountains. Having held this precious hoard for many years, he knew the gems could prove valuable to his daughter at some time in the future, but only time would tell if they were worth the cost.

Even now, as he unfolded the vellum to reveal them to the light, his fingers trembled with trepidation and superstitious awe. He instinctively knew that these jewels were blessed by some supernatural force and that no one should try to enrich himself through these particular ornaments. The heavy stones and the yellow gold had been wrought with secret women's magic and they were calling out to the light. Long hidden underground and then secreted in Pridenow's pouch, the gems hungered for eyes to see them and marvel at their beauty.

Creidne looked down at the pouch in her husband's hands

and she felt a weakening in her lower legs as if she was only barely able to stand.

'What are these, Pridenow?' she asked. 'Why do you bring them to me?'

Pridenow gave his wife a brief description of how he had discovered the remains of the murdered woman and recovered the remains of her jewellery. He explained that he became convinced that the victim was a Roman woman of Christian birth who had been sacrificed to the old British gods of bygone days.

'I could see that she had been placed in the ground in an upright position, as if she'd been interred inside a womb. It seemed to me that those who took her life wanted her to be reborn in some future life. I could feel a spirit of holiness when I entered that place, but it was a dark and poisoned religion and I knew that I had no business within that sanctuary.'

'I'm not certain that I'm happy to give these gems to our Ygerne,' Creidne cried out, her face suffused with doubt.

'I'd never seek to harm her, Creidne. But I believe that our daughter has a magic of her own that was given to her by She who must be obeyed!' Pridenow averred. 'Look at her now! She is happy as any child could possibly be.'

The babe had been laid out in her basket to keep her free from the chill of the roadway, while her wet-nurse was kneeling above the child and flashing one of the red jewels to keep her amused. She reached out for it, so the nurse placed the stone into the child's hands to sample its barbaric beauty.

Then, like a bolt from the blue, Pridenow had a vision. He could see that the outline of a black-eyed woman with rust-red hair had been superimposed over Ygerne's tiny face.

The prince flinched, but Creidne had noticed nothing of this exchange so he bit back an exclamation of fear. He knew instinctively that Ygerne and the jewellery had been wrought for each other.

'Why have you given her such magnificent jewels, husband?' Creidne asked. She doubted that Ygerne's fingers would ever be suitable for such bulky pieces.

'I can only ask that you lock them away in a place of safety in case I fail to return,' Pridenow replied and held his wife close.

'Ygerne should wear such gems as if they were hers by right. I've always hoped that I'd learn the name of the woman who entered the shades with these jewels. If so, I'd hope that the priests would find some way to bless her and free her from the resting place in which she was abandoned. Every person on God's earth is worthy of consecration and the hope of eternal peace.'

As she looked at the gold cross which still held several strands of the strangler's rope attached to it, Creidne swore mentally that she would never allow her daughter to touch these gems until she had learned and approved of their history. Then, with this vow, Creidne raised her face to kiss her husband's mouth.

She silently willed him to return safely to their home, for her life would be barren without Pridenow to show her the way.

In the courtyard of Corinium's hall, the women clutched at their menfolk and wept. Women know the true cost of war, for it is a debt that only the female of the species can pay, whether the conflict is for ill or good. Within the crowd, Creidne was simply one more patriot. To control her own fears, her fingers became entangled in the mane of her husband's horse as if she intended to keep him in Corinium and safety.

When the men pulled themselves free of their kinfolk and their horses broke into a trot, some of the women ran after them.

Creidne chose to stand spear-straight on the steps of the hall with one arm raised in a final farewell. As he rode away, Pridenow took comfort from his love for this woman whose honour was unassailable and whose courage matched his own.

Long after the column had faded into the distance, Creidne stood with her arm raised as if she bore a shining sword.

THE BATTLE FOR GLEVUM

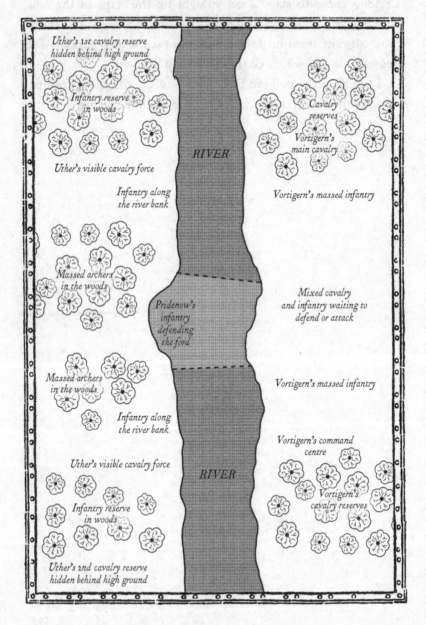

CHAPTER XXII

TO SEIZE A THRONE

Let your plans be as dark and impenetrable as the night
and, when you make your move, fall like a thunderbolt.

Sun Tzu, *The Art of War*

Lightning scissored through the sky and turned an old oak tree
into a blackened stump. The air was sick with the smell of ozone
and, for a moment, the earth was lit by a vast fire that seemed to
come from the depths of deep fissures inside the earth's crust.

Pridenow was afraid. Storms such as this rarely came to
Glevum and the prince hoped that he'd see no more of them
now that his men had established themselves in their bivouac. As
the tempest raged, his men had huddled together in the unnatural
light that seemed to presage some dreadful judgement from the
old gods of Britannia's pagan past. Yet he knew that God's wrath
and the rampant storm cells were quite capable of wiping out the
entire complement of men who were preparing for the coming
battle in their waterlogged tents.

For his part, Pridenow had been surprised to find that Ambrosius and Uther had kept themselves apart from their peers and it seemed as though Ambrosius and Uther were also avoiding the company of the common men they had recruited. Pridenow had felt his gorge rise when he thought of the risks he'd taken to demonstrate his support for Ambrosius.

Lightning struck again and the ground shook from the clap of thunder that followed. The time gap was almost instantaneous. Pridenow's face whitened with shock and fear, but his warriors had failed to see the trembling fingers that had been hidden inside the folds of his cloak.

Under canvas and leather, the volunteers that had gathered in response to Ambrosius's call for troops and supplies came from a multitude of backgrounds. Some of the landless men hoped to steal acres of their own, while others came to distinguish themselves in battle. If luck went their way, these warriors could find favour with the winning king. Other men, forever hopeful, came for much more intangible reasons such as love of country, tribe or personal honour.

In discussions with Paulus, the old decurion had tried to convince a younger Pridenow that unquestioning adherence to a cause was foolish and had no place in the repertoire of a soldier. But the prince was older now and he had learned from experience that Paulus's assertions weren't always right. Pridenow's personal view was that love of country and tribe was a purer emotion by far than the optimistic promises and sweet words of lesser men who promoted their political ambitions.

The evening landscape in the vicinity of Glevum was filled with a sea of the soldiers' lamplight. Yet thus far, though Ambrosius had recruited so many to fight the looming conflict,

Pridenow had failed to meet with either of the brothers or receive an invitation into the tents of the tribal chieftains, and had become a little miffed at these oversights. However, he kept himself busy with training exercises and tactical discussions with his officers, and familiarising his men with the intricacies of war.

Meanwhile, the camp grew in size, even as the storm clouds continued to advance.

Like the many lights of fishing boats that come to catch mackerel on that one day of the year when the sea gives up her bounty, the men of Glevum waited in their tents for signs from their betters that their presence was both required and appreciated.

Beside the warriors, servants and slaves whose skills were essential to the prince's success or failure were many common folk; men and women who offered their services as non-combatant volunteers. All were eager to help this golden-haired young man who had swept across the southern kingdoms of Britannia like wildfire.

Later that evening, once Ambrosius had established his headquarters under the smoky rafters of the ancient hall of the lord of Glevum, the British kinglets and many of the lesser chieftains were invited to a gathering that would determine the prince's order of battle. Pridenow joined the procession of warriors who were making their way to the king's hall to hear Ambrosius speak.

Ambrosius and Uther stood before the gathered throng and, without preamble, the elder brother spoke directly to his commanders. At first, many of the lesser kings and notables listened to his words with understandable caution. But their reserve was short-lived.

'Brothers! Friends! Men of Britannia! I have travelled many miles to mount this campaign against the tyrant, Vortigern, and to beg for your support. Unfortunately, you must judge me by my words, for I have precious little else to offer you. But one thing is certain – I will bear the weight of your suffering on my own breast – and in my heart!

'It could be said by my detractors that my brother and I haven't experienced the direct force of Vortigern's anger. It could also be said that my brother and I haven't shed our blood at the hands of that monster – and such criticism would be correct. In fact, I have little to offer our cause, except for my own life and that of my brother, Uther, who has been a tower of strength to me.

'I will gladly subordinate myself to a superior claimant if you should decide at this meeting of the tribal kings that another claimant is a more worthy candidate. Uther and I are agreed that Britannia will forever be our homeland for the remainder of our lives. And so it is that I stand before you as a petitioner. Uther and I have nowhere else to go.

'I may not have felt the tyrant's whip on my flesh, but my brother and I have known no peace during our lives. As children, we survived Vortigern's vengeance through the generosity of King Aeron of Corinium, a brave man who spirited us off to Hispania in a valiant attempt to save our lives. There, an old Roman decurion who served my father, Constantine, instructed us in the noble science of warfare and ensured we were educated in the social arts. He also prepared us for the duties of kingship to ensure that we were fully prepared for what would be expected of us during adulthood.'

'You'd have been better off thieving Hispanic and Gallic gold than chasing dreams of glory in Britannia,' one of the burly Brigante warriors shouted out. Many of the warriors in the audience snickered in amusement, but Ambrosius was undeterred by the interruption. The prince simply smiled and saluted the humour of the middle-aged tribesman.

Uther rose to his feet at this point, and the young man would have protested at Ambrosius's over-polite deference towards the assembled warriors if Pridenow hadn't restrained the young man with one hand.

'The truth is, my friend, that Britannia has called to me and her voice was strong. I was unable to forget the British people or the fate of my mother, Queen Severa. Throughout my youth, my kin spoke to me from the shades and told me of the injustices that had been inflicted on me and mine. Even the stones in the ancient Giant's Dance screamed out to me from over the waters, and those eternal sentinels decried the evil that was initiated by Vortigern.

'I am still a young man, but I possess a spirit that Vortigern will be reluctant to face. As a child, the usurper forced me to go into exile and remove myself from my people. Sadly, our departure from Britannia ensured that the impotent rage of the monster would fall on innocent heads.'

The crowd stirred like a swarm of angry bees that were striving to see their enemy. Ambrosius took two paces forward to unsheathe his sword. The dim light in the hall captured the outline of a massive weapon that flashed red in the light from the fire.

'There is no sword so strong that it will withstand this particular metal, for it is the blade of my grandfather, Magnus Maximus, the man who challenged the might of Rome. Macsen

Wledig, as he was called by the Britons of yesteryear, was a British hero. He was one of Rome's great generals who fought the Picts and won the Grass Crown of the Legions from his loyal warriors. One thing is certain! My love for Britannia is as deep and enduring as the affection for it held by Magnus Maximus.

'The blood of my mother, Queen Severa, has called to me from the shades. So, too, does the spirit of ancient Paulus, our decurion, and that of my father, Constantine. These ancients still yearn for the death of the Demetae monster.

'I cannot forgive the thief who brought our island to its knees. Britannia is so rich that its fields have presented us with gold and great wealth. Yet, our people are in decline and only blood that is spilled in her name can make the isles whole again.

'I ask you to march with me and feel like true men! Britannia needs you now, and she begs you to come to her aid. Today has drawn to a close and blessed darkness has come. The storms have passed now, so it is time to make our preparations for battle.

'Those of you who will stand with me shall be permitted to adjourn to your tents shortly so that you are rested for the combat that is to come. Those who reject my claim are free to depart and travel along our roads without fear of hindrance.

'Be assured that I shall not allow my warriors to shed the blood of true patriots.

'God save Britannia!'

Ambrosius turned and strode towards the back of the hall. As he walked away, those kings who were beset by indecision could see the shadow of a young man, and the figure they saw seemed much taller than the man they remembered as Magnus Maximus. This huge warrior-shape was a true Roman, and those chieftains with hesitant natures were enthralled by this great portent of success.

Finally, the last of the stragglers swore their blood oaths to Ambrosius, the newly chosen High King of Britannia.

Pridenow had barely managed to gather together his feelings of elation when a large warrior loomed out from the darkness adjacent to the hall's entry.

With the shock of nervous surprise, Pridenow realised that this warrior was Uther.

'Walk with me, Pridenow of Corinium! My brother wishes to speak with you in private before you leave to take your rest. He knows the hour is well advanced, but his business with you is a matter of some urgency.'

Uther's outline was menacing, especially as he possessed such huge shoulders and thighs. In the semi-darkness, his eyes seemed to be lit with a feral glow.

'I'll come at once if the High King has a need of me,' Pridenow answered in a voice that seemed to reverberate through his ears.

Uther nodded, but he made no other sign of acquiescence. He drew back so that Pridenow could lead the way into the battered tent that had once belonged to Paulus, but was now being used as an unpretentious command centre.

Conscious of Uther's proximity, Pridenow pushed aside the tent flaps that provided Ambrosius with privacy. The elder prince was sitting on a low stool, while feverishly examining several pieces of vellum on which charcoal writings displayed the topographical details of the terrain around Glevum. His large eyes glowed vividly.

'Pridenow! My friend! It has been many years since last we

met, and we could almost think that Fortuna has conspired to keep us apart.' Ambrosius laughed softly, as if he could see a joke that was beyond the understanding of other mortals. 'You saved our lives in bygone days, and it has now come to pass that I'm asking you to come to my assistance on one further occasion. Can I assume that you are totally committed to my cause?'

Such direct artlessness caught Pridenow off guard. Ambrosius's apparent sincerity was so disarming that he found himself stuttering in response.

'I've always been prepared to do anything for you that my foster-sister would have asked of me. I dared to defy Vortigern on your behalf when you were little more than a child, so I can do no less now, can I?' Ambrosius's candour demanded that Pridenow should respond in kind. If Pridenow lied, or sought to trap Ambrosius with insincere words, Pridenow would have proved himself to be even more dastardly than Vortigern.

'My mother was murdered – and this fate was inflicted on her with malice. Vortigern used the queen's vulnerable state to snatch the throne from our childish fingers. Neither Uther nor I have forgotten a single moment of our mother's pain. We'll never forgive the bastard!'

Pridenow felt, rather than heard, Uther's growl of agreement and his blood was chilled at the hatred that lay in the depths of the young man's voice when he spoke.

'Nor shall we forgive him until the day of his death and beyond,' Uther added from the shadows. His face was an inhuman mask.

'Your mother was always good to me, Ambrosius, so nothing you can ask of me will ever be refused. My family is indebted to you and yours and will remain so till the end of time.'

Pridenow was aware that he had just promised to cement a momentous bond between his family and that of Severa's children. He might have drawn back at this point to reconsider his words, but he heard the voice of Paulus as the decurion spoke to him from deep in the shades.

'*Each and every man is as nothing unless his word is strong,*' the decurion seemed to whisper. Ambrosius too was familiar with this ancient wisdom, but his knowledge of it had been derived through the influence of his father, Constantine.

Inspired by a determination to demonstrate his loyalty, Pridenow placed his fist on his chest in the classical Roman salute, a gesture that Ambrosius answered in kind.

Ambrosius smiled across at Pridenow, but a small frown creased his forehead.

'I have a task that I must place before you.' The prince paused and then selected the exact words he wanted to use. 'I need to dispatch a trusted envoy into Ordovice country to carry out an urgent mission of great delicacy. I have received conflicting information from the northern tribes and I've come to believe that those messengers we have dispatched to the region so far have been murdered by Demetae traitors. Regardless of the outcome of tomorrow's battle, I must send a man of substance to ensure that my mother's kin in Caernarfon are prepared to slam the gateway into the north if Vortigern should escape from Glevum.'

Surprised at this request, Pridenow remained silent.

'Would you be prepared to carry out this task for me?'

Ambrosius stared across at Pridenow with the same devastating candour he had displayed in their earlier conversation. Pridenow nodded wordlessly, although his every instinct urged him to turn on his heel and flee from the tent.

Uther smiled, his mouth as thin and as tight-lipped as a slammed door. He rested one hand on Pridenow's shoulder.

'Regardless of how we should fare in Glevum?' Pridenow asked.

Ambrosius nodded.

'Regardless! If I were to die in this battle, Uther would take my place and we are in total agreement as to any actions that must be taken. Our expectations would remain the same as they do today. I'll not lie to you, Pridenow! You'll have little chance of survival if you agree to undertake this mission, but your actions could influence the tide of Britannia's history if we can prevent Vortigern escaping from our clutches. He would forever be a thorn in our lands.'

'You will be well rewarded for your efforts,' Uther interrupted, and Pridenow recoiled with revulsion.

'I don't risk my skin for monetary reward, Uther. Such a suggestion is an insult!'

'Uther didn't intend to insult you with his words, Pridenow. You and your family are precious to me, and I'd be grievously wounded if any harm were to befall you during this mission,' Ambrosius interrupted in a conciliatory tone.

'So it shall be then,' Pridenow agreed and, as he left the tent with a scroll of vellum under his arm for delivery to the kings of the north after the battle. The young man could hear the creatures of the night as they called him a gullible fool.

'I'd rather be described as a fool than a dog whose word has little worth,' Pridenow muttered in response.

The wind soughed in laughter as the darkness of the night closed around him.

* * *

The night drew on and the campfires slowly guttered, while Pridenow remained watchful.

Meanwhile, his flesh crawled at the thought of an imaginary sword above his head.

Pridenow took out his battered writing tools and mixed up a small amount of black charcoal. He tested the ink's consistency and decided it would serve his purposes.

I go into the north on the morrow, dear wife. Something in the night air convinces me that I won't survive to see you again, so I beg you to take good care of little Ygerne. I can trust my father to keep my son safe, but my daughter was born under the comet's tail, and the portents surrounding her birth will follow her for all of her days.

Time is my enemy, so I have had no opportunity to organise her betrothal. She is so young that I thought I would have years to make such a decision, but I now find that I have but a single night.

Gorlois of the Dumnonii was present at the meeting of the kings, and I intend to seek him out and promise Ygerne to him. I'm aware that his wife died in childbirth, leaving him with no sons to perpetuate his line. I believe that Ygerne will remain safe under his protection.

I will speak to Gorlois on the morrow to gauge his thoughts on this matter. Be advised also, my love, that I intend to place you in his hands as your protector.

I regret that I can find no fond words of farewell that are worthy of you. My devotion to you has never changed. Farewell, my beloved.

Pridenow of Corinium

Written at Glevum.

Once Pridenow had used the last of his precious vellum, he felt as if the hardest part of his self-allotted task was over.

'It's done,' he said out loud to his pallet. 'All that remains is to speak to Gorlois on the morrow.'

Pridenow fell into a deep sleep as if all his worries were over. Around him, the camp was still. The only sound to break the eerie silence was the distant sounds of clinking harness as the pickets patrolled the perimeter of the camp. Within a few short hours, it would be daylight and Ambrosius would send word to his subordinates of the strategies that would be used by their units when they took to the field. It was obvious that Ambrosius's warriors would soon receive their marching orders from the officers who would position them inside the defensive line.

The long-overdue conflict to extract revenge from Vortigern for the wrongs he'd inflicted on Queen Severa was about to begin.

The queen had hoped that her sons would rule in their father's stead, and even the advent of Vortigern had failed to crush her ambitions after the death of Constantine had been confirmed. Eventually, she had given birth to three sons who, over time, would all lust after the Roman's poisoned throne. Had Paulus been alive, he would have warned Ambrosius against the acidic taste of power, but the decurion was long dead.

In any event, her sons would never have listened.

A heavy mist formed by the unseasonable cold began to dissipate as the breath from the Crone of Winter warmed the earth with a generous service of early-morning sun.

Fully prepared and ready for their final briefing, the local kings and a number of warrior chieftains were called to

Ambrosius's battle tent. Once the assembled officers had warmed their chilblained hands in front of a brazier, they craned their necks to peer owlishly at a large piece of vellum on which Ambrosius had drawn out his plan for the disposition of his troops and the likely dispersal of Vortigern's army. Most of the kings had little knowledge of reading and writing, but they were forced to make a feeble attempt at understanding the scrolls when the lives of their men were placed at risk.

Ambrosius felt a need to give a cursory explanation of tactics to his field commanders. 'The crucial part of this battle will occur when our troops make a feint attack against Vortigern's foot soldiers and our troops make their initial attempts to cross the river.'

A storm of protest followed Ambrosius's statement, but he raised his arms for silence. The clamour reluctantly abated.

'Vortigern will know if we try to trick him. He fought with the Eagles under Constantine, so he won't be fooled by any half-hearted shows of trickery.'

Ambrosius's face seemed unnaturally harsh. Unlike his brother, Ambrosius's features were soft, almost womanish, but on this occasion his expression was stern and implacable.

'Our infantry will attack Vortigern's main force on the far side of the river and make whatever inroads into Vortigern's forces are possible. It is likely that many of our men will die, but I want Vortigern to conclude that we've made a tactical error. He won't blunder into our trap unless he accepts that he has routed my foot soldiers. You, Pridenow, and you, Gorlois, can you put aside your natural concerns for your men and maintain control of our infantry?'

Both men indicated their agreement.

'You will have a combined force of Dobunni and Dumnonii warriors, as well as a number of volunteers from the other southern tribes. As this command will include the largest part of our force, I will be entrusting you with a vital part of my army. The wolf king must be fooled and he must believe he is hunting us down when he crosses the ford in pursuit of our stragglers.'

'I can carry out whatever task I am given,' Pridenow replied with a stark white face.

'And I,' Gorlois added. So too did the other kings as, one by one, they concurred.

'You'll be supported by one third of our cavalry force. These horsemen will attack Vortigern's foot soldiers when they reach our side of the ford and are established on dry land. Once again, we can expect a large number of casualties during this melee, but we must wait until we are fully ready before we spring my trap.'

'What sort of fool would allow his cavalrymen to attack a superior force of warriors?' the lord of Glevum asked boldly.

'I'm expecting your cavalrymen to volunteer for this task, since they're so familiar with the lie of the land,' Ambrosius retorted to the lord, who flushed an unbecoming plum shade at the commander's sarcasm. 'You'll note that I'm offering you the lion's share of the glory.'

The lord of Glevum nodded in acquiescence and Pridenow grinned from behind the back of his raised hand. Ambrosius had neatly trapped the bellicose man, leaving him with little room for complaint.

'We're about to enter into a life and death struggle for control of a large battlefield,' Ambrosius said confidently and glanced down at hands that had clenched themselves into fists. With a supreme effort of will, he forced his fingers to straighten and then resumed his explanation of the battle plan.

'At this point in the conflict, every occurrence will happen quickly, so much of our allotment of luck will depend on the good will of the goddess. Vortigern's cavalry and foot soldiers must be sucked further and further towards our side of the river bank, where I intend to allow the Demetae to see the true face of Britannia. Many of you might have wondered why I was prepared to accept so many of our common folk to volunteer for service with our army. Even in those early days when our planning was half-formulated, I envisaged a situation whereby our British peasants could demonstrate their mettle while showing their love for their native land.'

Ambrosius bent over and picked up a bow that was remarkably similar to those used by commoners for hunting. He raised the weapon above his head while the tribal leaders gaped at the possibility of using such bucolic objects as killing weapons.

'Every bowman at our disposal will be positioned along the elevated ground adjacent to the ford. I intend to use the weapons of the common folk to defeat our mortal enemy.'

A storm of irate argument filled the tent, but some of the tribal kings had noticed that Uther had failed to defend or reject his brother's proposal. Although they wondered at the young man's silence, Ambrosius ignored them and continued to speak.

'Our archers have taken as many barbs to their hides as they can carry and I've ordered them to target Vortigern's vanguard. Then, after the Demetae's reserves are fully stretched, Uther will carry out a flank attack on Vortigern's main force. If the usurper still has warriors in reserve, the last of our troops will be committed to the battle. These warriors will target Vortigern's foot soldiers, who can be isolated inside the ford.

'I'll be praying to God that we've met with success by this stage of the battle, for our total contingent of men will have been committed to the conflict. Like Caesar and the Rubicon, this will be our moment of truth. If we fail to achieve our objectives, the losses will be catastrophic.'

The silence that followed Ambrosius's explanation of the battle plan was total. The British chieftains could see how Vortigern would be ensnared, but what if the enemy commanders didn't react as Ambrosius expected? What if the cavalry failed to complete their allotted tasks? There were so many possibilities that could bring about a swift defeat to Ambrosius's fledgling army. Undeterred, Pridenow refused to contemplate any suggestion of failure.

The junior officers were dispatched to give heart to their warriors and acquaint them with the tactical information that the combatants would need during the coming battle. Meanwhile, other officers sought out those priests who always followed in the wake of armies. The sun was approaching its maximum height in the sky by now, so it was an opportune time for the men to make their peace with their gods. Shortly after noon, the foot soldiers would enter the ford and charge towards Vortigern's positions, a ploy that would force a response from the Demetae ruler.

Fortuna's dice had been cast into the air; who could guess at the number of warriors who would survive to greet the dawn of another day.

The madness of making an uphill charge against a defensive position would, hopefully, be explained away by the brothers' relative inexperience and their limited strategic knowledge.

Meanwhile, the cavalry contingents under Uther's command

had been inserted into the woods adjacent to the ford. The young prince had seen to their disposition during the hours before first light to ensure that Vortigern remained ignorant of Ambrosius's intentions. At the same time, other officers had secreted the teams of archers into an untidy phalanx above the ford where the ground rose upwards. With luck, Vortigern wouldn't anticipate their purpose before the barbs slammed into the bodies of his Saxon warriors.

All was in readiness now and the air was thickening with the accumulated fears of frightened humanity. Innocent or guilty, true or false, this upcoming battle was only making a minimal impression on Pridenow as he cast his eyes over the sloping ground that led into the wooded areas. His senses were so acute he could almost see the shiny black eyes of the carrion birds that had taken up their feeding positions in the trees near the killing fields. With a pang of precognition, he understood that the woods must be alive with these evil birds that were eagerly awaiting the coming meal. Shivering under the weight of his woollen surcoat, he prayed they would not feast on him.

Earlier, once he had seen to the disposition of his men, Pridenow had sought out his fellow commander on the front line that was forming in the open ground near the river ford. Gorlois's hulking figure, huge and menacing inside his chain-mail tunic, bore down on Pridenow.

'I don't believe I can help you with your problem, my lord,' Gorlois had responded after Pridenow initiated a discussion with his fellow commander and apprised him of his problems regarding his daughter. Sadly, the two men had never been particularly close, although their family history had frequently drawn them together.

But there was something about the sensitivity of Gorlois's features and his character that inspired Pridenow's confidence. I don't intend to make judgements about this man and there's precious little time to seek out a deeper understanding of him, Pridenow mused as he stroked his horse's mane and nuzzled its ear. Old Red, on his last campaign, was destined to spend this final battle in the rear echelon of Ambrosius's command so that Pridenow would have a fresh and dependable mount during the coming conflict.

Gorlois sniffed at the air as if he was forecasting the onset of inclement weather. 'There's snow coming, so I'm glad I've worn my woollen surcoat.'

Pridenow glanced upwards at Gorlois, for he was almost convinced that the other man must be laughing at him. But Gorlois's calm eyes were just like pools of clear water.

'My daughter's future is a serious matter, my friend,' Pridenow said. 'Fact is that I'd never have broached the topic on this day if the situation wasn't a matter of such urgency.'

Gorlois stared back at his older companion and raised his brows quizzically.

As he spoke, Pridenow's love suffused his face, so that Gorlois couldn't help but wonder at the charm of a child who was not yet a year old but could still generate such feeling.

'My family will see to the welfare of my sons, but little Ygerne will need a promised husband who can save her from harm during her formative years. You would be the perfect man to carry out this task if you were prepared to become my little one's protector. The betrothal, of course, would be in name only, because it would be some time before she grew into adulthood.'

Gorlois stared hard at Pridenow from under his tawny eyebrows.

'I'm near enough to your own age, Pridenow, so the last thing on my mind would be to entertain thoughts of wedlock with a babe in arms, even if such an agreement was a formalised betrothal by proxy.'

Pridenow's expressive face illuminated his own reservations and the concerns he felt about his proposal and the strange actions he was taking.

'I can't imagine that any man would shower love on my daughter and care for her with the intensity that I would bestow on her. Unfortunately, Ygerne was born under a dark star and I'm fearful that she will become the pawn of an unscrupulous manipulator if she isn't protected by a man of unimpeachable character and honour.'

'You speak as if the coming battle is destined to be the death of you.'

Suddenly shy, Gorlois looked down at his own sword-scarred hands in embarrassment.

'I've spent my whole life under the threat of Vortigern's sword,' Pridenow continued. 'The Demetae banished me and sent his Saxons to kill me on numerous occasions. Even now, he is planning how best to bring me to heel because he knows that where I go, so too do many of the rulers of Britannia. Most of the British kings are fools, so you can be assured that I'd never swear fealty to them. Vortigern knows I will not be foresworn, and, as yet, he thinks I will ultimately remain neutral. When he realises that I intend to ally myself with Ambrosius, he will try to make my Ygerne suffer if there is no man to protect her from his depredations.'

'Still, it seems wrong for a man of my age to marry a babe in arms,' Gorlois retorted. 'To me, it would be unchristian to allow strong feelings to develop during a union such as this. Will your wife approve of the bargain you intend to make?'

'Creidne understands my position and she'll do whatever is in Ygerne's best interests,' Pridenow said smoothly, but his eyes were stark from the pain he was experiencing.

Gorlois was dumbstruck by the enormity of Pridenow's suffering. Eventually, he could only accede to Pridenow's strange request. Later, Gorlois would wonder what chance, or mischance, had caused him to agree to this strange bargain.

'With luck I'll never know,' Gorlois wished out loud, and the intensity of his concerned words alarmed a young Brigante chieftain who had been standing beside him.

The weather gods must have heard his plea for understanding, for a light snow began to fall. The brief diversion allowed the foot soldiers to move out from their places of safety and make their way across the ford in ordered phalanxes.

Under a thickening shroud of snow, Death visited the Glevum battlefield as Pridenow's foot soldiers crossed the ford and ran, with unfurled tribal pennons, towards the distant cluster of tents that were laid out under Vortigern's banner. The snow silenced their movements and added a strange and surreal beauty to the physical exertions of the warriors.

Warriors began to stir within Vortigern's camp by now, for this was an unusual time of day for aggressors to mount an attack on an entrenched enemy. But this small element of surprise allowed the Britons to drive deep into Vortigern's territory before his Saxons reacted.

Pridenow's lungs seemed to burn from the effort of driving

his body over the uneven ground. The water in the ford had been icy, but it was shallow and didn't impede the warriors as they made their headlong rush to Vortigern's side of the river. Part of Pridenow's brain, like a high-flying raptor circling above the site of the battlefield, could visualise the bird's-eye view of the British warriors with their coloured garb and check designs associated with each of the tribes. The site was eerie, but very still.

Hot coals from Vortigern's cooking fires were sent flying as the Demetae's troops collected their weapons and formed themselves into the wedge formations that were favoured by the Saxon thanes.

'Christ! Vortigern must be anxious to get this melee over and done with! He's already sending his Saxons into the fray.'

Caught off-guard, Vortigern's response was immediate.

Only the complete destruction of these tribal upstarts would placate the Demetae's response to these British insults. The main contingent of hulking Saxons, in their furs and hides, screamed abuse towards the British warriors and hurled themselves towards the ill-disciplined rabble that Gorlois and Pridenow had led on to the battlefield.

Vortigern's Saxons struck back at their British enemies with all the force of a tidal wave. Taller and heavier than their adversaries, the giant northerners halted the British advance in its tracks. But, screaming at his men to adopt defensive positions, Pridenow managed to stop the Saxons from overrunning the British warriors by the sheer force of his will.

'They're not gods!' Pridenow roared as he hamstrung one of the Saxons who had attempted to disembowel him. 'These bastards are only men!'

'But they're so fucking huge!' Gorlois responded and Pridenow was pleased to hear some ragged laughter rise from British throats after this sally into humour.

Then the small melee became the grisly task of mass butchery as men fought against their enemies under the ashen sky.

'We were nearly overrun during that last charge, brother,' Uther muttered as he watched the ragged line of Britons who had been decimated under the sheer weight and ferocity demonstrated by Vortigern's Saxons.

'You can send in the first detachment of your cavalry now, but make sure they obey their orders this time,' Ambrosius snapped curtly. 'Send off a signal too that the first wave of our foot soldiers can make a tactical retreat and fight their way back towards the ford.'

'At this rate of attrition there won't be any survivors,' Uther answered, his brow creased in concentration.

'Just make sure that our cavalry don't become overeager and try to cross the ford. They must kill as many of Vortigern's men as possible while challenging the Demetae to expose his warriors to danger near the front line.'

Uther obeyed his brother's orders, although he hated to oversee the loss of so many good men. The carnage near Vortigern's command tent was horrific and Uther knew that few of the Britons would survive the retreat to the ford. During his exposure to the blood and death that was evident on the battlefield, Ambrosius had maintained an icy calm and Uther was struck by his elder brother's callous disregard for the lives of his warriors.

The newly arrived column of British cavalry charged through the shallow waters of the ford at a gallop and the horsemen's momentum carried them close to their defeated infantry who were trying to return to their own side. The cavalry was showing distinct signs of timidity, making Uther's heart beat faster as his confidence in Ambrosius's trickery returned.

Meanwhile, several tons of living and dead horseflesh impeded the path of the wounded Britons who were trying to make their way back through the ford. The battlefield was turning into a little hell of noise and carnage.

On the field of conflict, Pridenow suddenly regained consciousness after experiencing a sharp blow to the back of his scalp. He vaguely recalled being brained by a Saxon axe but, although he had struck back at the huge form, he could remember no more until he woke with the weight of a Saxon enemy on top of him. The stench of bear grease that the Saxon had used to darken his hair, in addition to the hot reek of blood and entrails, caused Pridenow to gag as his wits began to return.

The body of a dead horse lay across Pridenow's legs and the weight made movement difficult, yet he still struggled to free himself and move to safety.

'Give me your hand,' Gorlois's voice seemed to come to him from far away as he used his great strength to drag Pridenow free from under the dead animal. When he rose shakily to his feet, Pridenow suddenly felt the world spin dizzily around him.

'Show me your wound!' Gorlois ordered peremptorily and Pridenow obeyed without demur. 'It's a good thing you've got such a hard head, my friend, because you're going to have some interesting scars to impress the ladies.'

Gorlois used a strip of dirty cloth from a dropped banner to bandage the sides of a long gash that ran from Pridenow's forehead to his chin. 'You'll no longer be pretty, my friend.'

'What happened to me?' Pridenow yelled as he tried to make

his voice heard over the din that continued to come from the battlefield.

'Our warriors are almost spent! If Vortigern doesn't take the bait soon, we'll come to learn that today has become a good day for Britons to die,' Gorlois said with a limpid smile. His white teeth were sharply defined against the bloodstains that covered his face.

'Wait!' Pridenow interrupted. 'Look! Vortigern's thinking to finish us off.'

Pridenow stumbled and was almost knocked down by a small group of cavalrymen who were fighting their way towards the ford. Off to their right, an arrowhead formation of Vortigern's cavalrymen was cutting the remnants of the British infantry formation to pieces.

'Look! He's unleashing his fresh reserves! We've got him by the balls!'

There, with their horses' flanks inside the waters of the ford, Vortigern's best cavalrymen were inexorably driving Uther's horsemen into a full retreat. But, sadly, it was evident to Pridenow that few of the men in the first wave of Uther's attack would see the end of this battle.

The mud and soft earth along the margins of the ford were red with blood now and the shallows were choked with the bodies of the dead and dying. The noise from the melee was frightful as men and animals screamed out their defiance towards their impending deaths. Vortigern's fresh troops were destroying the Britons, regardless of the many acts of wild courage that Pridenow observed around him.

Shortly thereafter, Pridenow fell on to one knee after suffering a further wound from one of Vortigern's Demetae warriors. The pain was so severe that he missed seeing Uther's final charge with the last of his cavalry contingents strung out behind him.

Simultaneously, Ambrosius entered the fray at the head of the last of the infantry reserves.

Mindful of the battle plan that would come into effect when Vortigern's troops fought their way across the ford and the usurper was fully committed, Gorlois and Pridenow screamed at their troops to break for safety or take cover along the protected sections of the river bank.

Freshly lit signal arrows carrying warning messages cut through the slate-grey skies and, obedient to their orders, the Britons ran like the devil or threw themselves into a safe hideaway.

Then, forgotten and unappreciated by their erstwhile masters, the ordinary citizens of Britannia were given an opportunity to demonstrate their mettle.

As they rose from their places of concealment, a hundred archers drew back their bowstrings and fired their barbs. The powerful hiss generated by these underrated weapons was the last sound heard by many of Vortigern's warriors. Like an improbable shower of wood and metal, a hail of arrows swept through the Demetae's forces like wildfire. The attackers were tightly packed as they entered the ford, so the archers could hardly fail to find an attractive target. The waters in the ford began to run a rich red as the blood from Vortigern's casualties turned the verges of the river bank into slurry.

The Saxon warriors discovered, too late, that even shallow water can be a deadly enemy.

Pridenow watched as Ambrosius rallied his men and encouraged them to fight their way along the front line. Meanwhile, the British cavalry continued to cut down any of Vortigern's force that tried to escape from the shower of arrows. Suddenly, Pridenow noticed that Vortigern's showy banners had disappeared from the Demetae's ranks when a brace of horsemen hacked their way free from the mass of fighting men who surrounded them.

'The bastard's getting away! Vortigern's abandoning the field,' one of Uther's officers shouted as he alerted the other warriors in the front line. The British commanders were quickly acquainted with the situation.

With a dozen members of his personal guard flanking him, Vortigern drove his horse through the press of tightly packed combatants with scant regard for the safety of friend or foe until he reached the relative safety of open ground.

The wolf king's luck held and none of the many arrows that targeted him found their mark. The small group of warriors deserted their comrades and galloped into the west.

'Stop the bastard!' Uther yelled.

'We'll have lost him forever if he reaches the forest,' Gorlois added unnecessarily.

But Fortuna favours sinners and saints with even-handed justice. Unscathed, Vortigern fled from the field where his soldiers had perished to protect his throne.

Ambrosius offered an honourable peace to all except the Saxons who made up the bulk of his avowed enemies, but too many of Vortigern's British warriors were reluctant to accept the prince's good will. These men fought till the death.

In similar fashion, the aggressively foolish were cut down by volleys from the archers who possessed no squeamish reservations about the sanctity of life.

So, too, were the wounded put out of their misery; a boon

that allowed them to take their places among the honourable dead from both sides.

When the battle finally came to an end, it was time for the victors to restore the battlefield to normality. Neither Uther nor Ambrosius carried any physical wounds and, in a gesture of magnanimity, Ambrosius went to every wounded man to offer his hand in friendship and blessing. His generosity won him many friends but, in the messy aftermath of the battle, there was no trace of Pridenow among the living or the dead.

Then, after some hours, one of the warriors from Pridenow's unit approached Ambrosius with a memorised message from the master of Corinium. Gorlois was confused by its tone, but Ambrosius simply nodded his head in satisfaction.

'"Lord.

'"I ask you to recall your petition to me and, as I have survived the battle, I am leaving now with fresh horses to carry out your instructions. I pray that I will reach the Ordovice lands before the tidings of our battle reach our kinfolk in the north-west of Britannia.

'"As one last boon, I beg you to care for my people who have shed their blood on this day.

'"Pridenow, Master of Corinium."'

As Gorlois and the other officers puzzled over Pridenow's message, Ambrosius concentrated on those tasks that would restore the battlefield to normality. Long into the night, fires glowed redly and the air was filled with acrid wood smoke as unseasoned timber was burned to incinerate the corpses of the honourable dead. Great pits were dug to bury the dead horses, from which the smell of burning and rotting flesh eventually reached the citizens of Glevum, who were sickened by the stench.

Except for a small number of personal friends, few of the British warriors realised that Pridenow was missing. In accordance with Ambrosius's orders, regular patrols were carried out along the verges of the Forest of Dean in an attempt to kill or capture Vortigern, but no men were sent into the south of Britannia. Ambrosius had, with treaty and with force, secured the south under his banner. And so, sent into harm's way by Ambrosius, Pridenow prayed that his fresh horses would carry him quickly through the lands of the Ordovice and thence to Caernarfon without serious incident.

Even the poorest and most ignorant of peasants knew that momentous changes had taken place in the south of Britannia. The chill air and the black ash that was carried on the winds spoke mutely of the British people's struggle to determine who would become a worthy high king.

As he rode into the north, Pridenow prayed too that the voices in his head were wrong and the goddess would permit him to return to the safety of his wife's warm bed. All men wish for what they can never have and Pridenow was no exception to this rule.

Then, as his horse breasted the icy waters of a ford on the eastern verges of the Demetae country, he prayed that their sentries would be abed and fast asleep.

Sadly, Fortuna had turned her wheel and Pridenow's good luck came to an end.

EPILOGUE

I've seen a land that is bright with truth, a place where a man's word is his pledge and falsehood is banished. It is a place where children sleep safely in their mother's arms and never know fear nor pain.

Stephen R. Lawhead

A mud-spattered horseman entered the gates of Corinium with a ragtag group of small boys in hot pursuit as they played at a game of soldiery. Prince Gorlois, from the Dumnonii tribe of Cornwall, stood at the doorway of Pridenow's villa and tried to scrape some of the accumulated mud from his riding cloak.

'I bid you good day, my lord,' Creidne greeted her visitor. 'Tell me quickly! Do you bring tidings of Pridenow, my husband?'

On one hip Creidne carried her youngest child, a beautiful girl who was still learning to walk. Surprisingly, little Ygerne stared directly at her betrothed's face with eyes that were so limpid and adult that Gorlois felt his heart lurch with fore-knowledge of the friendship and love that would one day develop between them.

The prince bowed low over Creidne's proffered hand but he

473

immediately realised that this poor woman was shaking. She'd assumed that his arrival was an indicator that her husband was dead and her visitor might be the harbinger of bad news.

'You're wrong, my lady! Your husband lives. At least, he was alive when last I saw him after the Battle of Glevum. In fact, I came to Corinium to speak to you in person and gauge your feelings on a delicate matter that your husband raised with me. He asked me to become your daughter's betrothed, but I've been reluctant to consider his proposal if it might cause discord.'

Creidne ushered her noble guest into the atrium where a servant proffered food and drink in the name of hospitality. Gorlois repeated the substance of the discussion that had taken place with Pridenow before the battle, but he would prove to be mistaken if he expected Creidne to gainsay her husband's intentions. With a silent apology, the young woman left her guest to eat while she excused herself and returned to her apartments on a brief errand.

'My husband has always been a planner who tries to anticipate predictable eventualities,' Creidne explained on her return to the atrium. 'It's a thoroughly admirable quality. If he believes that you will make a good husband for our Ygerne, I will accept his decision without hesitation. With this in mind, I have some trifles to give to you for safekeeping.'

Creidne opened her hands and emptied a coruscation of colour into the lap of her guest.

Gorlois looked down at the cross, the chain, the uncut rubies and the other jewels that lay in his lap. The cold, unblinking brilliance of their cut was such they seemed almost reptilian to the young prince.

He almost recoiled from Creidne's offering.

'I don't understand! What are these jewels to me?'

He gingerly lifted each item from the hoard and placed it on to the bench that lay between Creidne and himself.

'My husband found these baubles in an abandoned mining shaft in the mountains that lie to the north of Corinium. I'll relate the full details of the discovery on some occasion when we have sufficient leisure to speak of it for longer. But, for now, suffice it to say that we determined that these jewels would become Ygerne's dowry at some future time. My husband is reluctant to send our daughter to her marriage bed without a gift that would make her a woman of value.'

Creidne allowed an impish grin to flash over her face.

'Fortuna gifted him with these stones so they could be presented to her betrothed husband.' She grinned again. 'It seems that you've been selected as her intended!'

In short order, a bargain was cemented between Gorlois and Creidne, the mistress of Pridenow's lands. For many years, Gorlois would protect his betrothed as his own child until the day came when she would be mature enough to travel to Tintagel.

As Ambrosius rode through the gates of Venta Belgarum to the cheers and adulation of its fickle citizens, Pridenow had penetrated deep into the north and had embedded himself among the rulers of the Deceangli and Ordovice tribes.

Ambrosius had assumed the role of High King of the South with his usual flair and grace, but Vortigern opted to carve out a new kingdom in the north that extended from Venta Silurum to Deva and westward to the coast. These lands would become his share of the Britannic spoils.

With self-satisfied smirks and titters of amusement, the citizens of Venta Belgarum referred to the wolf king as the High King of the North now, but they prayed with all their hearts and souls that they would never have to see him again.

Meanwhile, in the teeth of a northern gale, Pridenow experienced the doubtful hospitality of the kinglets who ruled Caernarfon. In bygone days, Magnus Maximus had stolen the heart of their princess, Elen, and she had died far from home in semi-abandonment. Her daughter, Severa, had been raised by strangers and had little interaction with her kin, further insults that slighted her clan. Old feuds and intangible rumours tended to fester in the north, so Pridenow's accusations of sinfulness against Vortigern were treated with scepticism by the local aristocracy.

Pridenow realised that the kinglets of Caernarfon hated all outsiders with cold disdain; as a result he was cynical about vague assurances that they would refuse to make treaties with Vortigern. This promise was however as much as the young master could expect, after which it was time for him to move on.

After this break from many days in the saddle and with a torrent of doubt, distrust and animosity washing over his head, Pridenow was grateful to be back on the road again. Within hours, he was forced to take shelter in a shepherd's hut overlooking the sea while a howling gale developed along the coast. Despite the spume from smashed waves and the fine mist that came with a thoroughly wet night, Pridenow believed he was safe, for he was far from the press of human habitation.

But he was mistaken.

How Pridenow met his end never became clear but he was captured inside the shepherd's hut where he had taken refuge by a band of Saxons who had arrived from the south after deserting Vortigern's forces at Glevum. The members of this rampaging patrol, carrying multiple wounds, thirsted for revenge after the pain that had been inflicted on them.

Pridenow had been recognised from his unusual eyes; the Saxons took their revenge immediately, and they targeted his injuries to cause him maximum punishment and pain.

In later years, the local peasantry repeated the tale of the suffering and death of the southern warrior they referred to as the sea king, and how this British warrior cursed his Saxon enemies and their Demetae companions with eternal damnation.

One curious boy from the fishing village had overheard parts of the stranger's torture in the shepherd's hut but, in later years, he was unable to recall everything he had heard.

He sometimes told his listeners how the Saxons had crucified Pridenow on a cross as a crude parody of the Christian symbol. Then, superstitious to the end, the Saxons had put out his eyes to avoid his icy stare. Still, antagonised by his bravery, they inflicted multiple wounds designed to bring about the prisoner's end with agonising slowness as he bled to death.

'Now that his eyes are out, he's just another short-arse Briton whose luck has run out,' one of the older Saxons had said from the best seat in the warmest corner of the shepherd's hut. 'See! He's just a man and he's bleeding like you or me! See, Ulf! Use your torch and make him scream a little. It might warm the bastard up!'

One of the younger warriors plunged a torch towards the gaping wound to Pridenow's face where his eyes had once been. The captive screamed and sagged on his cross in a dead faint.

Ulf laughed.

But all became silent in the room when Pridenow suddenly began to speak. It was almost as if the prisoner could see through every man in the room despite his ruined eyes. The Saxon's dread was such that none of the huge warriors possessed the courage to speak of him again.

'You think to take the British lands because you are tall and strong. Many men have made that same mistake before you and they have come to learn that Britannia places a high price on the rich flesh of her people. The Picts overran her and where are they now? The Romans were the masters of the universe when they became our protectors, but what has become of them? Where are they now? My people have fought over the centuries to keep these lands and, like you, we'd be lost if we failed to meet Britannia's exacting demands for the future.

'A long time ago, a wise man in Tintagel once challenged me and explained that no one owns the Britannic lands. We are simply allowed to borrow her bounty and we should be grateful when she permits us to live here. You may laugh if you will, but it has been foretold that one of my seed will stamp your women and your children, your warriors and your heroes into the dust. Sadly, he will also be destroyed by the British gods in the fullness of time.

'I, Pridenow, will give you warning! I am a man who is near to death, but I have no intention of deceiving you. You will all be dead before the onset of summer, so you can place no faith in Vortigern. All of this coast will be splattered with your blood when a man with grey eyes rides into these lands once more to lead our people to greatness.'

Pridenow began to reveal disturbing details of kin from each warrior's family and the destiny that would soon overtake each of these northerners. The men's laughter withered in their mouths until, terrified, Ulf panicked and killed their captive with a single blow from his axe.

If the Saxons were sorry to find that their captive had escaped any further torture, then they did not speak of it. But the listening boy heard every word and his heart and mind recognised the truth of Pridenow's words.

The boy's name was Myrddion Merlinus, a name that would echo down through the ages.

AUTHOR'S NOTES

This novel is the final offering in a trilogy I have called The Tintagel Cycle, historical fiction that features one of Britannia's major fortresses. The novels are set in a time period about which information is particularly lacking, mainly because record-keeping in the fourth and fifth centuries was marginal at best.

The Romans had departed from Britain at the time in which the novels are set, never to return, and the barbarians were nibbling at the island in earnest. The very beginnings of a racial and cultural war had started.

Severa was a real person, but I was forced to flesh out the bare bones of the tantalising glimpses of her which is all that remains after fifteen centuries. Women in those unromantic times had little status, even women like Severa, who was manipulated by a number of ambitious and unscrupulous men as a vehicle that helped them to seize the throne of Britain.

We know very little about Severa, so I have described her as a woman who is trapped by her biology. She is memorable as the British daughter of Magnus Maximus, the wife of Constantine II and the mother of three major kings: Ambrosius, Uther Pendragon and Vortimer. According to the legends, all three sons would serve as High King of Britannia in their own right.

During my early research, it became obvious to me that this book would rely on a great deal of speculative fiction, mainly because the records of this period were destroyed by Britain's ultimate rulers, the Saxons, in the centuries following the death of King Arthur. In addition, civil disturbances during the following centuries resulted in the records and libraries of any number of church and monastery sources being burned or destroyed.

I have already woven a web in other novels that involve the life and times of Arthur, Merlin and the Lords of the Arthurian Legends, so I wanted to ensure that the research used for this novel did not contradict information gained from other sources.

The book's complexity, as well as the limitations on the amount of information available to me, was a difficult problem at the time, but when brain injuries and physical problems were added to the equation, I began to fear that my task might never be completed.

For all that, I was to find that the characters in the history were so clearly developed within my own mind that it was a wrench for me to kill them off, especially characters such as Pridenow whose presence was fundamental to my interpretation of the entire plotline.

Some of the details in the legends and the rumours are clearly defined and I found that I could not tamper with them. Vortigern wasn't defeated at the Battle of Glevum so, for a generation, he was able to welcome Saxon mercenaries into his private army and maintain a separate kingdom in the north-west with only minimal harassment. Of course, I have added my own details to flesh out the myth because so little is known of Severa's sons and what they were doing when Vortigern was approaching the end of his life.

That Vortimer tried to kill his father is mentioned in the major treatises associated with the Arthurian legends. I tried to imagine what Vortigern would have been like as a man of his time, given the enormous authority of his position and his capacity to escape death in a violent age. I decided that, despite a penchant towards villainy, he was also a man who was driven by masculine desires. Men such as Vortigern are never satisfied with maintaining the status quo.

According to the legends, the widowed Vortigern would later marry a female relative of the Saxon thane, Hengist. In time, he would father two sons on this woman, although the British of the time would never have accepted a Saxon as the High King of Britannia.

The drive and ruthlessness implied in these facts present us with a special type of villain.

The children's journey into Spain was my own invention. Wace, Layamon and Geoffrey of Monmouth make no mention of the lost years so, given the ugliness of these times, I decided it would be necessary for them to reach adulthood far from Britannia where they might live in relative safety. As children, they would have been totally vulnerable if they lived in Britannia.

I gained a great deal of enjoyment from playing with the characters of Severa's sons. What made Uther so cruel? Why did Vortigern's sons try to supplant him? What actually happened to Severa? Did she meet with an accident?

I also enjoyed dropping hints of the boys' characters during their youth and knitting possible reasons together as explanations for the myths that abounded. In turn, I needed to lay the foundations for such women of the legends as Morgan le Fey, Morgause and even Iseult.

The sagas of these women have proved to be fundamental to the Arthurian story and a huge number of ancient poems, narratives and songs have been devoted to these women who were forced by their sex into positions of power within the Arthuriad. The parameters for their being insofar as the legends are concerned have been set, so my next task will be a trilogy on three special ladies who filled important roles within the Matter of Britain.

I have always been fascinated by order, so I enjoyed laying a coating of flesh over the skeletons of the past. Mostly, however, I've enjoyed creating common folk who are as important to my own mythology as the heroes who were fundamental to the Legends of Arthur. Targo, Paulus, Constantine, Merlin and the women of the legends who attended on them are the human faces of my personal mythology, so I hope you have enjoyed these characterisations.

I can say with some pride that I always relish a challenge. And so it was that overcoming a debilitating physical incapacity was very rewarding in itself.

The sudden onset of my illness left me partially blind and trying to cope with severely restricted hand–eye coordination. Unfortunately, an author who is unable to read or write loses most of the mechanical skills that are available to them.

It is especially frustrating when your mind tells you that all is well and everything is under control. But, in reality, the artist is unable to express themselves within their world.

I decided that I would refuse to allow Fortuna, fate, illness or my own bloody-mindedness to allow my characters to die on the vine. Severa, Pridenow, Gorlois and the other characters that fill these novels are as real to me as my personal family members and the friends who fill my private life with pleasure.

Ave, my friends! May we create many more!

M. K. Hume

June 2018

GLOSSARY OF PLACE NAMES

Abonae (Portus)	Sea Mills, Bristol, Somerset, England.
Adurni (Portus)	Portchester, Hampshire, England.
Anderida	Pevensey, East Sussex, England.
Anderida Silva	The wooded district surrounding Anderida in southern England.
Apollodorus	A large estate near San Sebastian, Spain. (See Donostia, Hispania.)
Aquae Sulis	Bath, Somerset, England.
Aquitania	Aquitaine Province, France.
Arelate, Gallia	Arles, France.
Armorica	A Gallic province in ancient France.
Atlanticus (Oceanus)	Atlantic Ocean.
Britannia	Britain.
Brittany	A province in France.
Burdigala	Bordeaux, France.
Caerleon (Isca)	Newport, Wales.
Caernarfon	Carnarvon, Gwynedd, Wales.
Calleva Atrebatum	Silchester, Hampshire, England.
Canovium	Caerhun, North Wales.
Cantabria	A province in Northern Spain.
Constantinople	Istanbul, Turkey.
Corinium	Cirencester, Gloucestershire, England.
Cymru	The Celtic term for Wales.
Cyrene, Africa	Cyrene, Libya, Africa.

Deva	Chester, Cheshire, England.
Donostia, Hispania	San Sebastian, Spain.
Dubris	Dover, Kent, England.
Durobrivae	Rochester, Kent, England.
Durovernum	Canterbury, Kent, England.
Dyfed	A kingdom in the west of ancient Britain.
Frisia	Modern-day Netherlands.
Gallia	The ancient kingdom of Gaul. Mostly France, Germany and Spain.
Garumna River	Garonne River, France.
Gesoriacum	Boulogne, France.
Glastonbury	Glastonbury, Somerset, England.
Glevum	Gloucester, Gloucestershire, England.
Hades	The Greek god of the underworld.
Hadrian's Wall	The Roman defensive wall that protected Britannia from the Picts.
Hibernia	The ancient name for Ireland.
Hispania	Spain.
Italia	Italy.
Liger River	River Loire, France.
Litus Saxonicum	The English Channel.
Loire River	Loire River, France.
Londinium	London, England.
Lugdunensis	Lyon, France.
Massilia	Marseilles, France.
Mediolanum Santorum	Saintes, France.
Middle Sea	The Mediterranean Sea.
Namnetum (Portus)	Nantes, France.
Pictavis	Poitiers, France.
Ratae	Leicester, Leicestershire, England.
Ravenna	Ravenna, Italy.
Red Wells	A legendary well in modern-day Somerset, England.
Rhodanus River	Rhone River, France.
Rome	The sacred city of the Seven Hills.
Rutupiae	Richborough, Kent, England.
Sabrina Aest	Bristol Channel, England.

Seven Hills (City of the)	Rome, Italy.
Tintagel	Tintagel, Cornwall, England.
Vandals	The ancient Germanic tribe which flourished in western and southern Europe during the early centuries of the modern era.
Vectis Island	Isle of Wight, England.
Venta Belgarum	Winchester, Hampshire, England.
Venta Silurum	Caerwent, Monmouthshire, Wales.
Verulamium	St Albans, Hertfordshire, England.
Vienna	Vienna, Austria.
Visigoths	An ancient Germanic tribe who flourished in southern France, Spain and Portugal from the second to the fifth centuries.

GLOSSARY OF BRITISH
TRIBAL NAMES

Atrebates
Belgae
Brigante
Cantii
Catuvellauni
Coritani
Cornovii
Deceangli
Demetae
Dobunni
Dumnonii
Durotriges
Iceni
Novantae
Ordovice
Otadini
Regni
Selgovae
Silures
Trinovantes

THE TINTAGEL TRILOGY

I
THE BLOOD OF KINGS

The first High King of Britannia is crowned. And he has
his eyes on Rome ...

II
THE POISONED THRONE

Britain is under threat from invaders. A bloody fight
to the death begins.

III
THE WOLF OF MIDNIGHT

The path lies clear for an evil betrayer to seize
the throne of Britannia.

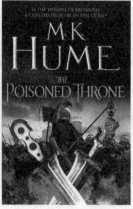

www.headline.co.uk
www.mkhume.com

THE KING ARTHUR TRILOGY

I
DRAGON'S CHILD

The epic tale of the man destined to become Arthur,
High King of the Britons.

II
WARRIOR OF THE WEST

Celtic Britain is under threat from within.
The legend of Camlann has begun ...

III
THE BLOODY CUP

King Artor has been betrayed. Celt will slay Celt
and the river will run with blood.

www.headline.co.uk
www.mkhume.com